THE BLOOD BROTHER

Gavin Esler is the BBC's award-winning Chief North American Correspondent. He lives in Washington DC. *The Blood Brother* is his third novel.

D1464351

GAVIN ESLER

The Blood Brother

HarperCollins*Publishers*

HarperCollins*Publishers*
77–85 Fulham Palace Road,
Hammersmith, London W6 8JB

This paperback edition 1996
1 3 5 7 9 8 6 4 2

First published in Great Britain by
HarperCollins*Publishers* 1996

ISBN 0 00 649304 1

Set in Linotron Sabon by
Rowland Phototypesetting Ltd,
Bury St Edmunds, Suffolk

Printed in Great Britain

For Mr and Mrs B. C. Warner

'And he will be a wild man; his hand will be against every man and every man's hand against him; and he shall dwell in the presence of all his brethren.'

Genesis 16, 22

PART ONE

Doubt

1

The first time David Kerr knew he had a brother was when he received a letter telling him his brother had died. The letter was in an envelope with a fancy seal, addressed to 'David Courtland Kerr' – so formal that he opened it first because it looked important. It made a change from the bills and junk mail that had piled up in his hallway when he returned to London after a week away. It was late and Kerr blinked sore eyes, reading slowly, gradually realising the letter was strange beyond belief.

'We regret to inform you,' it said, 'that your brother has died while on active service for the United States Air Force.'

That was it, more or less. There was a lot of bureaucratic huffing and puffing and regrets were expressed three times in four paragraphs, but death was the main point. Your brother has died. There will be a full military funeral at Arlington Cemetery in Virginia. The United States Department of Defense would be honoured by your presence. Further questions, please contact. God Bless America, and have a nice day. It did not actually say, 'have a nice day', but there was an infuriating mateyness about it which Kerr resented. He fingered the fine white notepaper, trying to work out what it meant, troubled by the obvious catch: he was an only child. And if you do not have a brother – neither American nor British, living or dead – then the sad news of a fatality in someone else's family is not going to mean very much. Kerr looked at the letter again and scratched his head in irritation.

'Bad joke,' he muttered and rolled his eyes to the ceiling as if to blame an eccentrically cruel God. 'I thought we

3

agreed I don't do death any more, okay? I resigned, right?'

He rubbed his shoulder. There was now a constant rheumatic ache round the wound which he called his Souvenir of Sarajevo. Two years before, Kerr had been hit by shrapnel from a Serb mortar while witnessing the evacuation of children from an orphanage in Bosnia. It had been his last assignment as a war correspondent for the *London Tribune* newspaper.

Kerr tried massaging the shoulder with his fingertips, but nothing seemed to do much good. He popped two painkillers into his mouth, washing them down with a sip of whisky. He pulled off his shirt and stood in front of the bedroom mirror for his nightly ritual of looking at the Souvenir of Sarajevo, hoping it might have disappeared. There was a patchwork of unnaturally pink and white skin across his shoulder and back. Another set of scars ran down his arm and ended on his right hand. The tips of his index and middle fingers were missing, where he held the letter in misshapen stumps.

'I'm resigning because I've been in more wars than I've got fingers left to count them on,' Kerr had told the *Tribune*'s editor when he was discharged from hospital. 'And you know the worst thing, Frank? After Belfast, the Falklands, Afghanistan, Iran, Nicaragua, El Salvador, Grenada, Angola, Panama, Iraq, and Bosnia? The very worst thing?'

'What, David? That you never sent postcards home? What?'

'I'm serious, Frank. The children. The dead children. I was lying there among all these wasted little lives in the orphanage playground, and the shock was realising I wasn't getting shocked any more.'

'You always write as if you are shocked.'

'That was professional shock. I mean human shock, Frank. There's a difference.'

And David Kerr was in human shock now. The letter from the American Embassy had made him angry and

4

depressed. He scrunched it into a ball and threw it across the room so the white paper bounced in the fireplace then out again on to the carpet. Kerr headed towards the drinks cabinet and poured another glass of malt whisky. He took a sip and let it tingle on his tongue, feeling much better. Some poor American had died and he was sorry, but it had nothing to do with him. It was like receiving the wrong credit card bill, best ignored. The telephone answering machine flashed the number two and Kerr pushed the play button to hear the messages. Colette had called. Since Sarajevo they had remained friends, but no longer lovers. Kerr believed she felt sorry for him – misplaced guilt, he decided, since Colette had been the Tribune's photographer working with him in Bosnia and the shrapnel which had hit him and the children missed her.

'Call me if you don't get back too late,' her message said. 'I want to hear how the new job is going.'

Kerr's new job, after months of indolence, was as publicity director for a children's charity. He had just returned from a fundraising trip in Scotland and was wondering whether he could admit to Colette how boring it was, when suddenly the answering machine beeped again and a deep bass American voice boomed out.

'Mr Kerr, this is Joseph R. Huntley at the American Embassy. Time is six twenty. I've been trying to reach you for several days but I guess you've been out of town. Hopefully you will have read my letter by now, but please contact me as soon as you can. It's to discuss your brother, Richard Rush. Again, our deepest regrets, especially for having to contact you this way.'

Joseph R. Huntley left a telephone number, but Kerr was so stunned that at first he did not bother to jot it down. Thanks to the United States bureaucracy, it looked as if he was going to have a dead brother whether he needed one or not.

He took another sip of his drink then replayed the

5

message, this time noting the telephone number. Presumably the US government had mixed up his name with some other Kerr, and the result was he was invited to a funeral at the Tomb of the Unknown Brother in Arlington Cemetery. It could be amusing, except that some real relative still did not know the news about poor whatshisname, Richard Rush.

Kerr checked his watch. It was late, and all he wanted was something to ease his shoulder and a good night's sleep. He unpacked his case and stood in the shower, washing the scars where the skin had healed over the shrapnel wound. It was an alien growth, part of him and yet somehow foreign, and as the water beat down on him, he began to feel a strange unease about the letter.

Regrets. Funeral. Most welcome to attend. Difficult time. More regrets. Sorry we could not meet with you. Your brother, Captain Richard Courtland Rush. A US Air Force training accident. Overseas. Your brother.

'Brother,' he said aloud, and the word had a strange echo in the thickening steam. He stood naked, patting the scar tissue dry, then towelling the rest vigorously. 'Brother.'

He shivered as something awful struck him, a ghost of a thought like a dead man's hand on his neck, a half-memory returning through the fog. He padded into the bedroom and pulled on a denim shirt and an old pair of jeans.

'Brother,' he repeated.

One of the few things Kerr knew for certain was that he had no brothers. But the blood thumped in his ears as he realised he damn well could have a half-brother, a half-brother christened with his own odd middle name, Courtland. It had been his mother's maiden name: 'Jennifer Kerr, née Courtland.' He remembered it from the old family Bible his father kept in the study back home in Edinburgh, a Bible which retained the memory of his mother even when his father tried to pretend she had never existed.

Brother. Natural mother. Family. The words came to him with all the happy associations of 'plutonium' or 'cholera'.

He sat down and rubbed his face in his hands, thinking of the list of marital break-ups and generational hatreds that ran like a battlefield history of the Kerr family. He re-read the crushed US Embassy letter once more, this time shaking with emotion. A half-brother! It was possible, maybe, but could it be true? His mother re-married? Produced another son? Could there be a brother who had died before Kerr even knew he had lived? Trembling, Kerr picked up the telephone and dialled the American Embassy inquiry number Huntley had given him.

'You have reached the voicemail of Joseph R. Huntley,' came the metallic reply. 'Please leave a message.'

Kerr hung up. He could not do voicemail. He looked at his watch.

'This is what families do to you,' he muttered, thinking how stupid he had been to expect any answer from the embassy at eleven o'clock at night. 'Brain turned to sauerkraut.'

Memories started to slip back into his mind like damp through a wall: his mother walking out on his father when Kerr was seven years old; how she had died that day, for him and for his father; how he felt it now like the rheumatism in his shoulder that would never go away. 'Family' had become a word like 'past' – something you tried to escape from, a genetic abnormality, a birth defect. It was like the night before he was hit in Sarajevo, tossing in the darkness, knowing his luck had disappeared and that in the morning he was going to wake up with everything going wrong in some awful, inescapable way.

He called Colette.

'Welcome home, David. How was Scotland?'

'Fine. I'm settling down. The job is not as bad as you said. But I think I probably have to go to the United States.'

'On business?'

'No. You might not believe this, but I may have to go to a funeral in Washington.'

7

'Who died?'
'My brother.'
'I never knew you had a brother.'
'Me neither,' David Kerr replied.

2

As soon as he saw David Kerr leave for Heathrow Airport and his flight to the United States, the Mormon put his Bible away. Scott Swett had parked his car so he had a perfect view of the front door of Kerr's red-brick semi-detached house in Chiswick, West London. He passed the time reading scriptures, spelling out every verse, his lips moving silently.

'And I saw a new heaven and a new earth; for the first heaven and the first earth were passed away and there was no more sea.'

Scott had been thinking about the new heaven and the new earth ever since he had arrived in London from America several days before. He could not decide what the problem had been with the old heaven. I mean, if it was heaven, right? Then it would be perfect. So why would you need a new heaven? Had it worn out, maybe? This was deep shit, and it made Scott's head hurt. He only ever read two books, Genesis and Revelation, the beginning and the end, figuring if he cracked these the middle would kind of fall into place. He was in London to track David Kerr, and now David Kerr had taken off for his brother's funeral in the United States, so Scott Swett had work to do. He squeezed his Bible into the glove compartment. It was a bitch because the gun kept getting in the way. The pistol was a Ruger P85, which Scott never liked wearing in a shoulder holster because it always made him think of cancer, kind of like a tumour in his armpit. The truth was he wanted to shoot David Kerr and get it over with.

Scott started the car and drove off, looking for a

9

telephone box to call his partner, Bob Allen. He was thinking of the verse from the Book of Revelation that Bob had shown him after they had killed two guys in Virginia, the week before Kerr's brother, Captain Ricky Rush, died. They had dumped them in the swamp. Scott and Bob had popped them with MAC 10s, neat little sub-machine guns, about twenty or thirty shots in each body, wrapped the corpses up in heavy-duty plastic and then thrown them in the Great Dismal Swamp. On the way back to Washington, Bob Allen had pulled out his Bible and read:

'But the fearful, and unbelieving, and the abominable and murderers . . . shall have their part in the lake which burneth with fire and brimstone: which is the second death.'

No shit, Scott thought. The second death. Maybe that's why they needed a new heaven. Two deaths, two heavens; stop it getting crowded up there; that would figure.

Scott saw a telephone box and parked his car. He didn't feel so good. He had a thick head from a cold, he had spent too much time trying to track down David Courtland Kerr, and London was like one of those Third World countries, Mexico or someplace, where things never worked right.

'Bob Allen please. Room 314.'

A sleepy man's voice answered his call. Bob Allen was in bed in the crummy and overpriced Cromwell Road hotel he and Scott had booked for a few days while they watched Kerr.

'He's gone to the airport,' Scott said. 'Call Washington and then I'll see you back at his place. And don't forget the tools.'

Scott Swett returned to his car, thinking how much David Kerr looked like his half-brother, Ricky Rush, and how pleased his bosses in the America First Corporation were going to be, knowing that Kerr was en route to Washington. He parked again outside Kerr's house and put the Ruger pistol in his pocket, waiting. When Bob Allen arrived they walked round the side of the house and pushed open an old wooden gate, which was so decrepit the metal lock fell out. There was one other small lock on the back door, a lot of glass, and no bolts. All they had to do was keep the noise down. Scott took the Ruger and stuck it in his belt, shed his coat and rolled it into a ball, inside out. He held the coat firmly on the door panel near the lock as Bob Allen prepared to swing the heavy masonry hammer.

'You hit any part of me,' Scott whispered, 'and you're a dead man.'

Bob Allen said nothing. He swung the hammer backwards in a wide arc then brought it down hard where Scott held his coat. The wood tore away from the lock, leaving it hanging on the door jamb. The two men waited, listening for noises. Nothing. Scott Swett shook his coat and let the shards of wood fall away, then he put the coat back on and pushed the door fully open with his foot.

'You first,' he said, ushering Bob in front of him.

Scott put his hand on the Ruger pistol, wondering if they had made a mistake. Maybe Kerr had a girlfriend inside? Or a cleaner come round to check on the place? What would it be like to kill a woman? He'd thought about it with his ex-wife a couple of times, maybe should have done it after she complained to the church about him disciplining her with the leather belt. He was her husband, goddammit, trying to discipline the bitch like it said in the scriptures. Made you sick. Scott stiffened as he heard Bob Allen swear softly.

'What's up?'

'Goddamn coffee table,' Bob whispered. 'Hit my knee.'

For such a big guy Bob Allen moved quietly from room to room, taking care of business, even though Scott was sure that what they were looking for would not be there – but they had to do a thorough search anyway so they could tell the bosses back home at America First they had checked.

Scott looked around the framed black-and-white photographs of war zones that decorated the walls, and their titles. 'Argentina, 1982.' 'Panama, 1989.' 'Kuwait, 1991.' Most of the pictures had captions, printed out as they would have been in a newspaper. Two of them were bigger than the rest, framed with a thick black border on grey paper. One showed David Kerr standing in what looked like a school playground between a crazy guy with a walrus moustache and a dark-haired little girl. There was another picture beside it where Kerr was on the ground, his face twisted and covered in blood, his right arm kind of blown away, the little girl looking pretty sick by his side. Dead, probably. The caption read, 'Souvenir of Sarajevo.' Scott didn't know about art, but he knew monkeys couldn't do it, and this was better than monkey-art. The pictures were really something.

Bob Allen came back into the room.

'Anything?'

Bob shook his head.

'Nope. He has a computer, a Toshiba laptop. Not what we're looking for at all. I flicked through his floppy disks. Nothing.'

'How about the video? You pick up any of the VHS tapes?'

'He doesn't have a video, not even a television.'

'C'mon, Bob, get real. Everybody has a television.'

'Not this guy.'

'I don't believe it.'

The two of them searched the house again. Scott pulled books from the shelves and threw them on the floor, but however angry he became, there was still no video recorder or television.

'The Tan Man will never believe this,' Scott said. 'What is this guy? Some kind of freak, doesn't believe in television?'

'Maybe we should steal something,' Bob Allen suggested.

'Like what? Books and shit? Maybe someone already stole his video. Come on, Bob, let's go. I told the Tan Man that we would get nothing here, that we would have to wait until Kerr gets to Ricky's funeral.'

They had started to move out of the house when Scott noticed the war photographs again, thinking of a good joke.

'They're really something, these pictures, eh? Looks like Ricky's brother is as wild as Ricky himself. They're even in the same business.'

Bob Allen stared back blankly.

'How do you mean, same business?'

This was like working with Mr Potato Head, Scott Swett decided. If you spoke slowly, maybe Bob could keep up.

'The dying business, Bob. The dying business. Aw, forget it. We're done. Let's get out of here and back to Washington before we catch something.'

3

When David Kerr arrived at Washington's Dulles Airport he was met by a US Defense Department driver who took him to a hotel near Dupont Circle. The driver handed over an envelope with a Pentagon seal.

'I'm real sorry about the death in the family, sir,' the driver said.

The note told Kerr to call a number at the Defense Department where a desk sergeant briefed him. The following day he was to take a cab to the Pentagon Mall Entrance for ten a.m. He was scheduled to meet his brother's former commanding officer, Colonel Noah McGhie. There was one surprise.

'So I just ask for Colonel McGhie?' Kerr said to the desk sergeant.

'No sir, for Mr Huntley.'

'Huntley,' Kerr repeated with some amusement. 'You mean, Joseph R. Huntley from the US Embassy in London?'

'Yes, sir, only Mr Huntley is home-based here. That was what he arranged. Have a nice evening.'

Kerr had talked to Huntley on the telephone in London before finally deciding to come to the funeral. Huntley had described himself as a Military Dependants' Officer and Kerr had assumed he was based in London – hence his bemusement over the move to America. It didn't quite fit. Whatever, he was tired and needed to sleep. He awoke early the next morning, unable to adjust to the new time zone. He searched for the hotel gymnasium and pumped his body through its regular exercises, finding the sit-up board and aching his way through a hundred repetitions then running to the canal in Georgetown, pounding the back streets and along the old tow path.

Over breakfast Kerr tried to read the *Washington Post*, but could not concentrate. Thoughts of his brother kept filling his mind, and the ghost of a memory of his mother who – Huntley had said in their telephone conversation – was listed as dead, leaving Kerr as the only next-of-kin.

'Why did Captain Rush never get in touch,' Kerr had asked, 'if he knew where I was?'

'Beats the hell out of me,' Huntley had replied. 'It looks as if he put your name on the next-of-kin form only three months before his death. Maybe it took him that long to track you down.'

Kerr arrived at the Pentagon Mall Entrance hoping for some answers. He walked up the steps and turned to look back over the Potomac river towards the city with the sun glinting on the Washington monument and the dome of the Capitol. As a building the Pentagon had no redeeming features, except one: it looked wonderful from the air, most memorably in spy satellite photographs, where the pentagonal shape was visible. From ground level it was a bureaucratic rat hole of seventeen and a half miles of corridors and 20,000 nomadic staff. A heavy black woman in her early twenties came to the reception area from Huntley's office.

'I'm Kyesha,' she said. 'Mr Huntley's assistant.'

Kyesha guided Kerr through the metal detectors and X-ray equipment, and led him past several layers of the Pentagon, moving from the outer 'A' ring towards the inner 'E' ring. They walked for what seemed like miles, until Kerr felt like Theseus looking for the Pentagon Minotaur, wondering if he should lay down thread so he could find his way out.

The walls of Huntley's office were cream coloured, the carpet a kind of green. There were no pictures or personal effects, though a sickly plant dropped yellowing leaves in the corner. The view from the window was filled by similar offices on yet another ring of the rat hole.

'Good to meet with you in person, Mr Kerr,' Huntley said cheerfully, transferring a lit cigarette to his left hand and shaking Kerr warmly with his right. He was in his late fifties, with a shock of long white hair and the lined face of a heavy smoker.

'I am trying to place your accent,' Kerr replied. 'Texas?'

'Right. Texarkana.'

Kerr sensed there was something about Huntley which just did not fit – his meagre, un-lived-in office, the way his eyes stared from behind gold-rimmed glasses as if he could see inside you, like a spider looking for a meal; the way he smoked when Kerr was sure smoking was banned in the Pentagon.

'You certainly get around,' Kerr observed. 'When we talked on the phone I assumed you were attached to the embassy in London.'

'No, I'm based here. But I felt your brother's case was one I should handle personally. Besides, when Uncle Sam is paying, who would pass up the chance of a trip to London, right?'

Now Kerr got it. It was Huntley's unblinking gaze that was so unnerving, and he found he could describe it perfectly as if for a newspaper feature that one day he might write: snake eyes. Definitely Snake Eyes, Kerr decided. He would count the blinks.

'Well, see here,' Huntley continued, taking a draw on his cigarette, 'I wanted to talk you through the funeral tomorrow, and ... Kyesha' – he buzzed through to the outer office – 'Kyesha, call Colonel McGhie and tell him Ricky Rush's brother is with me now, if he could spare the time?'

Huntley then ran through the procedures for the funeral, the Snake Eyes unblinking. It made Kerr wonder what kind of tongue might protrude from the grey face. Huntley stood

16

up to get a fresh cigarette packet from his coat which was hanging behind the door.

'When we talked in London,' Kerr said, 'you told me my brother died in a training accident but you had no more details. Do you have any now?'

Huntley lit the cigarette and smiled in a way which, on the whole, Kerr could do without.

'Next-of-kin have a right to know as much as possible,' he replied. 'Least in my book they do. The trouble is that some of the guys in this building . . . well, David, the truth is, I was taken to one side and told to butt out. They said there's no big mystery, Captain Rush died in a training accident, like I said, but the nature of that training involves matters that could be embarrassing if we made it public. It was in a foreign country, where they're cagey about admitting that we train on their soil.'

'I don't get it,' Kerr interrupted. 'How will it embarrass a foreign country that my brother died there?'

Prick, Huntley thought.

He sat down, remembering every detail of Kerr's file – expensive Scottish school, Edinburgh University, good degree, the *Scotsman* newspaper then Fleet Street. Half a dozen awards for war reporting before he went off the rails in Sarajevo.

'Your brother,' Huntley said, exhaling smoke.

'Half-brother,' Kerr corrected.

'Half-brother, right.'

Prick.

Huntley even noticed the family resemblance with Ricky Rush. They had the same straight black hair, they both looked fit, though he would describe Kerr as wiry whereas Captain Rush had been bigger and more heavy-set, with a quick temper and a big mouth.

'Your half-brother. He died during a training exercise at a US Air Force base outside the United States. I am not at liberty to tell you where that base is located. And to be

17

honest, David, I don't even know. They don't tell us low-grade paper pushers in human services diddleysquat, but they did say that this unnamed country does not publicise the fact that US troops are on its soil – most importantly, specialists like your brother.'

Kerr almost laughed.

'I still don't get it, Mr Huntley. I mean, who are the enemies now that we have to keep this secret from?'

Huntley drew deeply on his cigarette.

'The same people they always were, David. Foreigners. Isn't that where the enemy comes from?' He finished the cigarette and stubbed it out. 'And it would be helpful,' Huntley continued, 'if you would not press Colonel McGhie or any of the other men who worked with your brother on what happened, where it happened, or why it happened. They're as shocked as you are, you catch my drift?'

Kerr nodded.

'Were any of these others with Richard when he died?'

'No.'

'So he died alone?'

Kerr was irritated and wanted to tease. The snake eyes blinked for the first time, and Huntley reached for yet another cigarette.

'I did not say he died alone,' he protested. 'Because I do not know. But I know this much. Your brother would not have wanted details of his mission to become public knowledge. He was a patriot and a loyal American.'

Great, Kerr thought. My brother the war hero.

Huntley exhaled a cloud of smoke. 'What people here tell me is that Captain Rush was not the sort who would want anything negative that might affect his wider military family. I'm sure you can understand that.'

'Brothers in arms,' Kerr added laconically.

'If you like.'

The Texan did not smile, and Kerr was becoming increasingly tired of Huntley dressing up the Pentagon's best interests as if they were commandments from God. In the unlikely event that God had to have a nationality and was proved to be an American, Kerr supposed they might be, but for the moment he was doubtful.

'Look, Mr Huntley –'

'Joe.'

'Look, Joe. I don't know what all this is about, and I suppose in some ways I don't much care. It smells, that's all. But in one big way I do care. I want to learn as much about my brother as possible.'

'That's understandable, but –'

'Besides, I am grateful you contacted me, and I want to know how Richard lived more than I need to know how he died. Help me with that, and I'll keep out of the rest. Whatever game you and I are playing is obviously important to you, otherwise they would not have sent you to London to check me out.'

Huntley drew strongly on the Marlboro.

'Nobody sent me to check you out, David. I came because the US military looks after its own, and the families of its own.'

Kerr smiled, thinking, 'Sure, Joe.'

The conversation was cut short by a knock at the door and the arrival of a handsome black man in his late forties, wearing Air Force uniform.

'Noah,' Huntley drawled, relieved at the distraction. 'Good of you to come. I know how busy you are. This is Captain Rush's brother, David Kerr. David, I want you to meet the man your brother was probably closer to than any other in the service, Colonel Noah McGhie.'

McGhie pumped Kerr's hand firmly. He was the colour of slightly milky coffee, with an inner glow as if a lamp burned beneath the skin. There were a few grey wisps in his military-cut tight curls, and he spoke as if he was used to giving orders.

'Pleased to meet you, Mr Kerr, real pleased. We were

sorry to lose your brother. It's a bad moment for you all in the family, and it's a bad moment for us here. We looked on him as family, too.'

Kerr nodded. 'So Joe said.'

McGhie was taller than Kerr, with a boxer's build and the dignity of a man quite sure of his capabilities.

'Noah here won't tell you, David, so I guess I will,' Huntley was saying, suddenly all folksy. 'Ricky was almost like a kid brother to him. They were that close.'

McGhie grinned.

'Surprised?' he laughed. 'Well, I guess you should be. I'm nearly fifteen years older than Ricky, I am his commanding officer, and –' McGhie looked at the backs of his hands with a laugh '– and I guess there's a slight difference in skin tone. But the units we worked, the jobs we did, I guess I saw in him what I saw in myself years ago.'

'Which is?'

McGhie poured himself a coffee from the jug on Huntley's desk.

'Ambition, I guess. Determination. Striving to do something. Make a difference. The American way.'

'Be all you can be?' Kerr added, without irony. 'As it says in the military recruitment commercials on television.'

'If you want to put it that way, sure. Like the recruiting ads. Be all you can be. That's me. And that was Ricky. Helluva guy. I am so glad he has family coming to the funeral.'

At the word 'family', Kerr winced. Ever since his first conversation with Huntley he had turned over in his mind what he remembered of his mother. He had found himself on the journey to Washington thinking of a Christmas holiday more than thirty years before, when his father had picked him up from boarding school and announced that there was no mother any more. No mother, but in her place some woman produced by his father whom Kerr was instructed to call mother and who professed to love him.

20

Standing in the cold outside the grey granite of the school walls was the last time Kerr's father had ever acknowledged that his real mother had existed.

'You mean your bi-o-logical mother.'

He'd made it sound like germ warfare.

'My real mother.'

Kerr remembered it all now like ancient chisel cuts on soft stone, explaining a little of it to McGhie.

'Your bi-o-logical mother is a thrawn woman,' was the last his father had to say. 'She has left us and we need not think of her again.'

'Thrawn?' McGhie repeated, obviously in need of a translation.

Kerr awoke as if from a dream.

'Thrawn?' he said. 'It's an old Scottish word meaning stubborn beyond your best interests.'

Noah McGhie nodded. 'Your brother was thrawn all right. Ricky was stubborn as a mule.'

'It runs in the family,' Kerr added ruefully.

McGhie paused and sipped his coffee.

'I guess you're interested in discovering as much as you can about Ricky, finding out what he was like.'

'That's right. And how he knew about me, and why we never got together.'

'Ricky rarely talked about family,' McGhie explained. 'Played it real tight, even to me. Never spoke much of it, except when his mother was ill.'

'My mother,' Kerr interrupted sharply. 'She was my mother too.'

'I'm sorry,' McGhie apologised. 'I should have thought of that. It's like my own family, all bits and pieces. I never knew my own father. Maybe that's why Ricky and I always got along. I knew not to pry. There was some kind of hurt there.'

Kerr winced again. He did not know what to say.

'Maybe ... maybe when you have time I could talk to

you more, find out things ... meet the men Ricky was friends with.'

'Sure,' McGhie said. 'I'll fix it. How long're you in town?'

'I'm booked to leave in four days.'

'Come to dinner,' McGhie offered, 'out at my place on the lake. We'll fix the time tomorrow, after the funeral. Until then.' McGhie rose to go. 'I guess I've got work to do. I'm in the trenches today. *Mano a mano*, fighting the paperwork.'

Kerr thought he would push it. Just as he had taken an instant dislike to Huntley, somehow he believed he could trust Colonel McGhie.

'I'm told by Joe here I must not ask this, but ...'

McGhie smiled.

'Ask how he died?'

'Yes. Obviously I would like to know. If ...'

'So would I.' McGhie stiffened, and stared directly at Huntley. 'So would all his buddies. He was on secondment with another unit. I am told it is extremely sensitive. That's about all I know, and I am his commanding officer. Was, I mean.'

'And I'm his brother. What was he, anyway? James Bond? Why all the bloody secrecy?'

Kerr could see the snake eyes fixed impassively.

'You ever hear of SIGINT, David?' McGhie asked.

'Yes. Signals Intelligence.'

'Your brother was a highly talented SIGINT officer. His skills were very much in demand by agencies outside the Air Force. It was on one of these specialised missions that your brother died.' McGhie's voice was cold with anger. He turned his back to Huntley. 'He was not under my direct command at that time, and I know nothing about the circumstances of the accident, but if I could beat the answer out of some of the goddamn sons of bitches around here, I would do it.'

As rapidly as the anger rose in McGhie it subsided. So that

22

was it, Kerr thought. Somebody had hijacked his brother for a mission and got him killed, and in all the bureaucratic embarrassment they were covering their own backsides. The Enemy, Kerr remembered, was not as Huntley had said. It was not foreigners. They were merely the Opposition. The Enemy, as always, was within, and he was pleased to see McGhie knew it too. They shook hands.

'See you at the funeral,' McGhie said warmly. 'We'll talk again at length. Pleasure meeting you.'

'And you, Colonel.'

'Noah.'

'And you, Noah.'

As soon as McGhie left, Huntley lit another cigarette. He was about to hint that his meeting with Kerr was done.

'Just one thing, Joe,' Kerr asked. 'Could you tell me which undertakers – I mean funeral home – has my brother? I thought I should go and view the body. I don't want to do it, you understand, but I feel I've got to.'

Huntley protested that it was impossible.

'The accident was apparently very ... disfiguring,' he explained. 'It has been necessary to have a closed casket. I'm real sorry about that, but there's no choice. Had to be done. You heard from Colonel McGhie more than you should have, but I think you now realise the problem.'

Kerr looked across the plastic wood table and could not say exactly how it happened, but he knew at precisely that moment that Joseph R. Huntley was lying to him. In his surprise at the transparency of it all, Kerr arched an eyebrow and sat back in his chair.

'A closed casket,' he said blankly. 'For aesthetic reasons. Nothing to do with Signals Intelligence and national security this time?'

'Nothing,' Huntley answered briskly, thinking maybe he had underestimated Kerr. They were going to find their job more difficult than he had realised. Thrawn son of a bitch, to use that old Scots phrase, like his brother. 'Nothing at all to do with national security. But I have something for you if you are interested.'

Huntley pulled out a slim manila folder from his desk, opened it and pushed across to Kerr a typed page from Captain Richard Rush's last military resumé and a photograph showing him in his Air Force uniform. The man in the photograph had hair very like Kerr's own, but more closely cropped. His neck was thick like a body builder's and he looked tough despite his easy college-boy grin. Kerr thought Captain Richard Courtland Rush's eyes smiled at some private joke. He nodded at the photograph as if in a slightly distorted mirror.

'Hello, Captain Rush,' he said aloud and without embarrassment. 'Hello, little brother.' A few moments later he took the papers and shook hands with Huntley. 'Thanks for all your help.'

'No problem. I'll see you tomorrow at the funeral. Take care.'

As soon as Kerr left the room, Huntley lit another cigarette, took off his jacket, kicked back in his chair, and rested his feet on the desk, thinking of his next moves. Now he felt better than he had for two months. They might just be able to win through after all, with salvation coming in the unlikely form of Ricky's half-brother, the asshole ex-reporter. When he finished his private celebration, Huntley dialled a number in Virginia, just across the Potomac river from Washington.

'This is Huntley,' he drawled. 'Piece of cake. The guy's so excited he almost shit.'

There was a joke from the other end. Huntley laughed until the grey lines of his face cracked.

'Yeah, that's right, that's right,' he chuckled. 'Big Brother, *we're* watching *you*.'

4

Arlington National Cemetery was hot, and from its slopes you could see across the Potomac to the top of the Washington Monument and the United States Capitol. To the left, up the river, David Kerr could just make out the ugly tip of a massive skyscraper and television tower with a garish sign that read 'America First' in red, white and blue like a neon crown. A US Air Force band was playing hymns and the mourners sang along. Kerr stood with Noah McGhie and a bunch of uniformed Air Force personnel. Great guy, they said, Ricky Rush – a great guy. Kerr knew they were giving him the once over, but felt relaxed in their company. These were easy-going men who mourned his brother and yet were so habitually good-natured it shone through even at a funeral. Captain Tom Snow, tall, blond, with the appearance of a recruiting poster, said Kerr and his brother were very similar.

'You like beer?' Captain Snow asked. 'Ricky liked beer. And football. And –'

'And ass,' Major Steve Jiminez, a large-set Hispanic with a bent nose, butted in.

'Yeah, Ricky liked the ladies,' Snow agreed.

'They liked him too. We used to say his motto wasn't "E Pluribus Unum" but "Leave No Piece of Ass Untouched". Guess he'd like it on his tombstone.'

'So would we all.'

'A wild man,' Noah McGhie added affectionately. 'But a good man. Wild Ricky. We'll miss him.'

Kerr felt absurdly cheerful. The Air Force officers stood ramrod-backed, and when the band struck up the next hymn, they boomed it out. Trust in God. Do the Right. At the far end of the grave Kerr saw there was another group of men, civilians in suits, button-down shirts, a different kind of Washington uniform. Huntley was in the front, and below him were two strikingly beautiful women, one dark, Italian or Hispanic in a tight black dress with black stockings and a bright pink bouquet of carnations. She was leaning on the arm of a blonde in a flower-print dress with a broad-brimmed sun hat. Separated from the main group by several yards stood two more men wearing suits and sunglasses. One of the men was white, the other black. As the singing stopped and they waited for the preacher to speak, McGhie gently pushed Jiminez to the side and whispered in Kerr's ear.

'See the two empty suits?' He nodded towards the two men. 'FBI.'

Kerr blinked.

'FBI? What are –'

He felt McGhie's hand squeeze his elbow to silence him.

'We've got to talk privately about this,' he whispered.

'Meaning?'

'Meaning, don't tell Huntley. Okay?'

Kerr stared at McGhie. There was no danger of him telling Huntley anything.

'Okay.'

McGhie fell back into place. The Air Force preacher, an overweight man with a booming voice, waddled out from the side of the band and stood at the head of the grave.

'We come here today,' he yelled, gesturing to the pink flowering cherry trees around the hillside, 'to celebrate a good life cut short, like one of these blossoming trees, cut down before the ripening of the fruit. Captain Richard Courtland Rush.'

Kerr turned to his left. The two FBI agents were staring directly at him. He had an odd sense of foreboding, the feeling that he was effortlessly being sucked into something he could neither understand nor avoid. The preacher announced that the eulogy would be given by Senator Mark Barker and there was a ripple of whispering through the crowd. Kerr watched as a stiff little man with big ears and what seemed like a shaved head appeared from the group of suits surrounding Huntley and strode towards the preacher. They shook hands and Senator Barker smiled as if canvassing support. Kerr vaguely remembered the name, but could not place it.

'America First Corporation,' McGhie hissed in his ear. 'The building over there.' He nodded in the direction of the red, white and blue monstrosity of a television tower on the skyline. 'Co-chairman of the Senate Intelligence Committee, ranking Republican on trade, founder of the born-again America First movement, and Major League asshole.'

Now Kerr remembered. Barker was a big oil man from Oklahoma who had run for the presidential nomination last time round on trade protectionism, Japan-bashing and hatred for homosexuals. That in addition to abortion, liberals, immigrants, foreigners, the media and a few more people Kerr had forgotten. The rumour was, he was ready to try again.

'These are times that try men's souls,' Barker yapped over the Arlington hillside. The more grand his words, the more disjointed they sounded.

'And when we come here to bury. One of our own. Our souls are tried by doubt. Where does it fit. In God's plan? To take this American hero. From the bosom of his family . . . ?'

While he staggered on, Kerr remembered the news stories about America First. They were the nutters who pushed the president into what had become a worsening trade war with Europe, Japan and the Far East. Senator Barker was quoted as saying that a trade war would be a holy war against foreigners who had sucked America's lifeblood for years.

27

Kerr was intrigued: how did this fruitcake with the bad haircut know his own little brother?

'This young man,' Barker declaimed in the direction of the casket, 'died while doing the hard work of freedom . . .'

Kerr gazed to his right and saw the shock of white hair and grey face of Joseph R. Huntley, looking, he thought, in dire need of a cigarette.

'It is in Man's nature to search for reasons,' Barker yapped. 'Yet we must be content to say. As generations of American fighting men have before. In God We Trust, and America First.'

'No piece of ass untouched,' McGhie whispered.

Senator Barker stood back and the preacher boomed out a few more words as the casket was gently lowered into the Potomac earth. The trumpeter began to play Taps and for the first time Kerr felt like choking back a tear.

He arched his neck to point his eyes to the sky until he regained control, thinking how absurd it was to feel sad for a brother he had never met. When he looked down again, the trumpeter finished and the band struck up a sombre tune as the honour guard began to march away. The dark-haired woman stood clutching the pink flowers against her dress like a bridesmaid at a wedding gone wrong. She straightened herself and then threw the flowers down at the graveside. Her blonde friend was crying gently, as if in private grief. The dark one knelt and arranged the flowers on the grave, crossing herself. As she stood up, Kerr strode towards her, ignoring Huntley who hovered nearby.

'My name is David Courtland Kerr. Captain Richard Courtland Rush was my half-brother. Forgive me for being so direct, but I was wondering how you came to know him?'

The two women stared at each other.

'Hi,' the dark one said, extending her right hand. 'We heard maybe a relative was going to show. Good to meet you.'

Her eyes were a rich brown, yet lifeless. She spoke in a beaten monotone as if under the effect of tranquillisers.

'I'm Beatriz Ferrara. Your brother was part of my life for four years. I . . . loved him.'

She began to cry gently, arched her head sideways and leaned on her companion.

'Hi,' the blonde said, awkwardly shaking hands as Beatriz lay draped across her neck. 'I'm Lucy Cotter, Beatriz's friend. I knew Ricky real well too. You English? Ricky never mentioned he was English.'

'Scottish,' Kerr said adamantly. 'I'm Scottish.'

'Well, whatever, it's a great accent. And it's good to meet you.'

'Thanks. Listen, I'm in town for a few days. I never really knew Richard.'

'Ricky,' Lucy Cotter corrected, straightening her dress as Beatriz regained control. 'He was always Ricky. Nothing fancy, despite being so smart. And nothing straight-laced, despite being military, you know what I mean?'

'Ricky,' Kerr repeated. 'Anyway, I never really knew him.' He went through the story for what seemed the hundredth time. 'Maybe you can help me put a character to him, piece him together. For me it's like a jigsaw, you understand?'

'Sure,' Lucy said, smiling sweetly. Looking at her, Kerr realised she was one of the few women he had ever met whom he would describe as beautiful; a heart-shaped face, baby blue eyes, a perfect figure. 'Sure we understand. And we'd like to know you better. We can help, too. Can't we, Bea?'

'Yes,' Beatriz agreed, her voice still flat. She looked at Kerr but with her eyes focused in the distance. 'We can help. I can see part of Ricky in your aura. I can see the relationship.'

'She's kind of psychic,' Lucy Cotter explained.

'Psychic?'

'Yeah, she can detect things from your aura. Tell you when the balance is upset. That kind of thing.'

'Oh really,' Kerr replied doubtfully, wondering how much of an aura you had to see to work out that a man burying his brother might be upset.

'Call me tonight,' Beatriz said, her eyes re-focusing on the twentieth century. 'We'll meet. I'll help you in any way I can.'

'Thank you.'

She gave him a number which he wrote down in the back of his diary.

'I'd like to hear about Ricky's family.'

Kerr nodded, thinking, me too.

'It's been a pleasure to meet with you, David,' Lucy said warmly, with a smile that lit him up. 'Let me give you my number too, in case I can help.'

Kerr realised he was being picked up. The FBI, a crazy senator, a psychic, and now a flirt – some funeral. Only in America, Kerr thought, where everything was possible and most things were permitted. Lucy Cotter guided Beatriz towards a waiting black limousine. Kerr watched them elegantly slide their legs inside, and Lucy waved as the car descended the slopes of the gravesites towards Washington. Kerr folded the notepaper with Lucy's number and put it in his wallet with an intense sensation that he was being watched. He looked across the grave to catch Huntley's snake eyes boring into him, then flickering away guiltily. Half the crowd had dispersed, though there were small knots of men in and out of uniform chatting in the sunshine. It was almost noon and the sweat was making Kerr's jacket stick. He took it off, and a hand eased it for him. Colonel Noah McGhie was beside him with Senator Mark Barker. Up close the senator looked very much like a demented chihuahua.

'This is Rush's brother, Senator,' McGhie said, by way

of introduction. 'David Kerr. And this is Senator Barker. The senator was a big fan of your brother's.'

'Is that so,' Kerr replied. 'How is that?'

The chihuahua was a good six inches shorter than Kerr, with lively eyes and a perpetual grin. He seemed to be sizing Kerr up.

'Your brother did a lot of work on one of my favourite projects,' Barker rattled out like a machine gun. 'Keeping America strong. I met him a few times. Was very impressed. Fine man. Fine intellect. Pleasure to meet you, Mr Kerr. My regrets to you and the family. Fine man. Fine family.'

Senator Barker shook hands again, turned on his heel and left.

'Man in a hurry,' Kerr muttered to McGhie. 'He didn't say what kind of project, Noah. Any idea?'

'Later,' McGhie replied. 'Not here. I told you he was an asshole, didn't I? A very rich asshole. Come out and eat with my family and we can talk properly. I'll call you tonight.'

'Okay, but what's the big secret?'

'Maybe six weeks before he died, Ricky told me about you, about your mother, that he had traced you and was ready to make contact, then this happened.' McGhie gestured towards the grave and saw Huntley striding towards them, drawing from a lit cigarette. 'I'll tell you later.'

'I'm sorry about your loss,' Huntley butted in, exhaling smoke, 'but I think it was a real good send off.'

'Yes,' Kerr agreed, annoyed at the interruption. They chatted inconsequentially for a few minutes, until Huntley asked again when Kerr was returning to Europe. It seemed important to him.

'In a few days,' Kerr responded, not wanting to be specific. 'I'm thinking of spending time trying to meet more of my brother's friends.'

'That's good,' Huntley nodded. 'It's good that you met –' he faltered. 'What are their names, Noah? Ricky's buddies?'

'Snow and Jiminez,' McGhie said.

31

'Snow and Jiminez,' Huntley repeated. 'They were real thick with your brother. And those two beautiful women, Beatriz and Lucy. Fine women. I think they could be helpful. They knew him better than anybody. Make sure you meet up with them.'

'I will, Joe.'

Huntley took a quick pull of his cigarette, and put a hand on McGhie's shoulder, saying something about having to get back to work.

'Need a ride into town?' Huntley inquired. 'Ride with us.'

'No thanks. I want to spend a few minutes here, when it's all over, just to be at the graveside alone and think a little.'

'Sure. I understand. C'mon, Noah.'

They parted and Kerr walked towards the Custis Lee mansion, Robert E. Lee's former home, perched on the top of the hill at the crown of Arlington National Cemetery. Kerr's head was swimming and he was desperate to leave the crowd for a few moments to breathe. He walked round the old mansion until he thought most of the funeral party had gone, then made his way back to the grave, now fully covered with red-brown Potomac sand. He was alone. Kerr stood, head bowed, looking at the earth, and felt the tears come gently and naturally to his eyes, rolling down his cheeks without pain. He stood for perhaps fifteen minutes, watching the grave and thinking about what might have been, about his father and mother and half-brother, about death, and, for an instant, about Yasmin, the brown-eyed little girl who had died in his arms in Sarajevo. Her death lit up his own childhood, and he felt the past flood back like the sea forcing up an estuary against the flow of a river in a surge of unstoppable memories. He straightened up, blew his nose on a tissue and began walking down the hill, then heard footsteps behind him and turned. The two men McGhie had pointed out as FBI agents appeared as if from nowhere. Up close Kerr could see that one was a slim black man in a neat brown suit. He was lighter coloured than McGhie, so light there were freckles across the bridge of his nose.

Walking beside him was a younger, taller, and heavier white man wearing sunglasses and a light blue seersucker suit.

'My name is Harold Ruffin,' the black agent said. 'This is my partner, Brooks Johnson.'

Johnson nodded.

'How do you do? You friends of my brother?' Kerr asked innocently.

'Not exactly, Mr Kerr,' Ruffin replied. 'We work for the Federal Bureau of Investigation. We think maybe you could assist us and we'd like to talk to you, but not here. And not today, after a funeral. Could we schedule a more appropriate time?'

'Of course.' Kerr hesitated, then suggested meeting at his hotel the following day. 'Tell me, why the interest? Am I in some kind of trouble?'

Before Ruffin could answer Brooks Johnson stepped forward.

'Not so far as we know,' he said with an unpleasant smile. 'Leastways, not yet.'

Kerr looked at his reflection in Johnson's sunglasses.

'You sure you don't want to tell me about it here? I really don't mind. The funeral's over and I don't want us to waste any more time.'

'Not on the day you bury your brother, Mr Kerr,' Ruffin said. 'Nothing is that urgent. It's just a routine inquiry, is all.'

'Okay,' Kerr agreed. 'Tomorrow at four, then.'

'Fine.'

David Kerr turned to walk back through the gravestones, listening to the voice within him that had made him quit as a war correspondent after Sarajevo. The voice said that the most sensible thing he could do was to get on a plane and go home immediately, before another mortar shell landed. Kerr told the voice to shut up, this was family business.

5

Scott Swett said, 'No, we never saw Buckingdam Palace. We saw nodding.'

'Nodding?' the Tan Man laughed. 'How about Big Ben?'

'Nodding.'

'Harrods?'

Scott Swett glared in ill-tempered silence. He was glad to be out of England, but he still had a cold which made his voice strange, a headache and now jet lag. He could do without the Tan Man trying to be funny. The Tan Man's real name was John Oberdorfer, but as with everyone else, Captain Ricky Rush had given him a nickname. Oberdorfer had spent so long improving his skin tone under sun-ray lamps and with bottles of peculiar coloured liquids that he was now an odd shade of orange, and Ricky had been the only one brave enough to call him 'Tan Man' to his artificially tinted face.

There were five of them clustered round Oberdorfer's desk. They were in the penthouse at the top of the America First building, a few miles from Arlington Cemetery. The Tan Man presided from his padded leather armchair. The other four were the men Ricky Rush had nicknamed the Mormons: Scott Swett, Bob Allen, Brigham Y. Dodds and Ben Ritter.

Scott Swett blew his nose and tried not to be distracted by the magnificent view behind the Tan Man's head. He could see across the Potomac river into the heart of Washington, the Capitol, the Washington Monument and the Lincoln Memorial just a few miles away.

'Anyway, you were not in London to enjoy yourself,'

Oberdorfer said, standing up and beginning to pace in front of the picture window. 'You were supposed to find the videotape and the laptop, and you came back empty-handed. Senator Barker is mad as hell.'

Oberdorfer looked impossibly neat, as if he might recently have been disinfected. He was forty years old, his orange face thin and unhappy. He stood by a blackboard on which he had written a rota of who was responsible for surveillance of David Kerr over the coming week.

'We pursue a trickle-down policy here,' he snarled. 'In case you'd forgotten. Trickle-down happiness or trickle-down misery. Today it's misery, because none of you is up to the job the senator wants done, correct?'

The four men sitting round his desk nodded morosely. The dress code in America First was strict: dark grey or blue suits; white shirts; red or blue ties. Scott, Bob, Brigham and Ben were in their mid-thirties and never questioned the rules of the organisation in which sporting a striped shirt, a beard or long hair was cause for dismissal. Their uniformity gave them the appearance of factory products from under the Utah desert. Ricky Rush's nickname for them – the Mormons – stuck, even though Ben Ritter had a Jewish father and a Catholic mother, and the others were not exactly in the mainstream of Mormon theology.

'Let's get to business.' Oberdorfer clapped his hands. He was a Baptist who had never finally resolved the dilemma over whether Mormonism was truly a Christian religion, but was prepared for the sake of America First business to give Scott, Bob, and Brigham the benefit of his doubts. 'What have we got?'

Brigham began.

'As you know, Kerr looks a lot like Ricky. He has some of the same habits. Works out all the time. Ben and me caught him in the weights room at the hotel leaning back on one of those sit-up boards. Did a hundred reps, then spent thirty minutes with the weights followed by a long run. He's fit, though maybe not too alert.'

''Bout as bright as a forty-watt bulb,' Ben Ritter chimed in. 'Never saw us, never suspected nothing. We could have took him if we wanted, easy.'

'Meetings?' Oberdorfer asked. 'Who has Forty Watt been seeing?'

'He went to the Pentagon,' Brigham continued. 'Just as you said he would. Later he was trying to pick up a waitress over lunch. He seemed to be coming on to her real strong with, you know, the usual bull. Pretty little thing, too.'

'Just like his brother,' Oberdorfer reflected, running his hand across his tanned jaw. 'On a mission to get up every skirt on the planet. How'd Forty Watt do with the waitress?'

Ben Ritter shook his head.

'It was a no, but you're right. Kerr *is* like Ricky, so we're talking major league zipper problem.'

Along one wall of the office were a dozen small television sets, tuned to different channels, and in the middle a large screen on which played the America First Network's programming. It was a re-run of 'I Love Lucy', in the 'Family Values Hour'. The sound was turned down. Oberdorfer moved to a locked cabinet beneath the television screens and pulled out a large case. The four Mormons knew what was coming and shifted edgily in their seats. The Tan Man had done exactly the same thing before he ordered the killings in the swamp in Virginia. Oberdorfer drew the case towards him and put it on his desk.

'I figured you might need more firepower,' he said flatly, and produced four MAC 10 sub-machine guns, and four small plastic freezer bags filled with a white powder. Cocaine.

'Time for the Big-MACs,' Ben Ritter joked. 'I like mine with a small coke, too.'

'You trying to make out we're drug dealers again?' Bob Allen protested, uneasily. 'I don't like carrying no drugs.'

Oberdorfer put on the look of a hungry doberman, drawing back his tanned lips and showing his teeth. 'It worked before. You got any complaints?'

Bob Allen immediately backed off, which was what you did with Mr Oberdorfer, unless you were Ricky Rush and wanted to end up dead. Scott Swett was thinking of saying something about the killings in the swamp, but he decided to shut it. The air of crisis surrounding Oberdorfer was so strong you could almost smell the adrenalin. Senator Barker must have been real angry about the missing videotape. Trickle-down misery was right.

'Let me remind you,' Oberdorfer said, checking the MAC 10 sub-machine guns, 'that we have to find the video, and the laptop computer, before we can get rid of Kerr. You understand? First the laptop and the video, then we take Kerr down to the swamp and show him how the MAC 10s work. Right?'

'Right,' they all chorused.

Each man grasped a MAC 10 and a small plastic bag of cocaine. They signed for the guns and ammunition. Oberdorfer carefully checked the names, signatures, time and date, then he pulled out a box of eau-de-cologne tissues and wiped the gun smell from his fingers. His neatness, even by the scrubbed standards of the others, was obsessive. Scott remembered Ricky Rush had once jabbed a finger at Oberdorfer's lapel.

'Y'know, Tan Man, they say you iron your dick in the morning,' Ricky had bawled, in his best show-off fashion. 'That true? I got a question for you. Starch or no starch? My guess is heavy starch. I figure you need all the help you can get.'

'I'll see you in hell, Ricky,' was all Oberdorfer could reply. And maybe it was going to come true. The Tan Man clapped his hands.

'You want to revenge yourself on the Brits for their lousy hotels,' Oberdorfer joked to them now, 'just do the job, guys, okay? Get the goddamn video and laptop. The senator is giving me an ulcer over it.'

They nodded in unison. Scott Swett took a tissue from the box and blew his nose.

'Dokay,' he said.

'The guns,' Brigham Y. Dodds wanted to know. 'You want to enlighten us some more on rules of engagement? Instructions? And the baggies of coke?'

Oberdorfer said, 'Nothing's changed. Deadly force, if it comes to it, but only after we get the laptop and video. Until then, Kerr has to stay alive. The MAC 10s are to make it look like a drug deal, just like before with the guys in the swamp. If you have to use them, leave the weapons on the scene with the bag of cocaine. That ought to do it. And don't forget Kerr is going to help us,' he emphasised slowly. 'One way or the other.'

'Well, what if he does not? What if he just geds id the way?' Scott replied.

Oberdorfer thought for a moment, then drew a carefully manicured hand across his tanned jaw. There was that smile again, and the doberman teeth.

'If Kerr gets in the way,' Oberdorfer replied, 'we might have to consider the option of a family grave earlier than I thought. Now get on with it. And remember, around here I don't get ulcers. I give them.'

6

As soon as the Mormons left his office, John Oberdorfer returned to his desk and switched up the sound on one of the television sets. In the studio next door in the other half of the penthouse, the floor manager cued America First's president-for-life, Oklahoma Senator Mark Barker, at the start of the recording of his weekly cable news programme. Barker sat at his desk with the full panorama of the capital of the United States behind him.

'Howdy folks,' Senator Barker said with a grin, his Oklahoma yap exaggerated. 'I guess you could say that from where I sit, we look *down* on Washington, and you're right. What you see behind me is our nation's capital, home of Uncle Sam, the United States Federal Government, or for most of us normal people, home of the United States Federal *Mis*-government. Y'see . . .'

America First had constructed the tallest building in Virginia, much higher than anything permitted in Washington DC, with a spacious television studio at the top. The studio doubled as Senator Barker's office on the occasions he worked from the building rather than his Congressional offices on Capitol Hill. It was known locally as the Power Tower, from where Senator Mark Barker produced his weekly diatribes, lambasting the president for failing to stand up for American interests and allowing the decline of family values. The broadcasts were run on America First's own cable and satellite television channels. The senator was working himself up, yapping at the camera in his clipped tones.

'So all I am calling for now,' he said, pointing to a graph

showing the trade imbalances between the United States and Japan, coloured with the Stars and Stripes and a threatening Rising Sun, 'all I want is a level playing field. The White House –' he turned to point accusingly at the picture window ' – that's them behind me here, folks, you can just see the flag on the roof, and I guess it's the white flag of surrender, the surrender of American interests, anyways, the White House . . .'

Oberdorfer was thinking how funny it was that millions of viewers did not realise how small the senator really was.

'If they knew Barker was no bigger than a goddamn prairie dog,' he muttered, 'then maybe they wouldn't take him so seriously.'

John Oberdorfer ran his hand slowly across his tanned face, sniffed at the smell of the eau-de-cologne, then went to the office sink to scrub with soap and water.

'Are you aware, my friends,' Barker continued, 'how many Japanese businessmen and diplomats in this country are *spies* for the land of the Rising Yen?' (Pause.) '*All* of them. That's right. Every single one. We have in our midst – because this is a hospitable country, folks, right? – we have among us the agents of a foreign power, the raw fish eating crowd . . .'

The Tan Man mimicked the well-worn phrases and even the dramatic pauses in time with his boss, thinking of the occasion Ricky Rush had called Barker 'Mark the Bark, the demented chihuahua' and said he had a haircut that was so bad his head looked like a hand grenade with stubble. Oberdorfer laughed at the memory. Poor Ricky. Poor bastard.

'And now down in Florida,' Mark the Bark was saying, 'in Texas and California the left-liberal conspirators are trying to force Americans to listen to Spanish in schools. Spanish in American schools, folks! You believe that? The language that holds Christian people together has always been English. And if English was good enough for Jesus

41

Christ, it's good enough for me. Now, hear me on this one . . .'

Oberdorfer checked his watch. Just a few minutes left and then Barker would want a progress report on finding the videotape and the laptop computer. The Tan Man swallowed hard. He had nothing to tell Barker – except, maybe, that Ricky's brother did not own a television set or a video. Who would believe that? Where did this guy David Kerr come from? The Stone Age, maybe? Even the Flintstones had television, for Christ's sake.

'So, my friends,' Barker was saying. 'Here's what we do. We can keep the homosexual agenda out of our schools and out of our military. We can kick liberal abortion peddlers out of the Senate. And we can keep jobs in America for Americans. I'm not appealing for your money. I'm only appealing for you to pull out a pen and a piece of paper, or for you to pick up your telephone and call the White House and let them know what you think about their so-called trade bill. Trade war is holy war, my friends, and one we cannot afford to lose. The White House number is area code 202 456 1414 . . .'

Senator Mark Barker finished his appeal and then stood up, unclipping the microphone before waiting for a 'clear' from the programme director. He signalled impatiently to the make-up woman to clean his face.

The make-up girl was bending over the desk using the clean-wipes on Senator Barker as John Oberdorfer studied the roundness of her backside with a practised eye. He had tried explaining to her in the make-up room that if she would only be a little more friendly he could make things go well for her in the America First Corporation. He had tried putting his hand on her tail once or twice, but nothing nasty. He had even suggested they go take a room at the Holiday Inn to negotiate her next pay rise, but she had complained to Ricky Rush that the Tan Man was sexually harassing her, and Ricky had threatened him.

'You harass her again and you'll be eating your next lunch through a straw,' Ricky told him. 'Call yourself a goddamn Christian.'

'Aw, c'mon,' Oberdorfer replied. 'If God didn't intend men to harass women, he'd never have fixed them up with tits and ass. Chill out, Ricky.'

So maybe it was good Ricky had gone. Made life a lot simpler. Oberdorfer would have another try at the make-up girl, see if she had changed her mind about the Holiday Inn and the pay rise. But first, suddenly clean of powder, Senator Barker strode across the Power Tower penthouse towards his office area, and Oberdorfer ran to catch up. Behind the cameras, there was a desk, a sofa, a few chairs and a fifty-gallon fish tank.

'Great performance, Senator. The White House switchboard will be . . .'

'Get these people the hell out of here,' Barker said, pointing around the studio. 'We have to talk.'

'Yes, Senator.'

The penthouse office and studio were full of automatic cameras that could shoot Barker or the programme at any angle. The senator had a master switch on his desk which cut off – or switched on – all the fixed microphones in the studio. Barker called for his assistant, Janey, and ordered her to help Oberdorfer clear the place as quickly as possible. She tottered around on impossibly high heels and yelled at the crew to leave. At least, Oberdorfer thought, Janey was one woman who knew how to keep her job by keeping her boss happy. Barker walked to his fish tank and stared at the four large brutes inside, his nose almost pressed to the glass. Oberdorfer cheered up, because what was about to happen always put Senator Barker in a good mood. The fish were oscars, sullen, big-mouthed predators that hung in the tank like submarines. They were one of the few things in the world, short of oil prices going up ten dollars a barrel, that were guaranteed to calm Barker. The oscars eyed the senator with anticipation. He took off his jacket and told Oberdorfer to bring him the large plastic bag from his desk. The bag was filled with a dozen live goldfish.

'You know I got a pond at home,' he said over his shoulder, for what Oberdorfer knew to be the five hundredth time. 'They breed in their hundreds, the goldfish. Thousands, maybe.'

'Then what?' Oberdorfer asked, also for the five hundredth time.

'Then this.'

Barker put the plastic bag in the big tank and dug his nails in the side. The goldfish spilled out. The oscars looked at their lunch, waiting.

'They're in no hurry,' Barker explained. 'That's the great lesson of nature. Bide your time. Then you strike.'

The two men watched the fish in silence for a few minutes.

'Usually they suck out the eyes first,' Senator Barker explained. 'Then eat the rest.'

As he spoke, two of the oscars struck suddenly at the nearest goldfish, biting at their heads. In seconds the tank was a swirling mass of colour as the goldfish spun around literally in blind panic, the big fish sucking at them and swallowing them whole.

'Seen it a million times,' Barker confided. 'And it's still the greatest show on earth.'

'You are right, Senator,' Oberdorfer enthused.

'Okay,' Barker said, affably. 'Where are we on finding the video?'

Oberdorfer explained as best he could.

'We're still watching Ricky Rush's brother, David Kerr. The Mormons are all back from London now. We have a twenty-four-hours-a-day tail on him.'

'So you have found the video?'

'Not exactly, Senator.'

'The laptop computer?'

'Not yet.'

Barker hit his fist angrily on the desk.

'You know what's at stake here? Every goddamned thing. We're not playing in the Little Leagues. The future of this organisation, of the country itself, is in jeopardy, and if you're not up to it, I'll find someone who is.'

'Yes, Senator. I'm up to it,' Oberdorfer protested. He had been fired about as many times as he had seen the oscars eat lunch, but somehow he kept his office in the Power Tower. Somehow the Tan Man had made himself indispensable to Senator Barker's vision of America. 'We're on to it. We're working at it. We're almost there.'

If their future rested on finding the videotape, Oberdorfer would have liked to remind the senator whose dumb idea it had been to make the tape in the first place, but that would not have been very diplomatic.

'When the America First Movement reaches the White House,' Senator Barker explained, 'this videotape will be part of the history of the moral revival of the American people.'

'Yes, Senator.'

'But until then it could destroy us all.'

'Yes, Senator.'

'So find it, you son of a bitch, or else you're fired.'

'Yes, Senator.'

Barker had made the video himself, secretly, by switching on the microphones and the cameras in the Power Tower to record, as he put it, a meeting for future historians to ponder. The trouble was that Ricky Rush had decided to pre-empt posterity, and had stolen the tape, and they could not be sure its secrets had died with him.

'The missing videotape,' Oberdorfer mused, 'does *not* mean we have found our place in history. It means we *are* history.'

In the tank the oscars had eaten their fill. One small goldfish, only a little bigger than the size of a fin on the biggest of the predators, was trying to hide in the thick weed.

The big fish, their bellies swollen with food, paid it no attention until it made a fatal mistake. It broke cover from the weeds and tried to spurt away, but there was nowhere to hide.

'Hey, watch this,' Barker said, pleasant again. 'Watch this sucker go.'

The biggest oscar was too full to be hungry but it struck out anyway with a reflex action. In an instant it had sucked out both eyes. The goldfish spun blindly to the surface, gasping in shock. Senator Barker laughed and clapped his hands, then he put on his jacket and walked to the elevator.

'Remember,' he called out to Oberdorfer over his shoulder, 'in this world you either eat lunch or you are lunch, you follow?'

'Yes, Senator,' Oberdorfer said.

'So find the videotape.'

'Yes, Senator.'

'Janey, honey, get over here. We need to take care of a little business.'

7

New Age music jangled into the street; harps and bells, guitars and violins. There were two small speakers over the door of a red-brick building near the Potomac river waterfront in Old Town Alexandria, a few miles south of Washington. David Kerr checked the address, parked his rental car, and stared in the shop window. It was filled with pink and white quartz crystals, lush green ferns, and stiff little aloe vera plants. There were jars of vitamins and health pills, herbal remedies, books and music tapes, plus a large selection of colourful wall hangings, Native American rugs, framed nature photographs, and animal posters. The door said 'Harmony Supplies'. Beside the sign was a board shaped like a rainbow containing Hindu and Buddhist mottoes.

'You can never jump into the same river twice,' one read in deep blue tones. The small print underneath explained: 'You can jump in twice. But it is never the same river.'

A handwritten sign next to the platitude read: 'Closed Due to Death in Family.'

Kerr rang the doorbell and stood for a few minutes with the music wafting over him until a woman's voice answered.

'Who is it?'

'David Kerr,' he replied into the speaker phone. 'Looking for Beatriz Ferrara.'

There was a buzzing noise and the door sprang open. Kerr climbed the stairs and could smell cinnamon and other herbs and spices. The pleasant jangling music was turning into a kind of moaning which grew louder as he reached the inner apartment door.

Before he could knock or ring, Beatriz opened the door. She was dressed in a baggy white smock which flowed over tight pink leggings, pink canvas shoes, and a thick pink cloth tied round her waist. Even without make-up Kerr could see how pretty she was, exotically pretty, like the most beautiful of the Sandinista women Kerr remembered from the civil war in Nicaragua. Her face was drawn tight with tiredness and strain, and her voice was slow and soft.

'Come in.'

He followed her to where the jangling and moaning grew louder still. The sitting room was sparsely furnished, a couple of deep pink and maroon Indian rugs on a finely polished wooden floor, two settees and a chaise longue. A high-tech quadrophonic sound system hung in a glass-and-steel rack, and from the speakers in each corner the jangling ebbed and flowed. Dotted around the edges of the room were a number of low cherrywood tables on which sat large pink quartz crystals, pink pottery, pink geometric shapes, pink wall hangings, and a small, beautifully handwritten sign like a religious text in large italic letters which read simply: 'Think Pink'.

'Interesting music,' Kerr said, wondering.

'Whale Symphony,' Beatriz explained, in the emotion-drained voice he had first heard at the funeral. 'The composer combined the mating calls of humpback whales off the coast of Hawaii with his own synthesiser music to create something –' She took a deep breath as she searched for the word that would sum it all up.

'Pink,' Kerr wanted to say. But the word which completed the sentence after a long pause was ' – whole.'

Something whole, Kerr thought. Humping humpbacks. He tried to work it out, taking in the room again. The walls were pinkish white, a colour like that of the crystals, only softer. There was a large pendulum hanging over a sand pit in the corner. It was at rest now, but its point had left attractive geometric trails. Beside the pendulum was an expensive laser printer and computer system connected to a telephone line. The moaning of the humpbacks continued and Beatriz lay back on the chaise longue and closed her eyes, an American odalisque.

'You . . . like pink,' David Kerr observed.

'The gentle colour,' she responded, opening her eyes slowly. 'Warmth. Humanity. I can see a lot of it in you. It relaxes me. Thinking of the good things in life when so much is bad.'

For a moment, Kerr wondered if she was serious, but Beatriz looked so vulnerable he found himself pitying her eccentricities as if they were a defence shield. She picked up an infra-pink remote control and zapped the music down.

'Herbal tea?' she offered.

'That would be nice,' Kerr lied.

Beatriz retreated to the kitchen and he inspected the room for clues about his brother's relationship with this woman. A few days ago, he would have thought they were an unlikely match, but he'd hardly known he had a brother then. He looked at her bookshelves now, and found the titles were largely incomprehensible to him.

'*Chakra Medicine,*' one said. '*The Healing Crystal.*'

'*Shakti Woman – the Female Shaman.*'

'*Release your E-MOTION for Profit.*'

'*The Aura Guide.*'

'*The Deep Channel.*'

'*How to live your WHOLE life.*'

He opened the 'E-MOTION' book and began to read. A lot of it was printed in capital letters, like a written scream.

'Let me now tell you,' it said, 'the TWO greatest secrets. The first is that the SPIRIT OF EVERYTHING LIES WITHIN YOURSELF. And the second is that THE SPIRIT CAN BE CHANNELLED TOWARDS WHAT YOU DESIRE THROUGH E-MOTION OR ENERGISED-EMOTIONS.'

Then there was a series of mottoes.

'I use Money; it does not use Me. I control Money; it does not control Me.'

He flipped the page.

'I CAN. I MUST. I WILL.'

He watched Beatriz return with the herbal tea in a Japanese porcelain pot.

'A present from your brother,' she said. 'He was often travelling to Japan, picking up wonderful things.' She nodded to a silk screen painted with pink birds. 'That too. And silk kimonos. He loved me in them, don't know why.'

Kerr knew why.

'What did he do in Japan?'

'Air Force business. He never discussed it. Spent a lot of time in the Pacific. I knew he was a computer specialist, and that he spoke Japanese. When we first met he said it was boring backroom stuff, computer programs, signals maybe. Would that make sense? Then he said intelligence, whatever that is. Spying, I guess. I never asked any more, and he did not tell me.'

My brother the spook, Kerr thought.

'That his computer?'

Beatriz reacted oddly, as if embarrassed.

'No, no, it's mine. Ricky showed me how to use it. I keep all my business files on it.'

She sounded uneasy talking about the computer. He put the New Age books back on the shelf and studied her closely. British newspapers would call her 'sultry', but her beauty was under such stress it had the fragility of glass. Kerr recognised it was a beauty that could make men forgive anything, even humping whales and pink crystals.

'Was he into this?' Kerr said, gesturing at the books and crystals. 'My brother?'

Beatriz shrugged.

'Not really. Except that he hoped the store made money. He had . . .' She struggled for words again '. . . the habit of awkwardness. If anyone talked in a spiritual way, Ricky would be materialistic. If a person was a materialist, Ricky would speak philosophically or spiritually. He thought it was funny, but it always put people off balance. He swam against the tide, you could say.'

'I hope you don't mind me asking questions about Ricky,' Kerr added quickly. 'Even little things, like the Japanese tea set. It helps me draw a picture. It helps . . .'

'It helps you get in touch with your feelings,' she interrupted. 'So you can feel more comfortable about him, to be at peace like he is at peace.'

'Yes, I suppose . . .'

'I know.'

Kerr needed to move the conversation on.

'Two FBI agents came up to me after the funeral and wanted to talk. I fixed up an appointment to see them. They said it was not urgent, but it was about Ricky. I can't help being curious. Would you know what they want?'

Beatriz appeared to have been expecting the question.

'I better tell you a few things,' she sighed. 'Your brother was – or became – a fairly disturbed person. No one has said this to you?'

'No. Disturbed? How?'

'He did not confide easily,' Beatriz explained, 'even in me, but he was troubled, especially in the last few months we were together. Unbearable, finally. Anxious about his work, unable to talk about it, like he was a member of some kind of secret cult and had been sworn to silence. There was a hostility in him, you know? A disruption of the natural flow.'

Her eyes seemed to lose focus.

'When did you last see him?'

She hesitated.

'A while ago. A few weeks before that we had a falling out. It had happened before and I . . . I did not think much about it.'

'A falling out? About what?' Kerr felt he could be on to

something now, and didn't want Beatriz slipping back into the pink. She stared at him with some hostility.

'Sex,' she snapped. 'If you must know. Your brother was – what do his friends call him? – the wild man. That's how he liked to think of himself. Sexually omnivorous. I grew tired of it. And frightened. There are things you do not care to catch even from someone you love.' Now she'd said it, she seemed to calm down, but there was still some bite in her voice. 'His bad moods started more than a year ago when his mother took sick. They became unbearable by the time she died.'

'His mother?' Kerr interrupted, suddenly infuriated. '*Our* mother. My mother.'

Beatriz studied Kerr closely.

'I'm ... I'm sorry. Of course, your mother too. I never met her. Ricky and she did not get along. I think he felt guilty when she was dying. He hurried out to California and made peace. It was a long illness, then she died, and he was all mixed up. She told him about you, about her first marriage in Scotland, and there was a row between her and Ricky over it.'

'A row?'

'He told her she should be ashamed of abandoning her first son and running off to California. She said Ricky did not understand how it was, how she hated life in Scotland, how she had to leave.' Beatriz sipped her tea. 'Ricky thought about it for a while and began to track you down. In the end he said he had got a fix on you at an English newspaper, maybe three months ago. He was very excited, but then ...' She dried in mid-sentence and Kerr thought she was about to cry, but she held on, her eyes dipping in and out of focus. Eventually she went on, 'But there was more. There was something eating away at him from his work with ...' She spat out the phrase '... *those* people.'

'Which people?'

Beatriz shrugged. 'The Activity.'

Kerr looked at her blankly.

'I don't know much about it, except that Ricky was transferred into a new unit a year ago and he worked mainly with civilians. They called the unit the Activity. Then there were others that he really despised, not in the Activity but connected to the work. He called them the Mormons.'

'Mormons? As in, Jesus Christ and the Latter Day Saints?'

'I think some of them really were Mormons,' Beatriz replied. 'The rest just acted religious, quoting the Bible to him and things. Ricky was a great one for nicknames. But he could never bring himself to talk about the group. As if he was blocking, you know? It was a man thing.'

She stalled again.

Kerr said, 'I suppose it is difficult if your work is secret to talk it through with anyone.'

'Secret?' Beatriz laughed scornfully. 'I mean, what's secret now? I tell you, it was more like a religious cult than government work, as far as I could see, only . . . if I had been more understanding maybe none of this . . .'

Kerr was surprised he felt moved. This woman loved his brother, New Age freak or no, and on that point he was not entirely sure. Her voice was shaky.

'I was trying to get over it, but he left me . . . damaged. We dated and had lived together for four years, until this. He was such a gentle person, with me, anyway, until these moods.'

Kerr again thought she was going to cry, but there was steel somewhere behind the pink.

'And . . . that was when I decided I needed a new direction.'

'So you opened Harmony Supplies.'

'Yes.' She smiled at him. 'I'd been planning a retail business for years. I was just looking for the right opening.'

'I wondered if any of this would fit with my brother,' he said. 'It's not exactly the military style.'

Beatriz nodded, warming to him again.

'Right. He saw it as a marketing opportunity. I saw it as more spiritual, you know? Something to take me away from his life. But Ricky was one of a kind, finding the current and swimming against it, whichever way it was going. Like he wanted to prove himself, how tough he was.'

'Was he?' Kerr wondered. 'Tough, I mean.'

Beatriz choked up.

'He found it hard to get in touch with his feelings. When we first started to fight about his habits I told him I loved him but my body needed the equilibrium of celibacy for a while. He walked out. His anger was too high.'

The equilibrium of celibacy? Kerr almost laughed. He knew women who sometimes sounded as if they were speaking a different language, but nothing like Beatriz. She was the lover from another planet. He tried to imagine his brother, back from some God-forsaken foreign war and being preached at by Miss Quartz Crystal on the equilibrium of celibacy.

'So where did he go?'

'He spent some time with Lucy. You remember you met her? I think she was able to handle his hostility better than I. Or maybe she just took it less seriously. She lives life much more on the surface. It's what keeps her happy, and me miserable.'

Beatriz gave a nervous little laugh and lay back, closing her eyes.

'And the last you saw of him?'

'The last I saw was one day before he went overseas again, about three months ago. He came to the store when I was working. Said he had tracked you down to the newspaper in London and was going to contact you soon . . .'

'You loved my brother, didn't you?'

'Yes,' Beatriz whispered hoarsely. 'Still do.'

There was a long silence. Kerr stared awkwardly at one of the Indian rugs, embarrassed that he had asked such an intimate question, and finding that despite the occasional

54

lapses into hard-core psychobabble he was captivated by Beatriz. She'd said she couldn't live her life on the surface, like Lucy. She knew her awkwardnesses.

'In some ways Ricky was, you know, like a little boy. Then over the last few months something happened that meant he could not be a little boy any more. He was such a strange mixture. Loving, tough, in some ways, loyal. Stubborn.'

'Thrawn,' Kerr said.

'Excuse me?'

Kerr explained. Beatriz looked down at her hands. They were tiny and elegant. Her voice was almost a whisper now.

'The real reason I threw him out ... was not that he cheated on me ... it was because he brought guns back to the house.'

Kerr was stunned.

'Because he did what?'

'Brought loaded guns back. He said it was necessary to protect himself.'

She paused and Kerr waited a little.

'From whom?' he wondered.

Beatriz pursed her lips.

'I'm afraid to tell you, in case you think I'm even more eccentric than you already do.'

Kerr came over and knelt by her feet. She held her two hands together, as if in prayer. Her eyes were frightened.

'Protect himself from whom?'

'The Mormons,' she whispered. 'The short-haired, clean-living types who somehow became involved with Ricky's work in the Activity.'

'You keep saying Activity. What is it?'

'That's what he called it. That's all I know. He worked for the Activity, and some people he called the Mormons were trying to kill him. One night he came home with two cases. He opened one in front of me and inside was, like, a kind of pistol. Glick or something.'

'Glock.'

'Yeah, sounds right. Glock. Anyway, he told me he needed it and a shotgun for protection. I said I wanted no guns in my house. No guns, he said, means no me. I'm out of here. I said, okay, if that's how you want it.'

'And the other case?'

She shrugged again, then rolled her head forward so he could not see her eyes.

'A computer, a small laptop. And a video cassette, not the regular type but more like a professional tape. Ricky said he needed to find a safe place for them.'

'Where?'

'Well, obviously not here,' she sobbed. 'Maybe I got him killed.'

Kerr put his arms round her and hugged her. He felt her hold him tightly. 'Maybe if I had let him . . . He might . . . maybe . . . he would not . . .'

Eventually she stopped crying and Kerr rocked her back and forth then looked at her face, still pretty even though it was red and stained. She drew her fingers across her eyes and wiped away some of the tears.

'The best thing you can do,' she instructed him firmly, pulling herself together, 'is to go back to England as soon as possible. I can write to you or call you, tell you if I hear anything more, but please go back to England.'

'Are you trying to tell me my brother was murdered?' Kerr demanded. 'Is that why the FBI want to talk to me?'

Beatriz shook her head.

'I don't know, I'm not saying that definitely, but anything is possible. I only know he said he was in danger, and then this happened, and there's nothing you can do except complicate matters.' The tears had gone now and her dark eyes were staring pleadingly into his. 'Go home, David. That's the best for everybody.'

Kerr was puzzled.

'I don't understand. How is it the best thing?'

Beatriz tossed her hair backwards and began to cry again. Kerr moved away and sipped the herbal tea, which tasted like boiled grass.

'Is there anything he left with you?'

She shook her head and regained control.

'Nothing, not really. He took most of it, except a few photographs. If you want to see them, you are welcome. Happy memories. And he left me a couple of shirts, some books and things. I put them in a box. Want to see what I've got?'

They walked towards the bedroom. Above the bed was a geometric diagram with lines extending out of a crystal. Around it were more crystals, all aligned in the same direction.

'My meditation room,' Beatriz explained.

In the corner was a wide walk-in closet which Beatriz pulled open to reveal a stack of clothes and two cardboard boxes. She pulled out a photograph album from one of the drawers at the back of the cupboard.

'Take a look at these and if you want copies, I'll make them for you. As for the rest, look through the boxes and if there is anything you want, take it. I'm going to fix myself up.'

She left him alone, staring at the photographs. They showed his brother with Beatriz, looking like any young couple, happy, in love; Beatriz in a bathing suit; in tennis shorts; in a stunningly pre-celibate mini skirt with tight tee shirt; in evening dress. None of the clothes was pink.

There was a whole series of the two of them in scuba diving equipment on a wonderful beach; Ricky in his Air Force uniform; on holiday posing in front of a sign that said 'Rick's Bar'; at a barbecue; at parties; some with Lucy; one a foursome of Ricky, Beatriz, Colonel McGhie and an elegant black woman, presumably McGhie's wife. Then there was another series with Snow, Snow and Ricky in scuba diving gear, on the beach, in bars. The more Kerr saw, the less he could bear to look at them. He shuffled the photographs together and began to rummage through the cardboard cartons.

He pulled out two men's shirts and a pair of boxer shorts, running shoes and a couple of sweatshirts. He could hear Beatriz put on another CD. This time it was the cheerful sound of woodland birdsong arranged for synthesiser, beginning with the first chirpings of the dawn chorus. In the box there were a dozen or so books, a couple on economic theory, the rest on trade and the economy of Japan, plus a handful of paperback thrillers. Kerr picked up the photographs and walked back into the front room where Beatriz was still sipping herbal tea. She sat cross-legged, watching her smooth steel pendulum trace ever smaller ellipses on the sand, as the birds warbled on the CD player.

Kerr said, 'Do you mind if I make copies of these photos?'

'No,' she called out, her eyes fixed on the pendulum. 'But leave them here and I'll have it done for you, post them to England, then you won't have to wait around.'

'You still think I should go?'

'Yes.'

Kerr was losing her again. She looked down and began to cry, the sound like rain in a wheat field.

'Ricky said if anything happened to him before he tracked you down, they would find you.'

'They? Which they?' Kerr insisted.

'The Mormons. Or maybe the Activity people.'

'Beatriz, I don't know any Activity. I don't know any bloody Mormons.'

She shook her head.

'They know you, David, that's the point. They know everything about you. I can feel it. You must not stay here and get involved.'

'But get involved with what?' he snapped in frustration.

'Ricky told me –' her voice trailed off, then faded back.

'Told me if anything happened, to try to persuade you to leave.'

Kerr did not know what she was talking about. She seemed flustered and exceptionally anxious.

He said sympathetically but firmly, 'I am staying here until I find out as much as I can about my brother, from you, his friends, the military, the FBI, everybody. I want to know what the hell is going on, and I don't give up easily.'

Beatriz wrung her hands.

'You don't understand,' she shrieked, her voice suddenly strong and tinged with hysteria. 'You just don't understand. Go away! Go back to England! Go away!'

She closed her eyes and threw her head back as if he no longer existed. Kerr stood up and whispered, 'Goodbye for now, Beatriz. I'm sorry, but I'm staying. I have to find out more.'

Her face was like a beautiful death mask. As he walked from the room and down the stairs the sound of woodland birdsong followed him into the street, along with a cold feeling that Beatriz Ferrara was not the only one who had forebodings of the future. He wondered if he would ever see her again. Suddenly he felt desperate for a glass of whisky to chase away the taste of herbal tea.

8

David Kerr drove out from Washington to Virginia following Colonel Noah McGhie's directions. As he crossed the Potomac river at Key Bridge, he was amazed by the vastness of the America First Corporation. The building, with gardens and fountains below, was surrounded by hundreds of American flags, decked out at every level in red, white and blue, right up to the oversized Stars and Stripes hanging from the television mast on the roof. It looked, Kerr decided, like a star-spangled orgasm. There was a flashing neon sign along the side of the building with the electronic message of the day. It read: 'And God so loved the world that he gave his only begotten Son ... A message brought to you by the America First Corporation.'

'No,' Kerr muttered, 'a message brought to you by the Bible.'

Whatever Senator Barker's game, it obviously made money. Kerr took the road out into the Virginia suburbs. McGhie's house had a white picket fence and a large grassy front yard studded with trees. It ran down to a man-made lake, with a dozen or so other homes visible around the lake shore. McGhie's wife, the soignée black woman from Beatriz's photograph, had a wide smile and a gentle Southern accent. She greeted Kerr at the door like a long-lost relative.

'So sorry about your brother,' Arlene McGhie said, hugging him. 'He was family, so I guess you're family now.'

'I'm learning he was loved by many people, Mrs McGhie.'

'Arlene,' she insisted. 'And you're right. There was some-

60

thing in Richard that made people want to love him. His sense of fun, I guess. The kids . . .' She sighed. 'It was like losing their older brother.'

Arlene led Kerr through the house to a room filled with four children playing board games and doing homework. The children stood politely waiting to be introduced.

'This here's Richard's brother. Y'all take note of this fine man. He's from England.'

The kids looked at Kerr and shyly said hello. Arlene led him to the back porch where McGhie was sipping a Coke.

'I'm glad you could make it, David. Glad you found your way.'

'The others?'

'Others? Oh, you mean other buddies of your brother? Not tonight. They got sent to Fort Bragg on some business. 'Sides, I wanted a private talk.'

'And you pulled rank?' Kerr laughed. 'Sending them away.'

'Yeah, guess so.'

Kerr took a beer and McGhie used it as an excuse to throw away the Coke and open one for himself. They sipped from the bottles, making easy small talk about Ricky Rush as if re-living old times.

Kerr wanted to blurt out, 'Who are the Mormons?' or 'What the hell is going on with the FBI?' but the time was not right. Instead he said, 'Finding out about my brother is like being back at my old job.'

'Which was?'

'I was a newspaper reporter for fifteen years, a lot of it as a war correspondent. Finding out about Richard – Ricky – which is it?'

'His buddies called him Ricky,' McGhie laughed. 'Arlene calls him Richard because she thinks it sounds better.'

'See?' Kerr grinned. 'I don't even know what to call him. Anyway, finding out about Ricky is like piecing together a news story. You hear one thing, hear another, then it begins to make sense. For now, the more I hear the less sense it makes.'

McGhie laughed again.

'What's so funny?'

'That you and Ricky were in the same line of business,' McGhie replied. 'The information business. Quite a coincidence, or maybe it runs in the genes?'

McGhie explained how Ricky had been regarded as a high flier, a bright young officer, a credit to . . . and piled on the adjectives until Kerr thought he was back at Arlington National Cemetery listening to Senator Barker yap out the eulogy.

'Noah, you don't have to lay it on. Whatever my brother was like, I can't believe he was perfect.'

McGhie stiffened.

'I was just . . .'

'I know what you were doing, and I thank you for it. But I can take it if there are bad bits too.'

'You been talking to his women?'

It was not much of a question, more a statement. It made Kerr smile. 'How did you know?'

McGhie sipped his beer.

'Because some of us wondered whether your brother's dick would get him killed, or his mouth. It was going to be one or the other. He was a wild son of a bitch, that's for sure.'

Kerr was stunned by the change in tone, but before he could say anything Arlene called out that it was time to light the barbecue so the children could eat.

McGhie rose to comply as she appeared again with their four sons, eleven, nine, seven, and four, in a polite deputation.

'The boys want to ask a few questions about Ricky,' Arlene said.

Kerr told them the truth – that they knew Ricky better than he did, that he had never met his brother.

'You never met your own brother?' one of the boys said in disbelief. 'What kind of a family is that?'

Arlene said, 'That's enough, boys. Now go clean up.'

They scuttled back to their playroom, disappointed.

'I'm sorry,' Arlene said. 'Kids are so . . .'

'So acute,' Kerr interrupted. 'He's right. What sort of a family is it that can't keep together? I've been asking the same thing myself.'

Later, when they were ready to eat, McGhie led them in saying grace. They joined hands. Kerr felt the small fingers of the four-year-old slip between the stumps of his right fist, and it made his shoulder ache again. He closed his eyes in prayer and tried not to see the faces of the children who died when he was wounded in the grounds of the Sarajevo orphanage, but they swept back upon him. There he was standing among the blue berets of United Nations troops as they shepherded the children on to buses supposed to be taking them through Serb lines to safety and a new life in Austria. Colette Peters, two cameras round her neck and another in her hands, snapped at 1/250th of a second the upturned faces of children glowing with hope.

The orphanage director called a little girl from the line to talk to Kerr.

'This is Yasmin,' the director said, and translated as Kerr took notes and Yasmin clutched a battered teddy bear. She babbled about 'losing touch' with her family and what her new life might be like in Austria. Then the little girl put her fingers in Kerr's, holding his hand as McGhie's son was doing now. Yasmin talked cheerfully about finding her parents again, of a big, happy family, of her favourite toys, until Kerr had to blink back tears. And that was when he knew for sure that the attack was about to happen. There was an unnatural stillness and he felt the dull pressure round his temples like a thudding headache. Before he could call out a warning, they heard the crump of mortars. The girl's fingers tightened in his. She stopped talking, the dream frozen in her mouth, as the first of the shells hit the middle bus like a fist through a hen's egg. Kerr remembered the flash, the wailing children and the sound of his eardrums being torn. He felt the punch of shrapnel on his shoulder, then something worse, a tearing and a wetness on his hand. Colette was yelling, her mouth ugly, and he remembered a child's face, then another, and another, a swirl of children and nursery rhymes, and the uncomprehending look of Yasmin as the shrapnel killed her.

'Ouch,' Noah McGhie's four-year-old son wailed. 'You're hurting me.'

Kerr snapped awake and realised he was squeezing the boy's hand hard as if somehow to hold on to the memory of the children he had watched die.

'Sorry,' he apologised, letting go.

''S'okay,' the boy said, gripping Kerr's misshapen fingers again. 'Just don't squeeze so hard.'

'Sorry,' Kerr repeated.

Arlene's hand grasped his left, and Kerr felt his whole body tense as if waiting for incoming mortar fire as Colonel McGhie prayed to the family circle.

'Lord, we have the blessing of health, for which we thank you,' McGhie said. 'And the blessing of food, for which we are truly grateful. We think of those who are not so lucky, and we pray for the soul of our friend and brother, Ricky Rush. He walks with us still. Praise the Lord. Amen.'

Our brother, walks with us still. Suddenly the spell was broken and they began to eat, the boys diving towards the hamburgers and tomato ketchup, Arlene attentive to Kerr, handing him grilled chicken, ribs and salad. When they finished, Arlene took the boys to prepare for bed. McGhie suggested to Kerr that they walk down to the lake. The evening air was beginning to cool quickly as the sun set and the first small flies of spring danced in the light by the water. A rough track connected the houses along the shore.

'You can swim here in summer,' McGhie said proudly. 'Provided you don't mind the water plants.'

'It's very nice, very nice indeed. And I like your family, Noah.'

'I'm the real African-American hero,' McGhie added with a grin. 'A man with a wife and kids and a job and a home of his own. Not bad for a ragged-assed no-hope black kid from South Carolina.'

'Not bad for anyone.'

They stopped by a small wooden fishing platform and boat ramp.

'Your brother was murdered,' Noah McGhie said quickly, gauging Kerr's reaction. 'As far as I can tell.'

'Murdered?' Kerr gasped. 'Why?'

'I don't know. Not exactly, anyway.'

Kerr's voice came out strangled.

'You ... you said ... that one day his dick would get him killed or maybe his mouth, from talking too much. Are you saying ... ?'

McGhie waved his hand impatiently.

'I am saying I just don't know,' he repeated, stressing each word. 'There are one or two leads, but they are little more than rumours.'

'Are you involved in the investigation?'

McGhie shook his head.

'Not directly. I mean, no. It's difficult to explain without straying into classified areas, so let's make this real simple, David. You cannot tell anyone what I am about to say to you, understand? No one. Especially not Huntley. And most especially not any of the women your brother was with. I don't know what to make of them.'

Kerr shrugged. He didn't know either.

'Your brother disappeared six weeks ago. He had been working on an extremely sensitive mission in Europe and returned to the United States for some R and R. Then we lost him.'

'What do you mean, lost him?'

'A few weeks before he went to Europe he had a row with his girlfriend, Bee –'

'Beatriz Ferrara.'

'Right. He told me about it. She left him real pussy-whipped. Then he moved in with her pal, Lucy. I didn't think much about it, figuring it's not my business. Ricky had a – a big appetite. Anyway, after a few days, Ricky announces he's going scuba diving off the Outer Banks, North Carolina, down at Cape Hatteras. Scuba is a long-time hobby of his, but Hatteras is a tricky area for diving. So Ricky rents a room, alone. No woman, far as we know. Does not tell Snow, his usual diving buddy. His scuba gear, BCD, mask, snorkel, tanks – or pieces of them – get found by some kid washed up on the shore south of Hatteras. No sign of the body. His car's still at the hotel. His money, credit cards, everything still in the hotel safe.'

McGhie's eyes were sad, the words coming out slowly as if each syllable caused him pain.

'It's not like him. Nobody dives alone. Specially not off Hatteras. It's a bitch down there. And yet it's crazy to believe he just disappeared. His bank account is untouched. No money withdrawn recently. It's like aliens took him in a space ship or something. None of it adds up. None of it.'

Kerr asked, 'So what did we bury?'

'Rocks, maybe. Whatever it is they use when there's nothing to put in the casket.'

The deception made Kerr angry.

'So the funeral was nothing more than a bloody charade? I come all the way from London to bury a pile of rubble? Noah, I –'

'Shut the fuck up,' McGhie snarled a few inches from Kerr's face, flexing his body like a pit bull. 'I mean,' McGhie continued more emolliently, 'keep quiet, David. Don't go mouthing off until you hear the whole thing.'

Then he began to laugh, a full belly laugh. 'I'm sorry,' he

said. 'You just reminded me of Ricky. He used to say when I lost my temper with some white asshole that I was having a slave flashback.'

Kerr was amazed.

'He said that to you? To his commanding officer?'

McGhie nodded.

'And I guess slave flashback is not exactly a politically correct expression, but that was Ricky. Always on the edge, always living dangerously, and always treating everyone equally – that is, with no respect. He was lucky I've got a sense of humour. Follow me.'

McGhie led Kerr to the wooden slats of a fishing platform over the lake. They sat side by side, dangling their feet above the water's surface like children. So Beatriz was right, Kerr thought again. Even his own instinct after the funeral had been correct – he should have gone home when he had the chance. That was no longer an option. He was trapped by what McGhie had just told him.

'First the local police said it was a drowning accident,' the colonel said. 'They were looking for a floater, 'cause the bodies sometimes wash back inshore after a few days. Other times they get swept out to the Atlantic, and then it's over. Sharks, you know? It could have happened that way, but it doesn't square.'

Kerr watched McGhie's face as he struggled to make sense of it.

'The best dive sites at Hatteras,' he continued, 'are wrecks offshore, but you need a boat with at least one person on top plus a buddy underwater. This time Ricky had no boat, no boatman and no buddies. That's crazy, right? Then DoD security got spooked, because of the national security dimension, thinking he might have been kidnapped or something.'

'DoD Security?'

'Department of Defense. Like I told you, on paper I was his commanding officer, but Ricky got seconded to a new task force set up through the Economic Security Council. They reported a laptop computer missing. Also, two other men from the Economic Security Council were found murdered about a month before.'

McGhie took a deep breath. 'This is the weird part. The other two guys were called William Colvin and Peter Drysdale, both civilians. They were shot to death, their bodies dumped down in the Great Dismal Swamp a hundred miles south of here. There was a rumour about drugs, cocaine. That's when the FBI was brought in.'

'Was Ricky involved in drugs?'

'Hell, no,' the colonel scoffed. 'Drugs are for losers, Ricky knew that.'

'But he also knew the two men who were murdered?'

'Colvin and Drysdale? Sure. They were not buddies or anything, but he worked alongside them every day.'

'Does that seem like a coincidence to you?'

'No.'

McGhie paused and started rubbing the backs of his knuckles like a boxer checking for pain.

'This next part you have to forget immediately I tell you,' he insisted.

'Okay.'

'I sent Jiminez and Snow to Hatteras to check it out, because there's nobody else I trust. Not the FBI, not the DoD investigators. Not the local police. Nobody. You catching this, David?'

'I'm trying, Noah, especially since I don't know who to trust either.'

'Meaning me?'

'Meaning everybody.'

McGhie agreed.

'Yeah, I don't know what to believe, tell you the truth. I'm taking a risk talking to you, but I figure if I can't trust Ricky's own brother, then . . . there's nothing. Y'know what I mean?'

'I know.'

Now Kerr was embarrassed by his earlier outburst and apologised.

'Don't worry about it,' McGhie said. 'We're all strung out over this. Suicide isn't Ricky's style. Nor is getting careless and having an accident. That's why I figure somebody killed him – that and what happened to Colvin and Drysdale. But finding anything out from our own people, shit, those guys whine like a pig stuck under a gate every time they see me coming.'

David Kerr was listening but there was a buzzing in his ears as if this whole conversation were a bad dream.

'Noah,' he said eventually, 'don't do another slave flashback on me, but how come we took part in the staged burial of an empty coffin with full military honours? If there's no body, then what was Arlington about?'

'A decent burial for a good man,' McGhie responded firmly.

'But how many people knew there was no body?'

'We honour the dead even if technically they remain Missing in Action,' McGhie insisted. 'And your brother's MIA until I find out what really happened.'

'You have not answered my question, Noah. How many knew there was no body?'

'Maybe half a dozen. Me, Snow and Jiminez. Huntley and some of his people. You. That's it.'

'You never told Beatriz?'

'No.'

'But Huntley knew,' Kerr added scornfully. 'The Dependants' Officer. So what the hell *is* Huntley, anyway?'

'You know better than to ask,' McGhie snapped back. 'He ordered me not to see you without him being present, that I'd say too much. I told him I owed it to Ricky to tell his brother the truth. Guess Huntley was right.'

McGhie tried to rise but Kerr held his arm and pulled him down.

'I'm sorry, Noah,' he apologised again. 'I know you've taken a risk telling me anything. I didn't mean . . . it's just a shock.'

'Sure, but you are grieving over a guy you didn't even know. For us, we were his family. It's like losing one of my own boys. That mean anything to you?'

Kerr was struck dumb, because it did not. His family was so long gone, there was no sense of loss any more.

'You know, I don't remember ever having had a dinner at home with my real mother and father as we had with your family tonight,' Kerr said softly. 'Not ever.'

Noah McGhie looked at him in silence. The two men sat for a full ten minutes without saying a word, watching the last rays of the sun set and the flies land on the water.

Eventually Kerr said, 'So the FBI want to see me because there's an active investigation into the cause of my brother's death?'

'Active?' McGhie confirmed. 'Sure. We got *active* investigations like other people got mice. You ever hear of the Activity?'

Kerr shook his head. It would be better to keep Beatriz out of it. Things were complicated enough already.

'Never heard of it,' he lied.

'The Intelligence Support Activity,' McGhie continued. 'ISA for short. Or the Activity. Never run across it in your little wars?'

Kerr shook his head again.

'Not as far as I know.'

'Oh, it was there, all right,' McGhie continued in a low voice. 'It's a group of military and other personnel set up from different services to aid intelligence gathering and covert operations.'

'Sounds like the heavy mob.'

McGhie shrugged.

'Sometimes,' he said. 'Anyway, your brother was transferred to the ISA to help in their new technical role with the

Economic Security Council. This is where Senator Barker comes in.'

'The America First man.'

'Sure,' McGhie responded. 'Economic Security is Barker's latest crusade. He is the guy who arranged all the funding for the Activity through Congress. That's why he was at Ricky's funeral. He thought Ricky was one of his boys.'

'And was he?'

Noah McGhie shrugged.

'Ricky was his own boy.'

McGhie paused.

'Is that it?' Kerr wondered. 'Or are you part of the Activity too?'

McGhie ducked the question.

'I commanded your brother's unit, but was not involved in his most recent operation.'

'Which was?'

There was no answer. McGhie stood up quickly and Kerr scrambled to his feet after him.

'Let me repeat, in your brother's memory,' McGhie pleaded, 'say nothing about this otherwise I'm toast. If you hear anything from your brother's women, I'd be grateful if you'd let me know. They won't speak to me. They think I'm part of it, I guess.'

David Kerr could understand why. His head ached as if he had spent the day under an artillery barrage. McGhie stopped walking and stood right in front of Kerr, blocking his path.

'There's one other thing you got to know, David. One thing.' He paused for a second as if trying to think of precisely the right words. 'Where I come from,' McGhie continued, his voice dripping with menace, 'we have family and we have everybody else. When someone messes with family, we bear grudges. That's real family values, not the bullshit you get from people like Senator Mark Barker. I'm not going to let this rest.'

Kerr was still numb. 'Tell me, Noah,' he blurted out. 'Do you want me to stay here and help you or go back to England?'

'Help,' McGhie answered firmly. 'The more you stick around the more it might stir things up.'

'Is that good?'

'I think so.'

'Beatriz Ferrara said I should go home immediately.'

McGhie was interested in that. 'Oh, did she? Why?'

'She said something about dangers. She said Ricky had been worried for his life, worried about the Mormons. You know any Mormons, Noah?'

The colonel turned away and appeared to be staring at something in the trees.

'Mormons?' he answered, slowly. 'One or two, David. One or two.'

'Care to tell me about them?'

'No.'

They reached the house again.

'Noah.' Kerr tried again. 'I need to know who the Mormons are.'

'I have told you enough for one night,' McGhie replied.

Kerr knew he was about to overstay his welcome. He said goodbye to Arlene, then drove back to Washington, his head reeling with the new information. Behind him a large saloon car started up two hundred yards from McGhie's house, switched on its lights and threaded after Kerr through the darkened suburbs towards Washington.

'Mormons,' David Kerr muttered to himself. 'Where the hell would I find these bloody Mormons?'

9

David Kerr woke in the middle of the night dreaming of McGhie's dinner table, somehow relocated into the courtyard of the Sarajevo orphanage. He sat between McGhie's youngest son and Yasmin, the pretty Bosnian girl, who smiled vacantly at him. They looked to the sky. As if in a flickering old movie they heard the whisper of incoming shrapnel. In an instant it blasted into Kerr's shoulder and severed his fingers, painlessly, noiselessly. He found himself staring downwards as the corpses piled up at his feet: McGhie's son; Yasmin, whose head wound gaped open and bled on him; then Ricky, then their mother, who wore a Gorgon's head so frightening that Kerr found himself sitting upright in bed and calling out for it to stop. He was now so awake that he went to the hotel's exercise room and pumped his body hard, working with light weights on his shoulder, stroking the scar tissue.

There was a television in the corner. He switched on the early morning news where the lead story was Senator Mark Barker's latest attack on the White House for not standing up to the Japanese. He called it America's Economic Pearl Harbor.

'Sixty-four billion dollars trade deficit with Japan,' Barker said in his staccato way. 'No wonder they claim Americans are fat and lazy. The American people are not, but our government sure is. I don't see how we can blame the Japanese because we are dumb enough to let ourselves get taken. The problem is not in Tokyo. It's in the White House, and in Congress with liberals like Senator Hennington and his cronies. The president is the kinda guy, if he goes to a wedding he wants to be the bride. He goes to a funeral, he wants to be the corpse. Always has to be the centre of attention but never gets the job done. We gotta put America first, gotta . . .'

The interviewer tried to interrupt the monologue to ask if, as was widely reported, Senator Barker had really argued that the United States should send the Japanese government a photograph of a nuclear mushroom cloud with the words 'Made in the USA by fat and lazy American workers'.

Barker exploded.

'That's typical of the kind of unfair treatment I have to put up with from the liberal media. You folks should be ashamed of yourselves. If you spent more time listening to decent Americans rather than the east coast political elite, you might learn something. Anyhow, which Japanese corporation owns this network? Sony or Matsushita, I forget?'

The interviewer seemed painfully distressed but he tried to ask if Barker was thinking of running for the presidency.

'Sony or Matsushita?' Barker demanded again. 'Who owns you, friend?'

The interviewer became even more flustered and tried one more time with the running-for-president question. Barker's close-cropped chihuahua-head bobbed with laughter.

'I don't know anybody could do a worse job in protecting American interests than the guy in the White House right now. Since you won't say how much the Japs are paying you, maybe you could find out how much they are paying the president? What's it worth to destroy our economy, right?'

'But your own plans, Senator?' the interviewer persisted.

'My own plans are to put America first, always. The families of our people. Just watch this space,' Barker smirked. 'You'll hear soon enough.'

'We will watch, Senator. Thank you.'

The interview ended and they cut to a commercial for Toyota motor cars. What a malevolent little Nazi, Kerr thought. And my brother knew him? Jesus. He left the exercise room, showered quickly and caught a cab to where he had arranged to meet Lucy Cotter.

As soon as she saw him stepping out of the cab, she smiled, kissed him on one cheek and immediately took his hand teasingly, the mutilated right hand, appearing not to notice the stumps of fingers.

'And this,' she said, leading him away and up to the top of some steps, sweeping her arm around, 'this is the Jefferson Memorial. Named after, guess who?'

Kerr tried, 'Jefferson, maybe?'

'Wrong! President Memorial, dummy. You'll find things dedicated to him all over Washington. He's one of our favourites.'

Kerr began to loosen up, remembering how Beatriz had said something about Lucy living her life on the surface. So what? It was a great surface. She had honey-blonde hair round a heart-shaped face and the posture of a woman who suspected men were always looking at her. Which they were. As she walked round Jefferson's statue in her red dress, Kerr noticed more men staring at Lucy than reading the sonorous inscriptions from the Declaration of Independence. He could hardly blame them.

'Of course I miss him,' Lucy said when he asked her directly about Ricky. 'But there's no point in wallowing in it, is there, David?'

'You think Beatriz wallows in it?'

'She wallows in something, but I don't mean that cruelly. She feels guilt, as if it's her fault. She's been real strange for weeks. I don't . . .'

'Is it her fault? She said my brother was upset, feared for his life, that she would not allow him to bring guns into the house.'

Lucy shrugged her shoulders.

'He *was* upset,' she said. 'But whatever happened, I don't see how it could have been Beatriz's fault.'

Abruptly she changed tone, back to being a teasing tour guide. She pointed to the Jeffersonian quotations around the walls.

'They claim sound bites are a modern thing, made for television, but just read these inscriptions: "We hold these truths to be self-evident, that all men are created equal." Is that a good sound bite or what? And how about Lincoln: "Government of the people by the people for the people shall not perish from the earth"? We had sound bites before we had television, David. Is this a great country or what?'

Kerr laughed out loud for what seemed like the first time since Sarajevo. He felt a sense of liberation in Lucy's company that he had not known for years. He laughed so loudly he startled Brigham Y. Dodds, who was trying unsuccessfully to lurk behind a marble pillar. The Mormon could not imagine what was so funny about Thomas Jefferson, who, as far as Brigham could recall, was the serious-faced stiff on one of the dollar bills. He forgot which one. Brigham looked neat in his grey suit, white shirt and red tie, but he just knew that if any of the Mormons were going to get caught by David Kerr it would be him. Just his lousy luck. He sneaked back behind the pillar and shuffled his feet anxiously. Brigham carried his MAC 10 in a shoulder bag, just in case. He pulled back behind another Jefferson Memorial pillar and pretended to study his guidebook. The Brit was talking to Lucy like an old friend, looking relaxed.

'I saw Senator Barker on television this morning. It seems he is winding up for another run at the presidency.'

'Wouldn't surprise me,' Lucy agreed. 'He appeals to the worst in this country, to the Know-Nothings, to the foreigner haters.'

'Oh, so you really like him?'

'I despise him,' she said fiercely. 'You know he wears cowboy boots? There's a difference between farmers' boots and cowboy boots. With farmers' boots the bullshit is on the outside.'

Kerr laughed again, but he could see Lucy wasn't really joking.

'Barker must have known my brother well, judging from what he said at the funeral. How come?'

Lucy brushed back a wisp of blonde hair from the side of her cheek and spoke softly.

'David, as you probably figured out by now unless you're the dumbest reporter I ever met –'

'Ex-reporter.'

'Dumbest ex-reporter then – your kid brother was into electronic-computer-intelligence wizardry. Barker is co-chair of the Senate Intelligence Oversight Committee and ranking Republican on trade. He would have come across people like Ricky if your brother was involved in one of his important pet projects.'

'Such as?'

'I – I'm not sure.'

'Important enough to get him killed?'

Lucy turned away, saying nothing. She walked ahead to the top of the monument's steps with its view northwards across the tidal basin directly into the White House. Her body was backlit by the sun so Kerr could see her figure through her dress. Kerr walked up beside her, wondering if Lucy enjoyed the equilibrium of celibacy as Beatriz did. It did not seem likely.

Lucy said, 'You know Barker once argued that the only book a man needed in life was the Bible? He said everything you need to know is in the Good Book, and if it is not, then you don't need to know it.'

'Was that a joke?'

Lucy shrugged.

'I don't think so.'

Kerr decided to change the subject.

'Tell me about your family.'

'My family? Political. Politics in the blood. Dad worked on Capitol Hill as a lobbyist for the aerospace industry. Me, I'm with Senator Hennington.'

'Senator *Howard* Hennington?'

'You know any other Henningtons?'

'The one and only.'

'Right.'

Now it was all clear.

'No wonder you hate Barker so much. They must sit at opposite sides on everything in the Senate.'

'I would like to think so,' Lucy replied. 'Though Barker has become so strong, Senator Hennington has had little choice but to work with him on some issues.'

'Give 'em Hell Howie?' Kerr blurted out with amusement, remembering Hennington roasting Reagan officials for the massacres of civilians in El Salvador and the invasion of Grenada. 'The guy who takes up crusades against big government waste, especially in the Defense Department? You work for him?'

'You got it.'

Hennington was a walking paradox: a strongly pro-defence Democrat who had been in favour of every war against Communism, provided, as he used to bellow in his utterly uncompromising way: 'We pursue American values, not just American interests, and provided we have the wisdom to know the difference.'

Hennington had demanded the bombing of Serbia in retaliation for what he called their 'war crimes' in Bosnia, and every time some isolationist like Senator Barker claimed it was none of America's business, Howie would say that putting food in babies' bellies and taking out fascist monsters struck him as exactly America's business.

'It's what America was founded to *do*, Senator,' Kerr remembered was one of Hennington's more memorable lines. 'To do good. Or perhaps you have forgotten that?'

78

'And what's Howie giving them hell about these days?' Kerr asked.

Lucy Cotter laughed. He caught a whiff of her perfume.

'He's facing re-election in the fall. He's telling folks to raise less corn in Kansas and more hell in Washington –'

'I like it.'

'– more hell in Washington about foreign companies taking advantage of us, not paying their taxes here, and screwing us by protecting their home markets.'

'So he's stealing Barker's lines, about hating the Japanese?'

'No. But nobody can afford to be soft on trade these days, you understand?'

'That stuff big in Kansas?'

'It's big everywhere, David.'

'Maybe Howie should run for president,' Kerr joked. 'Against Barker.'

Lucy suddenly became serious.

'Don't say it, even in fun. Howie might do it and ruin us all. He's already appointed a new chief of staff, guy named Jim McCall, who once was a big-time campaign manager. I think McCall might persuade him to run for the White House, and I am not sure I could take it.'

They turned from the Jefferson and began walking arm in arm down the steps and around the tidal basin towards the Lincoln Memorial and the Vietnam Wall. It seemed so natural to be with her, Kerr almost could not believe that they had just met. Neither could Brigham Y. Dodds. He followed from a distance and scurried underneath the monument towards a row of public telephones, where he pretended to make a call, speaking instead into his radio transmitter.

'Jesus,' Brigham whispered. 'Love at first sight. Beats everything, don't it.'

From a bench on the far side of the tidal basin Scott Swett listened, then picked up his field glasses as if to observe the ducks on the water, watching Kerr and Lucy stroll under the pink cherry blossom, paying particular attention to Lucy's hips.

Kerr said, 'Can I ask you something?'

'Sure.'

'Something personal?'

'Go ahead.'

'Beatriz said she lived with my brother when he was in Washington.'

'Correct. Which was not often.'

'And that when they broke up, he moved in with you.'

She shrugged and squeezed his arm tightly.

'For a couple of weeks, that's all.'

'But you and Beatriz are friends?'

Lucy stopped walking and looked him in the eye.

'Listen, David, you British find it difficult to get to the point, don't you? Bea and I have been friends for ten, eleven years, since we were at Georgetown. We were together the night your brother and a friend of his, Tom Snow, picked us up in a bar over in Alexandria. She got Ricky, I got Snow. Could have been the other way round.'

'Fate?'

'Whatever. Snow and me, we lasted a few dates, nothing special. I don't go for military men. Bea and Ricky were serious. He was not your Grade A military clone, and she is the Nurturing Mother type. Wanted Ricky to settle down, get married, have a dog, a Volvo station wagon and ten kids all of whom would be honor students somewhere cosy. Your brother was never going to be that sort. For one thing, he never saw a pair of woman's legs he didn't want wrapped around his ears. Anyway, Ricky starts acting strangely because of his work, like he's being threatened. He won't say anything, but he starts taking precautions about his safety.'

'She told me.'

'Then there's a falling out between them and he has nowhere to go, so I took him in.'

The pressure had gone from his arm and she moved away to show him the pink-and-white blossom round the Potomac Basin.

'Wow,' Kerr exclaimed. 'It looks like Beatriz designed it. Think Pink.'

This time Lucy laughed.

'So where did you come in with Ricky?' Kerr persisted. 'You were his girlfriend?'

She turned and smiled.

'I did not sleep with him, if that's what you're getting at. He hit on me once, like he hit on everybody. I wasn't interested, that was it.'

Kerr was embarrassed because that was exactly what he was getting at. He wanted to know all about Lucy Cotter, and he could see she knew it too. They toured the Lincoln Memorial at the same high speed as at the Jefferson, while Brigham Y. Dodds scrambled to keep up. A group of Japanese tourists gathered round Brigham and insisted in broken English that he take a photograph of them. He tried to brush past but they kept bowing and smiling and getting in the way.

'Prease,' one said. 'Take photo.'

'Prease.'

'Okay, smile,' Brigham replied sourly, mocking their attempt at English. 'Smile for Mister Ablaham Rincon.'

Scott Swett had better luck. He followed a hundred yards behind, watching them traverse arm in arm along the black marble Vietnam Wall.

'Just like his darned brother,' Scott whispered to Brigham on the radio. 'Women won't leave him alone. I have him now, Brig. You take a break and we'll check in later.'

'Okay,' Brigham replied.

Lucy said to David Kerr, 'There is something you should know. Just before he died your brother asked me if Senator Hennington would meet with him, and I replied that the senator never met with anyone if he did not know what the

81

purpose was. Ricky said to tell him it's a national security matter. Tell him I've been ordered to do something ... something slimy. That was his word. Slimy. To tell him it's real important.'

'And?'

'And I talked to the senator and he said, okay, but he needed to hear more about it. He feared some kind of set-up, knowing Ricky was close to Barker's people. Anyway, when I came home to tell Ricky the news, he was gone. Next I heard was a few days later when the FBI came to call, saying he was dead. Then a couple of other guys came round asking more questions. They were from Defense Department Security. Gave me the creeps, if you want to know. Short-haired scary types, real Bible thumpers.'

'Mormons?'

Lucy looked puzzled.

'Could be.' She brushed back her blonde hair. 'They kept asking if Ricky had left any computer equipment or disk-ettes, or a video. I told them, no. So what's happening, David?'

Kerr shook his head.

'I have no idea. I don't know what is happening or who to believe. How about McGhie? Can I believe him?'

'There was a falling out,' Lucy replied, 'between your brother and McGhie.'

'About what?'

'I don't know. I like McGhie a lot, but Ricky claimed he was weak. He had to take a stand on something and would not do the right thing. Whatever it was, it seemed important to Ricky.'

Lucy looked at her watch. The senator was due back in his office after lunch and she had work to do. It was time to go.

'Can we talk about this more?' Kerr asked. 'Say over dinner?'

Lucy gave him a look as if he were transparent, and he

felt embarrassed again. She was more of a psychic than Beatriz.

'Okay, I do like being with you for other reasons. You make me laugh, that's all,' he explained lamely. 'I like being with you,' he repeated, as if to prove something. 'You cheer me up.'

'Okay. Come to my place. I'll cook. Eight o'clock.' She gave his arm one last squeeze and kissed him gently on the cheek. 'Only, here's the deal. I want the dinner conversation to be better than this interrogation, okay? Deal?'

'Deal.'

She turned and walked away. Kerr watched every step until she disappeared, heading towards the Capitol.

Scott Swett was also watching. He put his binoculars in his pocket and dodged through the crowds at the Vietnam Wall, trying to stay close to Kerr, wishing that it would soon be over and wondering whether they could dump Kerr's body where they had put Colvin and Drysdale. It was a big swamp, right? Only this time they could weight it properly so it was never found. Or maybe they should put Kerr in a bag and drop him in the Potomac, concrete round his feet, like in one of the Mafia movies? Scott decided he would like to see that, see how fast the body would sink.

10

As he trailed Kerr back towards his hotel, it never occurred to Scott Swett to consider that he himself might be followed. Instead he was thinking how it was a real miracle his head cold had gone. There had been a healing preacher on television that morning, the Reverend Willard McDill. Viewers could call in to the America First channel and say they had arthritis or bad knees or haemorrhoids and the Reverend Willard would offer a prayer and the sickness would be cured.

'Haemorrhoids,' the Reverend Willard had boomed, staring directly at the camera, his voice coming from a preaching tradition which did not understand the utility of microphones, 'haemorrhoids, *be gone*!'

And then the guy on the other end of the telephone wanting the call-in miracle confirmed it had really happened. He checked himself and said the haemorrhoids had indeed gone.

'It's a miracle. Thank you, Reverend,' he said. 'Thank you, Reverend. It's a miracle.'

Scott got so excited watching the show he spilled coffee over the Bible that rested in his lap, coffee right over Genesis 16. He got up and wiped it off and then blew his nose on the tissue, thinking maybe he should call the show and ask for a cure for his head cold. Then – like he is reading my thoughts, Scott concluded – the Reverend Willard asked people at home with ailments simply to touch the tube and pray, so Scott got down on his knees and tried it.

'Wow,' he yelled, wiping the coffee stain from his

trousers, as the miracle cleared his tubes. 'I can breathe, Reverend. I can breathe.'

For a moment Scott was so pleased he even considered sending in the requested fifty dollars to America First marked 'Reverend Willard's Christian Healing', but decided against it. He'd got a miracle on the house. So maybe he owed God one. And now as he trailed David Kerr through the streets of Washington, Scott had a spring in his walk, an unblocked nose and a clear head – not clear enough, however, to see what was coming.

A man wearing a leather jacket with a baseball cap pulled down over his eyes and carrying a Louisville Slugger bat on his right shoulder followed Scott at about the same distance Scott trailed David Kerr. He looked like a student athlete, wearing blue jeans and trainers and with an easy rhythm to his walk.

Instead of checking behind him, Scott was still practising breathing through his unblocked sinuses and beginning to fantasise about Lucy Cotter's body and how good she looked in that tight dress, and how Ricky Rush and Kerr had so much luck with women. There was nothing in the Book of Revelation that gave him any clues, and Scott could not remember anything from Genesis except begat this and begat that, but nothing about how to get started. Since his ex-wife had left him, he'd had little chance of begetting anything. Now Scott wondered whether asking the healing preacher for a few favours in that direction on his call-in show would amount to blasphemy. Guess not. At least, no more than having your haemorrhoids fixed.

Below-the-waist is below-the-waist, right? God would know this stuff, he reasoned, and if Scott got laid it might be worth the fifty dollars.

David Kerr crossed the road. Scott eyed him with contempt, thinking he had all the self-assurance of a sleep-walker who does not realise how brutal his awakening is going to be.

'Poor guy,' he muttered, buttoning his jacket and feeling the lump of the Ruger pistol under his arm. 'Won't know what hits him.'

Seconds after Scott followed Kerr across the road, the man in the baseball cap crossed too. Kerr was about two hundred yards in front as they walked past George Washington University, then he stopped and stared through the window of Tower Records. He stepped inside.

'What did I tell you,' Scott muttered. 'This guy's nothing but a goddamn tourist.'

The Mormon crossed to a pay phone to call Oberdorfer. As soon as he did so, the man in the baseball cap quickened his pace.

'Still nothing,' Scott reported to Oberdorfer. 'Kerr's buying a stack of CDs. Looks like he's heading back to the hotel. Spent a long time with Hennington's girl, so I guess she told him about little brother's approach to the senator. Kerr and she seemed to be getting on real well, you know what I mean? Feeling her up and stuff. It was getting hot, hot, hot.'

Oberdorfer tried to say something encouraging.

'Looks like we could be getting somewhere. Not long to wait now, Scott. One way or another, not long.'

'Right, not long.'

Scott Swett hung up the telephone and looked over 21st Street trying to work out where best to stand to wait for Kerr to come out. There were a few university buildings around, but with his jacket and tie he did not look like a college student, not in Washington anyway. There was a stockily built type with a leather jacket and baseball cap pulled down over his eyes coming towards him up 21st Street carrying a baseball bat – now *that* was what students looked like, Scott thought. Lazy, as if nothing mattered, scruffy and aimless, like Sixties liberals revisited.

Scott turned and spotted the perfect place to wait. As soon as he did, the scruffy student with the baseball bat seized his opportunity and broke into a trot. Scott moved into the doorway of one of the university concert halls from where he would have a clear view of the record store. The scruffy student was running now, turning the bat rapidly in his hands. Scott decided he would pretend he was reading the posters or programmes when Kerr came out of the store, but then his eye caught the flicker of the baseball bat and he tried to turn to see who was waving it in the air. It was too late. There was a brief moment of realisation when Scott heard the urgent shuffling of feet on the pavement behind him and guessed exactly what was about to happen and it amazed him. He tried to call out but the words died on his lips as he heard the rush of highly padded running shoes and a swishing noise as the baseball bat whirled through the air above him. Scott tried to reach for his gun. The student's face was contorted into a determined grimace as he swirled the bat full force, with the power, he hoped, to drive the Mormon's head for a home run into the oblivion somewhere between George Washington University and the state of Maryland.

The baseball bat landed on Scott's temple with a crack that could be heard across the street. As he fell, the student switched the bat again and struck two more blows, one of which glanced off the opposite side of Scott's head, the other beating on his shoulder-blade as he lay on the ground. Blood was already spilling out from the first blow, streaming across the grey concrete in a deepening red flow. As Scott slumped forward with a twisted smirk of realisation across his lips, the baseball player pulled his hat firmly over his eyes.

'Strike one,' he muttered, and began loping through the back streets towards Georgetown.

11

David Kerr emerged from Tower Records with a pile of compact discs and wondered what all the noise was about. To his left there was a disturbance a hundred yards down the street, a small huddle of people, a few police officers and two police cars, one with flashing lights on the roof. Kerr had spent half his life following police cars, and the habit would not die. He turned and walked to where there was a dark stain dripping into the gutter. It took him a moment to realise it was blood. The man on the ground was calling out something which sounded like, 'Heal me, Reverend.'

Then Kerr heard an ambulance wailing towards him.

'Heal me,' the man on the street was crying. 'Heal . . .'

'Broad daylight, man,' a black student said, still amazed at what he had just witnessed. 'Just clubbed him, you believe that? For what?'

'You saw it?'

'With my own eyes. Couldn't hardly believe it. Saw him run off with a baseball bat leaving this guy like he was dead. He dead?'

The cop said, 'Almost.'

'Looks like a lawyer from K Street.'

The paramedics started to load the body into the ambulance and the jacket fell open.

'Ain't no lawyer,' the black student said. 'Man's got a gun.'

The crowd fell silent as they looked at Scott Swett's shoulder holster.

'Shoulda used it. No point keeping it hid.'

'Use it or lose it.'

'Right.'

The paramedics quickly pushed Scott Swett inside the ambulance, shut the doors, and drove off.

'Broad daylight,' the black student kept repeating, shaking his head. 'What's happening to this place, you know?'

The policeman shook his head.

'This town's goin' to hell,' he said. 'Goin' to hell. Hey, what's this? Must've fell out of his pocket.' He picked up a small black book lying in the gutter. 'Jeez,' he said. 'It's a Bible. Killed a man carrying a Bible, you believe that?'

After Bosnia, David Kerr would believe anything. He turned and walked back to his hotel, tired from his early-morning start, too tired to care about Washington street violence, except for the nagging thought that death and spilled blood seemed to hang about him like a bad smell. He lay down on the bed and tried to doze, but what seemed like a few minutes later, the telephone rang.

'It's four o'clock, Mr Kerr,' the FBI agent Harold Ruffin said politely. 'We had an appointment.'

'Sure, of course, I was just dozing.'

It had been all of two hours since something extraordinary had happened and Kerr was beginning to expect a regular dose of surprises. He invited Ruffin up to his hotel room, but began to regret it immediately when the other agent, Brooks Johnson, started snooping around.

'Can I help you?' Kerr said pointedly. 'Maybe I can direct you towards whatever it is you are so desperate to find.'

Johnson took the hint and sat down on the couch.

Ruffin said, 'Truth is, Mr Kerr, we're not sure you can help us at all, but we're running low on ideas on your brother, and anything you can tell us could be useful.'

'Such as?'

'We understand you never met him,' Brooks Johnson butted in.

'That's right,' Kerr confirmed. 'I never met him.'

'Ever receive any communication from him?'

'Such as?'

'Telephone calls, letters, postcards, packages, presents, anything.'

Kerr shook his head.

'Until Joseph R. Huntley from the Pentagon – or whatever he is – contacted me, I didn't even know I had a brother.'

'But you came to the funeral?' Ruffin said.

'Wouldn't you?' Kerr smiled grimly. 'That's when I found out he had lived, when they wanted me to bury him. A little ironic, I suppose you could say. Do you mind telling me what this is about?'

He could see Brooks Johnson was going to make a snotty comment, but Ruffin put a hand on his arm to silence him.

'We know this is a difficult time,' Ruffin said. 'And we understand how awkward it must seem. We are investigating how your brother came to die, and related matters.'

'Was he murdered?'

Ruffin thought for a moment.

'Why do you say that?'

'Because I heard there was no body, that we buried a pile of stones at Arlington.'

Ruffin looked Kerr up and down, weighing how much to say. He preferred it if he did the investigating, but maybe Kerr was doing all right on his own.

'You still a reporter?'

'No, I'm in public relations.'

The more Kerr said it, the more it sounded as if he were lying, lying to himself above all. Of course he was still a reporter. It was a disease for which there was, as yet, no cure.

Ruffin said, 'Okay, but you understand the concept of off-the-record and deep background.'

Kerr thought that quite amusing.

'I understand the concept, Mr Ruffin.'

'Then off-the-record, this is what we have, or what we

don't have. We do not have a body. We do not have a very important computer containing classified information. And to tell you the truth, we do not have much help from your brother's co-workers and friends.'

'Huntley or McGhie?'

Ruffin smiled.

'Just leave it at co-workers and friends for now.'

'So is this a murder investigation, or not?'

Ruffin considered the question carefully.

'No. We were called in because your brother had disappeared, taking with him government property, the laptop computer and other documents. It was an investigation dealing with very sensitive matters of national security, but when your brother's diving equipment turned up at Hatteras we had to keep an open mind.'

'Meaning?'

'Meaning he could have had an accident, he could have committed suicide, he could have been murdered.'

'Of course,' Kerr interrupted. 'And he could have been vaporised by little green men from deep space.'

Ruffin patiently went through it again.

'You ever receive anything from your brother, any surprise packages?'

'No,' Kerr repeated. 'But maybe you could tell me if you are the only people looking.'

'Why do you say that?'

Kerr shook his head. 'I don't know exactly, except I have a strange sensation that I am being set up for something. Something nasty.'

Ruffin smiled. He liked this prickly Brit. Maybe they could do business together, if the Brit could manage to stay alive long enough.

'I do not know what to say, Mr Kerr. There's no reason why anyone should be setting you up for anything. On the other hand –' Ruffin shrugged. 'On the other hand, what can I tell you? That what we are looking for could be very valuable to other people. That you should take care. That you may be followed. That you may be at risk.'

'Oh, thanks,' Kerr said. 'Thanks for those words of comfort.'

'If you receive anything from your brother,' Ruffin went on, 'anything at all – in the will, maybe. Is there a will?'

'I don't know. I'm not expecting a legacy.'

'Of course not. But if anything does come to your attention, please give me a call.' Ruffin handed over a couple of business cards with the Federal Bureau of Investigation seal, and their telephone numbers.

As they stopped to shake hands at the door, Ruffin put his fingers to his forehead as if he had just remembered something.

'Oh, one thing, Mr Kerr, who was it told you we never found your brother's body?'

Kerr smiled.

'You familiar with the concept of off-the-record and deep background, Mr Ruffin?' he said. 'I'm thinking of going back to being a reporter, so I don't intend to reveal my sources. Do we understand each other?'

Ruffin had a look which suggested they did, but he would still like to know who told Kerr about the body.

'Okay, Mr Kerr,' he said. 'Have it your way for now.'

'Take care in this city,' Brooks Johnson warned. 'It's a violent place. They call it the nation's murder capital.'

Kerr stared back, not sure how to take the comment and not liking what he saw.

'I've been in violent cities before, Mr Johnson,' he said. 'But thank you for the advice.'

'You bet.'

12

After the FBI agents left, Kerr set off for dinner with Lucy
Cotter full of anticipation, of what he wasn't sure. He kept
reflecting on Harold Ruffin's oblique warning. Who else
was interested in his brother's death? McGhie? The Mormons? Huntley? Who were these people?

As he stepped out of the hotel elevator, Kerr felt as if he
had lost his lucky charm for the second time, as if the
darkness was about to swallow him again. He gazed around
the lobby then up and down the street, not even sure who
or what he was seeking. The FBI? The mugger with the
baseball bat? The ghost of Yasmin that he was sure would
walk with him forever?

'Oh, come on,' he muttered, trying to steady himself.
'Too much of this and you'll go crazy.'

He picked up a bottle of chilled champagne in a liquor
store near the hotel and walked towards Lucy's Georgetown
apartment. At every road junction he found himself checking behind him with the uneasy sensation that he was being
followed, yet there was nothing, no one, or worst of all, no
one Kerr could see.

'Jesus,' he muttered again, the hairs prickling on his neck.
'Paranoid.'

Lucy's apartment was in a fancy block on the harbour
overlooking the Potomac river from where Kerr could
clearly see the lights of the red, white and blue America
First Corporation skyscraper. There were clues there, he
was sure of it, but he had no idea how to get at them.

As he approached the apartment building Kerr did a
double-take. The paved area outside was decorated with

half a dozen life-size and life-like bronze statues – a white man in a suit sitting on a bench reading the morning paper; an elderly black man holding his granddaughter in the air; a young couple kissing in a doorway. The statues were all elegantly crafted, with a sense of fun, but in his current mood Kerr found them spooky. He hurried past the bronzes, the hair prickling again on his neck, to where Lucy's apartment entryphone hung on the outside wall. She pressed a button to let him in, reciting a five digit code for the key pad inside.

'To see you I need to know numbers?'

'If you want to get up here on the elevator you do.'

By the time he had negotiated the security hurdles and stepped out on the sixth floor, there was yet another locked door in front of him. Kerr picked up a second entryphone and Lucy buzzed again to allow this door to open.

'And I thought I was paranoid,' he mumbled.

It was only then that he reached the front door of her apartment, as secure as the keep of a modern castle. This one swung open with Lucy behind it, standing in figure-gripper jeans and an overlarge blue tee shirt which perched outwards on her breasts like a smock. She was smiling, cocking her head to one side coquettishly. It was worth the pain of getting here. She was beautiful.

'Hi, David.'

'You know, it's like trying to break in to a bank vault,' Kerr said. 'Everybody live like this in Washington?'

'Everybody who wants to stay alive,' she suggested. 'And welcome to our nation's capital, in which, in case you did not know, statistics show you were always much more likely to be murdered than by terrorists in Northern Ireland.'

'You are the second person in about two hours who has reminded me how dangerous it is here.'

'We like to keep our visitors informed.'

'And scared.'

'Right. Scared is good too.'

Kerr kissed her chastely on the cheeks. She smelled good. 'Wonderful. French champagne. I'll get glasses.'

Kerr walked through the apartment. It was big and airy, and, he was delighted to see, decorated in beige and a light pastel blue. There was no trace of the colour pink anywhere, which he took as a good sign that he would not find the equilibrium of celibacy here. A picture window opened to a narrow balcony. Kerr stepped out and looked below to the courtyard with the bronze statues and a small fountain. On the Potomac there was a party in progress on board a flat-topped riverboat, the dance music drifting towards the shore. To his left he could see in the sky the lights of aircraft slowly arcing behind the Kennedy Center to National Airport. Kerr turned back to the courtyard where he thought he saw the face of a man suddenly orange under the street lights. This was no statue. The man appeared to step out of the shadow of a doorway and look up at him, then dart back guiltily as if recognising he had been caught.

This time it was real.

Don't they say that even paranoids have enemies? Kerr moved quickly forward on the balcony and leaned over, trying to get a better look at the figure he was sure had been following him. Whoever it was did not show again. Nothing, except the orange glow of the lamps, the shadows around the bronze statues and laughter and music in the distance from the riverboat. Maybe it was one of Ruffin's people, or . . . Kerr started to think of who might have been able to put the fear of God into his brother, a fear that was so great he had brought guns home and then disappeared off Cape Hatteras. His mind raced through the possibilities again: Huntley, McGhie, and Senator Barker, plus faceless men in suits who had gathered for the formal funeral of an empty coffin in Arlington Cemetery.

Kerr's eyes darted round the streets below searching for Mormons. He could see nothing – only the lights from the America First building reflected in the stillness of the river.

He was almost beginning to believe he had imagined it again, when he sensed a hint of fragrance. Lucy was behind him with two foaming champagne glasses.

'Admiring the view?' she teased.

She handed him the champagne and he stared back at her, suddenly sure that the teasing was over, that she really wanted him now.

'Yes, it's a fine view.' He raised the glass and kept looking at her. 'In fact, let's drink a toast to it. You are a very beautiful woman, Lucy.'

Her face glowed with health as if she had just exercised. She smiled and her lips were moving gently towards him, close, very close.

'Thank you,' she murmured, and Kerr felt her breasts in the tee shirt push him as she softly brushed his lips with hers. 'And thank you for the champagne.'

Lucy took half a step backwards and Kerr blinked. The moment their lips touched was so short it was as if he had dreamed it, a passing breeze. He sipped the champagne and tasted lipstick, then wiped his lips slowly with his fingers, letting his tongue taste the kiss.

'I, um, I don't really know what to say.'

'Then don't say anything. That's the trouble with Washington. It's full of people who have nothing to say yet who say it anyway, usually on television and usually real loud.'

He stretched out his left hand and gently caressed her cheek. She edged towards him and he felt the press of her tee shirt again on his chest, then the curve of her jeans pushing into his hips. Her hands moved up his side and pulled him tightly into the kiss. The sudden leap of his blood excited him. When they broke free he took both drinks and put them on a small table. He could hear cheering and singing from the party on the riverboat and the noise of an aircraft landing in the distance.

'This is starting to get interesting,' Kerr said. 'It's almost worth coming to America for.'

'They don't do this in Europe?' Lucy asked playfully.

'Europeans? Sometimes. It's just here, I thought everyone was like Beatriz, seeking the equilibrium of celibacy.'

Lucy looked at him quizzically, turning her head to one side so the hair fell down in a shock of blonde.

'You really think all Americans are weird?'

'An old girlfriend told me I think everybody is weird, and it's true. It's just that Americans are just more public about it.'

'Old girlfriend?'

'Definitely.'

'Any wife? Kids?'

'Thankfully, no.'

There was a thickness in his throat and he pulled her back to him, wondering, since it was becoming so serious so quickly, what the man or men in the shadows might make of it. As they kissed, Kerr had an idea. He slipped his right hand behind Lucy's back and over the balcony rail so it could be seen most clearly by anyone watching from below.

Down below, Brigham Y. Dodds's heart was still beating fast from the shock of seeing Kerr stare right into his eyes. His first impulse had been to run, since Kerr's gaze made Brigham think of what had happened to Scott with the baseball bat. The poor sucker was still on a life support machine, according to Oberdorfer, his skull crumpled like a discarded Coke can. And now the crazy Brit was checking him out from the balcony of Lucy Cotter's apartment, like he wanted to come down and beat the crap out of him. It was scary. Jeez. Brigham pulled back deep into the shadows, deciding he would carefully reposition himself in case Kerr came running out of the apartment searching for him.

He could shoot him, of course, but Oberdorfer would go crazy, and Brigham's panic was made even worse by having to decide whether he was more afraid of Kerr or Oberdorfer.

It was not much of a choice. He was more afraid of which-ever one was nearer – which, right now, was definitely Kerr. He shifted into another doorway.

'Ah!' Brigham grunted in fear, startled by one of the bronze statues. 'Shit!'

He couldn't see the point of these goddamn things, put down to scare people. If this was art, give him the Mormon temple in Salt Lake City any time. Jesus. This was more like faggot art. He angled himself so he could look up to where Kerr and Lucy embraced on the balcony, yet would still be able to run if that proved necessary. After a while of watching, his heart stopped thumping. It was obvious Kerr had not seen him. At least, David Kerr was not going anywhere any time soon, except maybe into Lucy Cotter's pants. Brigham figured he could not be suspicious otherwise he would not be so casual. Then Brigham saw Kerr's hand slip round her back, doing something, and he got pretty excited, the more he thought about it. He knew Europeans had no shame, went topless on the beach and stuff. But were they – you know – going to do it on the balcony? Like one of those topless bars where you slipped them twenty bucks and they waved their titties in your face?

He felt a sudden pang of guilt that he was getting aroused. In the dim light he was not able to make out exactly what was happening, so he shifted position one more time, craning his neck to see.

Suddenly he realised that Kerr's hand was not unfastening Lucy's brassiere after all. Instead, as they continued to kiss, Kerr had moved his right hand behind her back. It dangled over the apartment balcony and David Kerr was carefully raising the middle finger in an unmistakeably obscene gesture directed downwards to where Brigham stood in the darkness. Brigham rarely said the F-word, but this was too much. He was stunned by Kerr's contempt.

'And fuck you too,' he whispered. 'You've got it coming, you fucker.'

In the shadows behind him a man in a baseball cap watched Brigham shuffle his feet nervously. This time the man had no baseball bat over his shoulder. He checked his pistol, and waited.

13

Brigham did not know what to do. Run away, maybe, only Oberdorfer would get mad and that did not bear thinking about. The Tan Man did not handle bad news very well, and the idea that Brigham stopped the surveillance because Kerr gave him the finger would be difficult to explain. But it was spooky the way it happened, as if Kerr knew everything about what they were doing, was always several jumps ahead.

Brigham rubbed his face nervously and thought for a moment longer. He could stay his ground and wait for Kerr to come at him. He put his hand on the butt of the Ruger pistol, and was ready to draw, then he thought again. Oberdorfer would be even crazier if he killed Kerr before he had led them to the video. Shit. Brigham took his hand off the Ruger again.

He looked from left to right. The bronze statue of the old black man playing with his grandchild seemed unoffended by Kerr's obscene gesture. The other statues were staring remorselessly at Brigham from the deep gloom. He felt the hairs prickle on his neck as he began to taste the queasy panic that swept up on him. Saliva filled his mouth. Something bad, real bad, was about to happen. He could smell it. Brigham decided he would call Oberdorfer for advice, so if he had to shoot Kerr it would not be such a big surprise. He would force the Tan Man to take a decision. Brigham looked up at the balcony to see Kerr's hand move over towards Lucy's butt, then he gazed around one more time at the statues before deciding to slip round in the shadows to one of the nearby restaurants and use their pay phone.

Most of all, Brigham realised, he wanted to kill Kerr, and get it over with, because Ricky's brother was bad luck, and if Scott Swett could get beat up in daylight, what could happen to Brigham now in the darkness?

He shivered and anxiously checked the Ruger pistol again. Brigham walked carefully through the shadows with his hand on the gun, slipping past the statue of the old man and the girl. He was coming upon the bronzes of the lovers when he noticed a statue he had never seen before. It was of a thick-set man wearing a pulled-down baseball cap, leaning on the brick pillar of an office block. The statue's right arm was extended, supported by his left, so that in the darkness Brigham let out a squeak of surprise. He could see the shape of a gun pointing towards him when the statue spoke.

'You even think about running away, you son of a bitch, and you're dead meat. Put your hands on your head where I can see them.'

Brigham tried to do as he was told but he felt his breath come in panicky gasps and a deafening rush of fear unblock his bladder, the warmth spreading down his trouser leg.

14

'The neighbours,' Lucy Cotter said, pushing Kerr away.

'They'll complain?'

'No, they'll be jealous.'

They paused and looked at each other.

'Can you believe this?' Kerr said.

Lucy smiled and said softly, 'Yes.'

From the balcony Lucy led Kerr inside and through to her pastel green bedroom. She pulled off her tee shirt and unpeeled her jeans until she stood in front of him in her underwear. The uninhibited way she did it made him forget the phantom face in the shadows, forget everything other than Lucy before him.

'Does this feel right to you?' she asked softly.

'Everything feels right.'

He began to unbutton his shirt. As it slipped off, Lucy saw the shoulder scar for the first time and stopped. Kerr could hear her sudden intake of breath and knew it must be a shock. He thought it probably disgusted her, but after a few moments her fingers trembled towards it. They felt cold.

'Maybe this doesn't feel right after all,' he said. 'I'm sorry.'

Lucy's fingertips gently traced down his right side from the shoulder, over the raised cut which fell to the rib cage in a white line and then across the patched road map where the last of the stitches had been removed.

'It feels just fine,' she replied.

She stopped and kissed the scar with a tenderness that made him gasp. He ran his hands down the smoothness of her back and she shivered, then he pulled her towards the bed. After some moments, she broke free, walking to a side table. He stared at her, bemused by her utter lack of self-consciousness as she pulled out a packet of condoms, selected one, unwrapped it and carefully unrolled it on him until he could take it no longer, hungry and desperate, falling upon her like a traveller finding water in the desert.

'Pursuit of happiness,' Lucy said, when their lovemaking was over, lying naked in his arms and running her fingers over the scar and the stumps on his right hand. 'I told you, it's what Americans are good at.' She twisted his chest hairs, running her tongue slowly along his skin. 'You want to tell me how you got the scar?'

'Not really.'

'Okay.'

Kerr paused and looked up at the ceiling. His shoulder did not hurt now, not at all.

'I didn't mean to –'

'That's all right,' he replied. 'It's my Souvenir of Sarajevo. Of course I'll tell you about it, if you want.'

He recounted the event plainly, stopping at the part where his dream always ended, the first punch of shrapnel on his shoulder and the look on Yasmin's face. In the dim light Lucy thought his eyes were glistening, and it made her want to hold him tightly.

'I don't remember after that,' Kerr explained. 'Except I was med-evacked out to Austria. I have enough shrapnel in my shoulder to make the metal detectors go off at airports.'

Lucy looked at him, curious. 'That's a joke, right? British humour?'

'Yes, that's a joke, Lucy.'

'And you still feel guilty about the girl?'

Kerr sighed.

'She would have had a chance if I had not been there. She was clinging to me.'

'Because she had no one else?' Lucy asked.

'I suppose so,' Kerr sighed. 'A few degrees one way or the other and I would have been killed, but she took it for me, took the blast. A few minutes later and she would have been gone, and ever since . . .' He lay back on the bed and put his hands to his eyes '. . . ever since, I wondered why a beautiful child is put into the world to die like that. What kind of God would let a child suffer and let me live?'

'You would prefer that you had died and she had lived?'

'Yes.'

He felt her lips brush the scar again and then kiss him. Her head came to rest on his chest.

'You British,' she scoffed. 'For Americans it's always the quality of faith that is important. For you it's always the quality of doubt.'

He brushed a stray tear from his eye, keeping his face from her so she would not see.

'What do you mean?'

'I'm thinking about you and Ricky,' she said. 'He was a lot like you – smart, good looking. But he always believed that if he did his duty for God and country, then God and country would look after him. I have to believe it was his faith that got him screwed.'

'And I'm not like that?' Kerr said. 'You know that already?'

Lucy laughed.

'Yes, I know that already. I think if someone told you it was all for God and country you would have to check it out. You always have to ask, why? What's this for? What does it mean? Before you decided to do anything for Him, you would want to interrogate God, make sure he was on the right side.'

'Maybe,' Kerr said. 'But that doesn't mean I don't get screwed too.'

'Of course you get screwed,' Lucy countered. 'But not by other people. You screw yourself with your doubts.'

'And what about you? Are you a Faith-person or Doubt-person?'

'I'm an American woman,' she giggled. 'Faith, Doubt, I can have it all.'

He pulled her on top of him.

'Look, I came here for sex,' he laughed, teasing her. 'Not psychiatry. So let's get on with it.'

They rolled together again. Eventually he said, 'Maybe you are right.'

'I'm always right,' Lucy replied. 'About what?'

'Well, if Ricky was too full of faith, then I certainly have doubts enough for both of us. If you combined us, you'd have a whole person. I have doubts about my job, doubts about my personal life, doubts about what I did in Bosnia, about what I'm doing here . . .'

She laughed again.

'What you are doing here, David, is getting laid. I thought we agreed on that.'

He stroked her cheek.

'I think it's more than that,' he said. 'It's as if I was asleep and you just woke me up. And I hardly know you.'

'Exactly,' she said. 'That's why I used the condoms. Come on.'

She slipped on a white silk housecoat, stood up and held out her hand. 'Come with me. I have a few things to show you.' She led him to the spare bedroom. 'This was where your brother slept,' she pointed. 'When he lived here.'

'You told me before.'

'I know, but I just wanted to make it clear. I liked him, but we did not sleep together, okay? Got the message?'

'Okay, Lucy, I've got the message. But I'm from the generation that reached puberty in the little window of opportunity after the invention of the Pill and before the discovery of AIDS. You don't have to explain anything to me. All I have to explain to myself is why I feel so relaxed with you.'

'Beatriz would say it's our auras.'

'Maybe she's not completely wacko then.'

Lucy opened a cupboard and rummaged around until she found half a dozen manila folders.

'Before he disappeared Ricky told me he wanted to leave some files here. I was to give them to no one, not even Senator Hennington.' She took another deep breath. 'To no one except you.'

Kerr was astonished.

'Me?'

'Like I said earlier, he told me he was on assignment in Britain when he found out you were a newspaper journalist. Then he called the newspaper and they said you had been injured and quit. He wanted to make contact but he was running out of time. He knew something bad was going to happen.'

'Meaning?'

'Meaning, Ricky would not tell me exactly, though I guess he had decided he was going to give Hennington the full story. He said they had lied to him, whoever "they" are. That they ordered him to do things he realised were wrong, but it was too late. Faith, you see? He believed in what he was doing. It's the American curse. The European curse is to wait for a good reason to do things, which is why Europeans are so goddamn inert. Anyway, whatever the slime was, it got to him. He wanted you to have these.'

She thrust a couple of computer diskettes into his hands.

'What's on them?'

'I didn't look.'

That struck Kerr as incredible. He would have.

'Why not?'

'Ricky told me not to. They were for his brother, like it was a private affair, family only. It could be about your mother. I never mentioned them to the FBI or anyone else, not even Beatriz. Family business is private business. If you had not turned up for the funeral I was going to look at them, but they are yours now.'

'Did the FBI ask you about the diskettes?'

'Not specifically. They were looking for a laptop computer.'

Kerr looked around. 'Do you have somewhere I can look at these?'

She pulled out her own computer, then left him alone. Kerr sat on the edge of his brother's bed and began listing the directories and files. They were all arranged by dates on an easily accessible word-processing program. The first few files carried a string of Japanese company names; some of them were banks, others were securities houses or industrial conglomerates.

There was a pattern to the entries but it was not clear what it meant.

'Nomura Securities. Eight days. $180,000. AFC x3.'

'Dai-Ichi. Six days. $225,500. AFC x8.'

There was a string of European company names, including aircraft manufacturers, half a dozen banks and securities firms, and profits in the tens or sometimes hundreds of thousands of dollars. Kerr keyed in a sub-directory marked 'Currencies' and opened the file called 'Sterling'.

'September 92: British pound sterling collapse; switch/ Deutschmarks. Check with JH, SS, Ob. AFC unknown. Check with Ob. Transcript FIVE Act. 154/2396b; Bundesbank 14–23 DM154/9893.'

Then there were numerous listings between October and December 1992 for US Air and British Airways, plus an overall figure quoted as '$115,000. AFC x5 est.'

And so it went on, including a lengthy section on the values of the French franc in the middle of 1993. Kerr scratched his head in puzzlement. It looked as if his brother had been working for a stockbroker or an international currency trader rather than Air Force intelligence. Was it a hobby, following the stockmarket? But why would his brother bequeath the diskettes to him? And the references to 'AFC' made him think only of Arsenal Football Club.

Kerr went through the files again carefully. The entries were similar in each: company names, notes about currency fluctuations, dates and statements from European central banks, plus a specified time period. The word PERSONAL or ACTIVITY was often typed in block capital letters. Eventually Kerr came across one which said 'America First Corporation'.

'Of course,' he exclaimed out loud. 'AFC. Bingo!'

The nasty little chihuahua, Senator Barker, really had something to do with his brother after all, something, in his brother's expression, that was slimy. And the connection involved a lot of money. When Kerr was sure he had exhausted every item on the diskettes he returned to the kitchen where Lucy was chopping salad.

'You sure you did not look at this stuff?'

'I told you I never read it. I don't lie, David.'

'It's about share dealings and currency information. AFC, which has to be the America First Corporation, is mentioned frequently, along with figures for profits. It looks like Ricky was monitoring the profits made by the America First Corporation from share dealing and currency trading.'

Lucy put down the knife and looked at him, aghast.

'You must be kidding.'

'Want to see? I think Senator Hennington might be interested.'

'I believe you . . . only . . . the time Ricky tried to fix up to see Hennington he asked that I tell the senator he had been assigned to the Economic Security Council.'

Kerr looked puzzled. Lucy tried to explain.

'The ESC is supposed to monitor our economic performance, that of America's competitors, and overall trade questions. I thought it weird, I mean, why would they need an Air Force officer? So I told Hennington and he said it figured.'

'Why?'

'Because the big money has been re-assigned to economic

intelligence. Hennington says the real hot button debate inside the National Security Council, the CIA and the NSA, is how far we should switch to economic intelligence, and if we do, who should benefit? The French do it; the Koreans and Japanese do it. So why not us? I don't know how far we've got, but it's so sensitive Howie just will not share much, except that the decision was to be left to the Economic Security Council.'

'And Ricky said he was being asked to do something slimy? Maybe spy on the America First Corporation because they are such a pain in the neck for the administration? There would be hell to pay if someone found out the White House was spying on a corporation run by a big-time Republican rival.'

'Maybe,' Lucy replied. 'Only how would that fit in with how worried Ricky was, or the way Barker seemed to like him?'

Kerr thought about it for a moment and decided he was even more lost than before.

'Beats me,' he replied. 'Except one way or the other I think I should try for a meeting with Senator Mark Barker.'

'Good luck,' Lucy said dismissively. 'You might be Ricky's brother, but Barker doesn't like journalists much. Plus you're a foreigner. I doubt if he will see you.'

'Who knows these diskettes are here?'

'You, me, that's it.'

'Beatriz?'

'I never told her. Maybe Ricky did, but I doubt it.'

'Let's keep it that way.'

'You think the diskettes are valuable?'

Kerr laughed.

'Valuable? They are the nearest thing I have to family heirlooms.'

15

Every few seconds something in Scott Swett's body caused an electronic beeping sound. A cathode ray oscilloscope at the end of his hospital bed traced a shaky wave. He lay on a life support machine surrounded by high-tech gadgets, all of which showed how barely he clung to life. John Oberdorfer stood in the private room in Georgetown hospital staring at Scott's body and listening to the woman doctor list his injuries as the machines beeped and buzzed. The doctor was quite taken with Oberdorfer. She wondered why anyone would want their skin to look quite so orange.

'Multiple fractures of the skull, broken jaw, shattered eardrum, broken collar bone, three broken ribs, plus facial bruises and swelling,' she recited.

Oberdorfer was thinking, you can live with this?

'How bad?'

The doctor exhaled air and shook her head.

'His chances?'

She shook her head again. 'We can pray for him.'

'Thanks, Doctor. I will. God bless you.'

Oberdorfer turned and walked briskly through the antiseptic corridors until he found a telephone, wondering how much worse it could get. Scott was barely hanging on, Brigham Y. Dodds was missing, and Oberdorfer expected that they would soon fish him out of the Potomac with a baseball bat shoved up his ass. There was no sign of the videotape, and there was the constant threat that the FBI would somehow link the deaths of Colvin and Drysdale in the swamp with the America First Corporation. The good news was that neither Brigham nor Scott had been carrying the MAC 10s or the cocaine when they got into trouble.

Oberdorfer had ordered them to use the shoulder bags and keep the MAC 10s with them at all times, but they had disobeyed him, praise the Lord. Scott's Ruger pistol was fully loaded, but the police did not seem much interested, figuring maybe a guy clubbed half to death needed a little protection. Oberdorfer called Senator Mark Barker at home and told him the news.

'Brigham is still missing, Scott is very serious in George-town hospital, and looks like he won't make it. Of course, Senator. Yes, Senator. I'll do that now, Senator. You want to use Scott's story? For a news broadcast? Of course, Senator.'

Oberdorfer could not believe it. The world was falling apart and the first thing Mark Barker thought of was exploiting the beating of Scott Swett as part of his goddamn television programme, a segment about crime in the city for the America First News Hour.

Un-freaking-believable.

Stunned even more by Senator Barker's reaction than by the attack on Scott, Oberdorfer put the telephone down.

'Arrogant *and* dumb,' he scoffed. 'Barker's a dynamite combination. Sweet Jesus, save us.'

The worst of it was that one day Joe Huntley would find out what was on the videotape – that Senator Barker had recorded their meeting on camera. And then he would find out that Ricky Rush could not wait for this meeting to achieve its rightful place in history, that he had stolen the tape. Oberdorfer did not want to be around to pick up the pieces if Huntley found out the tape existed before the Mormons got it back. It would be like Mount St Helens erupting again.

'It is really something,' Oberdorfer concluded, still mut-tering to himself, 'when you realise your boss is a goddamn liability.'

He took a deep breath and dialled another Virginia number, knowing his call would not be welcome.

'Huntley,' a rich bass voice answered.

'Hi, Joe,' Oberdorfer replied. ''Scuse me for calling you at home. It's John Oberdorfer. I know you said never to telephone unless the sky was about to fall, but . . . I think the sky *is* about to fall. The senator says we all have to meet.'

'Where?'

'At the America First building, right away. Scott's been hit on the skull and could die. He had a gun on him, and the DC police are all over the case. Brigham's missing. It's big time.'

'Was it Kerr who hit Scott? Does he know you are watching him?'

'No. We're sure of that. It was someone else.'

Oberdorfer could hear Huntley reaching for a cigarette, weighing his options.

'The senator is going to be there in person?'

'Yes.'

'In that case, so will I.'

'Drive into the underground compound,' Oberdorfer instructed. 'And remember, at least there's one piece of good news.'

'Good news?' Huntley exhaled slowly. 'Tell me.'

'The bait is working.'

'Sure,' Huntley sneered. 'The bait's fine, but nothing's been caught yet. Except us.'

16

David Kerr sat up in Lucy Cotter's bed, listening to the gentle rise and fall of her breath. He turned to rub his hand gently along the smoothness of her back. She moaned and rolled over and kissed him, still asleep, and he could imagine staying in this bed for a very long time.

A few moments later he blinked himself fully awake, sitting in the darkness, trying to think what to do next about his brother. His only inspiration was a belief that somehow he had to pursue Senator Barker and that he should have another talk with the pink princess down in Alexandria. The meeting with Beatriz nagged at him like a toothache. Why had she been so insistent that he leave Washington? Kerr decided he would call Beatriz first, then McGhie to see if he had found out anything in Hatteras. And there was one other thing he had to do. He had to visit his brother's grave. Whether it contained a body or just rocks, McGhie was right. It was as close to Richard Courtland Rush as Kerr could possibly get, and he wanted to see it again. He climbed out of bed and whispered to Lucy that he would see her later. He kissed her, then dressed and walked back to his hotel to pack his bags.

'You can stay here if you need to,' Lucy had said. 'For a few days. I mean . . . while you find out more about your brother. If it helps.'

'It helps not to pay a hundred and fifty dollars a night for a hotel,' he replied. 'And the entertainment here is better. Thank you.'

'This is so I can keep an eye on you.'

'You think I need mothering?'

'You need something,' Lucy replied. 'I'm not sure there's a polite word for it. Anyway, if you keep asking questions about your brother I'm frightened something bad might happen to you. Or to me. Call it a mutual support group if you like.'

As he prepared to check out from the hotel Kerr called McGhie, who was not at his Pentagon office. He tried his home, but Arlene said Noah had left town for a couple of days, Fort Bragg probably, and no, she did not have the number.

'Good to hear from you again, David. Come over for dinner before you go. And I'll tell Noah if he calls in.'

Kerr telephoned Fort Bragg.

'Colonel Noah McGhie? We have no Colonel McGhie listed. Which unit is he with?'

Kerr replied that he did not know, and felt the voice laughing down the telephone.

'You don't know? Do you know how many officers and men we have here at Fort Bragg, sir?'

Kerr did not want to play guessing games. He rang off and tried McGhie's Pentagon office again.

'He's on assignment, sir, like I told you before. I can't guarantee he will get any message.'

'What if his mother had died?' Kerr asked. 'Could you get a message to him then?'

'Are you calling on behalf of Colonel McGhie's mother, sir?'

'No, I merely wondered if you could get a message to him.'

'I'll try, sir.'

'It's very important.'

'I'll try, sir.'

The good mood Kerr felt after a day and a night with Lucy had begun to dissipate. He called Joseph R. Huntley, but Huntley also had disappeared off the map. Not even his secretary was available.

'This number has been discontinued, sir,' the Pentagon telephone operator told Kerr. 'Mr Huntley must have been re-assigned.'

'Where?'

'I do not have that information, sir.'

'How would I find him?'

'I do not have that information, sir.'

'Then put me through to the Intelligence Support Activity, please.'

There was a pause.

'We have no such Activity listed, sir.'

'How would I find the number?'

'I do not have that information, sir.'

'Well, thank you for your help.'

'You're welcome, sir. And have a nice day.'

Frustrated, Kerr called Beatriz Ferrara in Alexandria. Even she was not there.

'Hi,' her silky voice-message answered to a background of tinkling bells. 'This is Harmony Supplies. We can't take your call right now, but if you leave a message, Beatriz will call you back. Have a nice day.'

'Shit,' Kerr swore, then realised that word was the recorded message Beatriz would hear. 'Oh, sorry, Beatriz. It's David Kerr. I was wondering whether I could see you again. I'm going to Arlington Cemetery this morning about ten o'clock to look at Ricky's grave one last time before I return to England. If you can meet me, please leave a message with Lucy. I'll be staying with her until I go home.'

Depressed by his series of failed calls, Kerr checked out and drove west across Memorial Bridge to Arlington Cemetery, searching in his mirror repeatedly to see if he was being followed. The more nervous he became, the more he saw cars that were definitely following him – definitely – until they turned away, or he slowed and they sped past.

'Going crazy,' Kerr muttered. He was now absolutely certain something bad was about to happen. 'Going bloody crazy. I knew that this was what family did to you. They drive you demented.'

He parked at the cemetery entrance and wondered whether he could even find the gravesite. He remembered roughly the section and followed the signs up the hill past the eternal Kennedy flame towards the Custis Lee house. The sun glinted off the white gravestones as Kerr rolled up his sleeves and unbuttoned his shirt in the heat. At the top of the hill he turned to look back over the city, and then down to his brother's grave. He stiffened.

Something bad was about to happen, for sure. There was a man bending down at the grave. The distance was about five hundred metres and Kerr could not see clearly. He screwed up his eyes. Maybe the man was laying flowers. Maybe disturbing the sods of grass laid on top of the grave. Digging. Kerr walked quickly, trying not to run.

This had to be one of the men who had been following him, the one he had given the finger to. Kerr felt a rush of excitement as he lengthened his stride almost to a run. A Mormon. They were going to have a little talk, just the two of them. He was going to take this bastard warmly by the throat and shake some information out of him.

Suddenly the man on the grave stood up and looked back towards him.

Kerr was much closer now and could see that the man was wearing a white shirt and dark tie with grey trousers but no jacket. He had something in his hand. The man stared at Kerr, now less than two hundred metres away, then bolted towards a clump of trees behind the grave. Kerr began to run, trying to follow the white shirt as it blurred into the wood. There was a short trail then it split and Kerr ran left until he came out into the cemetery again in a section dedicated to the Korean war. Nothing. He cursed under his breath and turned to run in the opposite direction, angry with himself that he had made a mistake. This time he emerged from the wood on the far side among graves from the civil war. Still nothing.

'Shit,' he called out loudly, thumping his fists to his side in anger.

He doubled back and quartered the wood until he was sure the white shirt was not hiding behind a tree or lying in an obscure ditch.

'Shit,' he repeated. 'I've blown it, or this is Houdini.'

Kerr was sweating hard now from the effort and the heat. He wiped his face with a handkerchief and took off his jacket. Arlington Cemetery was so big and White Shirt's lead so great he did not think he had much chance of catching him now, but there was one viewpoint from which he could see almost down to the exit and the car park.

Kerr walked back uphill to the Custis Lee house, scanning across the gravestones below. Still nothing. Then he turned to the back of the house and glimpsed something white behind the treeline to his left. Sure of it this time, not imagining. White Shirt seemed to be circling at a distance. Kerr felt a frisson of fear like a hunter catching sight of a stalking big cat, unsure who was hunting whom.

He stood back and considered whether a dash downhill would be good enough to catch White Shirt, but before he could make up his mind the flash of white disappeared into the trees again. A couple of tourists looked at Kerr strangely, puzzled by his red face and air of anxiety. He turned away from them, walking briskly downhill, listening. The only sounds were the distant engine noise of a motorised lawn mower to his left, and in the trees the singing of a mockingbird. Now Kerr felt really unnerved, a throbbing in his head like the dull pressure of an impending storm. He scrambled round the side of the hill to the Tomb of the Unknown Soldier, looking to his left and right in the hope of seeing White Shirt again, his breath coming in shallow bursts, the sweat soaking through his shirt.

A small group of tourists lingered in the sunshine, waiting

for the changing of the guard. Kerr stood among them, transfixed by the ceremony, listening to the sound of heavy boots on concrete slabs, the dignified, robotic marching of the men who performed their tasks with the studied falseness of automata, as if dehumanisation were the highest form of military discipline. Maybe it was.

The new guard detail marched in Kerr's direction and then turned abruptly towards the Tomb. They took up position and the relieved guard marched out equally robotically.

The Activity, the Mormons, whoever or whatever they were, had made a big mistake. They had chosen his brother for some kind of dirty mission because he was the Unknown Soldier. After their mother had died, Richard Rush was an orphan. He had broken with his girlfriend, he had no known relatives, he had – what did Lucy call it? – the Quality of Faith. Whatever it was that Ricky had to do, if it all unravelled, he would be the ultimate automaton, marching like the honour guard to a secret rhythm whose beat eluded Kerr and everyone else.

The mistake was that the automaton discovered he had a brother, and even the hint of a family changed everything for Ricky as it had done for Kerr himself. It gave you faith where there were doubts, doubts where there was faith. It messed you up, as usual. Kerr rubbed his face with the palm of his hand, brushing the sweat from his eyes, desperate now to meet whatever was in store for him. He turned rapidly away from the Tomb and began walking slowly back to look for what he believed would be the last time at his brother's grave. As he came over the lip of the small hill immediately beside the site, he almost bumped into the man in the white shirt. Kerr jumped back in alarm.

This time White Shirt showed no desire to run. They looked each other up and down carefully.

The man was slightly taller than Kerr, just over six foot, lightly bearded, with a thick bull neck and a muscled stance.

He stood about twenty yards from the grave, calmly leaning on a tree. His hands were dirty with earth, there were patches of mud on his shirt and he carried a small trowel. The grave did not look as if it had been damaged, and White Shirt was totally relaxed.

Kerr clenched the disfigured fingers of his right hand into a tight fist and moved his left up a little, ready to adopt the boxer's stance. If the man was unarmed, Kerr thought he could take him. If he had a gun, then there was no point worrying about it.

'Who the hell are you?' Kerr called out angrily. 'What are you doing at my brother's grave? Why are you following me?'

White Shirt stood out from the tree and smiled. He made a full three-hundred-and-sixty-degree sweep with his eyes, checking that he and Kerr were alone, then he walked forward until they stood just two feet apart.

'Who are you?' Kerr repeated urgently.

White Shirt smiled.

'I'm your brother, dickhead. Who were you expecting? Batman?'

PART TWO

Faith

17

David Kerr stood in silence by his brother's grave, blinking at the man who was supposed to occupy it. Ricky smiled back. Now Kerr realised who he was, there was no mistaking the face despite the few weeks' growth of neat black beard. It was the face from the US military photograph Huntley had given him, a little older, more tired, the stiff black hair longer, but the same thick-set neck and shoulders, the same quick eyes and a handsome lopsided grin. Ricky was clearly amused.

'You look like you saw a ghost.'

'How am I supposed to look? I'm talking to a man I buried four days ago.'

'Aren't you going to tell me you're pleased to see me, or say how do you do, or whatever the English say?'

'Scottish,' Kerr corrected. 'Remember that, and the rest'll be easy.'

He held out his right hand and they shook. Kerr felt his heart was about to boil over. They both took half a pace forward and embraced in a bear hug.

'Listen, we have got to talk, big brother,' Ricky said. 'But not here. Too many uniforms. Too many ghosts.'

'Have you been following me for long?'

'Me and other people.'

'The FBI?'

'Not them, worse. I call them the Mormons, a bunch of thugs who have been hoping you would lead them to me.'

'That's absurd.'

'How is it absurd? You did. I'm here, right? Only, I caused

them so many problems they'll be off balance for a few more hours. You know how to get to Great Falls, Virginia?'

'I have a map. I can find it.'

'Meet me in an hour at the ranger centre. Don't call anyone or go back to your hotel until we have talked. They'll pick up the scent soon enough without you making it easier.'

'I wasn't planning to go back to the hotel. I –' He might as well say it. 'Lucy Cotter asked me to move in with her for a few days. I'm planning to stay with her tonight.'

Ricky laughed as if this was one of the finest jokes he had ever heard. He punched his brother lightly on the arm.

'Nice work, big brother, nice work. Now we split up and meet at Great Falls. Wait outside the ranger centre. We have a lot to get caught up on, and a lot to do if I'm going to stay alive for long.'

'It's that bad?'

'Yeah, it's that bad. Like it says on the cigarette packs, being related to me could damage your health.'

Kerr looked at the trowel in his brother's hand.

'You dig yourself out of the grave with that?'

Ricky grinned.

'Dug myself out of a hole, you could say. Maybe I'll tell you about it later. Now let's get going.'

Before Kerr could say goodbye, Ricky plunged into the light woodland that led from the cemetery towards the Potomac river. The white shirt disappeared again as if it had never been there.

Kerr walked quickly towards his car, feeling as if a wave had broken in his heart. He was happy beyond all expectation to find that someone of his own blood was still alive. Ricky meanwhile reached the Arlington Cemetery boundary wall, climbed over and walked through the brush to where his car was parked in a lay-by. He opened the boot and threw down the garden trowel, then he picked the baseball bat off the lumpy blanket inside. The lumpy blanket moaned. It contained the trussed, blindfolded and gagged shape of Brigham Y. Dodds who shook with fear, knowing that this had to be the moment when Wild Ricky was going to shoot him. Ricky slipped off the blindfold to check he was still alive. Brigham blinked in the bright light, and offered another feeble moan.

'Shut the fuck up, Brig,' Ricky said, grabbing him by the throat and pulling the groaning face to just a few inches from his own. 'You're giving me a headache.' Brigham stared back in terror. 'I'm not even going to shoot you,' Ricky continued. 'Leastways not yet, though you deserve it for what you did to Colvin and Drysdale. Remember them, you scumbag? Yeah, I thought you might. If I had more time I would torture you just for the fun of it, but not today, Brigham, so chill out, okay?'

Ricky pulled the blindfold back on and secured it tightly with duct tape. He grabbed Brigham roughly and hoisted him on his shoulder, walking through the scrub until he found a suitable bush to prop him against.

'Mainly I'm not going to shoot you because you never shoot the messenger. And you are my messenger, Brigham boy, okay?'

Brigham made no sound until Ricky punched him hard in the ribs.

'I said, okay, you pusbucket?'

Brigham nodded and made a low moan.

'Right. There's always joggers coming by here in the evening, Brig, so you're not gonna die. Not yet, anyway. The message is for Oberdorfer and Senator Barker: back off, then we can talk. If you keep up the pressure, I'll blow the America First Corporation apart. If anything happens to my brother, then you are all dead men. Remind them I've got the evidence they think I've got, and more. I can put everybody away forever. You remember all that, messenger boy?'

There was yet another low moan from Brigham which might have been the word 'yes'.

'Oh, and Brig,' Ricky concluded cheerfully as he turned for his car. 'Have a nice day.'

18

The National Park at Great Falls straddles the Potomac river a few miles from Washington, with Maryland to the east, Virginia to the west. Kerr walked to the ranger headquarters on the Virginia side and sat at a rough wooden picnic table, feeling dizzy and confused. After ten minutes that seemed like an hour he began to wonder if he had imagined the white-shirted ghost at the graveside, or whether he had been hallucinating. Suddenly there was a voice behind him.

'Let's walk,' Ricky called out. 'There's a trail towards the river where nobody goes.'

Kerr stood up to look at the handsome, bearded face. There was the hint of a suntan and laughter lines round the eyes.

'You don't look so bad for a dead man.'

'So there is life after death,' Ricky replied. 'What can I say? And maybe you don't look so bad yourself, for an old geezer. How old are you, anyway?'

Kerr told him.

'Wow. People can be that old? And still able to walk unaided? Jeez. You married? Kids?'

'No, and no. I'm still looking.'

'Maybe Lucy?'

'I said I'm still looking. But I have to tell you I like her a lot.'

Ricky nodded.

'Before we do serious getting-to-know-you, I have got to tell you something, bro. I'm in deep shit and just being with me puts you in it too. Part of me wants you to help, and part says the best thing I can do for my big brother is to tell you to get the hell out of here and come back once it's settled.'

'How will it be settled?'

Ricky shrugged.

'When I die for real, that'll finish it. Maybe not even then. But there's no reason for you to get involved.'

'Being your brother makes me involved, Ricky. And you are beginning to sound like Beatriz, saying hello and good-bye to me in the same breath.'

'That's what I told her to say,' Ricky replied. 'I wanted you to leave because you and me being curious about each other puts both of us in danger. Still, I knew you wouldn't go, not if we're any kind of kin at all. We just had to meet and screw up each other's lives, didn't we?'

'Had to,' Kerr agreed.

'And this is your last chance. There's at least two dead, three if you count me, and if you get out now, you're not part of it.'

'No,' Kerr said firmly. 'How could I leave when it's just started to get interesting? I spent years as a spectator of other people's wars, you don't expect me to miss this one? I will do what I can for my baby brother, how does that sound? Like a family, maybe?'

'Like a family,' Ricky repeated.

Up close Kerr could see a tautness around Ricky's mouth. His eyes flashed nervously as if expecting some terrible interruption.

'What are you scared of? That they are still following me?'

'No, I don't think so, not for a while. Like I said, I got a few of them real confused, and they're running out of people.'

'What do you mean, you got them confused?'

Ricky laughed uncomfortably.

'The people following you are playing for the highest

stakes. The prize for winning is that you gain everything. The prize for coming second is that you die. They have killed before, and they will kill you and me when the time comes.'

'Kill me when the time comes?' Kerr repeated, in disbelief. He had always reckoned on dying in some ghastly foreign war as a result of a mistake. He had never before considered the idea that someone might actually want to kill him on purpose.

'In a New York minute.' Ricky paused and put his hand on Kerr's shoulder. 'But I am not going to let that happen.'

'Great,' Kerr responded sarcastically. 'My baby brother is not going to let it happen.'

The trail forked past a group of old canal locks down to the river.

'They told me you had been murdered,' Kerr went on. 'First Huntley said –'

'Shit,' Ricky cursed. 'The Scumbag in Chief. What did he have to say?'

'He told me you died in a military training accident overseas, that it was a big secret. Then Colonel McGhie said maybe you were murdered, but there was no body. I was even thinking it might have been suicide. There were so many theories but nobody held out any possibility you were still alive.'

'They all thought it, though,' Ricky said, taking a deep breath and running a hand nervously back through his hair. 'They ever speak about the Activity, the Intelligence Support Activity?'

'McGhie did,' Kerr replied. 'But he told me almost nothing beyond the name and that you were part of it, that you were in Signals Intelligence.'

'I worked with McGhie for years,' Ricky said. 'He's a good man. Alaska – we were on the island of Shemya in the Aleutians together for eighteen months, watching Soviet missile tests. Japan, the Mid East, Cyprus, you name it.

Then I got re-assigned to economic intelligence. That's when the fun began.'

'The fun?'

'Yeah, the fun. They say I didn't play by the rules, but maybe that's because we made them up as we went along. I tried to tell McGhie, but he wouldn't listen.'

Kerr frowned.

'To tell you the truth, Ricky, I'm not sure I understand a word you're saying. Try it again slowly. Remember, I'm a journalist, and a good rule is to treat journalists like you would the average twelve-year-old, okay?'

To their left they had reached the first and most spectacular view of the falls. The air smelled damp and the brown river water cascaded between the rocks so fast the Potomac was a series of white blurs. Ricky led the way to an outlook and sat on the rock overhang, his back to the river so he could watch both ways along the trail, like a boxer on the ropes hoping for a lucky punch.

'Okay,' he said. 'What do I do? I help with economic intelligence for the Economic Security Council. They want to know – need to know – who is developing the newest technology, what our needs are, what technology we have to protect, you follow?'

Kerr nodded.

'So,' Ricky continued, 'in this new game, economic competitors happen to be military and political allies in NATO or the G7 or whatever. The one thing that must never happen is getting caught. They spy on us, we spy on them, and it's like cheating on your wife. Everybody knows it's going on but nobody talks about it, because if anybody did, the whole facade would fall apart. And I mean everything – right up to the White House.'

Kerr was bemused. 'Sounds like James Bond for accountants.'

Ricky turned serious.

'You still don't get it, do you, big brother? Bummer, eh?'

'No, I understand,' Kerr corrected hastily. 'At least I think I do. That's what the trade problems between the US, Europe and Japan are all about, right?'

'Some,' Ricky answered. 'Only now it has come to a trade war, that means we have failed. The idea is to work over our economic competitors so smoothly they don't even know we're doing it. We had a sign on our wall, the Activity's golden rule: "Do it to them before they do it to you – get your retaliation in first." And I'm proud to say that mostly we did.'

Kerr began to understand what Lucy meant when she talked about the quality of his brother's faith. This was like listening to a missionary.

'So why can't people read economic information in the *Financial Times* or *Wall Street Journal*?'

'Man, you're wicked, you know that? Wicked.' Ricky laughed as if this were a great joke. 'Let me give it to you like a college lecture. The Economic Security Council was set up to do for the American economy what the National Security Council has done for our defence – keep America first. Energy Security, means watching the Middle East and OPEC; Emerging Technologies is making sure no new Japanese computer chip or bio-engineered process leaves us behind. We have twenty people looking at biochips.'

'Biochips? You've lost me again. Potato chips, I know. Biochips . . .'

'Biochips are ways of combining genetic engineering and computer technology to magnify the power of a chip beyond belief. The buzz phrase is machines-that-think. Whoever gets there first will have the key to the next generation of computers. If it's us, then we screw Japan and the Europeans completely. If it's the Japanese, then our job is to steal it so we don't fall behind. You following this?'

The Potomac was in mesmerising spring flood. Kerr listened to the raw facts in his brother's voice with a peculiar sensation of numbness, wanting to ask about their mother, family things, not this. Ricky's words kept tumbling out as if he had wanted to confess to someone for months.

'Then there's our regional groups for Western Europe, Japan, and the Asian Tigers – Thailand, Singapore, Malaysia, Taiwan, Indonesia. There's the currency task force on exchange rates, and so on and so on. Like, we have this computer hacking project – you familiar with the term?'

'I know what computer hacking is, Ricky.'

'Right – so like I say, we have about three dozen personnel who work full time hacking into foreign corporations' data bases including the SWIFT network – that's the Society for World International Financial Transactions – so we can check out global business and bank deals. We've even got half a dozen guys infiltrating computer nerd groups on college campuses to see if the freelance hackers know more about it than we do. Some of them are better than the professionals. Am I making sense now?'

He was making sense, but Kerr could not see where it was leading, and the intensity of his brother's manner set him on edge.

'I understand what you're saying, Ricky. But how does any of this put you in trouble?'

'Item,' Ricky snapped, holding up the index finger of his right hand. 'We monitor trans-Atlantic and trans-Pacific fax communications plus selected telephone calls to check up on takeover activity and inward investment into this country. We have to know about big business deals and we do.'

Ricky cleared his throat, and held up a second finger.

'Item,' he continued. 'The collapse of the British pound and the shake-out in the European Monetary System. The central banks cooperate up to a point, but we needed to be sure what the Bundesbank and Bank of England were really up to. The collapse of sterling and of the European Monetary System in the middle of a US presidential election campaign would have produced Wall Street chaos, calls for higher interest rates, the works. Besides, we were trying to push the Bundesbank to lower rates, and needed to know what they were saying privately as well as publicly, and how they planned to screw the British, which, by the way, they did real well.'

'But how –' Kerr began.

'So we bugged them.'

'W-what?'

'We bugged their telephone calls and faxes.'

'You bugged the Bundesbank?'

'And the British Treasury, sure. All the players, in fact, including the British Chancellor of the Exchequer. You should hear what we found out about him.'

'B-but . . .'

'Item,' Ricky interrupted. 'The start of the trade war with the European Community. Apart from diplomatic gossip, we needed to know how far there were splits within the Community, whether their lead negotiator was in sync with Brussels – he wasn't – and mostly about the likely position of the French government. Our strategy was to make the British and Germans mistrust the French more than they disliked us. I helped provide the raw data that made that possible.'

Ricky smiled with pride and then paused for a moment as if everything was now clear. Kerr tried to keep his voice calm.

'How difficult is it to find out all this stuff?'

'Not very. The technology has always been available. What was missing was the will to employ it for non-military purposes. Now we use everything we'd use in a hot war, except live ammunition. The fancy name is national technical means.'

Kerr stared at the animated face of his brother. There was something about the way Ricky talked which scared him – not the secrecy or even the danger, but his religious fervour.

'After the hot wars and the Cold War,' Ricky grinned, 'we call this the Dollar War. Maybe that was the problem.' Ricky fell silent. He folded his hands in front of him, pausing to find the right words. 'The problem . . . the problem was, we all found out how much money could be made.'

'Illegally?'

Ricky raised his hands palm upwards and shrugged.

'What's illegal when you *are* the law? If everything you do is illegal but your government orders you to do it – wire taps, eavesdropping on microwave transmissions, computer break-ins – then where do you draw the line?'

Kerr blinked.

'You know better than that, Ricky. Using the information you are talking about to make investments must be like insider trading.'

'That's what they call it on Wall Street,' Ricky sneered. 'At the Activity we call it high-grade intelligence. Same thing, different angle. Only, whatever name you put to it, now it's got so big it's going to explode and people are getting damaged.'

'How damaged?'

'Dead damaged, David. Two of the guys I used to work with – William Colvin and Peter Drysdale – got careless and started spending too much, bringing money back onshore from the Caymans. The Drug Enforcement Administration took them for money launderers. Both the DEA and IRS started to investigate. Eventually so did the FBI, which is when I got scared. You don't mess with them.'

Ricky paused and took a deep breath. 'Colvin and Drysdale disappeared. For a few weeks I thought they'd skipped the country, then some redneck out duck hunting a hundred miles south of here stumbled into them. His dogs smelled their bodies. They were in the brush down at the Great Dismal Swamp, shot about twenty or thirty times each. Their tongues were cut out and there were a couple of little baggies of cocaine stuffed in their pockets.'

'Cocaine?'

'Yeah.'

'Were they involved in that?'

'Jesus, David,' Ricky snapped. 'They were Mormons, for Christ's sake. All they do is fuck and pray. They don't even drink coffee. Most of the team were like Sunday school teachers, decent all-American guys doing what they were told. They don't do drugs. The cocaine was put in their pockets in the hope that the FBI and everybody else would miss the point, like you just did.'

'I'm sorry, Ricky. I told you, I'm a journalist. I ask stupid questions for a living.'

Ricky cooled down.

'It's okay. I'm stressed out, right? It's not easy.'

'So who shot them?'

'The guys tailing you,' Ricky responded flatly. 'I call them the Mormons, only with them it's more of a nickname. They look like Bible missionaries, but they are killers, David. These guys work for the America First Corporation. You know who I mean?'

Kerr nodded.

'You were spying on America First?'

Ricky looked irritated by Kerr's question, as if wondering whether his brother might be mildly retarded.

'No, of course not. You read the computer diskettes?'

'Yes, but they didn't make much sense to me.'

'Well, a sworn deposition from me, plus Huntley's laptop showing all the bank account details – much more than I copied on to the diskettes – and we're talking millions, I reckon that's enough to sink America First.'

Suddenly Kerr got it.

'You weren't spying *on* them. You were spying *for* them?'

'Of course. America First turned tens of millions of dollars in profits from the information we supplied. In return, Senator Barker made sure the Activity survived the

Pentagon budget cutbacks. The White House wanted to disband us, but Barker did a deal. He made sure Congress appropriated enough money to keep us going and we provided information to him as a payback. Neat, eh?'

Kerr shook his head in disbelief. He could not think of anything to say.

Ricky continued, 'What you most need to know right now is that America First killed Colvin and Drysdale. They hoped that would cause the FBI inquiry to fade away for lack of evidence. They are so fucking dumb, you believe that? As soon as the bodies were discovered, the sky started falling. The Feds and the DEA and the IRS asked questions twice as often as before, talking to people in the Activity, wondering if we were into drugs. We all played like we were shocked about the two guys in the swamp – which was easy, since we *were* shocked, thinking it could be any of us next if Senator Barker and his Mormons had gone that crazy. Then one of the Feds, a black guy, could smell something wrong. Wouldn't leave me alone; wouldn't give up.'

'Harold Ruffin?'

Ricky nodded. 'Ruffin, right. Smartass son of a bitch. You meet him?'

'Yes,' Kerr said. 'At your funeral. He told me about the murders and the investigation. He seemed to be good at his job.'

Ricky laughed.

'Sure, that's the problem. I could see the others at the Activity watching him lean on me, wondering if I would talk. I started to get spooked and so did Beatriz. She told me I would be found out at Great Dismal Swamp with a nine mil through my brain, duct tape round my wrists and a little baggie of coke stuffed in my pocket. It wasn't the kind of career move I had been looking for, so I faked my own death and disappeared.'

Ricky was thoroughly alarmed now. There were small

beads of sweat glistening on the edges of his beard. He wiped them away brusquely with his fingers.

'Why didn't you talk to Ruffin and tell him the truth?'

'I'd be dead,' Ricky said.

'Don't the FBI have protection –'

'I'd be dead. You don't understand what Barker and the Mormons are like. You just don't get it.' Ricky looked at his watch. 'Listen, I haven't got time to explain it all. There's something I want you to do for me. If you can't, or won't, just say so and I'll figure another way.'

'What do you need?'

Ricky grabbed his lapels so tightly Kerr thought his jacket was going to split.

'You have to help me get a meeting with Senator Howard Hennington. If I talk to the FBI, any indictments will mean I have to tell an open court what I just told you. You think the Justice Department wants the world to know how we recorded conversations between the British Chancellor of the Exchequer and the Bank of England? You think anyone will let that happen? My only chance is to tell it all to Hennington, give him the proof and then disappear for a few more weeks until the Mormons are all picked up or the scandal is so big they can't cover it up.'

Ricky's words began flying out again like water over the Potomac falls. 'They even threatened Beatriz,' he went on. 'The white-shirted, white-bread family-values sons of bitches.'

'When?'

'The week I disappeared. A couple of them went into the store and started throwing the crystals around, smashed up pretty near everything and asked her where her boyfriend was. She said I was dead, and one of them said, if he isn't, and we find him, lady, he'll wish he was.' Ricky's face twisted with anger. 'If they go near her again I'll shoot every single one of the bastards and not wait to talk to Hennington.'

'Huntley?' Kerr interrupted. 'What's his role?'

Ricky grinned viciously.

'Let me tell you about Joseph R. Huntley,' he snarled. 'His official title is Director of the Intelligence Support Activity, but he lies so goddamn much if he ever catches himself speaking the truth he tells another goddamn lie just to keep his hand in. He's the one that scares me most. I can handle the Mormons, but Slippery Joe is going to take a full Senate inquiry to fix. He'll do anything to make me look unstable and unreliable. My only protection is if I get to Hennington first.'

'Huntley is that important?'

Ricky nodded in silence. There was a long pause in which they looked at each other. Ricky was wondering how far this stranger who happened to be his brother might help him. Kerr was considering why he felt so strong an obligation to a man whose existence he did not even know about a week before. Ricky spoke again, bitterly.

'When Mom told me about you I said, gee Mom, that's nice. I've got a brother that you locked away in your mind for thirty years, like in the basement or something. It was real intense. She only told me about you because she was dying. It was like her worst secret, that she had abandoned you. Now I'm telling you my worst secret, and I guess you must feel gutted.'

Kerr's body shook. He stretched his hand out to grasp the fence on the river overlook and steady himself.

'So what exactly do you want me to do, Ricky?'

'I want you to arrange through Lucy to take the diskettes to Hennington and explain they are just an appetiser. Huntley's own computer, tying in the Director of the Activity to illegal trading and the America First Corporation, is the entree. It shows who got what pay-off and when, and where the money went. Get Hennington to meet with me for an hour, then immediately afterwards I'll turn myself in to Ruffin and the FBI.'

Ricky dug in his pocket and produced a sheet of paper.

'You know how to use computer communications software?'

Kerr nodded.

'A little. I used to use Crosstalk to file my stories for the newspaper.'

'Good. This is how Beatriz gets in touch with me, on-line. Lucy also has a Communicator program on her computer, so it should be easy. Follow the instructions to this E-mail number. I read the contents twice a day, ten a.m. and ten p.m, calling in from so many different places that even if they knew this is how we communicated, Huntley's people would find it difficult to track me down. Now I've got to go.'

'We need to talk about family things,' Kerr protested lamely. 'You started telling me about our mother.'

'Our family's all dead,' Ricky said. 'Except you and me. Keeping us both alive is the family thing we have to do first, okay? We can reminisce later.'

It was impossible to argue.

'Okay, Ricky. Take care.'

Ricky opened his jacket to reveal a pistol in a shoulder holster. 'I intend to. Meet my good friend here, Doctor Glock. Doctor Glock, say hello to my brother, David.' He put the gun away, walked a few yards and then turned, calling out over his shoulder, 'You're the only flesh and blood I've got on this planet, David,' he yelled, waving his hand desperately. 'You have got to help me. Got to.'

'Of course I'll help you, Ricky. You can count on it.'

'And if anything bad happens to me, get them to exhume what they buried in Arlington Cemetery. I think they might find the corpse illuminating. You understand?'

Kerr did not, but he nodded anyway.

'Sure, Ricky. Exhume the corpse.'

He stood rooted to the spot, watching his brother's white shirt rapidly disappear down the trail. He thought of the wildness in Ricky's eyes and wondered what part of the whole truth Richard Courtland Rush was telling him. A shameful yet inescapable thought struck him. Ricky, beloved Ricky, his own flesh and brotherly blood, might truly have become unhinged.

19

Kerr was still trembling with shock when he reached his car. He took a deep breath and started the motor, his hands white-knuckled on the steering wheel. Ricky had done this, he had done that, he was guilty, but he was not crazy. He needed. He wanted. He said. He did. Kerr's head buzzed and ached. Ricky existed, that was the point, not an empty coffin and an old USAF photograph, but blood and bone, with the hunted look of an animal that had been beaten. A brother, an obligation.

Kerr drove quickly to Lucy Cotter's apartment, glancing round every so often to check who was behind him, detecting no one, in terror of men with white shirts and dark suits carrying Bibles and guns. He wondered how much his own presence in Washington had put Ricky in danger. Ricky had risked his life to come out of hiding to see him – no doubt exactly as Joseph Huntley had planned. And Kerr realised he had put his brother in jeopardy, just as he had with Yasmin, leading them out into the open so they could be killed.

Still trembling, Kerr parked in the underground garage, and hurried up to Lucy's apartment, to call her and tell her the news. Two messages flashed on the answering machine beside the telephone. Kerr hesitated for a moment, then hit the replay button.

A man's voice said:

'This is Colonel Noah McGhie for David Kerr. We need to talk, David. I'm at the office now, and I'll be home tonight.'

The message wound on. There was a second male voice, Ricky's.

'Hi, Lucy. It's me, Ricky, calling from the land of the living dead. This must be a shock, but I'm not a ghost, and I'm not joking. I am still alive, obviously. I met with David, told him about this miraculous resurrection . . . he will explain it to you. It's gonna be all right. My big brother's going to help. And –' here Ricky Rush's voice changed tone '– and to the rest of you listeners, tell Huntley the ghost says, don't fuck with me or you'll regret it. Goodbye.'

Kerr stepped away from the telephone as if it were radioactive. He did not like the casual way Ricky assumed the line was bugged, though if anyone should know, presumably it would be him. He decided not to take any more risks and to call Lucy later from a public telephone, though part of him found the idea of becoming a low-rent James Bond utterly absurd. He went into the study bedroom, switched on Lucy's computer and ran through his brother's list of instructions. The Communicator program came on the screen. The modem dialled the number of Ricky's electronic mailbox. Kerr could open it by typing the designated code, B-R-O-T-H-E-R. A full-screen display said simply: 'You have all the time you need to leave your message. It will take me only seconds to retrieve it. Don't worry – they won't find me. Best wishes, Ricky.'

Kerr began to type.

'I will do as you asked, and set up a meeting immediately. I cannot tell you how I felt when we met. I will do everything I can to help you, but if for any reason the meeting you request is impossible –' Kerr paused for a few seconds.

He did not want to annoy his brother from the start, but he had to write it.

'– is impossible, then I think you should contact Ruffin and explain it to him as you did to me. It will be all right, I'm sure of it.' Kerr typed in the telephone number from Ruffin's card, adding: 'There are so many things I forgot to ask you. Leave a message and I'll check late tonight.'

He paused again until he was sure he could think of nothing else to say.

'Remember, you are not alone. You took a risk to see me. I will do anything I can for you. Best wishes, your brother, David.'

He logged out of the E-mail and then connected Lucy's printer to the computer. He spent an hour printing out the contents of the diskettes Ricky had left for him, so he could give the copies to Hennington. Then he left to call Lucy from a public telephone in Georgetown.

'I met him.'

'I know,' she said. 'He said he left a message on my machine at home and then called here at the office. Isn't it wonderful?'

'Yes, wonderful. He wants to meet Hennington. Maybe I should come and talk to the senator first and try to persuade him. What do you think?'

'I've already fixed it. The senator is free at five thirty. You've got half an hour, max. Probably less.'

'What about the new chief of staff that you told me about? Mc-Something? Will he get in the way?'

'McCall,' she said sternly. 'Jim McCall. Of course he will get in the way. I fixed it with the senator first, then told McCall. He's pissed at me for going behind his back, and doesn't like the sound of Ricky. Thinks it could be trouble, or so he claims. If you ask me, the real trouble is McCall himself. I don't trust him, and you have to remember one thing – meeting Hennington may be good for your brother, but it could be fatal for my job if it goes wrong. If you care for me, you had better make it work.'

Kerr smiled. 'If I care for you? What do you think?'

'I'm not sure I know,' Lucy said coquettishly. 'You've had your fun, maybe that's all.'

'And you had yours?'

'Yes, but not enough.'

She turned serious again. 'Just remember, David, there's a lot hanging on this.'

Kerr put the telephone down and looked at the faces around him in the centre of Georgetown.

'So everyone keeps telling me.'

20

Joseph R. Huntley was desperate for a cigarette, but he took one look at Mark Barker and decided that if he tried to light up, the senator would go crazy. Or more crazy than he already was, which would be difficult to believe. Huntley could never figure out what it was that kept Barker going, beyond the dumb luck of being born into a billionaire oil family. The senator was always talking about 'rugged individualism' and 'American enterprise'. As far as Huntley could see Senator Barker's most rugged piece of American enterprise was to cash the cheques when the oil spurted out of the ground where his family had owned the drilling rights for decades, and to use the profits to buy his way into the Senate.

Huntley fiddled in his pocket for his nicotine chewing gum, knowing that *No Smoking* was Barker's eleventh commandment. The senator had dozens of immutable rules that he implied came directly from God, a possibility Huntley did not think very likely. The Director of the Intelligence Support Activity had noted that in Barker's universe God's laws and the senator's own best interests always seemed to coincide.

'It's a good trick if you can manage it,' Huntley once told Ricky Rush when he began to explain the relationship between the Activity and America First. He remembered Ricky's astonishment.

'You say they are nothing but a bunch of crazy religious headbangers, so how come we have to deal with them? It defies common sense.'

'Sure, but it makes perfect political sense,' Huntley had

responded, though now he looked at Mark Barker, he was not so sure.

Huntley withdrew two sticks of nicotine-flavoured gum and began chewing enthusiastically. There were three men in the senator's office-cum-television-studio: the senator, perched on a big leather armchair upon a raised dais so he looked like a leprechaun in a stage play, with the dramatic view of Washington behind him; Huntley himself, now chewing wildly, trying to suck the last of the nicotine juice from the gum, and John Oberdorfer who, Huntley thought, looked even more orange than usual. The Tan Man needed a respray in a darker shade.

The senator's private secretary, Janey, tottered in wearing white high heels and a tight black skirt to serve them cokes. Then she left, saying she was going to take the Cadillac and go shopping at Tyson's Corner Mall. Huntley put another piece of nicotine gum in his mouth, thinking how Ricky Rush had been right about all this. Senator Mark Barker was definitely one enchilada short of the combination plate.

'So then Ricky pulled the gun on him,' John Oberdorfer said. He was detailing Ricky's attack on Brigham Y. Dodds, who – just as Ricky predicted – had been found by a passing jogger, trussed up near Arlington Cemetery.

'He was a real mess,' Oberdorfer revealed.

'Ricky beat him?'

'No, Senator. He had a problem with his bladder and his bowels. Scared, I guess.'

'Scared shitless,' Barker snapped.

'Yes, sir.'

Huntley could not believe the kind of clowns Barker surrounded himself with. Oberdorfer, Brigham Dodds, Scott Swett, Bob Allen and Ben Ritter. They would be the Three Stooges, only there were five of them.

Huntley could not figure why a multi-billionaire felt so threatened by his employees that he always selected second-rate halfwits.

Loyalty over ability, he decided, maybe because Senator Barker's rules for America First employees outlawed the following: beards, drugs, cigarettes, booze, long hair on men, short hair on women and women wearing trousers – all of which cut down the potential recruits. What surprised Huntley was not how many Mormons worked for Barker; it was that anyone other than a Mormon could take the conditions. In fact the more Huntley thought about it, the more he desperately needed that cigarette. Oberdorfer was still describing the condition of Brigham Y. Dodds's underwear when suddenly Senator Barker stood up impatiently and walked to the fish tank. The oscars swam around in excitement.

'Nothin' for you right now, boys,' Barker said, his back to Oberdorfer, his attention on the big fish. 'Been so busy, I plumb forgot to catch your lunch. But I'll get something for you soon enough.'

Oberdorfer stopped talking, figuring if he could not hold the senator's attention over a bunch of the ugliest fish on the planet, then what was the point? Barker turned round and faced them.

'I'm in the picture,' the chihuahua snapped. 'Only it is not so pretty. So your boy Brigham shit his pants a little. And Scott Swett allowed Ricky to hit his head for a home run. And Ricky now is on the loose. Am I missing something?'

Oberdorfer shook his head.

'That's about it, Senator.'

'So you screwed up?' Barker went on. 'As usual.'

'I . . . that is, we . . .'

'Say it,' Barker instructed.

'S-say what, Senator?'

'Say you screwed up, you miserable piece of dog shit, and ask God to forgive you.'

Oberdorfer swallowed hard.

'I . . . I . . . that is, we screwed up. And I ask God to forgive me.'

Barker changed immediately to a more emollient tone and turned to Huntley, bobbing his crew-cut head enthusiastically as he spoke.

'First, Joe, I want to say I appreciate you coming here. I know the risks to your position if you were seen alongside all us crazies out at America First.' He chuckled. 'Second, we have to bring all this to an end and we're counting on you.'

'Bring it to an end,' Huntley repeated, now deeply suspicious.

'The only way this will work,' Huntley remembered once instructing Ricky, 'is that we feed Barker just enough to keep him on our side. But we don't get too close, ever. Get too close and he'll swallow us just as easy as one of his ugly goddamn fish.'

Ricky had replied, 'Getting too close to that slimeball is never going to be my problem.'

Right. Now Huntley cleared his throat.

'You are correct, Senator,' he said. 'The Ricky Rush business has to be ended now, but at the risk of stating the obvious, that is a matter for you. You have to get your people to find Ricky before the FBI or anyone else does. I don't think anyone will believe his stories if he surfaces again, even though he has stolen my computer. I have already taken steps to ensure people believe he forged the files and made up the conspiracy story to discredit me. His last fitness report now describes him as a homosexual. His faked disappearance proves he is mentally unstable. I was going to have to terminate him from intelligence work. And of course, faggots are notoriously unstable.'

Barker laughed.

'Very cool of you, Joe,' he said. 'Very commendable. Very neat. Security risk. You're right, can't have faggots in the military, corrupting people with their abominable practices. Typical of the low standards of these times.'

'Thank you, Senator,' Huntley responded. 'But that

means, when it comes to finding Ricky, I cannot help you. It's not strictly Activity business. It's America First business.'

Barker turned to Oberdorfer, his tone hostile again.

'What you are telling me is you cannot locate Ricky, right? No matter how much money we pump into it? Bottom line?'

Oberdorfer nodded.

'That's right, Senator. He must be using a completely new identity – new credit cards, bank accounts, driver's licence, paid for out of the profits he made. We cannot locate him anywhere.'

'So,' Barker sneered. 'He can find our people and hit them between the ears with baseball bats, but we can't find him, that what you're saying?'

'Yes, Senator,' Oberdorfer admitted.

Barker walked over to the desk and banged his fists on the surface. Oberdorfer jumped.

'Well, it's got to stop! Right now!'

Oberdorfer bowed his head penitently, until Barker banged his fist four times, punctuating every word.

'*I-want-him-dead!*'

Huntley was amazed by the puerility of the performance. Keeping the senator at arm's length had been one of his better decisions.

'We are trying to find him, Senator,' Oberdorfer pleaded bravely. 'But it's not easy. I have two independent detective agencies trying to locate him as well as our own people trailing David Kerr. But we do not have the resources of the federal government – and even they probably can't find him.'

Barker's anger subsided as rapidly as it came. He sat down and began speaking again, without any petulance.

'Okay, folks. What have we got here? How do we take the initiative back and stop playing pussy? Let's assume worst case, Ricky decides to go public, then the boy's still got a problem like Joe says, right?'

Oberdorfer looked blank, but Huntley explained.

'I have told Defense Department Security and the FBI that Ricky is to be considered a highly dangerous rogue operative who suffered a nervous breakdown. He pops his head up, we shoot it off.'

'Right!' Barker shouted. 'Right, Joe. But supposing he just disappears again with the computer, what do we do?'

'We wait,' Huntley said firmly.

'No, Joe, we can't wait.'

'Why not?'

Barker stood up and laughed.

'We just can't afford to,' he replied, walking around the office and inspecting the television cameras pointing towards where they sat. 'Can't afford to. So I have a different plan. We flush him out, and do it so there is no doubt he is a crazy man.'

Barker clapped his hands together and grinned, clearly believing his plan to be a masterstroke. Huntley shifted uneasily in his chair.

'Everybody has a pressure point, right?' Barker continued. 'What is there of Ricky's that he cares about? What could we destroy that would destroy him?'

Huntley chewed the nicotine gum nervously. Killing Ricky was bad enough, a necessary next step to protect them all, but he did not like the sound of this, especially the word 'we'.

'Any ideas,' Barker wondered, 'on what matters to Ricky? Where does he hurt?'

'Well,' Oberdorfer answered, 'there are three things we know he cares about: his money, which we can't touch because we can't find it; his brother; and his girl. She runs a New Age store out in Alexandria. The brother or the girl is what we can get to.'

'Right,' Barker snapped. 'That's it. That's it! Pick one of them, or both. Just make sure whatever you do leaves Ricky madder'n a nest full of hornets. Along with his attacks on our people, Scott Swett and Brigham, Ricky ends up looking like the guy from "Psycho". Am I right?'

Huntley really could use the cigarette now. Oberdorfer was nodding enthusiastically, like an orange-faced marionette.

'Wait just a minute, Senator,' Huntley said, trying to keep his voice calm. 'We should think this through. In the first place, if you stir up Ricky, it'll make what he has already done to America First staff look like nothing. You harm his girl and everybody will be a target, including yourself.'

'That's right,' Barker grinned. 'That's right. And who would believe a man who attempted to kill a US senator? Who would believe the information on the laptop computer was not faked?'

'But the girl is not involved in this,' Huntley protested.

'Like hell she isn't,' Barker rebutted. 'Like hell, Joe. She is part of this, and if America First is going to continue to do the good work we need to protect ourselves. The Lord helps those who help themselves. We need to do it, do you understand?'

Huntley eyed Barker coldly. For the first time he realised his problems were far greater than he'd supposed, and would not end when they caught Ricky. He would have Barker around him like a curse from now on, and sooner or later he would have to deal with it.

'The prophet Jeremiah,' Barker declaimed from the dais, 'makes clear the punishment for those that turn away from the right path. They will fall by the sword before their enemies. We are called to do this, Joe. Fall by the sword, Joe, before their enemies.'

Huntley felt the nicotine juice from the chewing gum dry in his mouth.

'Jeremiah,' he repeated.

'What we need from you, Joe,' Barker continued, 'is whatever you can learn of Ricky's whereabouts from the FBI or anyplace else. We can bring him to the surface, but we need the resources of the federal government on this.'

'Now wait a minute,' Huntley replied, stiffly. 'Our agreement does not cover anything more than economic information. That was always the deal. The Activity stayed strong, America First stayed strong, and the country stayed strong. You can't start telling me to do things just because you have had a conversation with fucking Jeremiah, for God's sake. If you had followed my advice and not killed the two guys in the swamp this would never have happened. Drysdale and Colvin would never have talked, but you had to make sure, Senator. You had to go too far, like you're planning now. And I can't afford to get mixed up in it.'

Mark Barker's stubby little nose twitched with distaste. Oberdorfer blinked in astonishment that anyone would ever argue with the senator, especially over the interpretation of Jeremiah, Chapter Nineteen, one of his all-time favourites. Nobody had ever questioned Senator Barker on Jeremiah before, or referred to him as 'fucking Jeremiah'. There was no telling what might happen now.

'You can't get mixed up in this?' Barker yapped back. 'You *are* mixed up in this, Joe, and you'll just damn well have to do as you're told.'

Huntley stood up, about to storm out of the room.

'Siddown,' the chihuahua barked again. 'We have not finished.' Senator Barker drew himself up to his full height on the raised dais. 'Listen,' he sneered. 'We're in this together, you and me, the Activity and America First, in lock step. If Ricky Rush nails me, he nails you, right?'

'But,' Huntley protested, 'you just said all he has is a bunch of wild allegations and a laptop computer full of information that I am telling you he could have fabricated. I don't see why you need to murder somebody else to make him mad when he is already discredited. He has no proof . . .'

Huntley noticed the strange way in which Barker and Oberdorfer were staring at him and the words dried completely in his mouth. He stopped chewing the nicotine gum and spat it out into a piece of paper.

'Senator,' Huntley asked, the truth dawning on him slowly. 'You want to tell me now how much Ricky *really* has on us?'

21

David Kerr caught a cab to Senator Hennington's office on Capitol Hill. He walked through the security check and across a cavernous lobby until he found the Senate office map and took his bearings. The elevator to the third floor brought him to the point where Lucy's directions began to make sense.

'You just follow your nose,' she said. 'Literally.'

'How do you mean?'

'Get out of the elevator and you'll understand.'

The air was heavy with a sweet smell. Hennington had a large popcorn maker of the type found in cinemas installed in his outer office. It was a gift from his home state inscribed with the words: 'For *Really* Putting America First. Give 'em Hell, Howie. From the grateful farmers of Kansas', and the hot buttered smell drifted along the corridors.

Lucy greeted Kerr with a formal handshake, looking efficient in her plain blue business suit. She led him into the senator's private office and motioned him to sit in a leather chesterfield. A tall, thin man walked in. He was somewhere in his late forties, wearing shirtsleeves, one thumb hooked casually behind bright red braces, the other hand carrying a sheaf of papers. The man had no hips, and he was so tall he reminded Kerr of a walking exclamation mark.

'This is Jim McCall,' Lucy announced. 'He's the senator's new chief of staff. Jim, this is Ricky Rush's brother.'

'Pleased to meet you,' McCall said, with a strong Texas accent and transparent insincerity. 'The senator is voting right now but he'll be with us momentarily. Is there anything you need, before we begin?'

'These are for you,' Kerr said, looking up six inches into McCall's eyes and handing him a sheaf of papers. 'My brother gave me this data on diskettes. The print-out shows the extent to which he says people illegally profited from the information they were providing to the Economic Security Council. He said it was very important he meet the senator to explain it further.'

McCall took the notes.

'We'll decide that in a moment. First I want to know what your brother was like.'

'In what sense?'

'Well, was he tense, nervous, was he –'

'Was he crazy?'

'Yeah, I guess that's what I mean,' McCall admitted. The more he talked, the thinner he seemed to get. With his reddish-blond hair and lanky body he began to remind Kerr of a used Q-Tip. 'Let me lay it on the line for you Mr –'

'Kerr.'

'Mr Kerr. My advice to the senator is probably not to see your brother. If what Captain Rush says is false, then obviously it is a waste of time. And if what he says is true or partly true, then it is still tainted. This is a guy who faked his own suicide. He stole government property, admits he was involved in the trafficking of secret information, and now there are reports he assaulted two of his former friends. One of them is in hospital, one is missing, and nobody has a precise motive, except that your brother has resurrected himself as the wild man of Washington.'

Kerr was stunned.

'What do you mean, wild man? What are we talking about here?'

'Just like I say,' the Q-Tip continued. 'A wild man. One white male aged thirty-two was bludgeoned with a baseball bat in the street near George Washington University. He's in Georgetown Hospital on life support, and they think he might not make it. The other victim disappeared almost twenty-four hours ago, another white male, thirty-one years old. Both men knew your brother.'

Kerr remembered Ricky saying he had been giving the Mormons something to think about.

'All the police in the District of Columbia are searching for Captain Rush right now,' McCall added. 'He is clearly a highly disturbed individual with a history of violence. His military record shows psychological problems dating back more than a year to when, I believe, his mother took sick and died.'

'Our mother,' Kerr corrected. 'It was our mother who died.'

McCall raised an eyebrow and went on.

'Even supposing there was a kernel of truth in his story, it would make Senator Hennington seem a fool to have anything to do with someone who faked his own death and is responsible for such violence. It's just too risky.'

'Physically risky or politically risky?' Kerr shot back.

'Both.' McCall was overtly hostile now. 'You understand what would happen if the United States was forced to admit to spying on the British Treasury? On the Bundesbank? On MITI? On the European Commission in Brussels? That agents of our government speculated on the collapse of European currencies?'

'I have some idea,' Kerr responded. 'But I'm mostly interested that you're so well briefed on this. You know what my brother is going to say before he says it. Who told you he was involved in these operations?'

The Q-Tip smirked. He put his hands down by his sides to where his hips should have been.

'I have my sources,' he smiled. 'And whatever cockamamie story your brother has concocted is not gonna save his traitorous butt.'

Kerr was going to hit back, but there was a disturbance outside. Senator Howard H. Hennington barrelled into his office followed by two junior aides.

'– you tell the White House the trade treaty is dead on arrival unless they move on farm supports, or screw more out of the Europeans on soybeans.'

'But you said –'

'Shut up, Marty. Just get Barker's office on the phone. We need to speak about the Japanese mini vans he says are flooding the goddamn market. Most of them are made in Tennessee.'

'But Barker's TV show just had another attack on you, and you said –'

'Get out of here, Marty, and do it. And don't tell me what I said all the time. If I want a tape recording of my words, I'll get one. Now call Barker's people and set up a meeting.'

'No, sir . . . I mean, yes, sir, Senator.'

'Senator,' McCall interrupted. 'Senator, this is Captain Rush's brother.'

The two junior aides scurried to their appointed tasks. Senator Hennington switched into a wide professional grin and shook hands.

'Howard Hennington.'

'David Kerr. Pleased to meet you, sir. In fact I'm Captain Rush's half-brother, and I've been a fan of yours for some time.'

'That so? How come?'

'Since your speech at the 1992 Democratic Convention.'

Hennington beamed. 'You liked it?'

'Well,' Kerr said, 'I liked the way you said the good news was that the Soviet Union had fallen apart because of Ronald Reagan, but the bad news was that the United States had fallen apart for the same reason.'

Hennington laughed loudly.

'It was a good line,' he admitted. 'Mainly because it was

true. Lucy came up with it.' He beamed at her, and she blushed, surprised he remembered.

'But now you're working with Barker on trade?' Kerr asked. 'I could not help overhearing.'

'You think I like that?' Hennington sighed. 'Well, I don't. But right now the prospect of the trade war deepening is such a clear and present danger, I'm hoping I can turn Barker aside from the wider tariffs by agreeing to the minor ones. Otherwise . . . well, I can count votes, and we're going to lose anyway.'

'Isn't that like saying you can get a little bit pregnant, sir?' Kerr protested. It was way off the point, but if McCall had already turned against him, he had nothing to lose. Hennington smiled. 'You are either for free trade or against it,' Kerr continued. 'You can't be a little bit protectionist, or a little bit pregnant. I'm surprised you don't just attack Barker and get it over with.'

'You speak your mind, don't you, son?'

'I'm Scottish, Senator. The English produced the diplomats. The Scots produced the fighters. Maybe I should keep my mouth shut. I'm sorry if I've been too blunt.'

Lucy hovered nervously in the background, sensing it was about to go wrong, but the senior senator from Kansas rubbed his chin thoughtfully.

'Don't apologise,' Hennington said. 'I like straight talk. It's kinda rare in this city. But protecting American jobs is popular back home, and so far Barker and his people are winning all the arguments.'

Hennington was a tall, tired-looking, handsome man in his late fifties, with a shock of long greying hair which fell over his face when he became especially worked up.

'But I hear what you're saying. The question is, how to kill off this America First garbage before it kills me, and the country.'

'Senator,' the used Q-Tip interrupted. 'I know Mr Kerr's views on trade are interesting, but you have another vote in twenty minutes. He's here to discuss the Second Coming, you know, the reappearance of that crazy guy who wanted to talk with you about economic spying.'

Hennington looked blank.

'Which guy?'

McCall reminded him sarcastically.

'This is the guy whose brother, Captain Ricky Rush, faked his own death, now he turns up Born Again, and wants to meet with you to tell you some sleazy story about the US government spying on its allies.'

Hennington laughed.

'Yeah, now I remember. Lucy mentioned it. And I said I hope to hell we *do* spy on our so-called allies. They need to be watched.'

Kerr smiled wanly, but Hennington cut him dead.

'I don't like traitors, Mr Kerr. I don't like dishonest men, cranks, or people who are close to Senator Barker. Folks who worked with your brother say he's all of the above. Ain't that the truth, Jim?' McCall nodded. 'And now it turns out that contrary to what was previously advertised, this brother of yours isn't even dead. No doubt all this makes sense to you, bein' family, and all. And I am real pleased you liked my speech to the 1992 Convention. But I think you should get the hell out of my office.'

'Ten minutes,' Kerr pleaded. 'You have twenty minutes before your vote. Give ten of them to me, and if you don't want to hear any more after that, I'll leave, of course. Ten minutes, you won't regret it.'

Hennington took a deep breath.

'You're a ballsy son of a bitch, I'll give you that,' he remarked. 'Your ten minutes begin now.'

Hennington looked at his wrist and set his stopwatch timer, warning Kerr out of the side of his mouth: 'Just don't piss me off.'

22

Joseph R. Huntley returned to his apartment a few miles from the Activity offices, took off his shoes and lit a cigarette as if it were his last. The conversation with Senator Barker had made him think that maybe it was. Huntley had given fourteen hours a day and often seven days a week to his job for as long as he could remember, and now the man who posed as the saviour of the Activity and all it meant – Barker – had provoked what could end up as its total collapse. Worse, its utter humiliation.

'And why?' Huntley muttered. 'Because he's a crazy, arrogant son of a bitch, is why.'

He padded to the kitchen and fixed himself a Jack Daniels on the rocks. If the video showed what Barker said it showed, and if Ricky had it, then they were finished. Simple as that. He took a gulp of the bourbon, then topped it up again. How could Barker have been so dumb?

It was an easy equation: video plus computer plus Ricky added up to the end for all of them. Ruffin would come up with a string of indictments, the Activity would collapse, so would America First.

'Unbelievable,' Huntley kept saying. 'Un-fucking-believable.'

He had tried to persuade Barker that it was all about to unravel, but the senator had been unmoved. Jeremiah had been talking to him again. Or Jesus. And Huntley could not compete.

'You pull your weight, Joe,' Barker had snapped, 'and it won't happen. You'll see. The Good Lord will provide. These people opposing us are gripped by a demonic agenda.

We'll beat them, because that is the Lord's will. I know it.'

A demonic agenda. Now how come Huntley hadn't thought of that? He knew about the problems with the FBI, but he hadn't counted on Beelzebub. Maybe they should put a wiretap on him.

'Demonic fucking agenda. Un-fucking . . .'

There was no swear word capable of expressing his anger. He walked back into the main room and opened a tin of peanuts, stuffed a handful in his mouth and began to chew gracelessly. Barker was talking to Jesus, that had to be it, though Huntley wondered if there was ever a conversation in which the Messiah got a word in edgeways. It did not seem likely. He gulped some more Jack Daniels, refreshed the ice and topped it up again.

'I did not come all the way from Texarkana, Texas to go down the tubes like this,' Huntley muttered into his glass. 'And I'm not going to roll over just 'cause Mark Barker wants it that way. Sumbitch.'

The bourbon was cutting his thirst and he began to think of the old Air Force term for when there were so many enemy troops needing to be killed you could hardly miss. In Vietnam they used to call it a 'target rich' environment. Target rich was right. There was Ricky, the computer, the video; and now Barker and Oberdorfer. That was the total of evidence against him, and he would have to make it safe somehow. All of it.

'Bastards,' Huntley told Jack Daniels. 'All of them. Bastards.'

Huntley's apartment was in a red-brick 1980s block in the built-up corridor between Washington and Dulles airport. After his wife died Huntley had assumed he would become a middle-aged philanderer. There was a surplus of eligible women in Washington, and at first he dated and bedded them with the enthusiasm of a teenager, but within a few weeks he always tired of their questions.

'So what do you do for the government, Joe?'

'I work for the Commerce Department,' he would say. Or sometimes it was: 'I work at the State Department in trade-related issues.' Or maybe, 'in the office of the US Trade Representative.'

And always they would say:

'Doing what?'

Stealing other countries' economic and technological secrets, darling.

He was tired of the bullshit, tired of the lies. It was easier to stay alone and to work, and work was all there was. Huntley fixed himself another Jack Daniels. He had half a dozen television sets so there was one in each room, plus a small set hanging over the toilet where he now he sat smoking a Marlboro, chewing the nuts and contemplating his future. He checked his watch and saw it was time for 'American Gladiators'. He finished in the bathroom, washed his hands and walked back to the main room where the forty-inch stereo television popped out from a teak wall cabinet. So what could he do? He had tasted defeat before in Vietnam and decided he did not like it. If the FBI got the video, it was all over. And if Barker got the video, he would have a hold on Huntley for the rest of his life. So that was decision number one. Huntley would get the video – nobody else – and then destroy it.

On television two of the female gladiators, both blondes, Storm and Viking, were posing in their tight bikinis. In this game they were supposed to prevent the competitors from running through a maze made out of massive padded cushions. There was a dark-haired contestant, Shari, who flung herself at Storm, catching her under her padding to send her flying so her legs splayed up in the air showing her butt. A-mazing. Women doing things like that on network television. No wonder Barker got so many viewers for his Christian broadcasting. The only butts you saw there were the preachers talking through their ass.

Huntley laughed aloud at his bad joke and lit another cigarette. Then he pushed his La-Z-Boy lounger back, thinking there was still a way out. It would not be pretty. It was something else he had learned in Vietnam. He called it the Huntley Doctrine.

'Overwhelming force,' Huntley muttered to Storm, who was sitting up, sticking out her chest and pouting for the camera. 'Overwhelmingly applied.'

Now the black male gladiator called Strike was explaining how he ate seven thousand calories a day, carbed up before a contest and never ate fruit because it was full of water.

'Water I can't use,' Strike said, pumping up his biceps with a grin.

Huntley thought Strike would understand the Huntley doctrine. Think what a few guys like Strike could do for the America First Corporation, instead of the white-bread Mormons who were so dumb Ricky was taking them out one by one. Strike would rip Ricky's head off, first sign of trouble, shove it up his ass then eat the goddamn video. And what would Strike have done when he found out that Barker had made the videotape that could blow them all away? What would Strike do with the crazy senator, huh? Huntley popped a can of Miller Lite beer and took a deep slug. Most of all he was angry with himself. He could not believe he had been so stupid as to sit in Barker's office in the America First building and not realise there were microphones and cameras everywhere.

'It's a television studio, for Chrissake,' he told Jack Daniels, and the ice nodded in the glass. 'So I figured the cameras were normal. Dumb, dumb, dumb.'

Huntley tried to remember the conversation, almost three years ago.

It was just after he had heard that the White House was going to scrap the Intelligence Support Activity, pleading lack of money – and lack of credible enemies – after the

Cold War. Huntley had gone to Barker's office to plead with him to persuade the Intelligence Committee to change its mind.

Barker had said, 'I'm sympathetic, Joe, I really am. But you need to switch more into economic intelligence. You do that, and I could swing everybody behind you.'

And Huntley had been so grateful he could have kissed Barker's bony little butt.

'Of course we need to expand our economic intelligence gathering, Senator. I would do anything to make it happen.'

And Barker had said, 'Anything, Joe?'

'Anything, Senator.'

'Then,' Barker concluded, 'maybe I have something for you. I have an idea. A neat idea.'

And that was where it all began, Senator Mark Barker's neat idea.

Huntley took a pull of bourbon. He could feel the alcohol now, dulling the pain, warming his guts.

''S like Barker had this death wish or something,' Huntley thought. 'Recording a meeting like that. Insurance, Barker called it. Insurance for what? The senator never answered when I asked him that question, mean little chihuahua. Never answered it. 'Nsurance, Jesus.'

Huntley slurped down more beer.

'Neat idea,' he muttered.

On 'American Gladiators' one of the male contestants tried to push past Strike to throw a basketball at a target. Strike hit him low and hard and the guy fell like a bale of hay. Couldn't even smile for the cameras, he was hit so hard. Yeah, Strike understood the Huntley Doctrine. Overwhelming force, overwhelmingly applied. Huntley took another beer and another bourbon. There was no food in the house except a jar of stuffed martini olives, potato chips, a tub of Cheez Whiz, and some salsa. The refrigerator contained a few six-packs of lite beer, a bottle of Stoli, some vermouth, cans of Coke and diet tonic water. Huntley pulled a pack of Doritos from the cupboard and emptied a jar of salsa into a soup plate, then his anger at Senator Barker flooded back upon him.

'Shit. Shit! *Shit!*'

Huntley punched the refrigerator door so hard he put a dent in it and drew blood from his knuckles.

'Shit,' he screamed, punching again. 'Shit. Shit! *Shit.*'

He wrapped ice in a towel, put it round his bloodied fist and returned to watch the end of 'Gladiators'. The more he looked at Strike the more he knew what he had to do. He would play along with Barker for now, do something to Ricky's girl, like Barker suggested. Maybe making Ricky real mad was not such a bad idea. It would flush him out, and they could finish him. Then there was one little trick Huntley had up his sleeve. He smiled into the bourbon.

'One li'l trick,' he said. 'My own neat idea.'

Strike was taking an amateur gladiator and beating him over the head with a giant pillow, beating the crap out of him. The amateur gladiator had been so destroyed by the pillow he fell over. Then they cut to Storm who was posing, showing off the shiny muscles round her chest in a way that made Huntley confused about whether she was good looking or not. He dipped a handful of Doritos in the hot sauce and swigged at his beer. The idea that had been slowly forming ever since the meeting at Barker's home suddenly became clear. Huntley laughed out loud, shaking so much that some of the hot sauce fell on the carpet. Barker had said it himself: nobody will believe Ricky if he attempted to murder a US senator. Huntley laughed.

'Attempted,' he giggled. 'Who needs "attempted"?'

A male contestant was trying to swing on hoops ten feet off the ground from one end of the gymnasium to the other. Strike came at him like a hungry alligator, trying to knock him into the safety net below. Strike hit the contestant with a scissor lock and after a few seconds, it was over. The man fell hard into the net.

'These guys are amateurs,' Strike said breathlessly, smiling at the television cameras. 'I'm a pro. That's the difference. However hard they try, I will always be better.'

Huntley vigorously crunched at the Doritos.

'Me too,' he said to the screen. 'Me too.'

23

David Kerr said, 'I met my brother for the first time today, Senator. And I do not recognise in him your characterisation of a traitor or a crank.'

Jim McCall's hostility was not surprising. Kerr had always found politicians' offices stuffed with aides with anti-freeze in their veins looking for reasons for their boss not to do things. It was Senator Hennington who disappointed him. Maybe Lucy was right. Maybe the senator had become so beleaguered fighting off Senator Barker's America First activists in Kansas and across the Mid West that he had buckled. He did not need any more crusades. But where was the tough old Hennington who had responded to one of Barker's tirades on homosexuals in the military by saying: 'I didn't know soldiers had to *be* straight, Senator; I thought they only had to shoot straight?' And Hennington had followed it up with a direct personal attack: 'I guess you would never know what makes a good soldier, Senator. What was it that kept you from service in Vietnam? A bad knee, was it? Or a billionaire father?'

Senator Barker had gone crazy, calling Hennington an apologist for homosexual perverts and child molesters. Maybe the thought of another unpopular burden and lost cause – Ricky – was too much. Whatever the reason, as Kerr spoke, Hennington looked on edge. McCall lounged back in his armchair, hands clasped, eyes fixed on an especially interesting ceiling tile.

The senator glanced at his watch.

'Your calculations of what is in your own best political

interest are obviously your own affair,' Kerr went on, desperately trying to strike a chord. 'I will simply tell you what my brother told me, and you can decide whether you are brave enough to run with it.'

Hennington jerked up at the implication of the word 'brave'. He leaned back at his desk, pulled his tie and unbuttoned his shirt collar. McCall twitched but kept his eyes on the ceiling tiles. Suddenly there was an interruption from the office secretary.

'Telephone call for you, Mr McCall.'

'I'm busy.'

'The caller said it was urgent. A private matter, but urgent.'

The used Q-Tip stood up and walked out to his office. Kerr seized the chance to present his case directly to Hennington. He began by explaining Ricky's role in providing technical assistance to the Intelligence Support Activity. Hennington interrupted tetchily.

'He bugs foreigners for their economic secrets.'

'Correct, Senator.'

'Then speak plainly for God's sake. It'll make the ten minutes go quicker.'

Kerr was rattled but tried not to show it. He listed, item by item, the operational areas Ricky had told him about.

'He is prepared to admit he personally profited from the data he collected.'

Hennington snorted.

'Now how exactly is that, Mr Kerr?'

'By using the information he acquired for the US government to speculate on the currency markets and deal in the shares of target companies. He said four senior ISA staff were involved. Two of them have since been murdered.'

Hennington sat bolt upright.

'Murdered?'

'Yes,' Kerr confirmed, looking at his notes. 'Their names

were William Colvin and Peter Drysdale. The two survivors are my brother and the Director of the Intelligence Support Activity, Joseph R. Huntley.'

Hennington was now as wide eyed as a child.

'Old Slippery Joe,' he said. 'Well, I'll be damned.'

Kerr thought, maybe we all will.

'And that's why my brother disappeared, Senator. He was in over his head. He thought he would end up dead like Colvin and Drysdale. He is a patriot who does not mind dying for his country in a real war, but does not intend to die to protect American industries in a trade war. Does that make sense?'

'And Huntley,' Hennington repeated as if wanting to savour it again. 'He . . . ?'

'He instructed Ricky to pass information to private businesses. He said there was no point the US government knowing about superconductor technology because Uncle Sam did not own the factories. The important thing was to deliver the information where it could do the most good for American business. Ricky started passing it on through America First, and then found they were being paid cash bonuses by the grateful industries.'

'He says he was suckered in?'

'Yes.'

'You believe him?'

Kerr shrugged.

'He's my brother, Senator. Of course I believe him. The point is, will you help him?'

Before Hennington could answer McCall returned from his private office and sat down.

'Excuse me,' the tall Texan apologised. 'Don't let me interrupt.'

The telephone call had apparently produced a profound change in McCall. He was no longer interested in the ceiling tiles, and Kerr was aware the Texan was staring at him intently.

Hennington sucked on his teeth. 'Quite a story, Mr Kerr. Can your brother prove it?'

'He says he can. Part of the proof is already here. I gave Mr McCall documents and computer diskettes.'

Kerr turned to the Texan, waiting for his scornful reply.

'The documents list companies and alleged transactions,' the used Q-Tip said mildly. 'I've only skimmed through them, but the information is along the lines Mr Kerr intimated.'

'Genuine?' Hennington wondered.

To Kerr's continuing surprise McCall was not especially hostile.

'Could be, Senator. Some of this has the ring of truth.'

'Mr Kerr said the files come from Joe Huntley. That he's dirty.'

McCall grimaced as if trying to look surprised.

'There's no written evidence I saw to prove that for sure, Senator, but . . .'

'So should I meet this Captain Rush, Jim? That's what I need to know.'

McCall cleared his throat.

'It could be very risky politically, Senator,' McCall reasoned, 'as I explained to Mr Kerr. However, if you could prove the corruption comes from the ultra-protectionist forces that have led us into the trade war, you might be able to get somewhere.'

'Why me?' Hennington suddenly turned to Kerr, who did not understand the question. 'Why am I so lucky that your brother is providing me with this treasure trove of information and not the FBI or the newspapers or some other equally worthy senator?'

'He trusts you,' Kerr replied slowly. 'Ricky believes you have shown you cannot be bought or bullied.'

Senator Hennington flashed his toothsome smile.

'And because Lucy is a friend of his,' Kerr added. Hennington looked at Lucy thoughtfully. 'And because there is nowhere else for him to go,' Kerr concluded. 'The FBI will arrest him eventually and he is concerned they will come under unstoppable pressure to suppress his information and dismiss him as a crank.'

'Why?'

'Because it would be too embarrassing to admit the degree of economic espionage which goes on between friendly countries.'

'And if we do nothing?' Hennington wondered.

Kerr sighed. 'Then my brother dies. And if that happens,' he said, 'the Activity is like Godzilla and will devour you all.'

McCall interrupted, the needle back in his voice.

'Sounds like your brother is a real crusader, Mr Kerr. Maybe he just wants to even some scores because he's pissed he didn't get promoted once his bosses at the ISA categorised him as unstable.'

'When did they do that?' Kerr asked.

'About a month before his disappearance.'

'Who told you that?'

McCall smirked and Kerr wondered what would happen if he punched the exclamation mark right in the teeth. Turn him into a question mark possibly. Hennington stepped in before it became really nasty.

'You told the FBI about your brother's resurrection?'

'Not yet.'

'You gonna?'

'I – I suppose so. I hadn't thought about it.'

'Well, let me put it this way. I can't hold public hearings if a federally targeted investigation is making progress. And I can't call as witnesses the defendants in a corruption case, you follow?'

'I plan to talk to the FBI after you have seen my brother,' Kerr answered quickly. 'How about that?'

'Good.'

Hennington turned again to McCall.

'I know you just skimmed them, Jim, but what do you make of the files? They the work of a madman or a patriot?'

'Both,' the chief of staff replied slowly, flicking over the pages. 'Captain Rush was highly decorated and well-regarded, but I am told he began developing psychiatric problems after his mother's death. Then there's his faked disappearance, and now his allegations, which, well, we could be talking major-league wacko here, Senator.'

'For example?'

'For example.' McCall shuffled the papers. 'The account of the manoeuvrings between the Bank of England, the British Treasury and the British Chancellor of the Exchequer – their finance minister – when the pound collapsed in September 1992. It sounds phoney. I mean the way the British behaved reads like the Keystone Kops.'

Hennington seemed amused rather than alarmed.

'They *were* the Keystone Kops, Jim. Those Brits do wonderful comedy shows. You ever been to their House of Commons?'

'And it is going to be difficult to evaluate,' McCall continued, without being deflected. 'For instance, there's all kinds of references to plans for high-speed trains, levitating monorails, hydrofoils, jet-propulsion systems, computer chips, biochips and superconductors. State of the art, cutting-edge technology. It will take dozens of experts in different disciplines to assess it for us.'

'Yes or no, Jim. Do I see this major-league wacko or not? In a word.'

McCall blinked.

'Regrettably, yes, Senator. You have to see him, because if it's true and you don't . . .'

'Then I could never live with myself.'

'Correct,' McCall concluded grudgingly.

Hennington rubbed his chin. He stood up and his long grey hair fell over his face as he paced the room. Kerr could see Lucy and McCall follow him with their eyes, waiting for a sign. Hennington walked to the window and paused for a few moments, looking out.

'I'm gonna have to see your brother,' he said as he turned back. 'Privately. See if he's a flake. And as soon as possible – say, this time tomorrow. I'm gonna give him a hard time. Tell him if he handles the pressure, we might talk about public hearings. But if Captain Richard C. Rush thinks my job is to bust open intelligence operations to save him from frying in the fire, he's wrong. I can't protect him from the FBI even if I wanted to, which I don't. If he did the crime, he'll do the time, you follow?'

Hennington moved brusquely away without waiting for a reply. The meeting was over. Kerr stood up and caught Lucy's eye. She winked at him and smiled.

'Thank you, Senator,' Kerr said.

Hennington turned back, grimly.

'You used your ten minutes well, son. Now tell your brother, if he does his disappearing act again, or does anything that makes him seem less than one hundred per cent American, I'll burn you both faster'n the British did the White House in the war of 1812. You got that?'

Kerr nodded.

'Yes, Senator. I think I got that.'

'That's it. Now get me Secretary Wallace on the line. Starsfeld Air Force Base is not gonna close while my tongue's good enough to shout about it.'

Hennington walked briskly out into his main office where Kerr could hear him greet a group of Kansas farmers, calling each man and woman by their first names like old pals, as he waited for the call to Defense Secretary Wallace to go through. The farmers were about to have their ten minutes of full laser beam attention from Senator Howard Hennington, before the next business began.

'He always like this?' Kerr whispered to Lucy. He could smell her perfume. She shook her head mournfully.

'This is a slow day. You should see him when he's busy. Hurricane Howie.'

'And what about McCall? How did he know about Ricky being categorised as unstable? Who has he been talking to?'

Lucy shook her head.

'I don't know, but I think I have a way to find out.'

She kissed him gently on the cheek.

'That means I'll be late home tonight,' she said. 'Don't wait up.'

24

The Harmony Supplies store was almost ready to close for the night. Music spilled into the street sounding like gentle rain in a tropical forest, punctuated by animal and bird calls. A grey car circled the block and the two men inside watched Beatriz Ferrara move around, rearranging crystals and watering the plants. She wore flared blue jeans, platform shoes and an oversize pink tee shirt with a rainbow and rainforest logo and the words 'Harmony Supplies' in multicoloured letters across her chest. The men got out of the car and were about to cross the road to the store when two teenage girls turned the corner, looked in the window of Harmony Supplies, nudged one another and walked inside. They wanted to know about the handcrafted Navajo silver jewellery. The two men walked briskly back to their car, started the engine and drove off. A few moments later a middle-aged hippy with long greying hair tied back in a pony tail arrived and asked Beatriz if aromatherapy was recognised as a cure for impotence.

'Like, I hear it can, you know, be effective?' the middle-aged man said in a sing-song voice, holding up an aromatherapy pack. 'If it's used the right way? Like with Vitamin E?'

The men in the grey car slowly rolled past Harmony Supplies, saw she was still busy, then set off for another circuit.

'Maybe,' Beatriz conceded, pulling out a bottle of Vitamin E pills. 'I've heard that it could be. Maybe you should try both.'

She looked at her watch, wanting to close up and leave

a message for Ricky. Ever since his telephone call she had been on edge. Ever since his brother had arrived, Ricky had broken every one of his rules.

'I'm surprised that you called,' she had told him. 'Because you said only communicate . . . you know, the other way.'

'They know, Beatriz,' Ricky insisted. 'They *know*.'

His tone made her even more alarmed.

'Are you sure?'

'Yes, I'm sure. Just like we suspected, David was the bait. They've always known, or guessed. That's why they went to such lengths to get him to the funeral. Anyway, David is going to help.'

She tried to sound comforted. 'What do you need me to do?'

'Nothing for now. I had to call to tell you I love you. I'd better go, before they have time to find me. I'll call when I have news, or reach you the other way.'

The 'other way' was the Electronic Mail system.

'I love you.'

'I love you too.'

He hung up, and she wondered how close he had been. His hearty manner always made him sound nearby, and it made her feel brave, as if he was watching over her. The middle-aged man with the pony tail caught her attention again. He decided to buy the aromatherapy book, a batch of oils and herbs, and the Vitamin E pills, despite Beatriz's insistence that it was not one hundred per cent guaranteed cure for sexual dysfunction.

'Do I need a partner for this?' he asked. 'Or can I do it by myself?'

'By yourself is fine,' Beatriz rapidly confirmed. 'To begin with.'

The teenage girls decided they could live without the Navajo jewellery, and left giggling together.

The man with the pony tail took his Vitamin E and aromatherapy kit and told Beatriz to have a nice evening.

She decided it was time to close and prepared to total up her cash receipts. Outside, as soon as they saw the customers leave, the two men parked the grey car again. They quickly checked each way down the street and walked across, pushing open the door of Harmony Supplies with such force it caused a dozen copper chimes to clang together. Beatriz jumped. Immediately she sensed something was wrong. The men's business suits looked as out of place in her store as the middle-aged hippy would have on Wall Street. There was something mean and anxious about the way the men looked at her. The older one closed the door and the younger pretended to study papier-mâché Guatemalan parakeets. He was late thirties, unseasonably tanned – from a bottle, Beatriz thought – with every hair in place and the aura of someone who was permanently unhappy. The older one, she had seen before. She was sure of it, but could not place him, except for his aura. It was grey, like death.

'What's the music?' the older one began politely, with a deep Texan drawl.

'S-sounds of the Amazon R-rainforest,' Beatriz replied, trying to control her nervousness.

She glanced at the telephone, wondering if she could call the police, then she thought of running for the stairs towards her apartment, bolting the door behind her. Let them wreck the store, she decided, if that was what they wanted. These were not the same two who had broken up the place when Ricky first disappeared, but, if anything, they were even more scary. The old one with the staring eyes, the younger one with the nasty look. She tried to keep her voice calm.

'Can I help you find something?'

'Not something,' the grey one said. 'But somebody.'

The orange tanned one locked the door and turned the Harmony sign to 'Closed'.

'Hey, what –'

'We need your undivided attention, lady,' John Oberdorfer said, a white-toothed grin across his face like a split in a melon, thinking: she's got great tits. He closed the window blinds and undressed Beatriz with elevator eyes, up and down. Joseph R. Huntley turned up the volume on the rainforest CD, pulled a cigarette from the pack in his pocket and lit it.

'I don't allow smoking in here,' Beatriz insisted.

Huntley grinned so she could see his yellow stained teeth.

'So call the police.'

He stared at her without blinking and breathed smoke. She watched his teeth as he curled his lip back over the cigarette butt, absolutely sure she had seen him before.

'Who are you?' she demanded.

The Tan Man pushed his face right up to hers with a leer.

'How about you invite us upstairs for some herbal tea, and we'll tell you?'

He dropped his hand to her buttock to give her a squeeze.

'Great ass,' he said.

Beatriz squirmed angrily and brushed him away.

'What the hell is this?' she screamed and dashed to the telephone. 'I will not be harassed by people like you.'

Oberdorfer pushed her hard in the chest so she stumbled to the back of the store. He pulled the telephone cord violently until it snapped.

'Is that so?' he sneered. 'You've been doing women's assertiveness classes, right? Self-esteem bullshit? I can always tell.'

He tried to grab her breasts but Beatriz darted behind the counter towards a second telephone. Oberdorfer was too fast. He kicked her hard in the pit of her stomach so she doubled up, gagging, then pushed her roughly back into the store room. Her head struck the door and she fell to the ground, moaning in pain. The Tan Man snorted with pleasure.

'Give me a few minutes, I'll show you about harassment. More than you'd ever want to learn.'

Huntley shut the store-room door and leaned over to grab Beatriz by the arm. He held her so close she could smell his odour of stale tobacco. He was all business.

'So where is Ricky?' Huntley asked slowly. 'Want to tell me now?'

Beatriz tried to break free, her belly aching from the kick, feeling as if she was about to throw up. Oberdorfer held her down by pushing both his hands firmly on her breasts and leering.

'In Arlington Cemetery where you put him,' she yelled, trying to push Oberdorfer away.

Suddenly she remembered where she had seen the older man. In the cemetery at the funeral, standing with a group of faceless dark suits. She had noticed him walk off and have a cigarette, thinking how disgusting he was, a smoker, a throwback with his grey aura like a ghost.

'Beatriz, honey,' Huntley said in a disappointed tone, twisting her wrist behind her back and breathing stale smoke in her face. 'We know for sure now what you have known for weeks, that Ricky's disappearance was a fake. You lied to protect him. I understand that, but he's a sick puppy. He needs treatment, and this is your last chance to get square with us. So let's hear it, hon, where is he?'

'I told you I don't know,' she screamed. 'And I wouldn't tell you if I did.'

Huntley quickly extended his right arm, crashing her backwards so her head hit a wooden shelf and she crumpled again at his feet. The rainforest sounds now included rumbling thunder and the heavy drip of rain through the forest canopy. Huntley took another pull on his cigarette and knelt down beside her. He could see the glint in Oberdorfer's eye, and it disgusted him. Almost gently Huntley ran his hand back across her forehead then grabbed a fistful of hair. She was a good-looking girl. What a pity. He pulled hard, yanking her head off the ground and drawing it towards his own face. The lit cigarette butt was an inch from her right eye and she tried to call out in terror, but no noise would come.

'Hon,' Huntley said slowly. 'I have to tell you, you're really pissing me off. It would be better for you to tell me. I'll torture you for the information, but my friend here'll do it just for fun.'

The cigarette smoke made tears come to her eyes and she tried to keep them shut. Then she felt Oberdorfer's rough hands pin her from behind and his knee dig in her back. She opened her eyes to see Huntley holding the cigarette butt by her eyelid.

'One way we could go,' he drawled, 'is call the FBI and let them take care of you. Aiding and abetting a fugitive, obstruction of justice, there's something to start with. The second way, is to listen to you tell us what you know, where Ricky is, and make sure he gets a fair trial. The third way we could go –' he drew on the cigarette until the butt glowed red and she could feel the heat on her eyelid '– is we beat the crap out of you, maybe let my friend here have his fun. If we do that, well . . . this time Ricky will need a real funeral in Arlington, you understand?'

'You can't do this to me,' she sobbed. 'I'll call the police, tell them everything about you.'

'Did Ricky leave any property around here?'

'No.'

'Any videos, maybe? A computer?'

'I told you, no. Search my apartment if you want. There's nothing.'

'Oh, you can be sure of that,' Huntley confirmed. 'We'll be taking the place to pieces.'

He could see Oberdorfer's eagerness was almost out of control. The girl was not helping herself any.

'She's all yours,' Huntley nodded to Oberdorfer in disgust, standing up and turning his back. 'I'm going upstairs to look around.'

Beatriz suddenly felt the knee stiffen on her back and

hands frantically pulling off her clothing from behind.

'Let me go,' she screamed as the Tan Man crushed her face to the floor. 'I'll tell the police everything.'

He punched her hard a few times on the side of the face so she quietened down. Her head jerked to one side.

'I don't think so, little lady,' Oberdorfer sneered, punching her one more time, then stripping off her jeans excitedly and pulling up her tee shirt so it covered her face like a bag. 'Fact is, you won't be telling anybody anything. They'll just have to take my word how much you enjoyed it.'

25

It usually took Ricky more than three hours to drive to where he was hiding out, a house he had bought on the remote Atlantic coast near Chincoteague under the false name Al Weinstein. He was in 'Al Weinstein's' electric-blue Grand Am, feeling more safe with every mile between him and the District of Columbia. The locals in Chincoteague treated 'Al' with exaggerated respect. 'Al' was a famous Hollywood screenplay writer, Ricky had told them, and they were too polite to say they had never heard of him or his (non-existent) hit movies, 'Devil Dogs of Death Valley' and 'The Wild Man', but they were impressed anyway. A writer, that was something to be. It explained how someone without any obvious talent could afford to buy a five-bedroom white clapperboard house with two acres, a view of the bay, and a large motor cruiser. But now as Ricky drove the first few miles towards Annapolis en route for Chincoteague and safety, he became increasingly agitated about Beatriz. She was such an innocent, and he should have warned her specifically that as soon as the Mormons found out he was still alive – by bugging the telephone, or following his brother – they would make trouble for her again. So would the FBI.

Ricky guiltily realised that he had been so concerned for his own safety, and that of David, he had forgotten to spell it all out for Beatriz. Maybe the best thing would be for her to move into Lucy's fortress apartment. David would protect her. Ricky turned off the freeway and drove into the centre of Annapolis, parking at the harbour. He found a pay phone near the fish market and tried her number several times, but each time there was a busy signal, which was weird.

In fact it was almost impossible, and it made his heart skip. Beatriz had a business system which meant if the line really were busy, calls would be diverted automatically to an answering service. It was not working. The blood began to pound in Ricky's ears like an approaching storm. He tried operator assistance. They checked and told him her number was out of service.

'How come?'

'I don't know the reason, sir. Out of service is all I have.'

Ricky paced up and down the waterfront, looking at the pleasure boats and the seagulls, thinking only of Beatriz and feeling almost physically sick. He could return to Harmony Supplies, but then he would be finished. By now the place would be staked out by the Mormons or maybe by the FBI. Or both. Yet the more Ricky thought about Beatriz, the more worried he became. He had not told her where his hideout was, nor details of his false identity, for obvious reasons. The way he planned it, the less she knew, the less she could reveal, the less danger she was in.

It had seemed to work – until now. Ricky's guilt came in waves, almost like a physical pain as he realised his mistake: he should have run away with Beatriz when it first happened, married her and made her Mrs Weinstein. A 'double suicide' would never have been believed, but the Mormons would still have had to catch him. With all the money he had salted away he could afford to buy safety, forever, and he could have protected Beatriz properly. But if he had done it that way, he would never have met his brother.

It was an impossible choice. Ricky shook his head at his failure to disconnect himself from the people he loved. He thought how he had been so clever to pretend he had broken up with Beatriz. He had been so smart, he had fooled himself.

'Dammit,' he cursed aloud. A couple of tourists on the

waterfront stared at him. He must be behaving oddly. He tried to pull himself together, or at least not to draw attention to himself, then he had an idea.

Ricky walked back to the pay phone. There was one other way to contact Beatriz. He had used it before. It was risky but probably could not easily be traced. Ricky took a deep breath and asked information for the Alexandria, Virginia number of Happy Harry's Ice Cream Parlour, across the street from Harmony Supplies.

'Harry? How're ya doing?' Ricky said, trying to sound cheerful. 'I'm Beatriz Ferrara's brother from Chicago. Yeah, Beatriz 'cross the street? We talked maybe a week or so ago 'bout the funeral of her boyfriend? Right. Yeah, but I'm having trouble getting through. It's like her line's broken again, and I was wondering if you have a minute you could go get her to the phone? Tell her it's her brother George?'

There was a pause on the other end of the line, a pause so profound Ricky thought Happy Harry had died in his ice cream shop.

'Hello? Hello? Hello, Harry?'

When Happy Harry's voice began to speak, it was laden with bad news. Ricky felt a hot knife twist in his guts, a wound so deep he doubled with the pain. He cradled the telephone and bowed his head forward into the open palms of both hands, sobbing with grief.

26

Lucy kissed Kerr goodbye again, standing at the elevator near Hennington's office.

'It is difficult to keep my hands off you,' she said. 'Even if you only want me for my political contacts.'

'Something like that,' Kerr said, then he paused. 'Lucy?'

'What?'

'We've only had one night together, but . . .'

She put her index finger across his lips.

'Don't say it, Mr Doubtful, or you might break the spell.'

'It's just that I'm too old for love at first sight.'

'Or too cynical.'

'Maybe. Either way, it has been too fast and I feel like an adolescent, but . . .'

'Look, David, I have work to do,' Lucy said. 'There will be time for us later. Everything in this town is like three-dimensional chess. Outsiders who play in just two dimensions think they know the rules, but they always lose.'

'Meaning me?'

'Meaning Ricky. I have to find out more about McCall and make sure the meeting is safe. I don't trust him. There's something going on, I can smell it.'

They kissed one last time and then Kerr took a cab to Georgetown, the taste of her lingering on his lips. He suddenly realised Lucy had said to him the kind of thing he had said all his life to every woman: I have work to do, there will be time for us later. And it was always untrue.

There was never time later. He paid the cab driver.

'Maybe the time for us is now,' Kerr muttered.

' 'Scuse me?' The cab driver looked perplexed.

'Nothing,' Kerr explained. 'I mean, sorry. I was just thinking about someone else.'

'I hope so, brother,' the driver said and drove away.

Kerr stood at the outside door of Lucy's apartment struggling with her written instructions for negotiating the codes and keys. Suddenly he heard a voice behind him.

'The elusive Mr Kerr,' Harold Ruffin said. 'I do believe it's time for another of our little talks.'

Brooks Johnson stood beside Ruffin and smirked unpleasantly.

'Ah, Mr Ruffin,' Kerr responded, trying to sound calm. 'I was just thinking of you. And your colleague, the elegant Mr Brooks Brothers. How nice to see you once more. And why am I elusive?'

'Because you checked out of your hotel and never mentioned it to anybody.'

Kerr hit the code for the elevator with Ruffin and Johnson by his side.

'Maybe I did not realise British tourists had to report their accommodation plans to the Federal Bureau of Investigation. Is this part of Senator Barker's influence on the trade war with the European Union? Are all foreign tourists suspects now?'

Ruffin smiled.

'Glad to see you're keeping your very British sense of humour, Mr Kerr. Country that gave the world Monty Python and Benny Hill. Got a lot to live up to.'

Brooks Johnson was not amused. He gave one of his tough stares.

Kerr said, 'Why do I think I am not going to like whatever it is you want to discuss, Mr Ruffin?'

'You're psychic, maybe?' Brooks Johnson muttered.

'Could be,' Kerr agreed.

He led the way to Lucy's apartment and offered them a drink.

'Nothing, thanks,' Ruffin said. 'But you go right ahead.'

Kerr wanted a whisky but poured iced tea from the refrigerator instead. He became irritated as he realised Brooks Johnson was doing exactly as he had in Kerr's hotel room, nosing around, picking up magazines, reading the message pad beside the telephone.

'Mr Ruffin,' Kerr said, annoyed, 'I am perfectly happy to talk to you anytime, but would you kindly tell your knuckle-trailing colleague to stop snooping around.'

Brooks Johnson glared back defiantly.

'You got a problem with me, doncha?' he growled.

'Yes,' Kerr agreed. 'So why don't you try very hard to give us your impersonation of a human being and stop creeping around.'

Brooks Johnson flexed his muscles, thinking of a smart retort, when Ruffin told them both to cool it.

'We got work to do, Brooks,' he said firmly. 'Sit down. You're making Mr Kerr nervous.' Johnson did as he was told. 'Makin' me nervous, now I come to think of it, all this testosterone rushing to people's brains around here.'

Brooks sat on a leather armchair and scowled. Kerr slumped in the sofa and glared back.

'Thank you,' Ruffin went on, all business. 'Now, Mr Kerr, maybe I should recap where we came in. First was the theft of government property from the office where your brother worked, a laptop computer carrying classified information. Then there were the murders of two government employees who worked with your brother. Finally, we go talk with your brother, and he dies on us. You with me so far?'

Kerr sat back and nodded.

'Yes, you told me.'

'So we hear that you've been meeting with the corpse.'

News travelled quickly in Washington.

'How did you hear?'

'Is your brother still alive, Mr Kerr?' Ruffin persisted,

dodging the question. Kerr decided there was little point in lying.

'He was alive this morning, yes.'

'You met with him?'

'I met him, yes.'

'You know how to get in contact with him?'

There was every point in lying now.

'No. He said he would contact me when he was ready.'

'Ready for what?'

'Ready . . . just ready. That's all he said. "I know how to contact you when I'm ready", those were his words.'

'And when will that be, Mr Kerr?'

Kerr shrugged.

'How would I know? I'm still trying to work out what is going on around here and who I can trust. At the moment, I don't trust anyone.'

'Even your new girlfriend?' Johnson interjected. 'You moved in here pretty quick, you must trust Miss Cotter a whole lot.'

Kerr glared back silently, then sipped his iced tea. For the purposes of this conversation, Brooks Johnson no longer existed.

'How did you know where to find me?' Kerr asked. 'And what business is it of yours what my sleeping arrangements are?'

'So tell me how you raise the dead,' Ruffin ploughed on, again ignoring Kerr's questions. 'How did you meet?'

'He raised me,' Kerr replied. 'That's what I'm trying to tell you. I went out to Arlington Cemetery to visit his grave and there he was, at the graveside, large as life you could say. I don't know how or why, he was just there. I was shocked. It was like seeing a ghost.'

'I bet. You tell anyone about your plans to go to the grave?'

'No. I mean, yes. I left a message on Beatriz Ferrara's answering machine.'

Kerr realised he should not have said that. Ruffin and Johnson exchanged knowing glances.

'That mean something to you?' Kerr inquired.

Ruffin explained that Ricky could easily dial in to hear messages on Beatriz's machine. 'On touch-tone phones all you need to know is the single digit code to activate play-back. Anyone can do it.' Then he asked, 'When was the last time you saw Miss Ferrara?'

'A couple of days ago at Harmony Supplies.'

'Today?'

'No.'

'When you saw your brother, did he have a baseball bat with him?'

'Baseball bat?' Kerr laughed nervously. 'Ricky and I were not playing games, Mr Ruffin. Unlike now, maybe.'

Brooks Johnson snorted but did not say anything. Kerr again sensed something wrong.

'What's the baseball bat for?'

'Oh, clubbing people round the head with, I guess,' Ruffin replied. 'You ever hear of the America First Corporation?'

'Of course.' Kerr stood up and opened the French windows, leading the FBI agents out to the balcony and pointing at the building. 'You can't miss it from here.'

'Your brother say anything about America First?'

Kerr looked thoughtful.

'No, he never mentioned it, except to say that Senator Barker – who gave the eulogy at his funeral – was one of the big supporters of the Activity and economic intelligence gathering. He apparently pushed through Congress all the money to keep them in business. So why are you interested? And what's that got to do with baseball?'

Ruffin walked back inside and sat on the sofa, bringing his hands together in an attitude of prayer.

'Name Scott Swett mean anything to you?'

'No. Is that a real name?'

'Yeah, it's real – and the man who owns it may be real

dead soon. He worked for the America First Corporation and we think your brother smashed his skull with a baseball bat near George Washington University.'

Kerr gasped. So McCall had been right. Ricky had gone over the edge.

'You know him, Scott Swett?' Ruffin persisted.

'I said, no,' Kerr repeated. 'Though I did see a man on the street with his head smashed in. Are you saying my brother did it?'

'We think so,' Ruffin confirmed. 'Then there was another America First guy, Brigham Y. Dodds, picked up by your brother at gunpoint and terrorised. We have a definite ID from Dodds that your brother did it.'

Kerr tried to suppress his alarm.

'Terrorised? Why? Does my brother know these America First people?'

'We think so,' Ruffin said. 'Though Dodds was not very cooperative and Scott Swett is too ill to say anything.'

'Mormons,' Kerr interjected. 'They would be the Mormons, right?'

Ruffin laughed.

'I don't think too many Catholic boys call themselves Brigham Young Dodds. Yeah, they'd be Mormons, Mr Kerr, or at least most of them are – more than fifty per cent of all America First employees. But you don't want to judge the Latter Day Saints church by what these guys do.'

Kerr shifted in his chair.

'Meaning?'

'Meaning most Mormons are God-fearing family people,' Ruffin said. 'Like the rest of us. The America Firsters are crazies, and some of them happen to be Mormons, but you should not judge a church or a group of people by the worst of the people within it.' Ruffin looked down at the backs of his hands. 'If you happen to be black, that's something you know.'

Kerr smiled. He had not expected folk wisdom from the

FBI. Worse than that, he had not expected to like Ruffin, but he did, and that could make lying to him even more awkward than it was already.

'Ricky *did* speak about the Mormons,' Kerr admitted. 'He told me they were trying to kill him and were responsible for the deaths of the two Activity members who were found dead in the swamp. He said these were the people following me. If Ricky attacked them it would be to protect me, correct?'

'Probably,' Ruffin agreed. 'And to protect himself. But you're a dangerous man to trail, Mr Kerr, which I'll bear in mind should the need arise. Little brother sure looks after you. Now, tell me what you think is the relationship between him and the America First Corporation?'

'You tell me,' Kerr responded. 'I have said three times now that he never mentioned it. You ask me again, and I'll say it four times.'

'Well, did your brother say why he faked his own death?'

'To avoid his real death. He didn't like the idea of dying in a swamp. Trying to keep yourself alive is not a crime, is it?'

Ruffin sighed in exasperation. He began counting on his fingers.

'Mr Kerr, I don't know how to put this, but we are not short of crimes where your brother is concerned. I'm thinking, assault, attempted murder, kidnapping, plus the national security offences. If you want to help your brother, now would be a good time for you to start helping us.'

'That might not be the same thing.'

Ruffin gazed at him thoughtfully.

'How many days have you spent with your brother?'

'Days? Only an hour or so. I was so stunned to see him I am not sure I listened carefully to what he had to say.'

'*Right,*' Ruffin said energetically. 'Now we're getting somewhere. And how many times have we met, you and me?'

'T-twice,' Kerr replied, catching the drift. 'Three times, counting the funeral. But I don't see –'

'Listen, David,' Ruffin said harshly. 'The truth is, you know nothing about me, after meeting with me two, three times. How come you trust this brother of yours after meeting him once following his –' he spat out the word '– resurrection? We're old buddies compared to that.'

'Easy,' Kerr shot back. 'Because he *is* my brother. That's all there is to it. And because I believe he needs help –'

'Psychiatric help,' Brooks Johnson scoffed. 'According to his military profile your brother suffers from mood swings, is likely to become unstable, has a propensity for violence, drinks too much. You want I read it to you?'

Kerr continued to ignore him.

'– he needs help,' Kerr went on. 'And I have tried to persuade him to give himself up to you because I believe the FBI is probably his only hope. But for now he is too scared.'

'I can see his point,' Ruffin said. 'When I think where this is leading, I get scared too.'

'Leading?'

Ruffin sighed. He was trying to think how much he should reveal. 'Suppose, Mr Kerr, suppose there was a link between a very powerful right-wing senator and a group of government officials. Suppose the senator was tough on trade and protectionism and might run for president. And suppose the government officials were directly responsible for collecting the information on which our trade policies are built.'

Ruffin stopped abruptly. He had already said too much.

'I see from the look on your face we are speaking the same language now. Your brother told you much more than you are admitting.'

'Maybe,' Kerr responded. 'But if we agree where this is leading, that would explain why Ricky doesn't trust anyone, including you.'

Ruffin shook his head.

'Listen, your brother is the key to unlock a whole lot of boxes for me. If we are going to fix this, I need him alive. If he does not trust me, then the Mormons will get to him first and … and that would be unfortunate. I'm your brother's only real hope, David.'

There was a deep silence, then Ruffin signalled to Johnson and the two agents stood up, ready to go.

'I just hope you have been paying attention,' Ruffin told him. 'We have enough information to put Ricky away forever, twice over, but that's not the point. If what I think is happening is *really* happening, then we are on the edge of something which has very serious consequences for this country.'

'Oh, come on,' Kerr scoffed. 'Where do you get this stuff from? Does someone write it for you?'

Ruffin glared back, deadly serious.

'Maybe your brother did not tell you everything. Maybe there wasn't time, but you'll probably figure it out sooner or later, David. I just want you to realise we are not playing pat-a-cake here. We can do it my way, or we can do it the hard way. Tell him, Brooks.'

Brooks Johnson grinned.

'The bottom line is that your brother better get his ass into our office and bring the laptop computer with him, and any other evidence, or else he's toast. It's either Great Dismal Swamp with a couple of nine mils in his skull like his pals Colvin and Drysdale, or maybe life in Marion prison – personally, I like the swamp better. The third way is he can talk to us. There's not much of a choice, and you being his only living relative ought to tell him that.'

'Thank you for explaining it so eloquently,' Kerr snorted.

Ruffin pushed in between them.

'I have a strange personal habit,' Ruffin said, moving his face so close Kerr could smell his aftershave. 'I understand brotherly love, but I get real mad when people jerk my chain. Don't jerk my chain, David. It's not worth it.'

'I'll remember that,' Kerr replied, thinking: no jerking.

'There's one other thing I have to tell you,' Ruffin concluded, his eyes looking straight into Kerr's. 'It's about Beatriz Ferrara.'

'What about her?'

'A couple of hours ago somebody tried to burn down her store in Alexandria. A woman's body was found inside. We're checking dental records.'

Kerr sat down, stunned.

'We're sure it was her, David.'

'You don't think Ricky . . . ?'

'No,' Ruffin said. 'Officially we've got an open mind. Unofficially, I don't think it was your brother. I think he's scared, and I think he is capable of almost anything, except that. You want to tell me where he is now?'

'I said I don't know,' Kerr snapped.

'Okay,' Ruffin continued. 'Okay, you stick with that for now. But we know how far Ricky was prepared to go to protect you. When he finds out what happened to Beatriz . . . Listen, David. If your brother begins a personal vendetta, starts acting crazy, he'll be treated as crazy, right?'

'What do you care?' Kerr snapped. 'It would be easier for you if he just died.'

Ruffin looked as if he had been slapped. His voice was cold with anger.

'What do I care? I need a witness, Mr Kerr. I don't need a looney tune with a baseball bat and I don't need any more corpses, you or your brother.'

'I-I'm sorry,' Kerr apologised. 'I just thought –'

'We know your brother bought a Glock pistol and a pump-action shotgun shortly before he disappeared,' Ruffin continued, his voice like ice. 'We know what he is capable of doing. You have to bring him in before he destroys himself.' Ruffin paused for a moment. 'And maybe destroys you too.'

'Me?' Kerr scoffed. 'Why destroy me?'

'Because now they've killed Beatriz, you are the only thing he has left to care about. You are the last piece of leverage they have. Remember that, and maybe you might stay alive.'

'Is that a promise?'

'I said maybe, David.'

Ruffin nodded at Brooks Johnson and the two agents walked away, slamming the door behind them as they marched down the corridor.

27

Ricky Rush walked up the side of the house in the darkness, checked the Glock pistol and then looked through the window. He could hear dumb middle-of-the-road music, Barry Manilow or Neil Diamond, filtering through the open door into the porch.

'Jeez,' he whispered under his breath. 'Man who listens to this shit deserves to die.'

He pulled his big hunting knife out of its sheath and cut through the bug screen, slipping his hand inside and opening the lock on the porch door. Easy.

Downstairs, Bob Allen was sitting on a rowing machine bathed in sweat. The basement of his Washington suburban home had been converted into a work-out and music room. He had a big hi-fi deck blasting out a CD of Andrew Lloyd Webber's greatest hits, while he worked on slimming down his beef-and-two-desserts-a-night belly. He reckoned he had time for a brisk work-out before the meeting he had planned with Brigham Y. Dodds and Ben Ritter.

Bob Allen was thinking how good it was that he had found a piece of England he liked, even if it was only the music. The great thing about Andrew Lloyd Webber was that the rhythm of his tunes always seemed to hit the rhythm of Bob's own exercise programme, a kind of one-two-three-four, in-out-in-out; one-two-three-four, in-out-in-out, like Lloyd Webber used a rowing machine to help him compose. Or maybe a StairMaster.

Bob was dripping sweat heavily now. Beside him was an exercise bicycle, a Nordic Track, a sit-up bench and a dozen or so small weights on a rack. Next to the weights was his

Ruger pistol, loaded and ready. Ever since the discovery of Brigham in the lay-by near Arlington Cemetery, Oberdorfer had become doubly nervous, unbearable even, and it had rubbed off on them all. Then they heard that Ricky had murdered his own girlfriend down in Alexandria and they knew he had really flipped. Oberdorfer told them Ricky was a sociopath, which sounded kind of scary, like that Hitchcock film with the scene of the woman getting stabbed in the shower. It was wild. Everyone in America First was now mobilised. Oberdorfer had taken to sleeping in his office in the building, and they were still nowhere near finding Ricky, his computer or the goddamn videotape. The Tan Man kept telling them how Ricky had freaked and they were all targets now.

'There's no point in tailing Kerr any more,' Oberdorfer said. 'We don't have to find Ricky. He will find us. And we don't want any more America First corpses, so be careful out there, okay?'

Like it was their fault.

'There are already too many questions being asked about Scott Swett,' Oberdorfer lectured. 'And about how come Scott knew Ricky. We're getting heat from the FBI on whether there was any relationship between America First and the Activity, and they are talking about the deaths of Colvin and Drysdale again. Until it cools down, you guys stay at home, stay armed, and stay alert.'

Right. And stay in touch. That was why Bob wanted to see Brigham and Ben.

One-two-three-four, in-out-in-out.

Figure out what to do next. Bob Allen looked across the room to check the Ruger pistol was where he thought it was. Stay alert.

One-two-three-four, in-out-in-out.

There had been some good news. Scott had staged a short recovery, though it was too fragile to put him out of danger.

Bob Allen had visited Scott when suddenly he opened his eyes and came out of the coma for a few minutes. He began to talk, though it did not make too much sense. Bob recalled something about whether they would have their part in a lake someplace, like in a timeshare.

'A lake which burneth with fire and brimstone, which is the second death.'

Scott kept saying that shit over and over again, until Bob Allen wanted to switch off the life-support machines. He kept calling out for someone called the Reverend Willard McDill and then he went back into the coma. Still, it was a good sign, Bob was sure of it, though he could do without the second death shit, which was Creepsville.

One-two-three-four, in-out-in-out.

And then, Bob thought, there was more good news. Ricky was now wanted for Scott's attempted murder, the kidnapping of Brigham and the murder of Beatriz. That was progress. Now every police department in the DC area was on Ricky's tail and he would be picked up sooner or later. Maybe they could stick him with the murders of Colvin and Drysdale too, if he really was a socio-whatever like Oberdorfer said.

One-two-three-four, in-out-in-out.

The only problem was the video. The goddamned video. Whatever was on it, and Oberdorfer would not say, it must really nail Barker. The senator was pissing his pants. Maybe it was a porn thing, little girls, though Bob Allen's imagination could not stretch to the idea of the senior senator from Oklahoma taking part in a video orgy. It was difficult to figure it all. But Bob decided he'd just do his job, as always, and leave the figuring to the Tan Man.

The local television news had shown pictures of the fire at Harmony Supplies, plus an interview with some ice-cream store guy who was wearing a tee shirt with smiling cows all over it. The smiling cow guy said he had seen nothing, heard nothing, until he saw the smoke and the store going up in flames. The firefighters found a woman's body half destroyed under it all.

'Beatriz was the nicest person in the world,' the smiling cow guy said, trying not to cry. 'In the world.'

One-two-three-four, in-out-in-out.

So all in all as he pounded along on the rowing machine, Bob Allen was feeling pretty good. One way or another, Ricky was cornered. The Feds would get him, and then they could all relax, so long as the videotape never turned up, and whatever was on it, Bob could not see how it affected him personally. That was Barker's problem. If the senator was into little girls, he had it coming, you know? Bob laughed at an outrageous thought. Maybe the little chihuahua was in a porn video all right, with fish, those ugly big fish he had.

That was it, Barker had videoed himself in the tank screwing his goddamned fish. Bob laughed so much he lost rhythm on the rowing machine. He would have to tell Brigham and Ben the joke.

Ricky Rush watched from the top of the stairs as Bob Allen stood up. He stretched and wiped the sweat from his face with a towel, moving over to the sit-up board and raking it back so it was at a sharp angle, hooking his feet under the straps to begin curling and uncurling his body. The Andrew Lloyd Webber CD was coming to an end and Bob figured he might finish the work-out if he could force himself to do fifty sit-ups. That son of a bitch Kerr could do a hundred. Ricky once did five hundred for a bet. Can you believe it? But fifty would be fine for Bob right now.

'Forty-six,' Bob Allen said, shrieking with effort, the sweat in his eyes making things look fuzzy.

Ricky smiled as he watched him suffer, thinking he would let Bob hurt himself a little before hurting him permanently. He had the Glock in one hand and the hunting knife in the other, wondering which to use. As Bob Allen uncurled, he took longer each time, exposing his neck as he lay back on the bench.

'Forty-seven.'

Ricky put the Glock in his pocket and switched the knife to his right hand.

'Forty-eight.'

Bob Allen uncurled and hung upside down, exhausted, readying himself for the final effort.

'Forty-nine.'

Ricky sprang forward. He grabbed Bob Allen's hair, wet with sweat from the work-out, holding his head back hard until the neck was fully exposed, then slashing deeply, jumping back at the first gush of blood. The Mormon lay gurgling, suspended by his feet upside down on the sit-up bench, blood pouring over his head and on to the carpet as he struggled to breathe, choking and drowning in the flow of red.

'Fifty,' Ricky said.

He watched the bleeding for a few moments then calmly walked over to the sink in the corner. He washed the knife and his hands, drying them carefully on the towel and making sure the blade was spotless before he put it away in the sheath. He had left no fingerprints anywhere, touching nothing except Bob Allen's head. Ricky picked up the Ruger pistol and stuffed it in his pocket. The last strains of 'Don't Cry for Me, Argentina' were fading on the tape deck as he climbed the stairs. He glanced back for a moment at what now looked like a scene from an abattoir and his eyes glazed over at the thought of how they had caused Beatriz to suffer. That made it simple. They all had to die now, every last one of them. They had sucked him in, destroyed his faith, and they were all going to pay. As Senator Barker used to say, it was just that simple.

Ricky checked his watch. He had never been to Ben Ritter's house but he had the address and was sure it would be easy to find. Ben Ritter next, and then Brigham. That would be enough for one night.

It was just that simple.

28

A rush of panic hit David Kerr as soon as the FBI agents left. It had been easy remaining calm when he was consumed by the effort of trying to handle them, but now he had time to think, the news that Beatriz had been murdered made him sick with anger and fear – anger that anybody could have done this, fear for how Ricky might react. At every stage Kerr felt he had been wrong. He was blundering about now as he had blundered in Sarajevo, taking risks, getting excited, missing the point. The point was that he knew almost nothing about his brother and was being drawn into a quagmire beyond his comprehension. The doubts hit him like a wave. What did Brooks Johnson mean about Lucy? Should he no longer trust her? In a few days he had thrown away all his reserve and caution and allowed himself to fall in love with her. What was he doing? Could he trust Ricky? Should he trust someone who had beaten up the Mormon in the street with the baseball bat? Kerr paced up and down, so confused he was not even sure which emotion was uppermost, only that he felt a pain in his soul as bad as anything he had ever felt in his shoulder. The Souvenir of Sarajevo no longer ached, but it had been replaced by something far worse. And yet . . . and yet . . . this was his brother. It was not just anyone, not just some stranger on the road or some helpless Bosnian girl for whom he felt endless pity but nothing more. This was an obligation. This was blood.

He walked to the balcony and looked across the river towards the America First building, hunched over Washington like a predatory beast. The puzzle that Ricky could unlock, Ruffin had said.

And they would try to turn the key tomorrow if Kerr could plan how to conduct the meeting with Hennington in safety. He walked to Lucy's cocktail cabinet and fixed himself a whisky. He was about to take the first sip when the telephone rang. Absently he picked it up, assuming it was Lucy. He was startled instead by a gruff man's voice.

'David,' Noah McGhie barked. 'We've got to talk.'

Shit, Kerr thought. The last man in the hemisphere he wanted to deal with now. He put the whisky down.

'Um, well . . . sure, Noah, it's late, past ten o'clock and um . . .'

'I mean right now,' McGhie insisted. 'For your brother's sake.'

'You heard?'

'Of course. Everybody heard.'

That was certainly true.

'And about Beatriz?' Kerr wanted to know. 'You heard about her as well?'

'Yeah, I can't believe it. Now we have to get together.'

'Of course, Noah, what do you suggest?'

What McGhie suggested was another visit to his home in Falls Church. 'Yes, Noah. Of course.'

Kerr left immediately. When he arrived McGhie was standing at the front door, clearly agitated. He led Kerr to the back porch. Arlene and the kids, he said, had gone to her mother's in North Carolina.

'Holiday?'

'Fear,' McGhie replied, not friendly.

'Of what?'

'Of your brother. They left an hour ago. I sent them away.'

'Fear of Ricky?' Kerr was amazed. 'I thought you said he was family?'

McGhie said nothing at first. He poured two glasses of fresh lemonade, gave one to Kerr and sat down in the porch. Kerr would have preferred the scotch, abandoned untouched in Lucy's apartment, but said nothing. McGhie's face was sombre and strained.

'Even family go wrong,' he whispered, as if to himself. 'Your brother is betraying us all. Huntley called and told me Ricky has attacked people he used to know, put one of them in hospital. Another guy, they found trussed up like a chicken by the roadside. What's happening to him?'

'They say Ricky is unstable,' Kerr replied. 'You believe that?'

McGhie looked doubtful.

'Wild, yes. Unstable . . . I never thought so, until now. Maybe.'

Suddenly McGhie's voice resounded with the timbre of a Baptist preacher spitting hell fire.

'Ricky betrayed us in so many ways I have trouble listing all of them.' He swigged the lemonade fiercely. 'Huntley said Ricky is threatening to talk in public before the Hennington committee, that he even discussed with you specifics of his work at the Activity. Talking to a foreign national about the economic security of the United States is as good a definition as any I've heard of treason.'

'Treason? Noah, I'm his brother, for God's sake. Be serious. He needs help, so he told me a few things to try to save his life. Is that so wrong?'

Kerr's desperate tone caused McGhie to sit back and be quiet.

'Besides, how did Huntley know Ricky wanted to meet Senator Hennington?' David Kerr asked. 'Does he have a source in Hennington's office?'

Now McGhie looked puzzled.

'I don't know,' he said. 'Huntley has sources everywhere. In this city, information becomes knowledge and knowledge becomes power. That makes Huntley one of the most powerful men in Washington. And he says Ricky has gone crazy, literally, like he lost part of his mind. Huntley said Ricky killed Beatriz.'

'You believe that?'

'No.'

'But you do believe he is dangerous – dangerous enough to be a threat to Arlene and the kids?'

McGhie was sweating gently now, small beads glistening on his smooth black forehead.

'I don't know,' he said. 'But I could not take the chance.'

Neither of them knew who they could trust any more, and each of them desperately wanted to trust the other.

'I have not got time to argue with you, Noah,' Kerr said. 'But I want you to tell me, what is your role at the Activity?'

'I can't answer that.'

'Ricky says you remained in charge of technical operations but always distrusted Huntley, that you were never directly involved in economic espionage.'

McGhie took a deep breath.

'I can tell you one small part of what you need to know,' he responded. 'Me and Huntley never got on.'

'Which is why, Ricky says, you never made any money.'

Now McGhie looked pained. 'I don't know what you are talking about.'

'Don't lie to me, Noah,' Kerr yelled. 'I told you, there isn't time. When did you find out Ricky and the others were making profits on the side?'

McGhie shook his head and said nothing.

'I know you fought with Ricky over something. It was this, wasn't it?'

Still no answer.

'Why did you not turn Ricky in if you knew? If you're so bloody straight why did you not break up the illegal use of information, this little business they all ran on the side?'

Now McGhie put his head in his hands.

'Stop it, David,' the big man cried. 'Stop it.'

'Noah, you have to answer me. Why did you not turn Ricky in when he told you about the profits and the links with Barker? You knew it was illegal.'

McGhie looked near to tears.

'I have known your brother for fifteen years,' he said slowly. 'I told you he was like a kid brother. When he confessed, spoke about the money he was making, I felt like something had torn my heart out. He came to me after the killings of Colvin and Drysdale in the swamp, scared, real scared. I ordered him to go to the FBI, but Ricky said that without hard evidence they would never believe him. He persuaded me to say nothing until he could steal enough of the evidence. Just give me two days, he said. I need to get a computer full of files and a video.'

'Video? I never heard about a video. What was on it?'

'He never said, but I told him he could have his two lousy days, then I would turn him in. Instead he disappeared off Cape Hatteras and I didn't know if Barker's people had killed him or not.' The big man's chest was heaving with emotion. 'I thought I had killed him, David, thought I had driven him to suicide, or maybe let him get killed. I thought I should have done more . . . Guilt? You bet I felt guilt.'

Kerr hated to do this to McGhie but he had to learn it all.

'So still you did nothing? You never told the FBI what he had confessed to you?'

Noah McGhie looked heartbroken.

'Like I said, I sent Jiminez and Snow down to try to investigate, only I never told them the full story. I went down myself to Hatteras but got nowhere. Now Ricky's back after pulling the disappearing stunt on us all. How do you think I feel?'

'Betrayed? Wasn't that your word?'

'Sure, David, betrayed, but also relieved he's still alive. I'm so mixed up I want Ricky to live so I can strangle him with my bare hands. Does that make sense?'

It made perfect sense to Kerr. He stood up and paced across the porch for a few minutes.

'You have to tell me more, Noah,' he said eventually.

'How did Ricky get sucked into this and you did not?'

McGhie rubbed the sweat from his face with the palms of both hands.

'All the documents we produced went to the Economic Security Council. Huntley instructed Ricky which ones were also to be diverted to America First. Barker's people were to be like a clearing house – delivering the information about foreign competitors to American businesses so they could compete better. America First got the credit, and if anything went wrong, the Activity could deny being involved.'

Kerr sat down.

'Who authorised it?'

McGhie smiled grimly. 'That's the sweet part. Ricky assumed Huntley's clearance came from the White House. Your brother was a good soldier and did what he was told. If you wrapped dog shit in the American flag Ricky'd eat it. Huntley made him eat it. There was no clearance from the White House. This was Huntley and Barker's little scheme. As soon as Ricky found out, he went off the rails.'

'But why were you never involved?' Kerr asked. 'You were Ricky's boss.'

'Huntley did not want me,' McGhie responded. 'He told Ricky that Barker didn't trust niggers. That's a direct quote. And you want to know something, David? Every night this nigger says his prayers to sweet Jesus thanking him that Senator Mark Barker is a racist son of a bitch, and for saving me from the hell Ricky's going through now.'

'The quality of faith,' Kerr interrupted. McGhie looked puzzled.

'That's what Lucy says drove Ricky,' Kerr explained. 'He always wants to believe in something.'

'And now he has nothing left to believe in,' McGhie answered. 'That's what makes him so dangerous.'

A cavernous silence fell. Kerr waited for five minutes.

He looked at the colonel, suddenly old, aged by disappointment.

'Noah, tell me exactly what Huntley said when he called you tonight?'

'He said he feared a scandal with Ricky, and said maybe Arlene and the kids were in danger. Then he asked me to call you to deliver an ultimatum: contact Ricky and get him to give himself up within twenty-four hours.'

'Or else?'

'Or else we could be attending his funeral all over again.'

It was as if the big man had shrunk like a balloon half-deflated.

There was one question left now.

'Which side are you on, Noah? Will you help me save my brother or not?'

McGhie looked as if he had just sucked a lemon. He slumped back in his chair, staring at Kerr and thinking about the question he had been dreading. He did not answer.

29

Just after eleven p.m. Brigham Y. Dodds and Ben Ritter met at the all-night Silver Dollar diner west of Washington on Route 7. The place was nearly empty except for a couple of middle-aged bikers who parked their Harleys outside, a chain-smoking thirtysomething woman who had walked out on her husband, and four hispanic teenagers who had come off shift at a nearby gasoline station. Ritter stared at the bikers, wondering if they were FBI. He saw government agents everywhere now, convinced that Ricky Rush had talked. But the more Ritter stared at the bikers, the less they looked like FBI, the more like corporate lawyers from Washington, pretending after dark they were Hell's Angels, red bandanas, Harley Owners' Group tee shirts, leather trousers, beepers on their belts, and – the clincher they were not FBI – Rolexes on their wrists.

In fact, Ben decided, he and Brigham looked more like FBI agents in their dark business suits, white shirts and ties. They asked for a table for three and checked watches. Bob Allen was late, as usual. They waited a further twenty minutes then ordered burgers, fries, milkshakes anyway. In the shadows outside, an electric-blue Grand Am rolled up behind a dumpster which smelled of rotting food. There were half a dozen cars in the darkness at the back of the restaurant including Brigham's Ford Taurus and Ritter's Oldsmobile Cutlass. The driver of the Grand Am killed his headlights and waited.

'Ricky's crazy, Ben,' Brigham said when the milkshakes arrived. 'You could see it in his eyes. He's not just a wild man any more, he's totally over the edge, like insane, you know? He wanted to kill me.'

Ben Ritter sipped his choc-o-malt then wiped his lips carefully on a napkin.

'If he wanted to kill you, Brig, you'd be dead. He wanted you to send a message to Barker.'

'And Huntley. He wanted Huntley to know.'

'Whatever.'

Brigham nervously looked at his watch again and stood up.

'I'm gonna call Bob one more time. There's three of us together in this and I want to hear from him as well.'

He made yet another call from the pay phone in the entrance to the Silver Dollar diner, but there was still no answer from Bob Allen's home. Outside the driver of the Grand Am took the Ruger pistol out of his pocket and stuffed it under the driver's seat. He had more guns than he needed, and Bob Allen's Ruger was just a distraction. Ricky stepped out of the Grand Am, watching Brigham talking on the telephone, wondering whether he should just shoot the son of a bitch through the diner window. Inside it was well lit, and at this range he could hardly miss. He opened the car boot and put the Glock inside, pulling out the pump-action shotgun.

Ricky decided to wait. He would take them when they left the diner. He had no quarrel with the chain-smoking woman or the bikers or the hispanic kids, and he worried they might be hit in the crossfire. This was strictly personal. The Mormons were going to die to make sure David stayed safe; then Oberdorfer and Barker, because they had ordered Beatriz to be killed. That would leave Huntley, and Ricky had decided to provide him with a personal hell.

Ricky would go through with the idea of talking to Hennington, knowing that a Congressional inquiry would ensure that Joseph R. Huntley spent the rest of his miserable life answering questions from Senate investigators, the FBI, the courts and the news media. For Huntley that would be permanent purgatory, having to explain himself to people who had never been sworn in to the cult of intelligence. Ricky touched the smoothness of the shotgun with his hands, and waited.

'Something's wrong,' Brigham told Ben Ritter in alarm when he returned to their table. 'Bob promised to be here by eleven. It's eleven thirty, and he's not at home either. There's no answer from his telephone.'

Ritter shrugged. Sometimes he wondered how he got mixed up with these guys. He thought it funny that Ricky referred to them all as 'the Mormons' despite his own pronounced Jewish name. In fact, he'd been brought up Catholic.

'Jewish, Catholic,' Ricky had told him. 'Once you start working for the America First Corp you're a goddamn Mormon asshole like the rest of them.'

'Thanks, Ricky.'

'You're welcome, Ben.'

When the burgers arrived Ritter said, 'So what do you think? You think Ricky killed the girl like Oberdorfer said?'

Brigham shook his head, pouring ketchup on his french fries. It gushed out of the bottle, covering everything in red.

'Shit,' he hissed. 'Nothing going right.'

'You're just nervous,' Ben commented. 'Stands to reason.'

'It's Oberdorfer,' Brigham whispered. 'Just you talking about him makes me nervous. I think he killed Beatriz to stir Ricky up. In fact, I'm sure of it.'

That was also the way Ritter had figured it.

'Yeah,' he agreed, stuffing french fries in his mouth as he talked. 'Yeah, if the Tan Man is trying to make Ricky go crazy, that'd be the way. But how come he didn't ask us? Why'd he do it himself?'

Brigham shook his head.

'Who knows what goes on in Oberdorfer's brain? Maybe

he just wanted a piece of pussy. You know what the Tan Man's like.'

Ritter considered what the Tan Man was like.

'How about this. Maybe Oberdorfer is using us like we used Ricky's brother. I mean –' the idea suddenly started making a lot of sense to Ritter '– I mean, once Ricky hears his girl is dead, who's he going to look for? The same people who did the business in the swamp, right? The same people who bust up her store last time.'

Suddenly Brigham did not feel hungry. He chewed a tasteless mouthful of hamburger then pushed his plate away.

'W-what are you saying, Ben?'

'I don't know for sure, Brig. I'm just thinking aloud here, but maybe Oberdorfer believes we can't find Ricky, and that if he rattles his cage enough, that Ricky will find us.'

Brigham began to see the light.

'C-could that be why Oberdorfer sleeps in the building now?'

'Say what?'

'He sleeps in the Power Tower,' Brigham repeated. 'Never leaves it. Told me he was too busy with crisis management.'

'Shit,' Ritter hissed, draining his milkshake and calling for the cheque. 'Crisis management my ass. Well, I ain't no human sacrifice. I'm out of here.'

Brigham looked thoroughly alarmed.

'You think Ricky'll come for us like the Tan Man warned?'

'Do ducks swim?' Ritter replied scornfully. 'What do you think? Is Ricky the type to want revenge, or what?'

There was no need for an answer.

Ritter said, 'He'll come for us, sure he will. Or he'll tell the FBI everything he knows. Or both. Either way, we're toast. You do what you want, Brig, but I'm not going to stick around to find out. I'm out of here.'

He paid the waitress and they stood up.

'I got the MAC 10, the Ruger and the cocaine baggies in my trunk. How about you, Brig?'

Brigham shook his head.

'Oberdorfer took the hardware back when Ricky kidnapped me.'

'You serious? He left you unarmed?'

'R-Ricky took the Ruger off of me, Oberdorfer picked up my car and got the MAC 10 out of the trunk. I never thought to ask for anything more . . .'

'What were you going to shoot Ricky with?' Ben Ritter asked in amazement. 'Your peepee? Okay, okay, you take my MAC 10. I hate the goddamn thing anyway. It's a pimp's weapon, if you ask me. I'll keep the Ruger. We'll go outside now and dump the baggies of cocaine in the trash, then we get the hell out of Washington until it cools down. I'm thinking maybe fishing in Idaho or someplace.'

Brigham nodded.

'Maybe Alaska.'

'Alaska is good.'

They left the diner and walked across the car park to Ben Ritter's Olds Cutlass. As soon as Ricky saw them he started to move slowly. He watched as Ritter opened the trunk and pulled out the shoulder bag with the MAC 10 and handed it to Brigham, then picked up the small bags of cocaine and prepared to throw them in the foul-smelling dumpster. Ricky slipped along the wall in the darkness between the diner and the dumpster holding the pump-action shotgun in both hands. His muscles were tense and ready to shoot. By the time he came to within thirty metres of Brigham and Ben he was preparing to rush and fire, when the two bikers stepped out from the diner and moved towards their Harleys. The movement caught Ben Ritter's eye and he dropped the cocaine back into his car until they passed.

His heart beat hard into his mouth. Maybe they were FBI after all. He started to reach for his gun. Then Ritter saw movement in the shadows. Brigham followed his gaze to the space between the garbage dumpster and the diner wall where the pump-action shotgun caught the light. Ricky broke into a run as Ritter pulled out his Ruger and Brigham levelled the MAC 10. Ritter fired a single shot at chest level but it strayed wide as Brigham loosed off a short burst which cracked through the diner window over Ricky's head. Now Ricky dropped to one knee and began firing blast after blast from the shotgun. The first shot clipped one of the bikers who fell forward as the other dived behind Ritter's car.

The second blast was better aimed and took Ritter in the stomach. He catapulted forward while Brigham opened up with a longer burst from the MAC 10. It started almost on target, but the gun was a bitch to keep down on fully automatic. The spray of nine-millimetre bullets ripped through the steel side of the diner. Ricky fired three more times with the shotgun, hitting Brigham each time so he jerked backwards in the air and then fell. Suddenly it went quiet. There was a moan from the biker who had been hit, then the other biker, who had been cowering behind the Cutlass, took off at a run down Route 7, screaming hysterically in the middle of the road.

It was so quiet now Ricky could hear his own footsteps. He turned and looked inside the diner. One of the hispanic teenagers popped his head above the counter then ducked as he thought it was about to be shot off. Ricky walked quickly to the back of the Oldsmobile where Ben Ritter was still moving. Ricky stood over him, looking into his eyes. Ritter struggled to move and say something but could not speak. His eyes stared up at Ricky in a silent plea for life.

'Please,' he moaned. 'Please, Ricky.'

'You get the same chance you gave Beatriz,' Ricky snarled.

'No,' Ritter gasped. 'I didn't . . .'

'Same chance, Ben.'

Ricky held the shotgun immediately above Ritter's head,

paused for a second, then fired one last blast at point-blank range into his face.

Everything went very quiet, everywhere it was still. Slowly Ricky pulled the shotgun back and cradled it on his shoulder.

He walked back behind the dumpster towards the Grand Am, put the shotgun on the rear seat and sped off towards the Beltway and the long trip to his beach house at Chincoteague. He did not bother to check his mirror to see if the police were on his tail. Somehow he felt he had a new aura, like a ghost dancer's shirt, which would protect him from everything they threw at him, until the very end.

His mind raced through each of the next steps he had to manage to nail them all. By now his computerised Electronic Mail should hold details of the meeting with Hennington, if David had managed to fix it. Ricky smiled, thinking of how it would be. When he told the truth to Hennington, he would end up destroying Barker and Huntley, America First and the Activity, knock them down like a stack of cards, Wild Ricky the Avenger.

'Destroy them all,' he repeated aloud. 'Every damn one.'

He looked in his mirror, caught a glimpse of his face in the amber street lights and was amazed to see he was crying. Tears glistened on his black beard.

'I am sorry, Beatriz,' Ricky muttered, trying to keep his misty eyes on the road. 'Oh, God, I am sorry, so sorry.'

30

David Kerr left McGhie's house thinking there was nothing as lonely as driving alone in the dark. He watched the lights of cars flash by in the opposite direction, the tower of the Washington Monument, the illuminated city skyline, trying to work out what connected him to anybody any more, a poor little orphan kid with a messed-up brother and a life that was falling apart. Go back to first principles, he told himself. Did Ricky kill Beatriz? No, why would he? He was angry, not crazy, even McGhie admitted that. Would he kill the Mormons? Of course, but that was justified to save himself and save his brother. Who has lied to me? Huntley? Yes. McGhie? No. Ricky? Not that I can prove. Lucy?

He took a long breath. Surely not? Lucy?

It was possible. Someone tipped off Huntley about the Hennington meeting. Someone talked to the FBI. McCall, Lucy? What did Brooks Johnson mean about Lucy? How well did Kerr know the woman he had been sleeping with? Maybe better than he knew his own brother, but still it had really been only a few days. And now the doubts. Always the doubts.

'Oh, God,' Kerr sighed.

It was like a teenage love affair in which every suspicion of betrayal now blared at him as if through a loudspeaker. The meeting with Hennington. Hadn't it happened so simply? Too simply? The easy way she had slept with him. Her offer for him to stay with her. Even the clever way she confronted him with his doubts. Was that a trick? Did it mean: 'Don't doubt me?'

When Kerr arrived back at the apartment, full of suspicion, he found Lucy sitting on the balcony overlooking the Potomac sipping a chilled mineral water, her bare legs crossed under a white silk wrap. It was late, but she looked pleased to see him until she caught something hostile in his manner. She stood up and they kissed briefly. Kerr found his whisky on the cocktail cabinet where he had left it untouched some two hours before. He took a sip.

'It was like coming home to the *Marie Celeste*,' she said. 'Finding your half-finished drink. You should have left me a note.'

'I'm sorry,' Kerr replied awkwardly. 'I was in a hurry to see McGhie.' He paused. 'Tell me what Hennington really thought of the idea of meeting Ricky.'

'I don't think there's a problem,' Lucy responded eagerly. 'The senator seems determined to go ahead as arranged tomorrow, and McCall recommended it enthusiastically. He's such a slippery sucker you can never tell what he's going to do. Anyway, he said he finally concluded it could make Howie's campaign if he ran for president on a clean-up Washington ticket after exposing a scandal like this.'

'That's all he thinks about?' Kerr said. 'Not right or wrong but what will look good?'

'Sure,' Lucy replied. 'McCall never uses words like right or wrong, only "appropriate" or "inappropriate". Anyway, Hennington repeated his one rule before the meeting: he wants Ricky to bring along every piece of evidence he can lay his hands on, walk us through it, the whole nine yards. What he would or would not say, if there were to be public hearings.'

'A dress rehearsal,' Kerr scoffed.

'Exactly.'

'In which Ricky has to bring along everything that proves his case – and without it, he would just be crazy Ricky, the man who pretended to kill himself.'

Lucy was exasperated by Kerr's tone.

'The senator's a lawyer, David. He needs to see everything, and he does not like surprises. It's his career on the line too, you know.'

She lay back on the seat, crossing her legs, and seemed surprised he did not go to her. Kerr watched the white silk part almost to the top of her thigh. Lucy caught the continuing chill in his manner and pulled the wrap back across her legs.

'Is there something wrong, David?'

He put the whisky down again. It tasted of nothing and there was no point drinking it.

'Lucy, I want to ask you a couple of things, and I don't want you to get angry, okay?'

'I'll try, but I can see you're in an awkward mood.'

'Yes.' He nodded.

She leaned forward. 'Did something bad happen?'

'Yes,' David concurred. 'Before I tell you, I need to know if you helped Ricky disappear? Helped him with his supposed suicide?'

'No.'

'But someone did. Beatriz?'

Lucy stood up. She came over beside him and put her arms gently round his waist and kissed him on the lips.

'I told you I do not like to be interrogated,' she said. Kerr stood, unresponsive, and she pushed him away at arm's length. 'Of course Beatriz helped him,' she replied irritably. 'What more do you want to know?'

'Just a little,' he went on. 'I thought they had broken up?'

'For someone so smart you can be real dumb,' Lucy snapped. 'Just like your brother. When he knew he was in trouble they pretended to break up, obviously to protect Beatriz. Ricky must have assumed they would stop at nothing to nail him, so he wanted to make her an *ex*-girlfriend. It was his way of loving her. He needed to know that she'd be okay.' Then she added with lofty condescension: 'I am sure you could work all this out for yourself if you tried very hard.'

It was clear now that Lucy had not yet heard about Beatriz's death. Kerr wanted to tell her, but he had to set his doubts to rest first. He stepped forward and put the flat of his right hand under Lucy's left breast, over her heart so he could feel the beat. She began to struggle, frightened by his movement.

'What are you doing, David? Why are you . . . ?'

He slipped his left hand round her waist and pulled her tight.

'David, you're hurting me.'

'I'm sorry, but I have one more question.' His tone was savage. He felt her heart leap under his hand. 'How did Huntley know that Ricky is trying to see Hennington? Somebody must have told him.'

Lucy fought to push him away, more angry than frightened now.

'You think that I . . . ?' She was almost speechless with fury. When finally the words came, they were half choked by anger. 'You think I would . . . ! Get out! How could you! How dare you? Get out of my house!'

Kerr let her rage while he calmly turned around and picked up the scotch again. He felt ashamed of his behaviour, but he had to know. She was either the greatest actress he had ever seen, or she was telling the truth. Lucy stood, white and trembling with anger, flailing her fists in the air. Kerr took a sip of whisky.

'Did you hear me?' Lucy shouted. 'I said, get out! Do you hear me, you bastard!'

Kerr sat down and drained the whisky then refilled the glass slowly. He bowed his head and pretended to study his drink, realising with horror that at precisely the moment he had found he could trust Lucy, his behaviour meant he had probably lost her.

'Lucy,' he pleaded. 'Sit down. I'm sorry.'

She was still so angry her words were swallowed.

'You think I would ... sleep with you ... to betray Ricky ...'

'I said, sit down, for God's sake,' he yelled. 'I am trying to tell you that I think I love you.'

Lucy folded her arms defiantly across her breasts and stood her ground, now utterly speechless. Men were unbelievable. If this was love, it was a curious way of showing it.

'You heard right,' Kerr repeated slowly. 'I said that I think I love you. I am ashamed and embarrassed at what I just did, but I had to check everything, to question everything. I owe it to Ricky.'

'You have to insult the woman you say you love?' Lucy asked sarcastically. 'This must be the great British idea of romance.'

'I ... I ... had to be sure. I ...' Kerr stuttered. He could feel beads of sweat on his forehead. 'It ... hasn't happened to me like this before. I don't know why I started to fall in love with you. But I did. The trouble is, I'm suspicious of everything and everyone, including myself.'

Lucy was astonished, unable to fathom such bizarre behaviour.

'Please sit down,' Kerr said. 'You and McGhie are the only two people I do trust, even if I have a strange way of admitting it. We have a lot of thinking to do before I contact Ricky on the E-mail.'

She was shaking now with so many contradictory emotions.

'But why did you say that thing? Why accuse me?' she blurted out, on the edge of tears. 'As if I would betray Ricky. How could you believe that? How could you even suspect?'

'Look,' Kerr admitted. 'I'm ashamed to tell you I doubted you because I thought you were too good to be true. I didn't believe my own good luck.' He bowed his head so she could not see his eyes filling with tears. 'I told you about Sarajevo.

That scene has been repeated throughout my life. Beautiful things have a habit of disintegrating in my touch. That's why I can't deal with them. It doesn't come easy.'

Lucy stood up and walked out to the balcony, gazing over the river. Kerr left her for a few moments and then wiped his eyes.

'I will leave here as soon as we have done what we can for Ricky,' he volunteered. 'If that's what you want, I'll do it and never contact you again.'

She turned to face him, aghast.

'But I thought you said you loved me,' she said quietly.

'Yes, I do,' Kerr told her emphatically, 'but if the habit I have of doubting everyone has killed any respect you might have for me, then the best I can do is to help my brother and leave.'

They looked at each other in silence for a full minute. Kerr's voice was husky. He very much wanted this woman to love him.

'What do you want me to do, Lucy?'

'I don't know,' she whispered. 'For now you had better stay here. We have so little time left to help Ricky. If something good between you and me can survive this, well . . . I can't bear to think of it now.'

He wanted to kiss her, to hold her, to beg forgiveness again, but she was right. There was not time for anything. He checked his watch.

It was just after one a.m., and there was too much he still had to tell her. They had to get on, impossible though it seemed.

'What did you find out about Jim McCall?' he asked directly.

'Enough to establish him as the link to Huntley.'

'How?'

'I can't tell you.'

'Oh, I see.' Kerr felt irrationally irritated now. 'I have to give you unconditional trust, but you won't tell me how you found out about McCall. I thought trust was a two-way street. Maybe I'm right to be suspicious.'

Lucy looked at him coldly.

'What I can tell you,' she continued, 'is that if this goes wrong, I will never work in Washington again. You will find out my sources on McCall before long, and see that they are credible. In the meantime, I changed the venue of the meeting between Ricky and Hennington. McCall thinks it is at five thirty tomorrow in Hennington's Senate office, and you can bet that is what he told Huntley and the America First people. But I told Hennington late tonight we had to change it. It will be at the same time but a mile away, in the office of a Congressman from Kansas, Bill Stewart. He's new and his staff would do anything to oblige Howie. If you agree the risks are not too high, we let McCall sit in Hennington's office waiting for the meeting, while the rest of us are on the other side of Capitol Hill, where it really takes place.'

She stretched over him and took a sip of his whisky. He felt her breast brush his arm and he realised how much he wanted her.

'It's that or nothing. We can't wait any longer,' she said. 'And you now have a choice, David Courtland Kerr. You go over to the computer and message your brother on the E-mail and tell him to meet me and Hennington. Or you decide not to believe me and call the whole thing off. It comes down to trust, as you said.'

He moved closer and tried to kiss her but she pulled away.

'Which is it, David?'

He smiled wanly.

'Are you trying to make me say I love my brother so much I can't trust you?'

She said nothing.

'Do you not realise why I am so upset?'

Still nothing.

'Okay, Lucy, let me tell you what I am going to do. I am going to message Ricky on the E-mail and tell him to meet you and Hennington in this Congressman Stewart's office at five thirty tomorrow.' Still silence. 'But I am not going to tell him the one thing which I have been keeping from you until now.'

'What thing?'

'The reason I went to see McGhie was that I learned something from the FBI. It is the kind of thing that explains why I doubt everything and everybody.'

Lucy looked up, concerned. 'What are you trying to tell me, David? That Ruffin was here?'

He nodded.

'And – there's no way of putting this gently – he told me Beatriz Ferrara has been murdered.'

Lucy stared at him for a moment as if in disbelief. He gestured to show her it was true and she lurched forward into his arms, her anger lost in grief.

31

David Kerr arrived alone at the Cannon office building more nervous than he had been at his own wedding. He hoped that today's ceremony would not end as badly. Ricky's message on the Electronic Mail had been three words: 'I'll be there.' Nothing more. No hint of whether he knew about Beatriz, or if it had affected him. Stiff upper lip, maybe, or ignorance.

Kerr shook his head, trying to clear it of apprehension for the day to come with Ricky, and the torment of the night before with Lucy. He could not believe how badly he had behaved. They had spent the night in separate rooms.

'I'm sorry I doubted you,' Kerr had apologised repeatedly. 'Please can we try again?'

She led him to the spare room where Ricky had slept.

'Your bed.' She pointed.

'Is it over?'

'Maybe,' she shrugged. 'Maybe not. Most people have a courtship, then go to bed together. We are going to have it the other way round. Goodnight, David.' And she'd left him.

And, when Kerr awoke at five o'clock the next morning, in the middle of a bad dream, it was not about the death of Yasmin, but about losing Lucy.

Kerr listened to the sound of his shoes on the marble floors of the Congressional offices.

Those on the House of Representatives' side of Capitol Hill were much smaller than those for Senators, but there were similarities. The Kansas state flag hung at Congressman Bill Stewart's door. He had the same sweet-smelling popcorn maker in his front office as Hennington had in his. The House was in recess and Congressman Stewart's staff had all left town, except for the receptionist, a carefully made-up blonde whose perfume hung in the air like a fog. She told Kerr that Lucy had already arrived and was busy briefing the senator.

'Like some?' the receptionist said, pointing to the popcorn. 'Help yourself.'

'No, thanks,' Kerr mumbled.

The receptionist showed him into a small conference room. It was already occupied.

'Sorry, I . . .'

Kerr saw Ricky sitting in a corner of the room, cradling Huntley's laptop computer as if it were the crown jewels. Maybe it was. To him, anyway. He wore a loose-fitting dark blue jacket over a shirt and blue jeans, and looked as if he had not slept for a year.

'Hi, bro. How's it going?'

Ricky's voice was rough, worn out, as if he had been crying. It was obvious he knew about Beatriz.

'Hello, Ricky. How are you?'

'Beatriz?' He mumbled, his eyes puffy, but his voice calm. 'You heard . . . ?'

'I heard, Ricky, I heard.'

The brothers put their arms round each other in a bear hug. Kerr thought his chest was going to explode with sadness.

'The FBI told me late yesterday,' he said. 'I didn't want to put it on the E-mail, until we could talk. It seemed too . . . antiseptic. I just can't tell you how sorry –'

'Don't,' Ricky said forcefully, holding up his hand. 'Just don't.'

His lips were quivering with strain. On the brink, Kerr thought. Ruffin was right about this too. Ricky on the edge.

'Listen.' Kerr tried to sound composed. 'I've never done a big brother act before, so I don't know how it will sound, but this is it, for the first and maybe last time: Hennington will be in here in a minute. You know it's your big chance, your only chance. You've got to relax, okay?' Ricky blinked, still clutching the computer. 'You want revenge on them,' Kerr continued. 'Everybody realises that. The way to get it is to nail them for breaking the law, not to turn vigilante and put yourself on the wrong side, you understand? You're in deep enough as it is.'

Ricky nodded vacantly, but seemed to be smiling at something.

'Not to turn vigilante,' he repeated. 'Ricky the Avenger.'

'Sit down,' Kerr instructed, like a parent to a child. Ricky did as he was told. 'You have to be very calm dealing with Hennington. Huntley is making out you're a dangerous lunatic. He says your last psychiatric evaluation described you as unstable. Don't let Hennington upset you. Don't make their case for them, okay?'

Ricky seemed to relax a little. The white knuckles on the computer softened their grip.

'Okay, big brother,' he said softly. 'Wise bird don't shit in own nest, right? Thanks for the advice. I won't crack up, not for at least the next hour.'

'Okay. Then we fix them over Beatriz. We will get our revenge, but legally. That's what she would have wanted.'

'What she would have wanted,' Ricky repeated, emptily.

Kerr stared at Ricky's rheumy eyes, expecting a tear, but he held back.

'You look as if you haven't eaten for a while.'

'I'm not hungry.'

'You get here okay?'

'Yeah,' Ricky responded with a yawn. 'I came in with a party of tourists, then slipped into the underground walkways and through to here. There's like a city underneath the city. I never realised there was a network of tunnels under the Capitol.'

'And on the way out?'

'On the way out I don't care any more,' Ricky said. 'They are not going to shoot me or try to arrest me in the United States Capitol or in a Congressman's office. Once I've talked to Hennington it doesn't much matter.'

'You know I'm hoping to persuade you to give yourself up to Ruffin,' Kerr lectured. 'As soon as you have made your speech to the senator, I think we should call the FBI to come round and pick you up. That way you'll be safe.'

Ricky stared back with a coldness that made Kerr's flesh creep.

'I'm not giving myself up to anybody.'

'But we agreed –'

'You agreed, big brother. I only said I'd think about it. I have. It sucks. They killed Beatriz, and Ricky the Avenger has plans for them, every goddamn one.'

His knuckles tightened white round the computer case, and then he fell silent.

'But you just said . . .' Kerr began, and then decided not to argue in case it set Ricky off before the meeting. Thrawn bastard. He would change the subject.

'Our mother,' Kerr continued. 'While we have time, tell me something about her. Tell me anything about her and you.'

Ricky relaxed sufficiently to put the computer case down on the table, though he rested his hand upon it.

'I was brought up in Bakersfield, California,' he recited. 'Mom taught French, German and Spanish in high school. Dad worked for California Data Systems as a computer salesman. What more do you want?'

'What did she tell you of Scotland?'

'That it was God's own country with the Devil's own people.'

'She said that?' Kerr laughed.

'Yes.'

'That's unfair. The Scots . . .'

'The Scots,' Ricky interrupted, mimicking a falsetto

Edinburgh accent, 'can never survive the fact that they're not English –'

'Aw, hold on, Ricky –'

'– and like the Irish, at home they appear narrow and unpleasant, riddled with doubts. But as soon as they leave their part of those peculiar little Atlantic islands, they are transformed into the finest people in the world.'

'You're making this up,' Kerr laughed.

Ricky smiled, wanly.

'Some. But Mom did bear grudges. She told me she hated your father so much it overcame her love for you, that he was everything bad about Scotland and it soured her on the whole place. The Thin-lipped Presbyterian she called him. Did he have thin lips?'

'No,' Kerr replied. 'But I know what she means.'

'She swore she would never return, and never think of Scotland again. She kept her promise. She was a stubborn woman.'

'Thrawn like all of us, especially you, little brother. What did she say of me?'

'That leaving you was worse than losing a limb or an eye. Worse even than the pain of the cancer which killed her.'

Kerr looked down at the stumps on his right hand. He could not imagine what the agony of separation might have been for her, and he tried not to blame her. If you could only connect the broken up pieces of their lives, he thought, the way you could stitch together an injured shoulder or the stumps of his fingers. Somehow it was impossible. Those scars never heal.

'At the end . . .' Ricky went on. He was trying to take it slowly so he did not upset himself. 'At the end she asked me to find you . . . try to explain that she . . . loved you . . .'

Kerr stared at Ricky until his eyes misted over and his brother stopped talking. They sat in silence for a few moments. There was a noise outside. Kerr wiped his eyes and glanced at his watch. It was now exactly five thirty.

'I'll tell you the rest later,' Ricky whispered, somehow more in control than Kerr himself. 'If there is a later.'

The door flew open, propelled by Hurricane Hennington. The senator led and Lucy followed with a female secretary who put a tape recorder on the conference table in front of Ricky, and sat down with a pad on her knee to take notes.

'The point,' Hennington was saying, talking about Ricky as if he were elsewhere, 'is that if Captain Rush is currently listed as absent without leave following a series of alleged crimes, then I am saying that it may not be wise for me to meet personally with a man who is technically a fugitive from military justice.'

'But we discussed that yesterday, senator. And you said –'

'Don't tell me what I said yesterday, Lucy. Makes you sound like one of those America First broadcasts pulling apart my record. This is what I am saying today. And where is McCall?'

The secretary was about to say something when Lucy interrupted.

'He was feeling unwell, Senator. Throwing up. Food poisoning, I think.'

The secretary looked at Lucy, puzzled. McCall had looked fine an hour before, sitting behind his desk in the senator's own office a mile away. This was getting weird.

'Jesus,' Hennington bellowed, his foul mood deepening. 'I think this guy – Rush – should get the hell out of here until I've had more time to think about it, and until McCall feels better. Sorry, Captain Rush. You better leave now.'

Oh, God, no, Kerr thought. Please don't, Senator, don't set him off.

Kerr looked at Ricky, expecting an explosion. The room fell silent except for the humming of the air conditioning. Suddenly there was a loud bang. Ricky smashed his fist down on the table.

'Now wait a goddamn minute,' he shouted. 'Throw me out if you want, but just remember, you were busting your balls to find out the information I had when you believed I was dead. Now I am alive, how come I am somehow less credible?' Ricky slipped his right hand into the computer case. 'In the past two days the sons of bitches have murdered my fiancée to get at what I have here.' He pulled out the laptop computer. 'So all right, Senator, there are risks in my being here. Sure there are. But you throw me out now after agreeing to see me, with the dynamite I've got in this laptop? Evidence so damning that people are prepared to murder to get at it? Jeez! I'd say that could make you look like shit.' Ricky put on a sneering voice. 'Give 'em hell Howie, the champion of the underdog throwing out of his office a man who came back from the dead to give him this.' Ricky's timing and sense of the dramatic was perfect. He pushed the computer out in front of him.

'In the hard drive you'll find enough information to blow apart the America First Corporation and Senator Mark Barker with it. You want his head on a plate, you got it. If you don't want it, tell me now and I'll see if the *Washington Post* is interested. Either way, make up your goddamn mind.'

Ricky folded his arms and sat back. Hennington looked as if he had been hit by Ricky's baseball bat. He slumped down behind the desk, turned brusquely to the secretary and pointed at the tape recorder.

'Is that thing turned on?'

'No, Senator.'

'Turn it on.'

'Yes, Senator.'

'You ready to write?'

'Yes, Senator.'

Then he addressed Ricky.

'Now listen up. This is on the record, a formal inquiry. If he had been here I would ask my chief of staff Jim McCall to put you under oath. But I guess I'm going to have to do that myself.'

Hennington pushed a Bible at Ricky.

'Put your right hand on that, son. Now do you solemnly swear in front of these witnesses and before God that what you are now about to say is the truth, the whole truth an' nothing but the truth?'

When they finished, Hennington took the Bible back.

'Before we start,' he said, 'I want to make one thing as clear as the headwaters of the Missouri river. You listening, son?'

Ricky nodded.

'That damn thing on?' Hennington repeated, pointing at the tape recorder. 'Okay. Well, Captain Richard C. Rush, US Air Force, after this is over I want you to give yourself up to the appropriate authorities and sort out your differences with the military, the FBI, the ISA and half a dozen other damn strings of initials that I don't rightly remember, you hear?'

Ricky nodded again.

'And let the record show I said all that, and Captain Rush signalled his assent. I am prepared in the interests of the national security of this country to risk my reputation for fifteen minutes with you, son, then you get the hell out of here and go see the FBI, clear?'

The secretary nodded. Lucy nodded. Kerr nodded. Ricky smiled and dropped his head in what could have been taken as a sign of agreement.

'And remember, Captain, I bore real easy. I don't like what you have to say, you're out of here faster'n a pig in a barn fire. Begin.'

Ricky opened the laptop computer, switched it on and loaded the files.

'My brother has told you the background about the Activity,' Ricky said. 'So I'll get to the point. This computer is small but it has a big memory, probably big enough to hold all the written files in this office, and then some. Half the used memory space is taken up with details of illegal or probably illegal transactions carried on in the name of the United States government by my co-workers at the ISA.'

Hennington sat back and opened his shirt collar, pulling down his tie an inch or two. 'And by me. I admit that I made a stash. Made enough to buy, under a false name, the place where I've been hiding out for the past six – seven – weeks. The other half of the computer memory details where the money went and how to find the bank accounts.'

He hit a few buttons and a text came on to the screen.

'Item,' Ricky said. 'The British foreign currency crisis. I like this one because it appeals to my brother here. Publicly the British government was saying it would keep parity with the German mark and other currencies in the European Exchange Rate Mechanism at three Deutschmarks to the pound. Britain's finance minister at the time said he was going to spend twelve billion dollars defending the pound. Can you believe this?'

Ricky's voice was full of humour now.

'The result was everybody who had any brains was speculating against the pound, driving it down, but timing was everything. The British were raising and lowering interest rates faster'n a whore's panties, but not so profitably. We were entertained for hours. The Economic Security Council knew more about the British plans than most members of the British Cabinet. While we did that I guess we made $400,000 in a week in currency dealings on the side.'

Hennington sat bolt upright.

'How much'd you say, son?'

'I said, $400,000 in a week.'

'Between how many of you?'

'Four in the Activity. The America First profits were counted separately.'

'And this was regular?'

'Nothing was regular about it, Senator. I'm just using the example because it was big news at the time in Europe. We kept ahead of the British, which was not difficult – and the rest of the market – and made everybody happy. It was sweet. I have fifty or sixty examples right here of the same kind of dealing. When it happened to the French franc in July and August of '93, because the Bundesbank refused to lower interest rates, we made sure we knew at each stage what the players were about to do. We made $600,000 that time.'

'Between four of you?'

'Yes, sir. We were better at it by then, or took more risks. Whatever.'

Hennington drew a deep breath as Ricky keyed in more letters and numbers. A bar chart popped up.

'Japanese automobiles sold in Latin America,' he said, 'before the agreement of a multi-billion dollar deal to export finished hard woods from the Amazon rainforest to the Far East.' He hit another button and the bar chart grew enormously. 'Import quotas after the deal.'

'I don't get it,' Hennington said. 'What has the export of Amazon timber to do with Japanese automobiles?'

Kerr was beginning to warm to the senator. When he was grumpy he showed it. When he didn't understand, he made sure everybody knew it.

'Well, sir,' Ricky explained. 'The Japanese and the Latin American governments tied one to the other, kind of like a barter arrangement. The result was shares in these three subsidiaries of Japanese auto manufacturers operating in Latin America jumped an average of eight per cent over-night following the announcement of the agreement.'

'Eight per cent,' Hennington said.

'Overnight,' Ricky repeated. 'That's a heap of pesos.'

'And the American manufacturers?'

'Our policy was not to collect losers' data.'

Ricky hit another set of keys.

'The re-convened GATT talks. Remember, this is how we got into the trade war.'

'I know how we got into the trade war, son,' Hennington muttered almost to himself. 'Tell me how we get out.'

'Sure.'

Hennington looked surprised by Ricky's arrogance.

The trade war had begun when the Senate demanded the renegotiation of a major trade agreement. Senator Barker – using the power of his television network and grass roots lobbying – passed a bill forcing the president to retaliate against any country that piled up a large trade surplus against the United States. In that way Barker bullied the president into imposing tariffs on Japan, China, Taiwan and also the European Community over the Airbus project. The foreign governments, not surprisingly, retaliated, leading to a recession which Hennington believed would eventually be as bad as the Thirties.

'Including the rise of a demagogue,' he mumbled.

'Excuse me?' Ricky said. 'I didn't catch that, Senator.'

'Nothing,' Hennington replied. 'Just thinking about my good friend Senator Barker and how he would fit in to the 1930s. Continue.'

'Here –' Ricky pulled out more bar charts. 'Here is data on soybean supports paid to French farmers.'

Terrific, Kerr thought. Soybeans. What next? Turnip quotas? Broccoli?

'By use of national technical means,' Ricky continued, 'we were able to establish precisely the degree of difference and ill-feeling between most western European states and the French government.'

'So how did that help us?' Hennington asked, trying not to sound too amazed.

Ricky cleared the screen.

'It made our bargaining position unbeatable in the trade talks. We knew exactly where to pitch our offer to divide French national interests from everyone else. The result, the French have been kicked in the balls and we might detach Britain and Germany from the European Union tariff bloc against us. If we can do that, we could end the trade war with Europe without a climb down.'

Hennington frowned.

'So why don't we?'

Ricky laughed.

'I guess some of this information must have got lost on the way to the White House. I know the America First Corporation got it all because I delivered it to them personally.'

'Barker knows we could end the trade war? He knows how?'

'Sure.'

'But the president does not?'

'Looks like it.'

Hennington scratched his head in irritation.

'Is Senator Mark Barker powerful enough to keep information from the White House?'

Ricky shrugged.

'Huntley is the link with the White House. I was the link with the private sector. I don't know who was told what, but I do know we could prevent the trade war from getting worse and probably settle it within weeks if we wanted to. Seems like nobody wants to.'

Hennington was stunned.

'Look,' Ricky explained. 'I do information, Senator, I don't do politics. But the way I figure it, Barker hopes the trade war will go on long enough to bring about such a deep recession he will be the saviour of this country. The guy wants to be president, Senator.'

Hennington sighed as if he already knew too much. His face was like that of a doctor performing an especially gruesome autopsy.

'I can figure out Senator Barker's ambitions for myself,' he said bitterly. 'That's why I mentioned the 1930s. Now tell me, all of your information gathering is illegal, I guess?'

'No, Senator. At least, in collecting the information we broke no laws of the United States.'

'But you eavesdrop on conversations?' Hennington persisted with evident distaste. 'National technical means?'

'Yes, Senator. We now routinely monitor trans-Atlantic and trans-Pacific fax transmissions. Plus we –'

'All of them?'

'No. I mean, we could record everything, but there is never enough time to read it all, so we have to be very selective.'

Hennington stood up.

'And you personally have profited from all this?'

'Yes, Senator. Along with Huntley and two others at the Activity, both now dead. I believe that Senator Barker ordered their murders when the FBI started to investigate us. That's why I disappeared. I was scared. I can make excuses, 'bout how naive or dumb or trusting I was, but in the end I did wrong. I expect to be punished.'

'Never mind that,' Hennington replied. 'If you spend your days in Congress, an admission of error is so unusual it sticks in the mind. The next question is, would the public interest be served by full open hearings – you telling all this on network television?'

Ricky was about to answer, when Hennington decided that was not a question for him.

'That's a question for me, son. I'm just thinkin' aloud here. Some days, any kind of thinkin' is good enough. Now, how clearly can we establish the connection to my good friend in the Senate, Senator Barker?'

Ricky gave a tortured little laugh.

'Senator Barker has been very good to the Activity.'

Hennington nodded.

'That I know. Every time it comes up he votes to increase your appropriations. Says y'all are doing the hard work of freedom. Now I kind of understand what he means.'

'Yeah. We are also doing the hard work of helping him get elected president. My figures suggest the America First Corporation has probably earned more than twenty-six million dollars in the past year directly from the information I passed to them, plus all the goodwill from any information they shared with other corporations. Barker has business friends on the evangelical right and he passes tips on to them. I don't know the names, but I knew it was happening.'

Eventually Hennington managed to find his voice.

'You . . . you mean . . .'

'Barker gave us political cover and ensured we had a good budget, and we helped him make enough money to keep his television channel on the air and run for president. He called it synergy.'

'Synergy?' Hennington spluttered. 'I can think of different names, son. Corruption for one. Maybe treason.'

Ricky smiled.

'Huntley kept telling me that our key problem was in the dissemination of information to the private sector. When we found out, say, about Indonesia's telecommunications contract going to the Japanese, or what Taiwan had bid for the construction of a new airport and port terminal in the Gulf, how could we put that information where it could do most good? That is, with American business.'

'And?' Hennington prompted.

'That was Huntley's genius. He used America First to disseminate the information for us, and act as a cut-out if anything went wrong. Huntley kept telling me that the business of America was business, that we were using our intelligence gathering to win the economic war, the Dollar War of the twenty-first century. Neat, eh?'

Hennington stood up and paced to the window, looking out towards the dome of the Capitol.

'I want you to agree to appear before my Senate committee in open televised hearings,' he said. 'And to use the computer as evidence.'

'Okay,' Ricky agreed. 'But for now I keep the laptop with me.'

He pushed five diskettes across the table.

'I made another copy of everything on the computer. I thought you should have it.'

Hennington swept the diskettes towards him.

'In the meantime, you better go see the FBI, son,' the senator advised. 'That's what will keep you alive.'

'Wouldn't that get in the way of you having hearings?' Kerr interrupted. 'If the FBI bring charges against Ricky or anyone else?'

'Maybe.' Hennington shook his head slowly. 'But that's not the point. I am trying to keep your brother here alive, that's all.'

'I have business to finish first,' Ricky interrupted.

'Such as?'

'Private business.'

Ricky stared ahead impassively. Hennington reached across and switched off the tape recorder.

'You don't get it, Captain, do you? When I first told you to go see the FBI that was to make sure I had covered my ass. Now I'm advising it not for my safety but for yours. People who know as much as you are not likely to live for long.'

Ricky stood up and shook Hennington's hand.

'Senator,' he said softly, 'thank you for listening to me. I hope my information might help you along the way, but you seem to care more for my life than I do myself. The only thing left for me now is revenge. I spent my life in the military doing the right thing, the patriotic thing, and I got screwed. Now I am going to do something for me.' He laughed bitterly. 'I just formed the Ricky First Movement, and I ask you all to join.'

Hennington did not even smile. He was weighing Ricky's words carefully, as if holding a timebomb.

'Supposing . . .' Hennington hesitated, his mind racing.

'Supposing something does happen to you, and Joe Huntley and Senator Barker say you made all this up, that you altered the computer data to make your case, that there was no impropriety. How do I nail them?'

'How do you nail them if I am dead?' Ricky smiled.

'Yes,' Hennington said.

'Well, you suppose something for a minute, Senator,' Ricky replied. 'You suppose that in order to protect himself and ensure Huntley's cooperation, Senator Mark Barker made a video in the America First offices of a meeting between himself and Joe Huntley. On that video you see them striking the deal to help each other. Supposing I had that video. How would that do as evidence?'

The room fell utterly silent.

'There is such a tape?' Hennington asked eventually.

'Yes,' Ricky replied. 'And I have it. Not with me, of course. But in a safe place. I'd be prepared to play it in open hearing of your committee.' He paused for a moment and looked at the stunned faces around the room. 'That is, if you think you would be interested.'

32

As they left, Ricky said, 'Looks like I upset your boss.'

He walked alongside Lucy to the elevator. David Kerr hung back nervously, hoping there might be a way to spirit his brother from the building, feeling the ache in his shoulder like a warning of something about to go haywire.

'Don't worry,' Lucy replied. 'After all these years of being targeted by Barker I don't think Senator Hennington really believes he's about to nail him. He wants to make sure there's no mistake. You take on the America First Corporation, it's like Dracula. You have to drive the stake right through the heart.'

'Right through the heart,' Ricky repeated, 'I'll remember that.'

'Will the video do that?' Kerr wondered.

'I think so.'

'You have it safe?'

Ricky smiled.

'Big brother, it's safe, and there are only two people in the world who know where that video is. I am one . . .'

He paused and waited for the inevitable question. A perfect sense of theatre, Kerr thought again.

'And?'

'And the other is you.'

'Me?' Kerr protested. 'But I –'

Ricky nodded, as if enjoying a huge joke, watching as Kerr began to think it through.

'You trust me that much?' Kerr said, realising what Ricky meant.

'Only with my life,' Ricky said. 'Nothing important.'

The elevator arrived and he gave Lucy a hug.

'Thanks for fixing up Hennington for me.'

'I'm just glad you're alive, Ricky.'

He laughed, the only one of them to be cheerful.

'Me too.'

She looked at Kerr.

'Well?'

'Well, if you're still talking to me, we have some unfinished business.'

'You two want to be alone?' Ricky asked.

'Yes, we want to be alone,' Kerr replied. 'But not here. I have been trying to tell Lucy that I love her. She is convinced I am too full of doubts to love anyone.'

Lucy blushed.

'I never said that.'

'It's getting hot in here,' Ricky grinned. 'I guess you two don't need me . . .'

'I'll see you tonight,' Kerr told Lucy. 'If I'm still welcome.'

'Of course,' she said. 'Now go, before Hennington calls the FBI.'

The two brothers descended in the elevator to the ground floor of the Cannon Congressional office building. Lucy hurried back to try to tell Senator Hennington that she had deceived McCall and explain why, but she could tell from one glimpse of the senator's face she was too late.

'I just talked with Jim McCall,' Hennington began, his voice a hiss of cold anger. 'I want to know what in hell –'

Lucy realised she was about to be fired, but there were more important considerations. To the senator's astonishment and before he could complete the sentence, Lucy turned and ran back down the corridor to try to warn Ricky. She was too late for that also.

The brothers walked together to the side exit from the Cannon building.

'How about calling Ruffin?' Kerr tried one more time. 'Giving yourself up?'

Ricky glared at him.

'No.'

'Nothing is going to happen to you, Ricky, if you call Ruffin,' Kerr replied. 'Hennington is on your side. They will look after you.'

'I told you I have business to finish. Ricky the Avenger.'

'Now, listen.' Kerr grabbed him angrily by the arm. 'If you try to take out your personal revenge on people then I don't want anything to do with you, understand? I want to help. But I am your brother, not an accomplice.'

Ricky looked as if he had been punched. He brushed Kerr's hand from his arm.

'Then fuck you, David. It's an accomplice I need. I got along for thirty years without a brother. You don't own me now. And anyway, the revenge has started.'

Ricky walked fast out of the Cannon building into the daylight. Kerr tried to keep up, regretting not what he had said but the unfriendly way he had said it.

'Ricky, wait.'

Ricky was almost running down the steps when he saw the black Jeep Cherokee with tinted windows speed in from his left. Twenty yards to his right two men jumped out of a Lincoln Town Car.

'Shit!' Ricky hissed, as one of the men reached to his shoulder holster. Suddenly the street was full of noises and doors banging, men running. Kerr whirled to see three more men leap from the Cherokee, all holding automatic pistols at chest height, yelling.

'Defense Department Security! Freeze! Freeze! Freeze!'

Two others, one a thick-set hispanic, the other white and built like a linebacker, also drew pistols and climbed into the flower beds to cut off a run to the right.

'Freeze! Armed police! Freeze! Armed police!'

There was a yell behind Kerr and he turned again to see his brother's knee hit deep into the crotch of the first man in a suit who was trying to level his gun at Ricky. The man grunted and went down, the colour draining from his face as he grasped the ache in his groin. To the right a fair-haired man in a grey suit struggled to pull out his pistol. Kerr leaped on him, locking his arms in a hug then headbutting him in the face so he fell at his feet. The thick-set hispanic pointed his gun at Kerr.

'Freeze or I . . .'

Kerr ducked and came at him under the gun, throwing him backwards into the wall and then pushing him into the Cannon building swing door with a force so hard the gun dropped to the concrete.

The blond linebacker ran at Kerr, who punched him in the throat and pulled him into the swing door, jamming it in a tangled heap of bodies. In the confusion, Ricky took off back into the building. The uniformed guard X-raying the bags of everyone entering the Cannon stood up when he saw Ricky running towards him then moved unconvincingly to draw his .38 revolver. He was unsure where to point it and Ricky's kick took him hard in the belly, sending the guard sprawling backwards across the polished floor like a deck quoit.

The .38 fell at Ricky's feet and he picked it up, one more for his collection. He raced to his right through the stunned crowds of Capitol Hill staff, clattering down the stairs to the underground tunnels in the basement, clutching the laptop computer like a football. Behind him, Kerr managed to hold on to the linebacker, who was struggling for breath through a smashed larynx.

The thick-set hispanic was wedged in the Cannon swing doors, holding them shut for thirty seconds, which was all Ricky needed to break away. Suddenly half a dozen hands grabbed for David Kerr's face and hair and finally broke his lock hold on the linebacker, sending Kerr sprawling on the concrete beside Ricky's first victim, who was still clutching his groin and sounding as if he wanted to vomit. The man Kerr had headbutted was on his knees, trying to hold his bloody nose together in a handkerchief. Inside on the floor the security guard moaned and held his belly. The two brothers had gone through them like dysentery.

Dozens of Congressional staffers scuttled back to their offices, while the corridors appeared full of running men, some in uniforms with guns drawn, others in smart suits that looked like another kind of uniform. So far Kerr had not heard any shots. Then he felt the thump of a knee in his chest, a fist at his throat and saw the muzzle of a pistol so close to his mouth that he had to cross his eyes to focus on it. There was the smell of stale tobacco.

'Move an inch, you miserable son of a bitch,' Joseph R. Huntley yelled, wheezing with effort, 'move an inch, and I'll blow your goddamn head off.'

'Huntley,' Kerr gasped. 'What took you so long?'

33

As Ricky ran he was exhilarated by the idea that he was living up to his reputation as a desperado. He burst from the bottom of the stairs into the basement corridor system, dodging and weaving through the crowds. In his headlong flight he hit into two female secretaries and sent one staggering backwards into a middle-aged man.

'Excuse me,' he called out lamely.

'Look where you're . . .'

'Hey, bud . . .'

'What the . . . ?'

'He's got a gun!'

He could hear gasps and screams as they saw the .38 dangling in his right hand, and their words trailed off into a shocked silence. He charged ahead through the sounds of chaotic pursuit, running full tilt without looking back, feeling the hardness of his breath and the dull thud of his feet on the marble floor, figuring if they were going to shoot him, he might as well take it in the back.

He decided he would prefer to die rather than risk killing innocent people. The guilty were something else. He slipped down a corridor and two security guards contemplated for a moment trying to block his path, but they were not completely stupid. They saw the gun and stepped back. As he passed, one yelled for assistance and the other, less timid yet slow, struggled with his own holster, but too late. The guard fired once and hit the sign which said 'Rayburn Building', about two feet to Ricky's right, putting a neat hole in the 'B'.

Ricky turned a corner and slowed down, then chose one

of three corridors which led him towards the electric train. The Rayburn was on the end of the underground service which connects the House office buildings with Congress and the Senate offices a mile away on the other side of Capitol Hill. As he reached the platform he slowed down to a brisk walk, stuffing the .38 in the back of his trousers and hiding it with his jacket. He tried to catch his breath as he stepped on the shuttle which was about to leave. The driver stared at him vacantly, as if lobotomised by his repetitive work. There were four tiny carriages, like electric golf carts joined together, one reserved for Members of Congress. The rest, Ricky thought, were for human beings. The train moved off within seconds.

He caught his breath and wondered if any of them would be quick enough to radio ahead, then he put his hand on the .38 and felt better. He was the thoroughly modern American male, he thought. One hand on a computer, the other on a gun. The train stopped and Ricky's breath returned in easier bursts, but he was still sweating hard. On the platform there were two small groups of Congressional staffers chatting amicably, rearranging thick files of paper, and waiting to get on the train. There was no sign of any extra security, just another catatonic stiff in uniform inside the glass box at the end of the platform. The guard, as lobotomised as the driver, was reading the *Washington Post* Sports section, sipping from a Redskins coffee mug. Ricky walked casually by, and the guard did not even look up until the telephone in the booth rang. He stretched out a lazy hand towards it. Ricky hurried past, knowing the call was about him.

He caught the elevator up from the underground tunnels to the ground floor and slowly walked out of the back of the Capitol across the grass towards the Supreme Court. As he reached the first of the trees on the edge of the Capitol Hill grounds Ricky turned to see dozens of uniformed police begin to cordon off the entrances and exits to Congress, sweeping inwards to look for him. At the front of the Supreme Court he zipped his light jacket and flagged down a taxi.

'Court House Metro Station in Arlington,' he said, the place where he had parked his car.

'Court House Metro,' the driver repeated.

'Thrawn,' Ricky muttered.

'Say what?' the taxi driver asked.

Ricky Rush smiled.

'Aw, nothing,' he said. 'Seems to be something going on up on the Hill.'

'Yeah,' the driver agreed. 'Always sumpin'.' Swarms of dark-uniformed police were scrambling, talking urgently into their radios.

'Must be another one of them terrorist alerts,' the taxi driver said, as they swept away towards the Washington Monument and the White House.

'That'd be it,' Ricky agreed. 'Goddamn terrorists.'

He rubbed his red eyes with his fingertips. He felt calm, almost cheerful, maybe because like most terrorists he really believed in his cause. And the cause, for the first time in his life, was not the flag or the Air Force or his buddies. It was personal.

He would like to tell David Kerr the whole story some day, but maybe it would not happen. They had spent their lives happily unaware of each other, and had brought each other nothing more than unhappiness in the short time they had been together. It was such a pity. He had not even managed to say a real goodbye to his brother.

The taxi sped across the Potomac and Ricky remembered there were others to whom he also had to say farewell, using the Glock 17 and the shotgun.

'You take on the America First Corporation,' Lucy had said, 'it's like Dracula. You have to drive the stake right through the heart.'

Or use silver bullets.

34

Kerr had never been handcuffed before and it was worse than he'd expected. They forced him on his front, jerked his arms back and produced not the metal handcuffs he had seen in every Hollywood cop movie, but toughened plastic of the type you might use to re-seal the bag round a loaf of bread. They threw him face down on the floor of the Jeep Cherokee where it smelled of carpet cleaner and shoe polish.

The Cherokee remained parked outside the Cannon building for about an hour while the fruitless pursuit of Ricky continued. The two men who guarded Kerr were eventually joined by five others who had chased his brother through the underground tunnels, and while they did not say much, it was clear they had failed. They were muttering despondently about Huntley's inability to organise the cordon, how their communications were on a different frequency from those of the Capitol Hill police, how they had been stuck on the Senate side, and other complicated excuses which contributed to their failure. To Kerr's delight an ambulance arrived and two of the men were taken to hospital for treatment.

'Hey,' Kerr called out, his face buried in the floor carpet. 'My arms hurt. Let me sit up.'

No one answered, and he twisted to one side so he could use the traditional British method of dealing with foreigners. He yelled out exactly the same thing three times as loudly.

'I said, my arms hurt.'

What used to work with colonials was not working any more. One of the men grabbed Kerr's hair from behind, pulled his head viciously backwards so he thought his neck was about to break, then rubbed his face deep into the smelly carpet beside someone's shoe, a dark tan tasselled loafer which jerked up into Kerr's teeth so he could taste the polish.

'Listen, butthead,' the man shouted. 'One more peep and we'll fill your motormouth so full of rags you'll have to breathe out your ass. Got it?'

Kerr got it, though he felt a sense of exhilaration he had not known since the last few days in Sarajevo. He was in danger with nothing except his wits to rely on, without hope, surrounded by hostile people, his arms and wrists aching where the Plasticuffs dug in. And somehow it was wonderful. No nightmares, no pain, and no trying to sell stories about the children's charity to local television stations and third rate newspapers.

One of the men pulled out a radio and called for instructions. Kerr heard what could have been Huntley's voice. The crackling reply was to proceed to Romeo One Zero location, and bring The Subject, which Kerr presumed meant him. The Subject. It was better than being The Object, but not much. The radio was switched off, the men piled on board and drove the Cherokee across Washington in silence. After half an hour of what for Kerr was a bruising ride, they reached McLean, Virginia, and stopped.

There was a short security check, then they were allowed to proceed down into a basement parking lot. The Cherokee stopped again. Someone slipped a hood over Kerr and dragged him awkwardly to his feet, pushing his head down so he ducked as he stepped from the vehicle. They led him to an elevator. One of the men produced a key, turned it in the lock, then pushed a numerical code to direct the elevator to the twelfth floor. They walked out and led Kerr through another security check, down a corridor to a room that smelled of cigarette smoke. He felt them ease him backwards into a chair. The hood was removed, and sitting in front of Kerr, just a foot or two from his face, was Joseph R. Huntley. The Texan looked tired, but his eyes were as snake-like as ever. He stared at the blinking figure of Kerr and pulled a cigarette from a Marlboro pack on the desk to his left, lit it, blew the smoke sideways, then stood up and began pacing the room. Kerr's eyes adjusted to the brightness of the anglepoise light shining towards him. He wondered if it was really necessary. He had seen American made-for-TV movies like this and did not think much of them, but he kept quiet. Then he felt someone undoing the Plasticuffs.

'Thank you so much,' he said politely, rubbing his wrists.

Behind Huntley, Kerr could see a younger red-haired man in civilian clothes, poised over a notepad, and operating a tape recorder. It looked like a formal interrogation. Two of the men who brought Kerr in, one carrying the hood, shuffled in the shadows, turned their backs and left silently. The room was quiet for a full five minutes, all except for the gentle pacing of Huntley on his rubbersoled shoes and the sound of Kerr's breath rising and falling with stress.

He shifted slightly in the chair to try to make himself more comfortable. Eventually Huntley finished his cigarette, and his pacing. He sat down in front of Kerr, folded his fingers together, and leaned forward confidentially.

'I suppose you know why you're here?'

Kerr wanted to snigger. He had been held by Argentine troops in Buenos Aires during the Falklands war and even they had not asked anything quite so imbecilic.

'Is that a metaphysical inquiry?' Kerr scorned. 'If it is a geographical question, Mr Huntley, then I'm here because a bunch of your mouth-breathing goons threw me in the back of a car and brought me here, no doubt according to your instructions. If, on the other hand, it is a question about the meaning of life, I suggest that I am here to make you realise you have just lost. Hennington knows all about you and your corruption. He has the evidence. You are finished, I'm pleased to say.'

Kerr felt his face flush hot. He remembered a police detective in Northern Ireland once asked him if he knew the most effective interrogation technique ever invented against terrorists. Bamboo shoots up the fingernails, Kerr wondered? A pistol to the head? The rack? Thumbscrews? Apparently not. The suspect, according to the detective, would be held, disorientated, regarded with silent contempt, but not maltreated in any way. There would be shuffling of papers and then at an opportune moment the interrogator would ask the first question, a question so naive it produced more confessions than any other.

'I suppose you know why you're here?'

And now Huntley was trying it, as if Kerr would reply: 'I'm here because I'm guilty.'

'I said,' Huntley repeated, 'that I suppose you know why you're here?'

Kerr narrowed his eyes.

'Anyone ever told you, Huntley, that you are a perfect bloody sphincter?'

There was no response from the Texan, who simply drew on his cigarette and stared back unblinking. It was Huntley's contempt which irritated Kerr most. 'Are you expecting some kind of confession?' he continued. 'Is that it? I have nothing to confess, but I will gladly take notes if you do.'

Eventually Huntley sat back in his chair, took a last draw on his cigarette and stubbed it out. The note taker scratched a few lines on his pad.

'Am I under arrest?' Kerr pressed on, disliking the whiny sound in his own voice but believing his situation was so hopeless he had no choice but to attack. 'Do I face criminal charges?'

Huntley stretched out a slow arm towards the Marlboro pack and lit up again. Serious outbreak of deafness, Kerr thought. Fuck them. Fuck them all. Minutes passed, then Kerr spoke again.

'If I am under arrest, then you should tell me why, and let me get a lawyer. And if I am not under arrest, then perhaps you might do me the courtesy of calling a cab and we can continue our discussions at a more convenient time.'

The greater the stress, the more pompous he sounded. Years of working in the Third World, maybe, where if you behaved like a complete shit sometimes they treated you like a colonial master. Huntley could see the tension in Kerr's eyes and pulled the chair round in front of him, scraping it violently across the floor. He sat legs astride, leaning on the back. Languidly he lifted the cigarette to his mouth and inhaled, letting the smoke drift from his lips.

'This,' he drawled, gesturing around him with the cigarette, his face just a foot in front of Kerr's, 'is where your brother worked. It's a bunch of offices out in Virginia that we know as the Activity. Since we're getting metaphysical, you can not be under arrest, I guess, because we don't exist. Right now, you're nowhere –' Huntley gave an awkward little laugh ' – you're nowhere, you're in Limbo, Virginia, a little suburb of Hell.'

Huntley was still grinning at his joke when he finished the cigarette and leaned over to the desk to stub out the butt. Then he rubbed his nose and sniffed.

'I had hoped to avoid anything unpleasant happening to you or Ricky. That's why we wanted to pick him up today, and why I still want you to cooperate. What I need is to tell you one big thing, and then maybe you'll be prepared to tell me a whole heap of little things. How's that sound?'

Kerr blinked, but said nothing.

'The big thing that I need to tell you,' Huntley continued, 'is that your brother is severely mentally disturbed. He is technically a paranoid schizophrenic suffering increasingly violent delusions, now with suspected homicidal tendencies.

We believe he has killed six, maybe seven, people – including four of his former friends at the America First Corporation. He used to socialise a lot over there. Alexandria police want to question him in connection with the murder of his former girlfriend, Beatriz Ferrara. And today he went on the rampage at the heart of American government, in Congress itself.'

Kerr gasped at the interpretation, but Huntley went on.

'He slashed the throat of one America First employee, left him like something from a slaughterhouse.'

'Bullshit.'

'He shot dead two more at an all-night diner, and the one he hit with a baseball bat nearly died.'

'I said bullshit, Huntley. Or maybe you're so old your ears need syringing.'

'Not to mention the murder of his girlfriend and two former Activity personnel a month ago, Colvin and Drysdale. I could string words together all day, Mr Kerr. Bottom line? Any police or law enforcement officer anywhere in the Washington area who sees the suspect is going to shoot first and fill in a few forms later. Armed and dangerous, take no prisoners. Y'understand?'

When Huntley talked, his lips moved a little but he held the rest of his body completely still except to take draws of the cigarette. The snake was waiting for Kerr to move so he could strike.

'In the entrance to the Cannon building,' Huntley went on, 'in front of a dozen witnesses, your brother assaulted two Defense Department employees, and one Capitol Hill police officer. You assaulted at least two more. We're still counting. Ricky stole a handgun and ran amok like a terrorist. We have reason to believe he may be trying to assassinate at least one United States senator as a means of drawing attention to his bizarre allegations about government conspiracies and cover-ups.'

Huntley paused to light another cigarette. Each word

came out slowly in his southern drawl, still portentously the voice of God.

'We are also concerned that you may be part of the conspiracy to assassinate Senator Barker.' For the first time in his life Kerr felt his jaw literally dropping open and his mouth gaping wide at the inanity of Huntley's words. 'We are asking for your help to locate your brother. Either you turn him over, or he will be shot dead.'

Kerr's mouth tightened. He blinked at Huntley. The man was serious, for God's sake.

'But this is just nonsense,' Kerr said. 'It's so ridiculous maybe I should laugh.'

'Did you know your brother was a homosexual, Mr Kerr?'

Kerr felt as if he had gone to sleep and awakened in Wonderland.

'What did you say?'

'I can see you are shocked,' Huntley said seriously. 'We believe your brother may have engaged in homosexual acts with these young men from America First and murdered them as a result of a love affair gone wrong. We believe he knew his homosexuality had come to the attention of his military commanders and that he would be removed from active duty pending disciplinary hearings.'

Kerr was so astonished he could barely find a voice.

'Are . . . are you on drugs, Huntley?'

The Texan leaned forward until their faces were only a few inches apart.

'Where is your brother hiding out, Mr Kerr? Unless we can find him we cannot help him.'

Kerr swallowed hard. He could feel Huntley's eyes bore into him through the cigarette smoke. Courage, he told himself. He took a deep breath of smoky air.

'You want to help my brother, Huntley?'

'Yes.'

'Then die of cancer.'

Huntley looked at Kerr with silent contempt. Without warning he pulled back his right arm and threw a punch which clipped Kerr on the left side of his head. Kerr's head bounced back and he felt his left eye-socket throb. He struggled to sit upright, rubbing at his eye with his hand. Now the Plasticuffs were off he could hit Huntley back, beat the crap out of the old man, half kill him until they pulled him away, but he thought better of it. Ricky would have hit Huntley until one of them died, but Kerr knew that way he would only lose. He suddenly realised that Huntley turning to violence meant the Texan was desperate.

'Do you really think,' Kerr said, trying to keep anger or fear from shaking his voice, 'that you can either beat something out of me, or provoke me so I hit you back? I demand –'

'Shut the fuck up,' Huntley said, rubbing his knuckles.

Kerr blinked, and tried to continue, but Huntley interrupted him again.

'I said, shut up. When I've finished with you, which will be in a few minutes, you will be turned over to the FBI and you can demand all you want from them. They love that shit. Right now, you just do as you're told.'

Huntley walked back to his desk and angrily picked up the telephone.

'It's Huntley. I want you to get him out of here. Take him back to DC. I'll tell Ruffin and get his people to pick him up. Appears he wants it the hard way, so we'll oblige.' Huntley put down the telephone and lit another cigarette. 'I'm not wasting any more time on you,' he told Kerr. 'There's a car that will take you back to Washington. I just want you to know how mad people are at your brother, and that rubs off on you. Senator Hennington has demanded Secret Service protection.'

'Hennington!' Kerr interrupted. 'But that's absurd!'

'And so, of course, has Senator Barker. He believes there could be a personal grudge. He's really pissed that we accorded your wacko homosexual brother full military honours.'

'If my brother happened to be homosexual,' Kerr said slowly, 'it would make no difference to me, though it might have confused Beatriz.'

'Okay, so he was bisexual,' Huntley decided. 'He swung both ways. That was what made him a security risk, a goddamn pervert. And it's typical of that faggot-lover Hennington that he agreed to meet with Ricky. Jeez.'

'You must be desperate,' Kerr found himself saying nervously, 'to make up stuff like this. But then, I suppose you know you are going to lose in the end. Especially as I have the videotape.'

'The videotape?' Huntley responded, putting on a creditable appearance of not being especially interested. 'What videotape?'

'Of you and Barker setting up your little deal.'

'I don't know what you're talking about. If there's anyone on drugs, it's you and your crazy brother.'

The door behind Kerr opened and two men came in.

'I've seen it, Huntley,' Kerr went on. 'The tape. You know you photograph really well, anyone ever tell you that? You could've been in movies if you weren't so ugly.'

Huntley sat staring at Kerr in silent rage.

Kerr said, ''Course the video is for the FBI, not you. I expect they'll appreciate your performance.'

Huntley signalled to the men. They slipped the bag over Kerr's head again, handcuffed him and led him from the chair.

'Get him out of here. Soon as you get to Georgetown, dump him.'

Kerr felt his handcuffed arms jerked high behind his back. He stopped in the doorway and yelled through the hood.

'It's over, Huntley. It's over.'

'Wait,' Huntley said.

The two men holding Kerr stopped in the doorway.

Huntley walked across to them. He drew on his cigarette until the end glowed red, and then grabbed at the hood, pulling Kerr's face towards him.

'I just figured it out,' he snarled. 'Even if I caught cancer right now, I would still outlive your brother.' He turned and walked back to his seat. 'That's worth thinking about, Mr Kerr. Wouldn't you say? Now, goodbye.'

35

A few miles out on Route 123 back to Washington they took off Kerr's hood again. He sat up in the back seat of a Lincoln Town Car between two of the men who had leaped on him at the Cannon Building. They did not look like Mormons, more like Marines, and neither did they seem about to make conversation. Kerr blinked in the sudden brightness.

'Where exactly are you taking me?'

Still no reply. The two men on either side of him sat square in their seats like heavyweight bookends. The driver, alone in the front seat, muttered:

'You heard what Mr Huntley said. Georgetown. Soon as we cross the river into DC, you're out of here.'

'And that was the Activity, was it?'

Silence.

'Well, it's very nice, I must say.'

The car slipped across Key Bridge into Georgetown and pulled into a back street.

'I live down the road at Georgetown harbour. Couldn't you pop down there and drop me off at the door?'

The driver winced.

'You heard. Soon as we hit DC, that's it. We don't waste government gas.'

'Okay,' Kerr agreed. 'But Huntley could afford it. You know he has been on the take for years. Hundreds of thousands of dollars. I expect he could spare a few pennies for the extra petrol.'

Silence.

'Huntley uses the economic intelligence the Activity

collects to play the stockmarket on his own account. He's going to prison.'

'Personally,' the driver said, 'I couldn't give a shit if he eats babies.'

He stopped, pushed Kerr out and the car roared off back towards Virginia.

'You should check on it,' Kerr shouted after them. 'Because one day you'll read all about it in the newspapers.'

He began walking through the late afternoon shopping crowds towards Lucy's apartment, slightly dazed and wondering if he was really in trouble with the FBI. He touched the bruise over his left eye where Huntley had punched him and reckoned he would need ice. His right hand felt sore where he had hit the linebacker at the Cannon building and he had a bruise in the middle of his forehead where his head had met an unfriendly nose. If he was sore, he wondered what the nose must feel like. Kerr even cracked a smile, thinking how odd it was to be free after what he had done. If the FBI really wanted him, he assumed Huntley would not have let him go. Ruffin could have picked Kerr up at the Activity's offices instead of allowing him to be released and possibly flee the country ... He could go immediately to Lucy's apartment, pack his bags and head for Dulles airport, be on the overnight British Airways plane and get back to London before anyone missed him. There was nothing more he could do for his brother, and nothing more he could learn about his family while Ricky was on the run. So what was keeping him here? In Sarajevo he had stayed too long, pushed his luck, and been hit. He did not have to make the same mistake twice.

The trouble was that in Sarajevo he had no brother. And no Lucy. Kerr was still pondering how to persuade her to forgive him as he turned into the Georgetown harbour development, walking past the life-size bronze statues of the old black man playing with his grandchild and the lovers kissing on the park bench. He neared Lucy's apartment building and realised it was too late. Two men waited by the front door and another two walked rapidly towards him from his right, trying to cut off any retreat he might have contemplated. Ruffin was not with them, but thankfully neither was Brooks Johnson. As all four men approached, Kerr decided to do nothing. He put his hands up in the air as a kind of joke surrender and tried to look as relaxed as anyone about to be arrested by the FBI.

'David Kerr?' one of the men said.

'Yes. Guilty.'

Now these FBI agents looked like Mormons, he thought. Grey suits, white shirts, red and blue ties. Maybe the FBI was stuffed full of well-fed America Firsters.

'Please come with us.'

'Right,' Kerr replied. 'I know. Another day, another interrogation. Can I at least leave a message for my girl-friend in the apartment?'

'We will see she is informed.'

'But could I –'

'You heard me, Mr Kerr. Get in the car, or we will put you in it by force if necessary.'

Don't argue with the FBI, the voice told Kerr. Don't jerk Ruffin's chain.

'Where's Ruffin?'

'You'll find out soon enough.'

They walked briskly towards a black Lincoln Continental and Kerr was bundled into the back seat, squeezed between two of the men, the mirror image of his trip from the Activity to Georgetown.

'You're not going to believe this,' Kerr said cheerfully. 'But I have just come all the way from Huntley's office in Virginia in this position. Why they didn't just drop me off at the J. Edgar Hoover building and save you all the trouble, I don't know.'

The man in the front passenger seat turned round and grinned. He was immaculately dressed, as if he had been newly dry-cleaned from head to toe, but he had a very fake tan. It was orange and ended at the back of his neck where the skin became white. The orange man laughed heartily as if at some private joke, but said nothing. The car turned around and even with Kerr's limited knowledge of Washington geography, it was clearly not heading downtown towards the FBI headquarters but out of town, back towards Virginia.

'I don't get it,' Kerr said. 'The J. Edgar Hoover building is that way, right?'

The man with the fake tan fumbled under his jacket and produced a 9mm pistol. He leaned over the seat and pointed the muzzle between Kerr's eyes.

'I wouldn't know,' John Oberdorfer responded with a grin that cut into Kerr like a saw. 'I've never been there. And on this trip, the location of FBI headquarters is not going to be of much interest.'

36

Kerr looked at him and said calmly, 'You would be the Mormons, right?'

The Tan Man scowled but did not reply.

'I thought so,' Kerr continued, sounding cooler than he felt. 'My brother described you as America's Hezbollah, the Party of God. I'd guess we are going over to meet the Ayatollah in the America First Corporation?'

The Tan Man looked away. They drove back across the Potomac to Virginia and, as Kerr had predicted, into the underground car park of the America First Corporation. He was taken to the top floor, one man holding each arm, the Tan Man in front, a fourth man behind, and led past a television control room full of flickering screens then through a set of bullet-proof glass security doors. There was a brisk walk down a corridor filled with what Kerr realised were extremely expensive works of art, sentimental pictures, cowboy bronzes, a bust he recognised as being of Theodore Roosevelt with the words 'Rugged Individualism' on a bronze plaque beneath. The corridor led into a large office which widened out into a television studio. Kerr was thrown down on a couch facing a glass tank filled with three or four dopey big fish. The bronze-coloured man now sat opposite him. The others who had picked Kerr up hung around the edges of the room, not directly threatening him but making clear he was not going anywhere.

'My name is John Oberdorfer,' the bronzed man said. 'I am a friend of your brother.'

'Ah,' Kerr said. 'The Tan Man, of course. I should have

recognised you from my brother's description. He said you were an odious little jerk.'

Oberdorfer offered an unpleasant smile.

'I see humour runs in your family.'

'Ricky said you are the America First Corporation's link man with the Activity – his counterpart in the private sector. You're the one who gets the inside information from Huntley and then you pass it to Senator Barker. Must be a nice little job, if you don't mind me saying. Pay well?'

'Ricky told a lot of people a lot of things, but nobody will believe him. Not after what he has done.'

'I believe him,' Kerr responded. 'Senator Hennington believes him. That's a start. I expect the newspapers will too.'

The Tan Man shook his head.

'Senator Hennington is still in shock after the incident on Capitol Hill. It doesn't matter what Ricky told Hennington, he'd never buy it now. Did your brother mention to Hennington he murdered four America First employees?'

'You want something from me?' Kerr shot back. 'What is it? I have things to do. The FBI are scheduled to arrest me next, and I wouldn't like to keep them waiting.'

'We were hoping we could get you to contact your brother for us.'

Kerr laughed acidly.

'You too? Sure, why not? There's Huntley's band of criminals, there's the FBI, and now yourselves. You better join the end of the queue, Mr Oberdorfer, though I think it's all too late. No matter what you say, Hennington is about to brief the press on what the truth really is.'

The Tan Man looked especially annoyed.

'Only God knows what the truth really is, Mr Kerr,' he said. 'And you want my advice? You better get right with God before this is through. You're going to need the kind of help only the Lord can provide.'

'The chances of you knowing much about God strike me

as rather thin,' Kerr responded. 'But I'm sure God knows about you.'

Oberdorfer glared back angrily.

'You are going to help us one way or the other,' he snapped, 'playing the role you managed so well before.'

'Which is?' Kerr stared at him, the question hanging.

'Bait.'

Oberdorfer raised his hand and Kerr turned round in time to see the fist that caught him on the side of the head and knocked him from the sofa on to the ground. He rolled sideways and hit Oberdorfer with a sharp punch to the gut and watched him fall, gagging. But before Kerr could turn, there was a scurrying of feet and someone kicked him from behind as a rain of blows pummelled his back and chest. He thought he was going to die, but desperately did not want it to happen. It was worse than the mortar fire at the orphanage in Sarajevo because for the first time in his life Kerr wanted to live not for himself, not from mere force of habit, but for someone else. Lucy. Kerr kicked out hard and struck one of the Mormons with his left elbow, splitting open a nose that gushed blood. He was not going to make it easy. He just needed to talk to her and apologise. He felt a knee clip the side of his head. There were too many of them and they were too vicious. One of them kicked him in the back and he toppled forward and knew then that he was finished.

He tried to fold himself into a ball as they beat him, wanting to live a few seconds longer to show his defiance, to tell Lucy he was sorry.

At first there was pain, but Kerr was being struck so many times by feet and fists that his body could not even register the worst of it, only the thumping rhythm, and Lucy's face appearing like a rock music video, until finally the video and the face faded to black.

And over the blackness a voice within him said, 'If you survive this, you're back.'

37

From behind the trees on the lakeshore, the man watched Noah McGhie, noting that he looked distressed. McGhie came out of the back door of his house and began walking on the rough path round the lake. As soon as McGhie was at a safe distance, the man crept inside McGhie's house, sat in the main room and placed his gun on the table, waiting.

McGhie walked slowly. He had forgotten how empty his life was without Arlene and his children. First he wanted them to be with him, then, as he remembered what was likely to happen, he wished even more fervently that they would stay away. Arlene used to read horoscopes to McGhie for fun, until he objected that they were stupid to the point of religious blasphemy. Nobody could predict the future. Nobody. And yet McGhie was beginning to think maybe he could, and if he was right the way the planets and stars were lining up looked like disaster. The story about Ricky running amok on Capitol Hill had been on the evening news along with his military ID picture. The television report had shaded Ricky's face, saying he had grown a beard, making him out to be a cross between Billy the Kid and an axe murderer. Alexandria police announced Ricky was wanted in connection with the murder of his girlfriend, now positively identified as having been badly beaten, raped and her body burned. Washington DC police said they wanted him for the murder of an America First employee, found with his throat gashed while he exercised on a sit-up board. They also wanted him for the attempted murder of Scott Swett. Then Arlington police were investigating a possible connection with a double homicide at an all-night fast food restaurant on Route 7.

Watching the television reports pile up on Ricky Rush was like seeing a file from the FBI's most wanted. The news reporter quoted police sources as saying they believed Ricky had a grudge against unnamed senators, though how that squared with a chase through the House of Representatives' offices, McGhie did not understand. Then, the reporter said, there was also an unexplained link with two men whose bodies were found shot to pieces in the Great Dismal Swamp.

'Anybody else?' McGhie mumbled. 'Like maybe he killed Kennedy?'

Walking round the lake was the one place where McGhie could fix his mind on what was really important. His wife, his kids, a career, the smart house, two cars – everything the raggedy-assed kid from the broken home had built up over twenty-five years and that over the next few hours he might piss away. And for what? To back up the story of Crazy Ricky that no one wanted to hear? Crazy Ricky who Huntley now was trying to tell people had turned homosexual? Could you believe it? McGhie was so upset and confused he did not know what to think. When David Kerr asked him which side he was on, McGhie had said, 'God's side'.

Kerr had looked at him as if he were crazy.

'Like Abraham Lincoln in the civil war,' McGhie explained. 'I am not asking God to be on my side, but praying I am on God's side. There's a difference, right?'

Senator Barker, now, he never would understand the difference, not in a million years.

Barker was the kind of Christian who believed God was just another supporter lining up behind America First, just another voter to keep sweet every election time. The colonel stood at the water's edge and took a deep breath of the clean Virginia air. There was only one solution, he decided.

Someone had to bring Ricky in, to save him from himself.

'Like it was that simple,' McGhie whispered into the twilight air. 'Finding Ricky and handing him over.'

He turned back towards his house, his mind filled with memories of Ricky, memories he could not reconcile with the television portrait of the demented fugitive Captain Richard Courtland Rush, Ricky the desperado, Ricky the queer, Ricky the liar, the treacherous, the corrupt . . .

'Hate the Sin,' McGhie muttered. 'Love the Sinner.'

He rounded the turn of the lake and walked up to his house. Before going inside he looked around him as if for the last time. A few lights were going on around the lake. There was the smell of burning charcoal and barbecuing chicken from a neighbour's back yard, the sound of a lawn-mower motor in the distance, someone cutting grass before it became too dark. There was normal life in a neighbour-hood so safe you were able not to lock the door at night. But now McGhie felt he had seen his horoscope again, and it scared him. It was as if all around this lake, this little patch of the best in America, there was an inescapable and deepening cloud of the worst in America. He put his hand on the back door and gently turned the knob, knowing with a dumb-animal sense that there was someone inside.

Huntley, maybe. Or the bastards from America First. For a second he thought he should not go into his own house, that it might be better to start the car and drive to a hotel, call the police, maybe call Ruffin for advice. Maybe drive south and stay with Arlene, and run away and forget what he knew. He paused for a moment and realised there was another choice. Duty and Country. Noah McGhie took a deep breath and opened the door briskly, switched on the kitchen lights and recovered his composure. No one. He walked to the main room and bent down to turn on a table light when a man's voice slashed through the silent air like a whip.

'Don't.'

McGhie stiffened and stood upright. He turned to where the voice had sounded, and could see in the shadows a man sitting in an armchair, his right arm bent at the elbow resting on his knee and pointing towards McGhie. There was a glint of metal at the end of the arm and a gun muzzle aiming at his chest.

'I was expecting you. I don't know why.'

'Sit down, Colonel,' Ricky Rush said. 'We need to talk.'

McGhie stayed where he was, not defiant exactly, just not doing as he was told. Ricky was not sure how to handle it, figuring that once McGhie realised he didn't want to kill him, what then? What's the point of showing the gun unless he decided to use it?

'In case you can't see in the darkness, Colonel, there's a fully loaded .38 that I borrowed from Capitol Hill police pointing at your guts. I don't miss from this range, so just take things easy.'

'Sure, Ricky,' McGhie said, without a hint of surprise or fear. 'How've you been? You sound screwed up.'

'Thanks, Colonel. I'm bad, you're right. As bad as you can imagine.'

McGhie said, 'I heard about Beatriz. It was on the evening news. I'm sorry.'

As his eyes adjusted to the darkness, McGhie could see the end of the gun wobble. He thought he heard the sound of Ricky trying to choke back tears.

'You want to tell me,' McGhie went on, 'about the killings?'

Ricky shrugged.

'What's to tell?' he asked. 'After they murdered Beatriz, I decided to kill them all. There will be no justice for me except if I do it myself. Do it thorough. Do it right. That's the American way. That's Life's Golden Rule. Do it to them before they do it to you. I don't even know why I went to see Hennington, except Beatriz always thought it was a good idea. I tried to tell her, we're living outside the law, there's no way that Hennington could make a difference.'

Ricky's voice seemed so distant in the darkness it was as if he had forgotten about McGhie's presence, that he was speaking directly to Beatriz herself.

'I loved her and yet I could not protect her. I killed her just as surely as if I pulled the trigger.'

'You lied to me Ricky,' McGhie said, quietly. 'You told me you were going to get the laptop and the video, collect the evidence, then go and see Hennington, but you disappeared instead.'

Ricky held the gun tightly in his grip, still pointing it at McGhie's chest. At this range the .38 would take out McGhie's stomach and backbone. The colonel realised that anything he said might make the finger tighten on the trigger, but he would say it anyway.

'I was real disappointed in you, Ricky. Using me like that. I felt so guilty I almost threw up from the pain. You know I figured they had killed you? You know I was sure I was responsible because I should have protected you? You know any of this? And that when you came back from the dead, why, I was so angry I wanted to kill you myself. You believe that?'

'I believe it,' Ricky croaked. 'And now?'

'And now,' Noah McGhie responded, 'I'm disappointed in you, but I realise you maybe thought you had no choice. I want you to tell me a few things. Huntley now says you're homosexual, Ricky. Is that true?'

Ricky Rush looked astonished by the question.

'No,' he replied. 'It's not true.'

'They say that's in your files, that they were going to deny you security clearance and you got mad, that's what set you off.'

Ricky stood up and paced the room.

'Jesus Christ, Noah! I'm no faggot, I got enough problems. Why are they saying these things?'

'Because they are trying to destroy everything about you,'

McGhie snorted. 'Even our memories of who you were. You're being demonised so you turn into the monster they need.'

'You believe this shit?'

'No I don't, Ricky. But even if I did, it would make no difference. I want to help you. You have done wrong, and I want you to give yourself up.'

There was no response, though maybe the gun muzzle twitched a little.

'Or, y'know we could pray together,' McGhie offered. In the gloomy light he could make out that the gun twitched again then drooped in Ricky's hand. McGhie knew he could take it away if he wanted. 'Put the gun down, Ricky, so there's no accidents and we'll pray first, then figure out where we're going.'

'We, Colonel?' Ricky's voice was weak and reedy, as if he had snapped out of a trance. 'You know I've never been big on praying. And the more I dealt with Barker's people the less I believed there was a God anyway. Leastways, if Barker was on God's team, maybe I should be rooting for the other guy.'

'I understand that, Ricky. But if you won't pray for yourself, do it for your brother. Huntley's people picked him up at the Cannon, then they claim they released him, but he never showed up anywhere. He's off the map.'

'Where did Huntley take him?'

'First to the Activity. Then they let him go, and he's disappeared. Huntley is saying he went home to England.'

'Good,' Ricky said. 'No sense in him staying to get caught up in this.'

'Only I don't believe it. Lucy says David's passport and clothes are still at her place, so it doesn't make sense.'

'What were you going to do?'

'I was about to call Lucy again to see if David had returned, and maybe work out a way that between us we could save your ass.'

'Where do you think he could be?' Ricky wondered.

'I guess we both know the answer to that,' McGhie responded. 'Oberdorfer will have picked him up, and they'll beat the crap out of him trying to find out where you are, which is why you have to turn yourself in, for your brother's sake.'

Ricky shook his head in disbelief but knew it was true. They had got his brother now. They had it all. McGhie took a deep breath.

'Put the gun down and let's pray, Ricky.'

Ricky hesitated. 'I told you I wasn't too good about praying.'

McGhie stood up and switched on a light. Ricky jumped, waving the gun in his face.

'Hey, what are you –'

McGhie interrupted. 'If you want to kill me, Ricky, get to it. If you don't, put the goddamn thing away and get down on your knees and ask the Lord God to find a way to forgive you.'

Ricky stared at him for a full minute, his eyes flashing anger and hatred. Then he began to waver and put the gun down on a side table underneath the light. He reached into the pocket of his jacket and pulled out the Glock pistol and set it beside the .38 revolver.

'I don't want to kill you,' he said. 'Waste of a bullet. You're not on the list. You're not important enough.'

McGhie said, 'Thanks.'

Then Noah McGhie knelt on the floor and Richard Courtland Rush looked down at him for a moment before finally bending his knees.

'Forgive us, Lord,' Noah McGhie boomed out. 'Forgive us our suspicions of one another, and give us courage to do the thing that is right; not just the thing that is convenient. And give us the humility to know the difference.'

38

Senator Howard Hennington yelled out for Lucy Cotter to get her butt into his office. It was just after seven a.m. and they were scheduling a seven thirty staff meeting followed by a nine o'clock news conference. The television networks were setting up their equipment in the Senate television gallery. CNN said they would take it live.

'I said, get your butt in here, now.' It was not Hennington's usual way of addressing his staff, but he was bordering on panic. 'Right away,' he shouted.

'Right away, Senator.'

'Siddown,' he barked. 'I'm real surprised you have the nerve to show your face here again, but now you have, maybe you'll be kind enough to tell me exactly why you exposed me to Butch Cassidy and the Sundance Kid.'

Behind Hennington, Jim McCall sat in his shirt sleeves, one thumb hooked under his red braces, pretending to eye some documents. Lucy could swear his expression was half concern, half smirk.

'Wh-what?' she stuttered. Hennington was almost speechless too, but in his case it was from rage. He pushed the *Washington Post* story towards her.

'This . . . this . . . this goddamn armed lunatic. They say he wants to kill me.'

'Ricky does not want to kill you,' Lucy protested. She had already read the story. 'If he did, you would be dead.'

That sobered Hennington a little.

'Well . . . well . . . they are all saying he tried to kill me.'

Lucy glared back at Hennington, unable to keep the contempt from her voice.

'Saying and doing are two different things, Senator. I'd have thought a politician would know that. And who are they?'

Hennington did not take kindly to Lucy's tone. McCall was right. She should have been fired yesterday. He would do it himself now and then announce it at the staff meeting, blaming Lucy in the news conference for the errors of judgement.

'CNN,' he answered. 'Associated Press. The *Washington Post*, here. The television networks. Here, the *New York Times*. The BBC, for God's sake. They are all calling the office demanding a full account of the attempt on my life by some homosexual madman who assaulted a Capitol Hill police officer and ran amok in this building. They are calling him a . . . a . . . goddamn Washington serial killer.'

Lucy was amazed. This man who had pretensions towards the presidency believed what reporters were telling him rather than the evidence of his own eyes. She glanced at McCall. The mock concern had evaporated but the smirk was still there, and it made her mad as hell.

'Senator!' she called out firmly. 'For God's sake, think!'

Hennington blinked in alarm. The exhortation was uncommon in the Senate.

'What – ?'

'I said think, you dummy! Captain Rush risked his freedom, and quite possibly his life, to try to bring you information of the biggest financial scandal to hit this city since Teapot Dome. Somebody –' she glared at McCall '– somebody tipped off the Activity that Ricky was here. They want to destroy him, have him categorised as insane.'

'He acts insane,' McCall suggested. 'They say he was a homosexual whose liaisons with –'

'Shut up, McCall,' Lucy yelled with such violence that the tall Texan did exactly as he was told. Hennington looked stunned. He wanted this crazy woman out of his office immediately. 'You can account for your behaviour later,' she yelled at McCall.

'And you better account for lying to us both,' McCall snarled back, recovering. 'Exposing the senator to that bozo Captain Rush, threatening his reputation and . . .'

'Now hold on here, folks –'

Fearing a physical fight, Hennington tried to interrupt in his best folksy manner, but Lucy clapped her hands together so violently both men twitched. If it came to a fight, Hennington was thinking, Lucy would break McCall like a stick of celery. Oh, God. Blood on the office carpet. What would he tell the news conference?

'Why don't you explain to the senator about your most recent job offer, McCall,' Lucy spat out venomously, and the atmosphere immediately changed.

'Job offer?' Hennington's eyes suddenly lit up. What the hell was going on? McCall too? Were they all now insane? 'You been searchin' around, Jim?'

Before McCall could speak, Lucy said, 'You could say that, Senator. Want to tell him, McCall? Or shall I?'

McCall sat mute, reddening. Lucy Cotter continued like a lawyer outlining a case.

'McCall's scheduled to become Deputy Director of the Economic Security Council, working alongside our good friend Joseph R. – as in Rat – Huntley in the Activity. I've been checking around and the word, Senator, is that your loyal and recently appointed chief of staff will resign within a month, citing irreconcilable differences with you –'

'Now just a minute!' McCall protested.

' – citing differences that will screw your chances of ever running for the presidency, and therefore helping Barker immeasurably. By a remarkable coincidence that's the same Senator Barker who has been lobbying hard for McCall here to take his great talents from this office and put them to work at the ESC. And believe me, McCall deserves his reward. He has been passing information on you to Barker's people at every step.'

Hennington now was stunned speechless. Lucy kept talking.

'You accuse me of lying to you. Of course I lied – so this snake would not know where we were meeting with Captain Rush; so he would not tell his pals in America First and get Ricky killed. As soon as you telephoned and told McCall where we were, the goons turned up. Is that a coincidence or what?'

'This is an outrage,' McCall blurted out, getting thinner and redder by the minute. 'An outrage. You have no right . . . You could not possibly . . .'

One glance at McCall's face was enough to tell Hennington that Lucy had hit the target like a laser-guided smart bomb. The senator bowed his head for a moment then ran his hands through his long white hair. He took a deep breath.

'Don't lie to me, Jim.'

McCall stopped blustering.

'No, Senator.'

'You tell America First or the Activity about Ricky Rush coming round?'

McCall looked as if he suffered serious indigestion.

'I want you to tell me yourself, Jim. You tip 'em off?'

McCall spoke haltingly.

'Captain Rush is a madman, Senator. You said so yourself. Of course I spoke to the proper authorities. He killed his own girlfriend, for Pete's sake.'

'He did not,' Lucy stood up and shouted. 'Whatever else he did, he did not do that. She – was – my – best – friend . . .'

Despite her efforts, Lucy's words started to disintegrate into tears at the thought of Beatriz's death. But Hennington stuck to the point.

'And you talked to Huntley, Jim? Told him when Captain

Rush and his brother were coming round, even though you knew what that would mean?'

'Ricky Rush is absent without leave, Senator. He's a . . . a fugitive. Wanted on espionage charges. He . . .'

'Yes or no, Jim? I need to hear you say it.'

McCall hesitated. Senator Hennington waved a hand in the air to signify that the silence was eloquent enough.

'I'm asking you one last time,' he said slowly. 'Did you betray to anyone the fact we were meeting with Captain Rush?'

'How can you ask if I betrayed a murderer, Senator?' McCall argued. 'I mean –'

'God damn it, McCall,' Hennington roared, white with rage. 'I did not ask if you betrayed *him*. I asked if you betrayed *me*, betrayed this office.'

McCall took a step back as if he had been hit, but still would not reply.

Lucy said, 'Let me answer it, Senator. McCall deals directly with the America First Corporation. Your new chief of staff is a plant from Barker. He's their creature. The FBI have been investigating Barker for months and have logged a dozen visits by McCall to Barker's office plus more than a hundred telephone calls. Barker bought him up. There's $400,000 in payments so far, and more once he defects. This is Barker's pet poodle.'

Hennington's face turned grey.

'So that's my answer,' he murmured. 'You got anything to say, McCall?'

Still there was silence. Hennington managed a weak smile.

'The best I can tell you, McCall,' he began slowly, 'is you've got fifteen minutes to clear your desk. You show your face round me or this office any time from now till the Second Coming, I'll fry your Judas ass. Now get out.'

McCall stood up and appeared to be trying to say the word 'but', as if in protest, but it came out as a babyish 'ba ... ba ... bbb ...' until Hennington picked up the telephone and called the front desk of the office.

'Candi, Mr McCall will be leaving us in a few minutes. Permanently. If he is still around these offices –' Hennington checked his watch ' – by quarter of the hour, call me first then call security and have him thrown out. Yes. Yes, I said permanently. McCall's fired. Tell the rest of the staff there is to be no contact with McCall on any subject, ever. I'll explain at the full staff meeting.'

'Yes, Senator.'

Candi then told Hennington that a Joseph R. Huntley was holding for him on line two.

'Did he say what it was about?'

'Only that it was urgent. I said I would interrupt your meeting.'

'Tell him to hold.' Then, to McCall, 'Goodbye, Jim.'

'I think I should hear what Huntley has to say.'

'Then call him on your own time, not mine. Get the hell out of here before I throw you out, you goddamn stick insect.'

Jim McCall backed out of the office and shut the door behind him. Hennington looked at Lucy and sighed.

'We have got only a few minutes to decide how to play this. First, how did you know about McCall?'

'I heard, that's all.'

'Are you working for me or for the FBI?'

Lucy crossed her legs, nervous under his stare. When Howard Hennington was removed from all the stupid distractions of politics, she thought, he could be a very fine senator indeed.

'In this case, Senator, I am working for the good guys, that's all. And thankfully so are you. Don't weaken. We are on the right side, we have more friends than you can possibly know about, and we are going to win.'

Hennington stood up.

'How are you sure this guy Ricky did not murder your friend, Beatriz?'

'He loved her, Senator, but . . . they had problems.'

'Problems that would make him kill her? That's the theory the police are working on.'

Lucy shook her head again.

'Ricky would never harm her, never.'

'And how about that he is unstable?'

She nodded.

'He is now, I guess. But not before.'

'Homosexual?'

She took a deep breath.

'No, they're just making it up. Unreliable, mercurial, unfaithful, maybe, but homosexual, no. That's just another one of the unprovable things they are saying to blacken his name. And yours. You're the faggot-lover, remember?'

Hennington sat back and smiled wryly.

'And he trusted me – ?'

'He thought you were honest, is all. And you are, if your staff will let you be.'

The senator stood up and paced behind his desk.

'Then I have to congratulate you, young lady,' he murmured. 'What you did to McCall was the most professional knife job I've seen in all my years here. It was him or you, and I had made up my mind it was him. You persuaded me otherwise. Now, what do we do about Huntley?'

Lucy took a deep breath.

'Senator, you have to trust me that the FBI are closing in on Huntley and Barker.'

Hennington looked at her blankly.

'That's their business. What do I have to do? And remember, if you screw this up you might be working for the ex-senator for Kansas. I have to appear on live television in just over an hour.'

'You have two choices,' Lucy replied. 'You can roll over and let Huntley and Barker dictate how this falls apart, which – from your performance a few minutes ago with McCall, Senator, seems unlikely. Or you put out a statement which blows the whole thing open.'

'Saying what?'

'The truth. That Captain Richard C. Rush – a highly decorated Air Force Signals Intelligence officer, with citations from the Gulf War and the invasion of Panama, came to see you to make serious allegations about corruption inside the Economic Security Council. On leaving your office, a fight broke out between Rush and his former co-workers and you have no evidence that Captain Rush was making any attempt on your life whatsoever.'

'Anything else?' he responded drily. 'Shouldn't we refer to his reputation as a mass murderer?'

'Ricky will pay the price, Senator. You can be sure of it. If they ask, say you don't know.'

'The homosexuality allegations?'

'You know nothing about them either, but say that a person's sexual preference is no litmus test of truth or guilt.'

Hennington looked at her thoughtfully for a moment or two.

'You're quite a piece of work,' he said softly. 'Anybody ever tell you that?'

Lucy smiled faintly but did not reply. Then Senator Hennington picked up the telephone.

'Put Huntley through, Candi.'

Hennington pushed the speakerphone button so Lucy could hear the conversation, putting his finger to his lips so she would remain silent. Then he pressed the 'record' button on his telephone answering machine so the conversation would be taped.

'Mr Huntley,' the senator began affably. 'I'm sorry to keep you holding. How's it going?'

'It's going well, Senator, real well,' Huntley drawled. 'But the reason I called was to apologise.'

'Apologise, Joe? What for?'

'Ricky Rush. I know he came to see you yesterday. Ran crazy through the Cannon building. The boy's got problems, Senator. Deep personal problems. I know I can't be held responsible for everything members of my team do, but I feel responsible for this, and I wanted to apologise personally, and say we're doing everything in our power to catch him.'

Hennington smiled like a big cat being stroked.

'Well, that's real mannerly of you to take the trouble to call, Joe, what with you boys bein' so busy ahead of the Pacific trade summit and all. Real mannerly. But help me with a couple of things, will you?'

'Certainly, Senator.'

The big cat suddenly looked hungry.

'The boy, Rush? He came in here, showed me a computer, said it belonged to you? Claims it showed how you and your team at the Activity have been making money by using the kind of intelligence you're gathering. What d'you say to that, Joe?'

Lucy Cotter could hear a long intake of breath at the other end of the line.

'Like I said, Senator. Captain Rush has a history of mental instability and homosexual activity. We were trying to get him severed from the service. Lost his mother a year ago to cancer. What can I say? He's a crazy, Senator. Been peddling that computer story for weeks while he has been murdering and killing around him. If there's files on that computer, then he put them there. Nothing to these allegations.'

''Course not, Joe, just asking for the record. Second thing – was it some of your boys trying to pick up Ricky Rush over here at the Cannon?'

'Er, yes, Senator it was.'

'Now why exactly was that, Joe? If you don't mind me asking?'

Huntley was slow to speak. Hennington asked again. 'Y'see, I'm wondering why you did not leave it to the FBI to pick up Rush? That would be the regular way, right?'

'Yes, Senator, but you see –'

'And did you inform the FBI that Rush was alive and was coming to see me?'

'No, sir.'

'Now why exactly was that, Joe? Help me out, here.'

The big cat was ready for the kill. Huntley said something about there not being enough time.

'We got a tip-off, and –'

'From my chief of staff, McCall?'

'I can't say, Senator.'

'My former chief of staff, I should say.'

'Excuse me?'

'I just fired him, Joe. Confidence in government demands confidentiality in this office. Rule one. McCall broke it, so I broke him. Now to get back to your own particular matter, why exactly did you not call law enforcement about Captain Rush?'

'Because I thought he might respond better to some of his co-workers at the Activity.'

Hennington laughed so strongly Lucy thought the old boy might burst something. Then the claws came out again.

'What?' he guffawed. 'He might respond better to co-workers he claims are corrupt? Told me as much to my face. You bullshitting me here, Joe?'

'No, Senator. I . . . I mean, I thought . . . that is . . . He's unstable and flaky, and I . . .'

Hennington's good mood vanished as quickly as it arrived. The big cat struck.

'Now listen here, Joe. Until this telephone call from you I was not sure exactly what to do about Ricky Rush. Flaky? Sure he's flaky. Loses his mother, then finds he's in a government department where the office lottery is worth hundreds of thousands of dollars every month for Senator Mark Barker's presidential election campaign.'

'That's not true, Senator,' Huntley pleaded. 'There is nothing to his allegations, I swear it.'

'I'm delighted to hear that, Joe. Because that's exactly what I want you to do. Swear it at my full-scale public hearings under oath. I want you to turn over to the committee all relevant documents and computer files about your relationship with the America First Corporation. If you don't want to help, I will subpoena you. I intend to say so on CNN in just over an hour's time. I suggest you watch it. Should be a good show.'

Huntley was stunned into silence.

'By the way, Joe,' Hennington concluded mischievously. 'Have you seen the video of yourself discussing all this with Senator Barker? I'm no real judge, but I guess the video is the thing that nails you.'

'Wha-what video?' Huntley asked hoarsely. His voice had lost all its richness, like an opera singer with a bad throat.

'The video Barker made to make sure he could keep you in line. You aware that Captain Rush has it? He couldn't fake the video, Joe, could he? Not unless he got a double to play your part.'

Huntley was stunned into silence. He dropped the telephone into its cradle. Hennington listened to the dial tone and then looked at Lucy Cotter.

'He's gone,' he said, putting down the telephone and switching off his answering machine. He popped out the tape and labelled it with the date and time, then stood up and went to the drinks cabinet, pulling out a bottle of club soda. The early Washington morning seemed calm.

'Want one, Lucy?'

'No thanks.'

Lucy marvelled at Hennington's easy performance. She had once described him as the piano player in the Congressional whorehouse, the last honest man on Capitol Hill, and now she wanted to hug him.

'Are you really going to announce open hearings?'

He sipped the soda water.

'Yes,' he responded, 'though mainly I'm thinking that this is the moment when my thirty years in public service could go up in smoke, unless you are right about the FBI closing in on Barker and Huntley.'

'They are, Senator. Trust me.'

He smiled.

'An hour ago I was going to fire you. Now I have to trust you. Isn't life swell? Can I ask you something?'

'Of course.'

'Why are you doing this?'

Lucy stood up.

'Because it's the right thing.'

'And the pain you are risking?'

'The pain of doing the right thing is always more bearable than the pain of doing nothing.'

'You love this guy, Ricky?'

'No, Senator. Though I might be in love with his brother. I don't know exactly.'

'I see.'

Hennington turned his back on her, walking to the window to stare out at the dome of the Capitol building whose cornerstone had been laid by George Washington himself. His mind was still struggling, trying to work out how it would sound to the American people when America First Television cranked up their campaign to portray Hennington as the defender of a sexual pervert, a traitor and murderer.

'Or maybe,' Senator Hennington said out loud to the dome of the Capitol, 'maybe the American people are better and brighter than Mark Barker thinks they are.'

He took a sip of club soda.

'Let's hope so,' Lucy said.

39

Noah McGhie called the Activity number.

'Joseph Huntley's office, please.'

'This is Huntley.'

'Joe? It's Noah McGhie. Got someone here wants to speak with you.'

Ricky took the receiver.

'I want my brother,' he said.

Huntley laughed, a smoker's laugh which turned into a cough. Senator Hennington was just about to blow the Activity and the America First Corporation sky high on CNN, and all this dumb-ass son of a bitch cared about was his brother.

'Well, I haven't got him, Ricky boy,' Huntley responded. 'But if you want me to help you find him, I guess you should come out here and bring what I need to have. Then we'll see what we can do about helpin' you track him down.'

Huntley's forced good humour set Ricky on edge. Was the man never scared? Did he not know what he was facing?

'Where is he? Where's David?'

'Looks like he disappeared. It's pretty hard keeping track of you boys sometimes. Elusive sons of bitches, whole family.'

'What have you done with him?' Trying not to sound too anxious, coming over as hysterical. 'You picked him up on Capitol Hill. Where is he?'

Huntley's voice cut in like a saw.

'You know what I need from you. When I get it, we'll all help you find your brother.'

There was a long pause. Ricky could hear Huntley slowly

light a cigarette. The bastard was sitting smoking, relaxed like he was talking to an old friend of the family.

'Huntley?'

'Yes.'

'You still there?'

Huntley smiled at the edge in Ricky's voice.

'Yeah, I'm still here, Ricky. So what's happening?'

'What do you want for my brother?'

'I told you that I haven't got him.'

'Then you handed him over to Oberdorfer. Neither of us has time for games. I asked what you wanted for him.'

'I need you to return my computer, and I want the video. If I can track down Kerr, I'll try to get him released, but you also have to retract all the allegations you made to Senator Hennington, about us making money on currency dealings. I've got the statement ready for you to sign and people willing to witness it.'

'What do I get?'

'We'll find your brother for you,' Huntley replied. 'Undamaged. I'll even try to square the FBI so he faces no charges. If I can.'

'And me?' Ricky asked plaintively.

'You?' Huntley replied.

'Yes, me. What do I get?'

'It's what you don't get, Ricky. Maybe you are lucky and you don't get your brother killed. You, nobody makes any promises.'

Ricky thought for a moment. The palms of his hands were sweaty and he rubbed them on his trouser legs. There was one more thing he could try.

'I'm holding McGhie,' Ricky said. 'Right now he's got a Capitol Hill police .38 right at his belly.'

Huntley thought for perhaps half a second.

'So shoot the bastard,' he chuckled. 'Who gives a fuck?'

Then he slammed down the telephone.

40

What Ricky Rush had just told Huntley was almost true. McGhie did have a .38 revolver at his belly. The colonel had picked it up from the table and was checking it, wondering, when the moment came, how far he would go to protect Ricky.

'He told me to shoot you,' Ricky said, putting down the telephone. 'His exact words were, "So shoot the bastard. Who gives a fuck?"'

'Is that so?' McGhie replied. 'I always knew Huntley figured there were too many nigger colonels in the Pentagon. Now I know for sure.'

'So where does that leave us?'

McGhie put the .38 back on the table between them, beside the Glock.

'If David has been handed over to Oberdorfer it means he is playing the same role as he has played all along. He's bait, Ricky. Bait for you.'

'Well, if you're not going to help you won't be needing the .38.'

'I never said I wasn't going to help, only I'm not going to do things your way, storm into the America First building like the two of us are the 82nd Airborne.'

'You got a better idea?'

McGhie smiled.

'Of course I got a better idea. That's why I'm the colonel with the fancy house in Falls Church and you're Captain Psycho.'

So it was professional now, Ricky thought. Maybe it was going to be all right.

'You want to explain?'

McGhie rubbed his chin thoughtfully.

'I think we want them all, don't we? Barker, Huntley, Oberdorfer. Why don't you call Oberdorfer and say you are willing to trade the computer and the video for your brother. The deal is you will do it in the America First building but only for Barker and Huntley in person.'

'Huntley will say yes, but what if Barker won't play?'

'He'll play,' McGhie responded viciously. 'He'll want to save another sinner washed in the Blood of the Lamb.'

'How come you hate Barker so much, Colonel? I mean, I hate him, but that's personal. *You* hating him is something else. You don't hate anybody.'

'I've been thinking and praying a lot,' McGhie replied softly. 'About you, about what you told me, about what we do. I watched Barker and listened to him talk about God and God's will and God's view of this and that, and I'm thinking, I don't know God, Mr Senator, though I try. But I know enough to say to Barker, you ain't Him.'

'Whatever God is,' Ricky agreed, 'chances are He is not a freakin' chihuahua.'

McGhie drove Ricky in his Oldsmobile station wagon to a ribs and chicken restaurant on Route 7. The colonel called Oberdorfer and delivered his ultimatum: the computer and video for David Kerr, otherwise they were going straight to the FBI. McGhie said they would need an answer in one hour. They ordered and ate and as soon as they'd finished dessert, McGhie called Oberdorfer again.

'Barker will play,' McGhie told Ricky when he returned to their table. 'I guess there'll be him, Huntley, Oberdorfer, the security people at America First and any of the Mormons still alive.'

'Damn few of those,' Ricky said, sipping his coffee. 'You know I never killed anybody before, Noah. Not in Panama, not in Kuwait. Never had to do it. I just looked after the electronics.'

'And you feel bad about killing them now?'

'I feel bad I couldn't make it more painful.'

Ricky pushed the coffee to one side. It tasted of nothing.

'When they murdered Beatriz they destroyed my life, Noah. You understand? I had something and they destroyed it all, and . . .' Ricky looked at Noah McGhie for a long time without finishing the sentence.

'I know,' McGhie said eventually, 'I know what you had. I have still got some of it to lose, Ricky, okay? So play it like we agreed, right?'

Ricky nodded slowly. McGhie checked his watch.

'Party time. You ready?'

'Yeah.'

'I need to call Arlene.'

'Tell her I love her.'

'I will, Ricky.'

McGhie left the table again, made the telephone call, and a few minutes later they set off for the America First building in Arlington. McGhie nervously steered the Oldsmobile wagon up to the Power Tower and round the back, as instructed by Oberdorfer, to the underground car park.

'I feel like we're going into the headquarters of the Ku Klux Klan only worse,' McGhie whispered. 'At least the Klan have the decency to wear white sheets over their faces.'

There were two armed guards, one in a hut behind a bullet-proof glass screen, the other standing beside a heavy metal parking barrier.

'Colonel McGhie?' the guard read on his ID. 'Oh, you're expected.' He bent down to look in the car at Ricky Rush, who nodded and said nothing. As they drove through the barrier, Ricky could see the second guard behind the bullet-proof screen pick up a telephone and talk. Ricky fingered the .38. Its size meant it stuck half out of his leather jacket pocket, showing just the way he wanted it. He tucked the

Glock under the front seat. As they parked, the colonel glanced at Ricky's bearded face and the red eyes which were twitching with fatigue and stress.

'You look like shit, Captain.'

Ricky stood up straight and saluted.

'Thank you. I suppose you think you look like Sidney Poitier, Colonel?'

McGhie grinned. Ricky picked up the computer case. They walked towards the elevators.

As far as McGhie could tell the basement was empty, though at any minute he expected a single shot from somewhere into Ricky's head, maybe another into his own.

Ricky said, 'You think maybe you get closer to God in the Power Tower?'

McGhie snorted. 'The Lord must have a sense of humour, otherwise what they'd be getting close to is lightning strikes.'

When the elevator arrived Ricky pressed the top button.

'Top of the Power Tower,' he said. 'Where Barker and Oberdorfer have their offices.'

'You been here a lot?'

'Enough,' Ricky said. 'I used to brief Barker here in person once a month.'

McGhie shook his head. If ever he could get out of this, he and the Lord were going to have a serious talk about the way things were going in this country, and the way they ought to be. When the elevator opened at the top floor they stepped out and walked past the television control room with its bank of flickering screens, most tuned to the America First channel's programming. They were showing Flintstones cartoons. Ricky and McGhie were then confronted by a bullet-proof glass door. McGhie heard the clicking of locks as they were opened automatically from inside. They were being tracked by closed-circuit television. Ricky made sure the .38 did not fall out of his pocket. They stepped into the long atrium and followed the route Kerr had taken past the large Remington bronzes of cowboys and indians, buffaloes and broncoes, massive bronze eagles with outspread wings, Teddy Roosevelt smiling grimly.

McGhie was astonished by the richness of the sentimental American paintings on the walls, the Norman Rockwells, the idealised small-town life, doting parents and wide-eyed children. Then there was a group of paintings of Vietnam veterans and photographs of war memorials and military statues.

'So this is the White American Dream.' McGhie nodded at the pictures. 'No brothers of mine here, Captain.'

There were no black faces in any of the paintings and the Vietnam Vets looked as if they had won the war. In fact, Barker believed they had. McGhie remembered that at least once a month Barker argued on his television programme that except for what he called 'the stab in the back from the politicians and the media', the United States had proved victorious in South-East Asia. In the paintings around him McGhie noticed that the biggest sin was not violence or drugs or poverty, but one of the Rockwells showed a doe-faced child in shock after realising there was no Santa Claus.

'All originals,' Ricky said. 'Barker only likes the best.'

'Yeah,' McGhie whispered. 'So did Hitler. This is not the place I'd have picked to die.'

'You're not gonna die here, Colonel,' Ricky said.

'Guess not,' McGhie muttered. 'Barker wouldn't want nigger blood messing up his carpet.'

At the end of the corridor the boardroom doors were open and a group of men lined the walls. In the middle John Oberdorfer stood in his shirt sleeves and greeted them.

'Good to see you, Ricky,' he said with an attempt at bonhomie. 'You must be Colonel McGhie?'

McGhie nodded. Instantly he decided Oberdorfer was a creep. Fake tan, male model, or something worse.

'My name is John Oberdorfer. I'm vice president of the

America First Corporation and America First Broadcasting. And what would that be, Ricky?'

He pointed to the bulge in Ricky's pocket.

'That would be a .38 revolver,' Ricky replied casually. 'I was planning to shoot your pecker off, if I can find it.'

'Your brother is behind these doors,' Oberdorfer said quickly. 'And if for any reason there was to be . . . an incident, he might well find himself falling twenty storeys down into the good Virginia dirt. Give me the gun, Ricky, so we can prevent accidents.'

Ricky did not move. Oberdorfer grew impatient and nodded to the men standing around the room, all of whom drew pistols.

'Ricky, if you came for a fight, I'm sure we are able to oblige, but even at this time of night there are twenty security guards on duty, all armed, as well as the men you see here and the two with your brother. The gun, please.'

Ricky handed the computer to McGhie, took the .38 out of his pocket and gave it to Oberdorfer, with a deep sigh. The Tan Man carefully unloaded it, checked the chambers were clear, then handed the empty gun back to Ricky.

'You'll get the ammunition when you leave.'

'You are going to allow me to leave?'

Oberdorfer gave a creepy smile which made his face look untidy so he straightened it.

'If it was up to me, Ricky . . .'

'Yeah, I know,' Ricky said. 'I'd be put on a plane to South America with a million bucks in my pocket.'

Oberdorfer nodded.

'Something like that. Now search them both.'

The four guards roughly frisked Ricky and McGhie from their ankles to their heads. Ricky turned to McGhie.

'This guy is real interesting, Noah,' he explained, nodding in Oberdorfer's direction. 'Spends all his time wearing a fake tan, like he wants to turn black or something, only he ends up orange. Pretty weird, eh? He look like a brother to you?'

Oberdorfer twitched. Ricky kept talking.

'Me neither,' Ricky said. 'I always figured he was a closet queen or a child molester. How about it, Oberdorfer? Is it young girls or boys?'

'Let's go in,' Oberdorfer interrupted, trying to keep his voice level.

'Also a butt-kisser extraordinaire,' Ricky continued. 'Watch him press those orange lips to Barker's ass. Mmmmm-mmm.'

They walked through the boardroom to Senator Barker's office, followed by the other four guards. Oberdorfer sat down in front of the fish tank where the big oscars swayed in the bubbles of the aerator. Beside the tank, Huntley stood chewing nicotine-flavoured gum. To his side sat Senator Barker, rubbing his chin.

'A full house,' Ricky said.

'How are you, Ricky?' Barker asked.

'I'm fine, Senator. You?'

'I've been better. I'm wondering why you got me out of a lunch at the US Trade Representative's house to come running over here, Ricky. We were planning the nex' step in the trade war with the Japs ahead of the Pacific conference. An economic Hiroshima I call it. But I 'spect you've got some good reason, so let's hear it.'

'I want my brother. I was told he was in here.'

'I understand,' Barker said.

'So where is he?'

'He is close. Where's the computer and the video?'

Ricky put the computer on the table.

'The deal is, my brother leaves with Colonel McGhie. I stay here with you and the computer. As soon as McGhie calls me and says that he and David are away safely, I'll tell you where the video is. The terms are not negotiable.'

Barker said, 'Well, isn't that dandy. How about if we said no?'

Ricky shrugged his shoulders.

'The trouble with threatening me,' he said, 'is that I have lost everything already. I don't care if you shoot me.'

'How about if we also shoot your brother?' Barker said.

'Then Hennington and the FBI get the video. You shoot David, it would be like you kill yourself. And Huntley. And –' Ricky waved his arms around pointing to the Power Tower '– and you might as well blow this place up, because it's history.'

'Your brother for the video,' Barker repeated. 'That's the deal?'

'That's the deal. Take it or leave it.'

Barker nodded.

'Okay, Ricky. We will accept your offer and pray that the bloodshed you have caused may now be brought to an end, praise the Lord.'

Oberdorfer handed the computer to Huntley, who switched it on and began checking through the data.

'Is it your computer?' McGhie asked.

'Looks like it,' Huntley replied.

'The data all there?'

'It will take me a while to check,' Huntley said, pulling out a box of computer diskettes, then adding, for McGhie's benefit, 'but I doubt if it is my data. It's Ricky's data. He put it in himself to back up his crazy story. I want to clean house so I'm going to perform a little trick with it.'

Senator Barker interrupted.

'For those of us too old for computers, what are you doing, Joe?'

'I'm re-formatting the hard drive, Senator. That is, I'm wiping it clean of all Ricky's lies. It will be like he never existed, you understand.'

'I understand,' Barker repeated, 'but why do you think Ricky here did not make copies of these – these lies?'

Huntley laughed.

'You make copies of this, Ricky? Give them to Senator Hennington?'

'Of course not.'

Huntley laughed again.

'You see, Senator? He's a lying son of a bitch, but any information coming from the Wild Man of Washington isn't worth shit. I'm just cleaning out the infection, is all. It's as if I'm pouring disinfectant down the drain to clean up Ricky's stink.'

As soon as Huntley had finished the process, he nodded to Oberdorfer, who produced several sheets of paper.

'Sign,' he ordered Ricky. 'Three copies. Then, Colonel McGhie, we'd like you and Senator Barker to sign as witnesses.'

'What does it say?' McGhie asked.

'That Ricky here freely admits that due to pressure of work and other emotional problems, including his mother's death and his own aberrant sexual behaviour, he made a series of false accusations about the Activity and its alleged relationship with the America First Corporation; that he unreservedly and without any pressure being brought to bear, retracts these allegations.'

'What aberrant sexual behaviour?' Ricky demanded.

'It's not negotiable, Ricky,' Senator Barker said. 'Just like you said, it's a take it or leave it deal. Once in a lifetime.'

'My brother,' Ricky added. 'I don't do any more until he's here.'

Oberdorfer nodded to one of the guards. A few minutes later Kerr was led into the room, handcuffed and blindfolded.

'Take the cuffs and hood off,' Ricky ordered.

The guards waited for Oberdorfer's signal, then obliged.

'Now he leaves with Colonel McGhie,' Ricky said.

'After you sign,' Oberdorfer insisted.

'Before. McGhie can witness my signature before I make

294

it anyway. What does it matter? It's all a goddamn joke.'

'He's right,' Barker said, eager to finish it. 'It doesn't matter which way we do it.'

Barker walked over to where Ricky held the papers and signed three times where it said 'First Witness' then pushed the paper across to McGhie, who also signed it. Ricky looked at his brother's face, bruised and swollen. Both eyes were puffy and blue, and his nose was twisted.

'You okay, David?' Ricky asked.

Kerr smiled, pushing his tongue through a gap in his teeth at the front where two had been knocked out.

'Never been better,' Kerr replied. 'Only don't give these bastards anything. Don't sign the paper, and remember I told them nothing. Nothing, Ricky.'

'I have to do it,' Ricky explained. 'To save your life.'

'Don't,' Kerr pleaded. 'Please don't, Ricky.'

'It's done now,' Ricky answered. 'They're going to let you go. Did they tell you I was homosexual?'

It was as if the room had become electrically charged. Everyone stood still waiting for Kerr's reply.

'Yes.'

'You believe it?'

'I told them I didn't care what you were as long as you were my brother. If they kill us I confidently expect we'll stand together in Heaven and piss on them in Hell.'

Ricky grinned. 'I'm not a faggot.'

'I told you I don't care.'

Kerr looked in need of medical treatment but seemed perversely happy.

'The worse they treat you,' Ricky remarked, 'the harder you become. You're a thrawn son of a bitch, David Kerr.'

Kerr tried to smile but his swollen lips hurt too much.

'Runs in the family,' he replied, with an effort.

'You can go.' Oberdorfer nodded at Kerr. 'And you too, Colonel.'

'I want my brother to come with me,' Kerr argued.

'Tell him, Ricky,' Oberdorfer ordered.

'Just go, David,' Ricky responded. 'I'll be fine. Noah will take care of you.'

'I'm not going without you.'

'You have to go,' Ricky told him. 'You can do no more for me now.'

McGhie put his hand on Kerr's arm and nodded for him to leave.

'I mean it,' Ricky added. Kerr walked up to his brother and embraced him as if for the last time. 'We'll talk about it later,' Ricky said.

'Okay, Ricky.'

McGhie put his arm on Kerr's shoulder and led him away to the elevators. He was so bruised on his back, ribs and legs he hobbled down the corridors. His right hand was swollen where he had tried to punch his way out of the Power Tower.

'He's sacrificing himself for me,' Kerr whispered through his cracked lips when they reached the Oldsmobile.

'Maybe,' McGhie replied. 'Maybe not.'

'He could have gone on the run. He would have made it – nobody knows his new identity.'

McGhie shook his head.

'He has plenty to run from,' he said slowly. 'But nothing to run to. He wanted to do some good for his brother, is all.'

They sped out through the security gates. McGhie drove fast back across the river into Georgetown.

He pulled the Glock pistol out from under the seat and put it in his lap, checking the mirror to see if they were being followed. He parked at a pay phone off Wisconsin Avenue, pushed the Glock into his pocket, then called the America First building.

'Ricky,' he said. 'It's me, McGhie. They kept their word, far as I can see. I'm with David. We are safe, and I don't think we've been followed.'

'Let me speak to David.'

Kerr picked up the telephone.

'Whatever happens now,' Ricky told him, 'just believe I tried to do the best I could.'

'I believe,' Kerr said. 'You're my brother. Always will be.'

'You can say that after all I have done?'

'I told you, you're still my brother, and that's what matters.'

'And you are mine. Whatever else, they can't take that away from us. Take care, David.'

In Senator Mark Barker's office in the television studio at the top of the Power Tower, Ricky Rush put down the telephone. He looked at the faces of Oberdorfer and Barker and Huntley and the goons surrounding him, then pulled the papers towards him. With the sense that he was authorising his own execution, in triplicate, slowly and deliberately Ricky Rush signed each one.

'Now,' he said, 'I expect you'll want to know about the video.'

41

Huntley pulled a piece of nicotine-flavoured chewing gum from the pack, carefully unwrapped it and stuffed it in his mouth. Following Ricky's directions, John Oberdorfer had taken four of the men from the America First security staff over to Arlington Cemetery to try to dig up the videotape from Ricky's grave.

'Just don't get caught,' Senator Barker snapped. 'I don't want people thinking you are grave robbers, especially since we got the body right here.'

'We won't get caught, Senator. I promise.'

That left Huntley alone with Senator Barker and Ricky. Barker was pacing up and down by the fish tank, talking to the oscars. Ricky sat in a stiff-backed wooden chair handcuffed as his brother had been, with the cuffs through the wooden slats of the chair, pinning his arms behind him.

'Talk out of turn, Ricky, and we'll tape your mouth and put a bag over your head,' Huntley told him, and then proceeded to check the .38 revolver Ricky had taken from the Capitol Hill police. Huntley counted out the bullets Oberdorfer had removed from the gun and carefully reloaded it.

'You should have seen Hennington this morning,' Huntley drawled cheerfully to Senator Barker as he pushed the bullets into the chambers. 'At his news conference. What a Grade-A asshole, trying to convince the news media that Ricky is not so bad after all.'

'I heard it,' Barker called out over his shoulder, still engrossed in the fish tank. 'The reporters ate him alive.'

'Yeah,' Huntley laughed. 'Without Ricky or the computer or the video I'd say Hennington's gonna look all sizzle and no steak. Nothing to back it up. He's done.'

Huntley finished re-loading the .38 and spun the chambers with his fingers, pointing it towards Ricky. 'I hope you are not lying about the video, Ricky,' he drawled, slowly masticating his gum. 'At this stage in the game, that would make us real mad.'

Ricky stared back in silence.

'I mean,' Huntley went on. 'Don't get me wrong. It's a nice touch, burying the videotape in your grave, and all. If that's what you did. And you say your brother knew all the time?'

'Yes.'

'Then he's some kind of guy. After what Oberdorfer put him through, I'd have thought he'd a cracked. They beat the shit out of him, and he refused to talk.'

Still Ricky said nothing.

'I guess he wanted to do the best for his brother, you believe that? Oberdorfer and some of the goddamn Mormons would sell their grandmothers to a troopship for five bucks, and yet your brother, good ol' David, lets them spoil all his good looks, kick out his teeth, and he never says diddleysquat. Jesus, that's loyalty, right, Ricky? You must be aware of the concept of loyalty, Ricky? Even though you don't practise it any?'

Ricky tried to avoid eye contact. He knew something bad was about to happen, and just hoped he would be as tough as his brother when the time came. Huntley did not look in the mood for delay. The Texan got up and walked over until he stood right in front of where Ricky was cuffed to the chair. He pushed the gun muzzle on to the side of Ricky's nose and almost playfully pushed Ricky's head from side to side.

'Scared, Ricky?' Huntley said. 'Gonna piss your pants maybe, like you made Brigham do?'

Ricky kept looking away, trying to forget the gun and focus on Barker and the fish tank. Huntley checked his watch.

'Oberdorfer's been gone more than an hour,' he said, still pushing Ricky's nose with the gun barrel. 'If he doesn't call soon, I'm going to have to assume the worst. The worst for you, that is.'

Ricky kept staring into space. Suddenly Huntley pushed the barrel up Ricky's nostril, forcing his head up until their eyes met.

'That's better,' he said. 'I wanted to see whether you'd like to hear what we did to Beatriz.'

Ricky felt hot blood sweep to his head and he pulled back from Huntley. Even Barker noticed the change in tone and turned away from the fish to watch the scene.

Huntley said, 'Maybe you'd like to hear what Oberdorfer did to her before he killed her? How when he put it in her he asked her to yell out your name?'

Ricky roared and tried to stand up, struggling to free himself from the handcuffs. He wanted to tear Huntley's head from his body, but as he tried to get to his feet Huntley kicked behind his knees and he fell to the floor, pulling the chair on top of himself. He landed on the ground face down, the chair over him, his hands locked through it in the handcuffs. Huntley took a pace backwards, chewing the gum and laughing.

'She squealed a lot,' he said. 'Yeah, she was a squealer all right. Put up a struggle, but Oberdorfer just kept putting it into her. Wanted to do things I never knew people did to each other, man and woman things. I mean, it was an education. Down in Texarkana we never knew about stuff like that, 'cept maybe between black folks or something.'

Barker walked over from the fish tank, amazed at Huntley's tone and fascinated by what was about to happen. He could taste the violence in the air.

'I think by the end,' Huntley said slowly, 'she was starting to like it. I really do, Ricky. Really do. Like she died with a smile on her face, y'know?'

Ricky ground his head into the carpet and closed his eyes. He could feel tears of anger and he prayed for a superhuman burst of strength that would enable him to leap from the chair and kill Huntley. McGhie had planned it all and prepared him for every kind of torture, except this. He wanted Noah to get here now, so he could kill these bastards.

''Course,' Huntley went on, 'we find out you're lying to us about the videotape, and we'll make what happened to Beatriz seem like pat-a-cake.'

Ricky pushed his face deeper into the thick pile of Barker's carpet.

'And I know what you are thinking,' Huntley said. 'That you don't care what happens to you. It's your brother I'm talking about. There's nowhere for him to hide. You lie to us about the videotape and next time we pick up Kerr we won't be looking for information. We'll just torture him for the heck of it.'

Barker stood at the fish tank, his hands by his sides.

'This is nearly as good as feeding the oscars,' he said. 'It's like giving them raw meat.'

Huntley smiled back wanly. 'Tell me something, Ricky,' he asked, kicking the side of Ricky's face with his shoe. 'You think Beatriz enjoyed rough stuff?'

Ricky could not answer. He kept grinding his face deeper into the carpet, hoping they would all disappear.

'Maybe she found in Oberdorfer what she'd been looking for all these years,' Huntley went on. 'You know what I mean? A real man?' He turned to open his attaché case. 'You know what this is?'

Senator Barker watched closely as Huntley held up a large pink quartz crystal. Ricky kept his eyes shut. Huntley walked over and laid it by Ricky's nose, then kicked it into his face.

'I said, you know what this is, Ricky?'

Ricky moaned but still said nothing. He was thinking, if David can take it, so can I. His head began to feel sticky. Blood flowed out from above his eye where the quartz had gouged into his forehead.

'Well, let me tell you, Captain Rush, this here's a little souvenir I picked up from Harmony Supplies, just before it went up in smoke. And right now I was planning to make sure you have it on you, just in case anything should happen. Maybe the police might decide you really did kill Beatriz after all, and how you were about to kill the senator here when I came in and saved him.'

Ricky blinked open his eyes to see the quartz crystal through the blood, then he shut them again.

'Oh, did I tell you,' Huntley concluded. 'Oberdorfer said she was a great lay. Beatriz, I mean. Said she was so grateful for it.'

Barker laughed his chihuahua yap. Huntley sat back in his chair, and chewed impassively, looking down at the helpless body of Ricky on the floor. The telephone rang and Barker picked it up.

Oberdorfer talked excitedly. He said, 'We got the tape.'

'You checked it?'

'I put it on the portable player we took with us, Senator. It's the one, all right. You and Mr Huntley, large as life, sitting in the office where you are now and talking about how you will help him if he will help you. Time code on it and everything. It's the one.'

'Then bring it back here right now.'

'Okay,' Oberdorfer said. 'Only it'll take some time. I'm on the portable phone in the middle of Arlington Cemetery.'

'Just do it,' Barker snapped, and slammed down the telephone.

'He got it?' Huntley asked, looking down at the loaded .38, his heart pumping hard. It was the endgame now, time for Wild Ricky to attempt his escape and time for Senator Barker to have a big surprise.

'Yes,' Barker smiled, for the first time truly happy. 'So let's see. He's got the video. We have wiped the computer. We've got the signed statements from him. That means there's nothing left as evidence against us, except maybe this turd on my carpet.' Barker pointed to Ricky on the floor. 'Now we have to sweep up the turd, right, Joe?' Barker winked.

'Right, Senator. You think he could have made copies of the videotape?'

'It's a professional Beta standard,' Barker responded. 'I doubt if he has the equipment. Why don't you ask him?'

Huntley kicked Ricky hard in the face.

'Make any copies, Ricky?'

He kicked him again, this time in the ribs.

'I said, you copy the video, Ricky?'

'N-no,' Ricky moaned.

Huntley kicked him once more for good measure. What else would Ricky say? There was a risk, but there was no choice except to assume that there were no other copies. Huntley picked up the quartz crystal, making sure he kept the blood stains from Ricky's smashed forehead away from his own hands and clothes.

'You want to kill him now?' Barker asked.

'In a moment, Senator. Got a few more surprises first.'

God, these amateurs. Huntley had planned to put the pink crystal in a place that really would surprise Barker, only he had to time it right, get it done before Oberdorfer returned. First he placed the crystal on top of his attaché case and then asked Barker to help him pull Ricky's chair back into an upright position.

'So he can see better?' the senator sniggered.

'Right,' Huntley agreed.

'I think you're going to like this,' Huntley said. 'You're going to like it a lot.'

42

The way Oberdorfer had planned it was for two of them
to keep watch while he and the two other America First
security guards dug up Ricky's grave with shovels.

'Like Barker said, we don't want people to think we're
body snatching,' he joked. 'So everybody keep their coats
and ties on, and we just make out we're FBI or something,
doing an exhumation.'

'A what?' one of the security guards asked.

'Digging up the body,' Oberdorfer explained. Jesus.
These guys were dumber than Scott Swett. And he was in
a coma. The plan had started to go wrong when they were
unable to drive their cars through the cemetery to the
graveside without an official pass.

'No, sir,' one of the Arlington National Cemetery guards
explained. 'Nobody drives through here, only funeral parties. Is this a funeral party, sir?'

The Tan Man had to admit it was not.

'The parking garage is over there,' the cemetery guard
insisted. 'You better use it.'

Then when they walked in with the tourists, the Tan Man
tried to hide his shovel in a large sports bag, looking casual
– as if everybody came to Arlington National Cemetery
with a bag full of tennis equipment. As soon as they reached
the grave he ordered one of the others to dig. Thankfully it
took only a few minutes to move enough loose earth from
the top of the grave to uncover the videotape. They pulled
the tape free and shovelled back the soil.

'Paydirt,' the Tan Man said. He turned to the security
guard who carried a portable professional beta-player and

was about to insert the cassette to check it, when he noticed three cars sweeping towards them along the pathways, from opposite directions.

'Now how come they can do that, Mr Oberdorfer?' one of the America First men asked. 'And we can't? They got pull or what?'

Oberdorfer did not know, but his first instinct was to reach for his gun. His second instinct – and a voice from a megaphone – told him if he moved, he'd be dead.

'Armed Federal Agents – freeze. Armed Federal Agents – freeze.'

Groups of FBI agents in bullet-proof vests were now running in from over the hill, threading through the gravestones. The three cars spilled out a dozen more, all armed. A helicopter swept in across the trees and hovered fifty feet above them, almost knocking Oberdorfer down with its blast.

'FBI, get down on the ground! Federal agents, get down on the ground!'

The yelling was so loud and came from so many directions at once that Oberdorfer thought he was going to be sick. He fell to the ground, his neat grey suit lying deep in the mud. He pulled his hands over his ears, wishing the noise would go away. The FBI agents swarmed everywhere, frisked and handcuffed them all. Then Harold Ruffin appeared and separated Oberdorfer from the rest.

'W-what do you want?' Oberdorfer asked. 'We never did anything. I was only –'

Ruffin tried not to laugh. Here was the Tan Man standing by Ricky Rush's grave in Arlington Cemetery, looking so bewildered even the fake colouring on his face seemed to have turned pale, his suit stained with Potomac dirt, in his right hand, the video. Slowly, as if talking to a child, Harold Ruffin explained how it was going to be. Oberdorfer swallowed hard.

'Y-you m-mean you want me to lie to Senator B-Barker?'

'You got it,' Ruffin said.

'A-and if I d-don't?'

Ruffin stood in front of Oberdorfer with a look that said, don't even think about it. He did not have to speak.

'G-give me the telephone,' Oberdorfer decided. 'What do you want me to tell the senator?'

Ruffin explained it one more time, and Oberdorfer did exactly as he had been instructed. He blanched as Barker shouted at him to return to the Power Tower with the tape immediately.

'Of course, Senator. Right away, Senator.'

Ruffin marvelled that even as he betrayed Barker, Oberdorfer could not bear to disagree with him. The FBI agent took the portable telephone from the Tan Man and handed it to Brooks Johnson.

'Good doggie,' Ruffin told Oberdorfer, in his most condescending tone. 'You did okay. Now you get your dog biscuit.'

He turned to a group of other FBI agents.

'Take this bozo away, Mirandise him, and tuck him up somewhere safe until we come back from the America First building. Time's running out. We have to move.'

The agents swarmed around Oberdorfer and led him up from Ricky Rush's grave to where the nearest FBI car was parked on the service road. The men from America First security stared at Oberdorfer gloomily from the back seats of the other cars, each with his hands cuffed behind his back. A black Lincoln drew up. Kerr, McGhie and Lucy stepped out. Kerr tried to talk through his puffy lips and broken teeth.

'You think we can still save Ricky?' he asked Ruffin.

'I would not have done it this way if I thought he would die, David,' Ruffin replied. 'But there is a risk we could be too late. We better get going.'

McGhie, Lucy and Kerr joined Ruffin and Brooks Johnson in the lead car. Three other cars followed them out of the cemetery towards the America First building. The cars carrying Oberdorfer and the guards peeled off towards Washington. Kerr felt Lucy's hand search for his until she grasped his fingers, then she raised them to her mouth and kissed them gently. Maybe it was going to be all right.

'What makes you so sure we're going to be in time?' Kerr asked Ruffin.

'I'm betting Barker won't do anything until he sees this for himself,' Ruffin replied, holding up the muddy video-tape. 'He's waiting for showtime. What he does not know is how we're gonna rewrite the final act.'

'Maybe,' Kerr retorted. 'Except that Barker and Huntley could be working from a different script.'

Harold Ruffin said nothing, and stared straight at the road ahead.

43

In the Power Tower at the top of the America First building Ricky Rush now sat upright in his chair, still handcuffed, watching Huntley. All around him the cameras in the Power Tower studio stood in their transmission positions, like electronic sentries. They gave Ricky the creeps. Barker was getting excited, flitting around because he was ready to feed more goldfish to the oscars, playing with the television studio control panel on his desk, unable to settle. Ricky could see Huntley was getting irritated. He asked Barker if it was all right to wash Ricky's blood off the quartz crystal in the fish tank.

'Sure,' Barker responded, clearly amused. 'See if the smell of blood turns 'em on.'

It did not – not human blood anyway. The big fish swam for cover as Huntley carefully washed the stain from the rock and set it down.

'We should kill him now,' Barker said. 'Get it over with.'

Huntley frowned. 'After we see the video, Senator. That's what we agreed, right.'

Imbecile.

'Right,' Barker admitted. 'That's what we agreed.'

He was getting nervous, looking for something to do.

'Why don't you feed the fish,' Huntley suggested, trying to keep the disdain from his voice.

'Good idea, Joe. Feed the fish. Yes.'

The little chihuahua rummaged behind his desk for a moment and emerged with a plastic bag with half a dozen goldfish inside. He took it over to the tank, floated it in the water and then split it apart.

'Let's see if this gets more of a response than Ricky's blood,' Barker laughed. The goldfish spilled out and the senator settled down to watch the fun. Huntley kept checking his watch to work out how long it might take Oberdorfer to return from Arlington Cemetery. Another fifteen minutes at most, he figured. He paced up and down nervously between the cameras at the top of the Power Tower, then he walked back to where he had left the pink quartz crystal. He picked it up and held it in his right hand.

Barker changed position to the back of the tank for a better view of the goldfish being torn to pieces by the oscars.

'That goddamn Janey,' Barker muttered, referring to his personal assistant. 'I told her to get more fish. What does she bring? Just six. Sorry, boys. Look on this as something to snack on. I'll do it myself tomorrow, okay?'

'It's a-mazing,' Huntley said, tossing the crystal from hand to hand. 'To think Beatriz made her money out of selling rocks like this. You ever think of that, Senator? Money out of rocks?'

Barker was too interested in the fish to reply. The biggest oscar was pecking at one goldfish, sucking out its eyes. Then he switched to another. Then a third, pulling it from the mouth of another oscar.

He was not eating, just attacking, as if for sport, a new kind of viciousness.

'Guess not,' Huntley said, answering his own question. He walked round behind Barker. 'Guess if you figured you could sell rocks instead of gas you wouldn't have bothered with all the expense of drilling for oil in Oklahoma. Is that right, Senator?'

Barker mumbled something indistinct, his interest still absorbed by the killing in the tank. He was bent almost double, trying to catch the best angle as he viewed the swirling water.

'Never seen it like this before,' he said. 'See, the regular way is, the oscars attack when they are hungry, and when they are not, they just sit awhile. Right now the big one is playing, but he's not eating. It's acquired behaviour, I'm sure of it. Not instinct.'

The biggest oscar was pecking at the gills of the smallest goldfish, drawing blood, but still not going in for the kill. Huntley stood behind Barker, pretending to get a better look.

'Go on, my beauty,' Barker whispered in encouragement. 'Go on, there's one that can still see.'

Huntley was now staring at the back of Barker's head, not at the fish. He raised the quartz rock high in his right fist.

'Go on, go for the eyes,' Barker called out excitedly. 'Sink him.'

Huntley brought the pink quartz crashing down on the back of the senator's skull.

'This should sink you, you bastard.'

Barker grunted in amazement then fell to the ground. Huntley climbed on top of him, pounding his head until there was nothing but a pulp under the force of the rock, the pale pink dripping red between the Texan's fingers.

He stopped for a moment and stood up, panting for breath and looking for somewhere to clean himself. His eyes locked on to Ricky, who met his gaze calmly. Ricky smiled, realising it all now.

'It's a good try, Huntley,' he said. 'But you still lose.'

'Oh,' Huntley replied, still breathless from the effort. 'Is that so?'

In the tank the youngest oscar had now joined in the fight, sucking at the last remaining goldfish, pulling it apart between himself and the big fish.

'I don't lose,' Huntley snapped, his strong voice made ugly by tension. 'It's not in my nature. Now Barker, he lost. And you, you're a loser, Ricky, always were. Me, I'm the spirit that made this country great, the can-do spirit. People like me don't lose. Overwhelming force, overwhelmingly applied. The Huntley doctrine. Remember that.'

'I'll remember that, Joe. I'll tell them about it in court.'

Huntley dipped his hands in the fish tank and washed the blood again from the quartz crystal, then he threw it down on the bloodied mess that had once been the senior senator from Oklahoma.

'I think this is going to be perfect,' he said. 'Just perfect. Ties up all the ends. What do you say, Ricky?'

Ricky said nothing. Carefully Huntley washed his hands once more in the tank until they were clean, and then wiped them on his jacket. There were splashes of blood on his trouser legs, but he planned to kneel beside Barker's corpse to offer assistance, he would say, and that would explain everything. It was all fixed now. He had the computer, Oberdorfer was on his way with the videotape, and Wild Ricky was about to perform a great service for God and Country. Huntley began to laugh. He spat out his nicotine gum and lit a cigarette. It tasted so good now, smoking in Barker's own office.

Like dancing on the old bastard's grave. He dropped a little ash on the carpet by the senator's body.

'I hope you enjoyed the show,' Huntley said to Ricky. 'At least, I guess you enjoyed it better than the senator did. I came to realise he was crazier than you are, Ricky. Something had to be done.'

'You never should have got mixed up with him, Joe. He ate you up, like one of those little goldfish in the tank.'

'He never ate me,' Huntley protested violently. 'I ate him, Ricky. He's the corpse. I'm the one who's going to make it, right, Ricky? I ate him.'

'I don't think so, Joe. It's over.'

Huntley quickly checked Barker's body, then his own watch.

'So you keep saying, but not yet, Ricky, though it soon

will be. That bozo Oberdorfer won't be long, and I intend
to conclude with your starring role, your big finale.'

'Which is?'

'Which is, Wild Ricky, the scapegoat on whom all sins
can be laid.'

Huntley stepped over Barker's body to where Ricky's .38
lay. He spun the chambers one more time.

'This is the gun you took from the guard on Capitol Hill,
right?'

Ricky knew he had to keep Huntley talking to give the
FBI a chance to arrive, but the Texan was moving along
fast in ways he could not predict. Now he was pointing the
.38 at Ricky's chest.

'Isn't that a-mazing,' Huntley said, as if rehearsing for
the police report. 'Damnedest thing I ever saw. Senator
Barker decided you were no risk to anyone, and so he took
the cuffs off you. Trusting son of a bitch, wasn't he? Goddammit, he should have known how crazy you were, Ricky.'

'Crazy?' Ricky said. 'Sometimes, Joe, I realise I'm the
only one round here who's sane.'

Huntley laughed loudly. 'Sane? You crazy asshole. You
call hitting that guy over the head with a baseball bat sane?
Or the one with his throat cut?'

'Yes, Joe, that was sane, because I did it to protect people
I love. You're doing it for what? Money maybe? Ambition?
You still think you can get away with it and call that sanity?
Then give me crazy every time.'

Huntley was moving around the room quickly now, looking for the keys to Ricky's handcuffs.

'This is the way it goes, Ricky,' he explained. 'Barker let
you out of the chair and you murdered him with the rock
you used on Beatriz. Then you tried to come for me, only
I blew you away with the gun of a law enforcement officer
you assaulted a couple of days back. I told you it was neat,
eh? Now I just have to do it.'

Huntley found the key and held it up to check it.

'You going to take these cuffs off first?' Ricky asked hopefully.

Huntley shook his head. 'You really must be crazy, Ricky, if you think I'm so dumb as to give you the slightest chance. Overwhelming force, Ricky, overwhelmingly applied.'

Now Ricky began to laugh, a laugh so low and bitter Huntley's finger relaxed on the trigger of the .38.

'I say something funny?'

'I'm just thinking about the tape,' Ricky guffawed, playing desperately for time. 'And how you were fooled by Oberdorfer.'

Huntley let the gun drop for a moment to his side, puzzled. Ricky was surprised how much, suddenly, he wanted to live. Even if he spent the rest of his life in prison, he wanted to live now, to deny Huntley anything like a victory.

'Meaning?' Huntley asked, confused.

'Meaning, like I said, you're finished, Joe,' Ricky sneered. 'Oberdorfer is with the FBI right now. He was picked up at the grave. It must have taken Harold Ruffin about a nanosecond to explain to the Tan Man that if he cooperated he might avoid the death penalty for the murders of Colvin and Drysdale.'

'W-what do you mean, Ruffin? Oberdorfer said he had got the tape.'

'Oh, Oberdorfer got the tape. Then Ruffin got Oberdorfer.'

Ricky's laughter resounded in the empty room.

'Y-you're bluffing.'

'Right, Joe. You're right, always right. I'm bluffing.'

Ricky laughed again and again until Huntley started to get angry.

In his rage he hit the butt of the .38 into the side panel of the fish tank. The glass smashed and fifty gallons of water spilled on the floor. The fish thrashed in the blood and water round Barker's body. The biggest oscar was washed into the crook of the senator's arm where it gasped and flapped, covering itself with his blood.

'You lying son of a bitch,' Huntley snarled. 'You lying traitorous son of a bitch.'

'It's the truth, Joe. It's finished. You might as well release me now.'

Huntley levelled the gun at Ricky's chest.

'That's not what I had in mind,' he said.

44

The first truckload of agents in black uniforms with body armour and the initials 'FBI' in bright yellow fluorescent paint hit the security post at the America First car park. The guards were so startled they came out with their hands up, begging to be arrested. The second FBI team secured the outer perimeter of the building. In the air, an FBI helicopter circled the roof. All the America First security guards were disarmed and made to squat facing the wall, while agents clipped their hands together with plasticuffs. The car carrying Harold Ruffin, Brooks Johnson, Lucy, McGhie and Kerr swept up to the elevators in the underground car park.

'Colonel McGhie, you stay in the car, please, with Miss Cotter. David, you come with us.' Kerr bounded out after Ruffin and Johnson.

'Keep behind us,' Ruffin ordered, nodding to the Power Tower. 'I don't know what we'll be dealing with up there, what state your brother will be in. I want you to do precisely as you are told but to be on hand in case Ricky needs someone he trusts to talk to him, understand?'

Kerr nodded.

'Okay,' Ruffin ordered. 'Let's do it.'

FBI agents swarmed up the stairs and the team led by Ruffin commandeered the elevators, using priority keys to reach the twenty-first floor. The doors opened at the top of the Power Tower and Harold Ruffin burst out at the head of the first team of agents. The second elevator exploded open and another team spilled out. From the stairwells the leading agents in uniform smashed through the locked fire doors, panting with the effort of having cleared so many stairs so quickly. Every conceivable escape was now cut off.

'Up,' Ruffin ordered, and two teams ran to the roof to check it. In front of him the bullet-proof glass security doors leading to Barker's office and the television studio were closed. Ruffin told the battering-ram team to smash through the plasterboard wall to the side instead. Walls were usually weaker than doors.

'Look,' Kerr said. To his left he could see the banks of television screens in the television control room. About half were showing the network transmission – a re-run of the 'I Love Lucy' show in the 'Family Values Hour' – but the rest of the screens showed the scene from inside Barker's office. The bank of beta-recorders was running, recording the camera transmissions from inside the Power Tower. On a dozen screens they could see Ricky Rush handcuffed to his chair in animated conversation with Joseph R. Huntley. Huntley was waving the .38 in Ricky's face. Kerr could not hear the sound.

'Hurry,' Ruffin yelled at the battering-ram crew, but they were in trouble. America First Security had put chicken wire between the plasterboard walls of the Power Tower to protect Senator Barker, and the ram could not push through.

'Wirecutters,' Ruffin ordered.

'For Christ's sake do something,' David Kerr yelled. 'Look.'

On the screen Joseph R. Huntley appeared to have finished his argument with Ricky Rush. He smashed the side of the fish tank and the water and weeds and fish poured on to the floor.

'Oh my God,' Kerr said. 'Hurry.'

The tip of Huntley's .38 revolver no longer twitched. He levelled it at the centre of Ricky's chest.

45

Kerr looked in silent desperation from the television screens to the FBI team as their cutters snipped at the chicken wire. He pushed open the control-room door and turned every button on the sound desk in front of him until he found one which boosted the volume from the ceiling microphones in Barker's office.

'You lying son of a bitch,' he could hear Huntley snarl in Ricky's face. 'You lying, traitorous son of a bitch.'

'It's the truth, Joe,' his brother's voice said. 'It's finished. You might as well release me now.'

Behind Kerr the wirecutters had finished. They pulled back and the battering-ram team gouged a massive hole in the wall, allowing the agents to pour through. Kerr turned to follow them then stopped abruptly when he heard Huntley say, 'That's not what I had in mind.'

He glanced back at the screen where Joseph R. Huntley's blank eyes stared straight ahead as he pulled the trigger, firing the revolver at a range of just a few feet, firing it until there were no bullets left.

'No,' Kerr gasped. 'No.'

He pounded on the television screen with his fist, tears of frustration and pain flooding his eyes. Huntley was standing pointing the empty gun directly at Ricky, panting with excitement.

'I always told you, Ricky,' Huntley gasped. 'One day your mouth would get you in trouble. But you never listened. You never listened to old Joe.'

46

Kerr bowed his head in the television control room, as if he was about to be sick. Behind him Ruffin froze.

'Shit,' he said, as Brooks Johnson prepared to leap off towards the sound of gunfire.

'No,' Ruffin ordered. 'We're too late. Wait and see what happens next.'

With the bullet-proof doors breached the uniformed FBI agents fanned out in the corridors at the top of the Power Tower but had not yet reached Huntley. He quickly moved towards the chair in which the body of Ricky Rush sat slumped and bloody. He unlocked the cuffs and slipped them into his pocket. Ricky's body immediately fell face first on the floor. Huntley moved off-camera as he dragged it towards where Barker lay. Kerr watched as Huntley rolled Ricky's body a little in something on the floor, carefully pressing Ricky's right arm down. Then Huntley stood up and they could see clearly that he walked across to a raised partition table on which sat the shattered fish tank. He unfolded a pocket handkerchief and picked up what looked like a pink quartz crystal.

'A rock?' Brooks Johnson said. 'What the – ?'

Ruffin watched in silence as Huntley walked over to where he had dumped Ricky's body and placed the rock down by Ricky's right hand.

Then he knelt and appeared to be rubbing the rock in something on the floor. He stood up, put away the handkerchief and pulled out another cigarette.

He lit it, placed the .38 on the table beside the fish tank and then calmly walked across to the armchair beside

Barker's desk. He sat down. A few seconds later the first of the uniformed FBI agents had threaded through the corridors into Barker's office and studio.

'Federal agents,' they yelled at Huntley. 'Freeze.'

The Texan stood up and held his hands in the air, the cigarette dangling from his lips. He stood directly in front of one of the cameras and Kerr watched a smile spread across his face.

'Thank God you're here,' he said. 'Pity it wasn't soon enough to save the senator.'

Ruffin signalled to Brooks Johnson to come with him then turned to Kerr.

'David,' Ruffin said firmly. 'I want you to stay here.'

Kerr said nothing, too stunned to move or to think. Ruffin and Johnson climbed through the hole in the wall and walked slowly towards Barker's office. As they stepped inside Huntley was in the middle of explaining something to the uniformed agents. Ruffin tried to take in the red mess on the floor, the two bodies in a welter of blood and weed and water and gravel and dead fish. One of the fish was not quite dead. The biggest of the oscars flapped occasionally, smacking his tail on the waterlogged carpet. Huntley's grin disappeared when he saw Ruffin and he took a long draw on his cigarette, slowly exhaling the smoke.

'Wild Ricky,' Huntley signalled. 'I was just telling your co-workers here, Mr Ruffin. He killed the senator with that pink rock. Beat his head in. I struggled with Ricky, got his gun.' Huntley looked down at the mess on the floor. 'Then I had to shoot him, had to do it. You could say it was like a mercy killing. It put us out of his misery.'

'Yeah, I guess so, Mr Huntley,' Ruffin said. 'Leastways, that's one way of looking at it. But tell me something.'

Huntley shrugged.

'Sure.'

'When Ricky did all this,' Ruffin asked slowly, pointing

at the mess on the floor, 'was he wearing a set of handcuffs and maybe a chair?'

Huntley took a step backwards. The smoke from his cigarette curled in swirls above his head and his face twitched as if in pain. Before he could respond, the door behind Ruffin opened and David Kerr stepped through. In his right hand he held up a television videotape.

'I told you to stay out of here,' Ruffin ordered.

Kerr shook his head.

'Senator Barker is a creature of habit,' he said slowly. 'He not only videotaped the meeting when you set up your deal with him, Huntley. He also recorded his own murder, and that of my brother. It's on this tape. I just checked it, saw the whole thing, twice over. I will be seeing it in my dreams for the rest of my life.'

Huntley took the cigarette from his mouth and exhaled smoke, but said nothing. Harold Ruffin walked over beside Kerr and gently took the tape from him. Huntley's face at first looked like grey granite, but as Kerr stared at him, he was in no doubt. This time the snake eyes blinked.

47

The waves on the beach at Chincoteague, three hours' drive east of Washington, had been whipped up by an early summer storm out in the Atlantic. A few gulls caught the wind and glided back over the sand dunes in widening arcs. In the old graveyard, David Courtland Kerr held Lucy Cotter's hand tightly and watched the sand filling the hole above his brother's coffin. The pastor said a few words, closed his Bible and walked away. Harold Ruffin, Brooks Johnson, Noah McGhie and his wife and family stood together for a moment, their heads bowed in prayer. Senator Howard Hennington stood apart, gazing down at the grave, then he walked up towards the sand dunes to think. One by one the other mourners came to stand by Kerr. Arlene hugged him.

'Richard would have wanted it this way,' she said. 'To be buried near the sea. He loved it so much.'

'I know, Arlene.'

Noah McGhie hugged him too, and Kerr bent down to hold each of his sons in turn. The youngest, Robert, asked if Ricky was going to be cold under all that sand. Kerr smiled.

'Like your daddy said, it's only his body that's here. His soul is in Heaven, Robert. He walks with us still.'

Little Robert McGhie hugged Kerr again. Arlene took the children back to the car and Noah said, 'He changed me, your brother.'

'He changed all of us, Noah. How did he change you?'

'In the way that because I knew him, I could forgive him almost anything. Do you understand that? When people do bad things and you still want to help them?'

Lucy said, 'It's called love, Noah.'

'I guess.'

'Think what I have had to forgive in the name of love,' Lucy added, squeezing Kerr's hand.

'How come around you two I always feel uncomfortable?' McGhie asked. 'Like I'm interrupting something?'

'Because you are interrupting, Noah,' Kerr said. 'Now, go away so I can take this woman home.'

Lucy looked at him.

'More of that British romance, huh?'

Kerr grinned. His mouth still showed the gaps where his teeth had been knocked out.

'Of course,' he said. 'What woman could resist a smile like this?'

McGhie kissed Lucy on the cheeks and hugged Kerr.

'You going to be around for a while?' he asked.

'I have to go back to London in a few days to tidy things up, then, if I can find someone to employ me, I think I might work in Washington for a while. I'm going back to being a freelance reporter.'

'Any special reason,' McGhie asked, smiling at Lucy, 'for you choosing Washington?'

'The climate,' Kerr replied. 'It's good for my shoulder.'

'Right.'

'See you around, David.'

McGhie walked back to join Arlene. Harold Ruffin took his place.

'I almost can't believe Barker switched on the cameras so they recorded everything,' Kerr said.

'If you're going to do it, do it on television, I guess,' Ruffin replied. 'He believed everything should be preserved for posterity, including his own death. He called it living history in the Video of the Recording Angel.' Ruffin smiled. 'In the Bureau we call it evidence. He was one sick puppy.'

Kerr shrugged.

'It still doesn't bring Ricky back.'

'No, but he was on the right side in the end. That's maybe all you need to know about him. That he was with the good guys.'

'He was like a comet coming into my life and then disappearing,' Kerr said.

'I'm sorry,' Ruffin began.

'Don't be,' Kerr interrupted. 'I mean, it's better to have seen the comet for a few seconds than not at all. Does that make sense?'

Ruffin nodded.

'All the sense in the world.'

Brooks Johnson came up, wanting to shake Kerr's hand.

'Listen,' he apologised. 'About our misunderstandings . . .'

'Forget it, Brooks,' Kerr said. 'Like I said to Harold here, I only have to put up with you being an asshole once in my life. He has to make a career out of it.'

Brooks Johnson looked stunned.

'It's a joke, Brooks,' Harold Ruffin said, and even Johnson got it this time.

'British humour,' Brooks Johnson decided. 'Monty Python, right? Kind of grows on you, doesn't it?'

'Precisely, Brooks. Kind of grows on you.'

They walked away, leaving Kerr and Lucy together by the graveside, until Senator Hennington walked towards them.

'Thank you for coming Senator,' Kerr said. 'I know how busy you are.'

Hennington swept back his mop of grey hair. 'Least I could do, son. The way it worked out your brother was maybe a better patriot than anybody I ever knew. He gave his life for his family, and his country, only in a way that won't lead to any medals.'

'Are you going ahead with your hearings?'

'I doubt it,' Hennington replied. 'The White House decision to disband the Activity by executive order is good news. And America First is nothing without its Bigot-in-Chief. There would be no point in rehearsing our dirty little secrets in public.'

'But it will all come out at the Huntley trial?'

Hennington smiled.

'They say Huntley is going to plead guilty to the murders of Barker and Ricky and they will drop the corruption charges. I wouldn't hold your breath for anything much coming out. It's in no one's interest to publicise this.'

'And the economic intelligence gathering?'

Hennington brushed his hair back from his eyes and thought for a moment.

'I am sure those responsible for the economic security of this country,' he concluded carefully, 'will act in the best interests and traditions of the United States of America.'

Kerr said, 'That's what worries me.'

Hennington was not sure whether Kerr was joking. Neither was Kerr.

'I thought you liked America?' Hennington wondered.

'I do,' Kerr admitted. 'The people, the country, the ideals, the culture. Love it all.' Then he paused. 'Only, the government I can't take. It stinks.'

Now Hennington laughed.

'Spoken,' the senator said, 'like a true Kansan. Marry this boy, Lucy. He's more American than he thinks.'

Senator Hennington shook Kerr's hand.

'I wish I could say it has been a pleasure,' he said grimly. 'I guess I should just say, it's been an education, and leave it at that. You will understand that I never want to discuss this matter again?'

'I understand,' Kerr said. 'Goodbye, Senator.'

'Goodbye, Mr Kerr.'

Hennington turned on his heel and walked across the graveyard back to his car. Lucy took Kerr by the arm and led him up to the sand dunes where they stood in the brisk wind coming from the Atlantic, watching the surf break on the shore.

'Did I hear you right?' Lucy asked. 'You are thinking of staying here for a while?'

'Yes. If you want me to.'

'That's called a commitment, David. You know, the kind of thing that demands faith rather than doubts.'

'Don't romanticise it,' Kerr replied. 'Without doubts, faith is just stupidity. Didn't we learn that from Barker? I still have doubts about everything.'

She put her hands on his hips and looked in his eyes.

'Everything?'

He could feel with his tongue the gaps in his teeth.

'Well, nobody's perfect,' he said at last. 'Let's say, almost everything.'